I0671030

The Kate Huntington Mystery Series:
MULTIPLE MOTIVES
ILL-TIMED ENTANGLEMENTS
FAMILY FALLACIES
CELEBRITY STATUS
COLLATERAL CASUALTIES
ZERO HERO
FATAL FORTY-EIGHT
SUICIDAL SUSPICIONS

The Kate On Vacation Series (novellas):
An Unsaintly Season in St. Augustine
Cruel Capers on the Caribbean
Ten-Gallon Tensions in Texas
Missing on Maui
(coming 2016)

ECHOES, A Story of Suspense
(a stand-alone ghost story/mystery)

SUICIDAL SUSPICIONS

A Kate Huntington Mystery

Kassandra Lamb

SUICIDAL SUSPICIONS
A Kate Huntington Mystery

Published in the United States of America by *misterio press*,
a Florida limited liability company
www.misteriopress.com

Suicidal Suspicions is a work of fiction. All names, characters, and events are products of the author's imagination (as are most of the places). Any resemblance to actual events or people, living or dead, is entirely coincidental. Some real places have been used fictitiously.

~~~~~~~~~~~~~~

Edited by Marcy Kennedy

Cover and interior design by Melinda VanLone,
Book Cover Corner

ISBN 13: 978-0-9908747-5-1 (misterio press LLC)

ISBN 10: 0990874753

This book is dedicated to my readers.
Thank you so much for your support!.

PROLOGUE

Josie jolted upright, blood pounding in her ears. A vise squeezed her chest. Her hands fisted around clumps of damp, rumpled sheets.

The shadows shifted, morphing into the dark outlines of her bedroom furniture. The vise loosened. She sucked in air.

"Crap!"

She'd had the damn dream again. And just when she was starting to feel better.

She shuddered. The dream often foreshadowed the beginning of another bout of depression. Which would be so freaking unfair, since she was just coming out of one. The lows didn't usually come so close together.

There'd be no going back to sleep right away. The best thing to banish the dream, she'd discovered by trial and error, was to read for a while. She turned on her side and reached toward the lamp on her nightstand.

No! No lights! The stern, male voice from the dream.

Adrenaline shot through her. She'd never heard the voice while awake before. She fumbled for the switch on the lamp, almost knocking it off the little table. It rocked wildly. Finally she got her hand wrapped around its neck. Her thumb found the switch.

Light flooded the room.

No lights! the voice screamed in her head.

Her heart pounded, threatening to explode in her chest. She leaned back against the headboard and tried to take a calming breath, like Kate had taught her.

That usually helped. But this time the anxiety wasn't

subsiding, not even a little bit. She was about to jump out of her skin. Fear closed her throat. She tried to swallow but her mouth was too dry.

No more voices yelled at her, but she had the gut sense that she wasn't going to feel better until she turned the light off. She did so with a shaky hand. Her eyes darted nervously around in the blinding darkness. But the rest of her began to relax, her body shifting from full-alert terrified to moderate jitters.

Maybe she should call Kate. What time was it? She didn't have an alarm clock. The natural one in her head always woke her when she needed to be up.

She felt around on the nightstand for her watch, found it, and pressed the tiny button that backlit its face. She held her breath, waiting for the voice to object.

Silence.

It was two-thirty in the morning. She couldn't call Kate. If she was suicidal, yeah, but not over a stupid dream. And she'd have to give the whole background on the dreams–dreams she'd never mentioned to Kate before because they hadn't come all that often in recent years.

And because a previous therapist had told her the dreams were symbolic of some kind of unconscious wish fulfillment. How could her psyche be secretly wishing to be scared witless?

Of course, that therapist had turned out to be a jerk, so why had she believed him about the dreams? She would tell Kate about them during their next session.

The fear raged back, flooding her system.

No, you can't tell anyone! The disembodied male voice again.

Why couldn't she tell Kate about the dreams?

The vise returned, squeezing her lungs. Panic was building in her head. Voice or no voice, she had to have light.

She threw the covers back and dropped her feet to the floor. In the darkness, she fumbled her way down the hall to the bathroom and flipped the light on.

The voice in her head was silent. Apparently bathroom lights were okay.

The puppy rustled in his crate in the living room, letting out a low growl.

"Shh, it's okay, boy. Mom just had a bad dream."

More rustling, then he settled down again.

Josie ran water into a glass and popped a Xanax, wishing she had taken one at bedtime. Maybe then she wouldn't have had the dream.

And now she would be groggy in the morning.

Leaving the bathroom light on so she could see in the dim hallway, she headed back to her bedroom. Her feet stopped of their own volition next to the linen closet door. On a shelf behind that door lay the Mickey Mouse nightlight she'd bought when one of her college friends had come to visit, along with her three-year-old daughter.

Heat rose in her cheeks. *I'm such a wuss.*

Nonetheless, she opened the closet door and located the object of her shame. She took it into the bedroom and plugged it into an outlet near her bed. The light shone softly, revealing a silently laughing Mickey.

No objections from the voice.

Suddenly she was exhausted, too tired even to contemplate reading. She laid down on the bed, praying to a God she sometimes doubted existed that she would be able to go back to sleep.

Sure enough she started to feel drifty. *Huh. There is a God after all.* She snuggled deeper into her pillow and sighed.

Gotta remember to tell Kate about the dreams.

Her body tensed.

No. The voice was a whisper, so low she was probably imagining it. *You can't tell. You can't remember.*

The Xanax was kicking in. Her eyes drooped despite the tension in her body. All she wanted to do was sleep.

Okay, okay, I won't tell.

You can't remember. The slightest breath in her ear. *You can't remember.*

She was drifting. *Okay, I won't remember.*

Good girl! Go to sleep now, little one.

Warmth spread through her body, relaxing her muscles. She was a good girl.

CHAPTER ONE

Kate watched the confusion of emotions play across Josie Hartin's face, and mentally held her breath. Two weeks ago, the combination of the young woman's bipolar disorder and her controlling mother had conspired to throw Josie into another bout of depression. Kate hoped the analogy she'd just suggested would reframe Josie's perspective on her mother.

The client's eyes lit up and a soft smile spread across her face.

Kate continued to wait silently, a well-practiced expression of warm neutrality on her own face. She wasn't quite ready to breathe a sigh of relief yet.

"I can do that." With a slender finger, Josie hooked a strand of dark blonde hair behind her ear and then nodded. "I can love Mom the way I loved Buster."

Buster had been Josie's dog as a teenager, a rescued mutt who had no doubt been abused. He'd had a tendency to resort to growling and snapping at the slightest provocation. But even as a teen, Josie had understood he did so out of fear.

Josie had loved the dog fiercely, and his reciprocal adoration had been her salvation during a particularly rough adolescence. He'd been dead for eight years, and the young woman still talked about him as if they had romped in the yard just yesterday. Indeed, she talked more about Buster than she did about her current canine companion, a Great Dane-Black Labrador mix she'd named Sphinx.

"I felt a little hurt sometimes when Buster snapped at me," Josie said, "but I always realized that he was just scared." She tilted her head again in a small nod. "Yup, I think I can do this. Thanks, Kate."

A quick glance at the clock on the wall told Kate that they had five minutes left in the session. Earlier, Josie had mentioned she'd been having some recurring dreams. Then she'd become agitated and changed the subject back to her mother.

Kate had let it go, making a mental note to come back to the topic. But now, with so little time left, was it prudent to bring the dreams up? Maybe it would be better to end on a happy note.

Josie made the decision for her. She jumped out of her chair.

Kate also stood. At five-seven, she was no shorty, but Josie's lean body towered over her by several inches.

Josie launched herself across the space between them and gave Kate a big hug. "I'm so glad I found you." The young woman's exuberance indicated she was now moving toward the other end of the bipolar spectrum.

Kate smiled. "I'm glad you did too. I enjoy working with you."

"Really? I'm not a pain?"

"Not at all. You're a delight." And Kate meant it. Josie didn't have many friends. Her intense mood swings could be off-putting. But Kate found her charming. Her downs were sometimes scary, but when she was up, she bubbled with enthusiasm for life.

The ups also fueled her creativity. During her manic episodes, she produced brightly colored abstracts and Impressionistic-type landscapes that Kate loved. Of course she was no judge of art. But the owner of the small gallery in Baltimore—where Josie worked part-time—was willing to display them.

Kate ushered her client to the door.

Josie stopped to give her another quick hug. "See you next Monday."

On Tuesday, Kate checked her office voicemail after her last client had left. Despite her end-of-the-day fatigue, she smiled at the sound of Josie's cheery voice.

"Kate, you're the best therapist ever. I just got off the phone with my mother. She was harping again about my, quote, 'silly little job.' And what you suggested, it worked! I let her words roll on by, 'cause I know it's just her way. It's all she knows, as you've said so many times. Oh, I need to change my appointment for next week. Marilyn needs me at the gallery on Monday. Do you have anything else open next week?" She rattled off her phone number.

Kate looked at her watch and groaned softly. Josie definitely sounded like she was heading into a manic episode, or was already there. And that meant it could be difficult to get her off the phone.

Would she feel rejected if Kate didn't call her back tonight? Maybe. She tended to be hypersensitive at times.

And she was making progress. Kate didn't want to jeopardize that.

Taking a deep breath, she punched Josie's home number into her desk phone. Three rings and it kicked over to voicemail. She relaxed. She was going to get away with leaving a message.

A beep in her ear. "Josie, this is Kate. I'm afraid I don't have any openings next week. I'm booked solid. If you're still feeling good, would you be okay with waiting until your regular Monday time the following week? But if you start to feel the least bit down or anxious, let me know. I'll juggle things around and get you in sooner. Call me back and let me know if that's okay."

Kate disconnected and quickly gathered her things. Tonight was the elementary school's play, *The Princess and the Pea*, and her nine-year-old was playing the princess.

Kate dared not be late.

The gold flecks in Skip's hazel eyes sparkled with amusement as they made their way through the crowded school parking lot after the play. They each led a tired child by the hand. Skip had Billy and Kate, the princess.

Edie was both exhausted and excited–a dangerous combination. She was talking a mile a minute, while dragging her feet.

Skip leaned down a little and whispered to Kate, "Isn't that story considered sexist these days?"

She raised up on her toes to reach her husband's ear. "That wasn't the original story they performed. It's the Broadway adaptation, in which the feisty, tough-skinned princess foils the evil queen's plans."

Skip grinned, skimming slender fingers through the straight brown hair that perpetually flopped down onto his forehead. "With a little help from the prince's friends. The jester trying to cram that vibrating jackhammer under the mattresses was a hoot!"

Kate returned his grin. Then in a low voice, she said, "I was kind of surprised that Maria didn't come with us tonight."

"Didn't you know? She had a date."

Kate stopped in her tracks. "Seriously?"

Edie looked up at her with glazed eyes. Kate started moving again.

"Some guy she met at church," Skip said.

"Maybe we should check him out?"

"Darlin', Maria's thirty-four years old. I don't think she needs our protection."

"Yes, but she's never dated, at least not since she's worked for me, and that's going on nine years now. She's pretty naive."

"And why are you assuming that?"

That gave Kate pause for a second. Why *was* she assuming that? "She hasn't had much experience with men."

Skip shook his head. "She grew up in Guatemala, one of the most corrupt countries in Central America. I doubt she was naive much past the age of four."

"Point taken. But I can't help being curious about this guy."

"He picked her up a little bit before you got home. Seemed nice enough. Hispanic, about fortyish. She said something about him being a widower with three kids."

Uh, oh. He's looking for a mother for his children.

But Maria might not mind that. Her whole identity was defined by taking care of people. And she might want to have children of her own, before it was too late.

Kate's stomach clenched. She glanced down.

Edie had fallen silent, worry in her eyes as her gaze darted back and forth between her parent's faces.

Kate decided to change the subject. They'd cross the "losing Maria" bridge if and when they got there.

A week had gone by when Kate realized she'd never heard back from Josie Hartin. On Tuesday morning, she made a mental note to call her again at lunchtime.

Turned out there was no need. When she checked messages after her last morning client, there was Josie's cheerful voice. "Hey Kate, just dawned on me that I never called you back. Skipping this week is fine. See ya at eleven next Monday. And maybe by then, I'll have something very interesting to tell you." Her voice dropped to an excited whisper. "I think I'm on the verge of a major breakthrough, but I need to check some things out first."

A faint noise in the background, then another voice, muffled, said, "Who are..." The rest was indecipherable as Josie whispered a hurried goodbye.

A major breakthrough? Wonder what that's all about?

Josie could be talking about her art work or her therapy, or some other wild project she'd latched onto in her manic state.

Kate shrugged. She'd find out next week.

A mechanical voice gave the day and time of the next message. "Tuesday, eleven-ten a.m." Several clicks in a row. A hang-up.

No doubt a telemarketer. Kate checked caller ID. Sure enough, it read NUMBER BLOCKED.

There were no more messages. Kate sank deeper into her desk chair and let out a long breath. For once she'd be able to eat her lunch in peace, without having to wolf down her sandwich between returning phone calls. She erased Josie's message and the hang-up, then fished her lunch bag out of her desk drawer.

The following Monday, Kate sat at her desk with her office door ajar so she could hear the outer door open. She was trying to focus on paperwork, in between frequent glances at the clock on the wall.

Eleven-fifteen. Josie was late, which was out of character.

Unless she's gone into full-blown mania.

If that were the case, the woman's behavior was unpredictable. She certainly wouldn't intentionally blow off an appointment, but she could have gotten caught up in some manic-driven project and lost track of time.

Kate called Josie's cell phone. It rang several times and went to voicemail.

That didn't make sense. The ringing said the phone was on, and Josie had a Bluetooth in her car, so she would have answered even if she was driving to Kate's office.

She waited for the beep. "Hey, it's Kate. Just wondering where you are."

Josie never did show up. And no call came in from her during Kate's afternoon sessions.

This is totally unlike her!

Worrying her lower lip between her teeth, Kate called her again, got no answer and left messages both at her home and on her cell phone.

After a moment of hesitation, she looked up Josie's parents' number in the young woman's file. Her call to them went to voicemail as well. She wasn't about to identify herself as Josie's therapist so she left a message saying she was a friend who had been trying to reach their daughter and was concerned that perhaps she'd been taken ill or had an accident. She left her cell phone number rather than the one for her office.

By lunchtime on Tuesday, no one had returned her calls. Kate left messages again on both of Josie's numbers and on her parents' voicemail.

When she finished up with her clients that afternoon, she

immediately checked for messages, praying there would be one from Josie with a logical explanation for her long silence.

The third message made her heart stutter in her chest.

"Mrs. Huntington, this is Pernette Wells, Mrs. Hartin's personal assistant. You have made several attempts to reach her daughter. I regret to inform you that Josephine has passed away. Please do not try to contact the family. They have no desire to talk to you."

CHAPTER TWO

Their seven-month-old Labrador mix greeted Kate at the door with his usual enthusiasm, which she most definitely did not share this evening. When she didn't freely offer an ear scratch, Toby nudged her hand with his nose.

"Out of the way, boy." She pushed past him to hang her coat in the closet near the door.

When she turned, Toby placed a big paw on her pants leg and tilted his cream-colored head to one side.

"Down!" Her voice was sharper than she'd intended.

He dropped the paw to the floor. His ears sagged. Big brown eyes stared mournfully up at her.

"Sorry, boy." She patted him quickly on the head, then bee-lined for the study and her computer.

She called up the *Baltimore Sun*'s website and searched for news about Josie's death. Her stomach churned.

She had lost a few clients in the past—one in a car accident, another to a heart attack. A few years ago, a former client's previous profession as a CIA covert operative had caught up with him, with fatal results. But they had all been middle aged or older.

Josie was only in her early thirties and was finally reaching a level of mental health that allowed her to truly enjoy life. How cruel that she should die now.

Peaches the cat jumped onto her lap, rubbing her head against Kate's arm. Kate absently stroked her silky fur as she scanned the newspaper's site.

She was about to give up when she found the small notice

among the obituaries from the previous Friday. It was not particularly helpful. There was no cause of death listed and the memorial service was to be restricted to close family and friends, by invitation only.

Somehow that didn't surprise Kate. Josie's upper-crust parents wouldn't want her riffraff artist friends showing up.

Kate wouldn't have gone anyway, not after the message from the snooty PA, Ms. Wells. The leave-us-alone part of that message hadn't surprised her either. Josie's mother had never approved of her daughter being in therapy.

Where to look next?

The police blotter. She went back to the newspaper site's home page and found the link for it. She searched backward from Friday to Tuesday, when Josie had to be alive because she'd left a message on Kate's office voicemail.

Finally she spotted the report of a woman found dead in her apartment Wednesday evening–no signs of foul play, identity being withheld pending notification of next of kin. She sat back and tried to process what that might mean, if this report was indeed referring to Josie.

Her thoughts stalled as her mind conjured up an image of Josie, lying perfectly still, eyes closed, skin pale. Dead.

A lump grew in her throat. Her eyes stung.

Hands descended on her shoulders. She jumped. The cat bolted from her lap.

The hands pressed gently downward. "Didn't you hear Maria calling, darlin'?" Skip kneaded her muscles with his long, slender fingers. "Supper's ready."

"Sorry. I was absorbed in what I was doing."

Toby bounded into the room and tried to insert himself between them. Skip gently blocked him with his knee. The dog settled for pushing his head under Kate's elbow and bumping it, a not-so-subtle hint that she should pet him.

Feeling guilty about her earlier neglect, Kate scratched behind his soft ears. The dog closed his eyes and made a sound very much like a human moan of pleasure.

Skip's thumbs continued to massage away the tension in Kate's neck. She leaned back against him and let out a soft moan of her own.

Skip chuckled. "What are you doing?" He bent down a little and squinted at the monitor.

Kate instinctively moved to block him from seeing it, then realized there was nothing on it that identified her client.

Unfortunately.

"Why are you looking at the police blotter?"

Kate took a deep breath and let it out slowly, debating with her conscience. Technically, confidentiality did not end with the death of a client, but she trusted her husband's discretion. And she didn't need to give him any names. "It's complicated. I'll tell you about it after the kids are in bed."

After reading the children their bedtime stories, Skip found his wife on the living room sofa, her legs tucked up under her. The dog was curled up on the floor nearby, doing what dogs do best–sleeping.

Kate was staring into space, her eyes the washed-out gray they became when she was stressed or worried.

He sat down next to her and gently hooked a stray strand of hair behind her ear. He noted some gray scattered amongst the dark curls. He knew the gray hairs bothered her some but he thought of them as silver highlights. Besides, he had a little salt in his own hair now.

Dropping an arm around her shoulders, he said, "Penny for your thoughts."

She tensed, rather than relaxed. "Okay, what I'm about to tell you is confidential."

Aw, crap! Could he take his metaphorical penny back? Every time she said those words, they ended up in the middle of somebody else's mess.

"One of my clients was found dead last week."

Skip's stomach clenched. The last time she'd said *those* words, they'd ended up being chased by international thugs. It had been one of the scariest experiences of his life, and that was saying something considering his was a somewhat dangerous profession.

He hoped his dismay wasn't showing on his face. "What did he or she die of?"

"Well, that's the problem. I don't know." Kate stopped and took a deep breath. "The last communication I had from her was a call to my office last Tuesday morning. She was confirming a scheduling change. But then she didn't show up for her appointment yesterday. I kept leaving messages on her voicemail because it wasn't like her to just not show up like that. Finally I left a couple messages at her parents' home. Today I got a message back from them, saying she had died and to leave them alone."

Skip's jaw tightened. "That's pretty rude."

"Yeah well, I'm used to families not liking me. All too often they're part of the client's psychological problems and they often object to the client being in therapy."

"Why wouldn't they want their loved one to get better?"

"They don't want anyone rocking the dysfunctional family boat."

"Ah." He tilted his head in a slight nod. "So what did you find in the newspaper's files?"

"An obit from Friday that said nothing. And a police report that a woman–no name given–was found dead in her apartment Wednesday night, no sign of foul play."

Skip used his fingers to comb back the hank of hair hanging in his eyes. "Could be her."

"So what's the best way to find out more about that woman?" Kate asked.

"Dolph may be able to find out. He's still got some contacts with BCPD."

"Can you ask him?"

"Sure. I'll make it his morning assignment." A retired Baltimore County police detective, "Dolph" Randolph now worked for Skip's agency as a private investigator.

"Oh, no!" she said. "I don't want to take up agency time with it."

Skip shrugged. "Not a lot going on tomorrow anyway. He'd just be sitting around eating donuts." He smiled down at her. "Think you can put it aside until we know more?"

"Yes, now that I know we can probably find out more. The not knowing what happened is driving me crazy."

"Good, 'cause I've got something else important to ask you."

"What's that?"

He leaned down and nibbled on her ear, then whispered, "How soon do you want to go to bed?"

She let out a low chuckle. It stopped abruptly when he kissed the sweet spot where her neck met her shoulder.

"Now would be as good a time as any," she said in a husky whisper. Then her tone shifted to teasing. "Unless *you're* not ready yet."

He pushed himself to a stand and pulled her to her feet. Wrapping his arms around her, he grinned down into her face.

Toby jumped up and tried to nose between their knees.

Skip ignored the dog. He leaned down and swept Kate up into his arms. He ignored the twinge in his back as well. "Darlin', I'm *always* ready."

~~~~~~~~~

Dolph had come through in spades. Not only had he gotten a verbal rundown of the case, he'd somehow gotten his hands on a copy of the responding officer's report.

"It's kinda gruesome," Dolph said as he handed it across Skip's desk.

Skip read through the first part of the report. The woman had been found on the floor, an almost-empty bottle of vodka next to her, as well as two empty pill bottles.

Skip shook his head slightly, wondering why Dolph had called it gruesome. It definitely wasn't good though. If this was Kate's client, it looked like she'd committed suicide.

"You get to the part about the dog yet?" Dolph asked.

"No." He skimmed down the page. He stopped at the words *barely alive* and then backed up. The woman's dog had been found locked in a metal crate. It was covered in its own filth, its food and water bowls empty. The report said they had received a call from a neighbor that the animal was "howling pathetically."

He grimaced, then handed the report back to Dolph. "Stick this in a file somewhere, just in case we end up investigating it."

"Why would we investigate a suicide?"

"Long story."

Which I can't tell you, Skip added mentally. "Hopefully, we won't have to get involved," he said out loud.

Dolph nodded and left his office.

Skip glanced at his watch. Four-ten. Kate would be headed home by now. She had taken the afternoon off to participate in some activity with Billy's second-grade class.

He called her cell phone. As it rang, he decided to leave out the part about the dog. She would be upset enough that her client had done herself in.

"Hey there," she said.

"Hi. Are you home yet?"

"No, on the way. I really love this Bluetooth in my new car. So cool to be able to talk while driving."

She sounded so chipper. He hated to deflate her good mood.

He took a deep breath. "Is your client Josephine Hartin? If so, the news isn't good."

Silence.

"You there, darlin'?"

"Yeah, but maybe this conversation needs to wait until you get home." Her voice was shaky. "I've got the kids with me, and little pitchers have big ears."

"It's kinda quiet around here," Skip said. "I think I'll come home early. See ya there."

"Okay." Silence, except for the sound of the children squabbling in the backseat. "Thanks for finding out for me. Love you."

"Love you too." He disconnected.

Don't need to tell her. She already knows.

~~~~~~~~~

Kate's eyes stung. She slowed the car as her vision blurred. The woman in that apartment had been Josie. "No sign of foul play," the newspaper had said. If it had been an accident, Skip would have said so right off. Or a heart attack or stroke, not that thirty-one year olds often dropped dead from those causes. That only left one alternative.

Edie had broken off her argument with her brother and was telling her something.

Blinking hard, Kate tried to tune in to what she was saying, but the words wouldn't register. "That's nice, dear," she said, hoping that was an appropriate response.

She'd been denying her fear that Josie had committed suicide. She hadn't wanted to believe it, although it would explain the family's attitude toward her.

Kate shook her head. Why hadn't Josie called her? She'd done so before when she was down. And her message the day before had sounded cheerful enough. But she'd mentioned some kind of breakthrough.

Had her psyche coughed up some realization that had thrown her into a downward spiral?

Of course, some people with bipolar committed suicide while in a manic state. But they weren't usually the ones who had been in therapy for a while and were responding to treatment like Josie was. They were the desperate folks who believed there was nothing that would help them, and they couldn't take the out-of-control roller coaster of mood swings anymore.

Had there been a note?

Kate blew out air and willed her tense fingers to loosen their death grip on the steering wheel. She'd have to wait until Skip got home to learn more.

Maria had been Kate's housekeeper and nanny since Edie was a baby, before she had married Skip even, and the plump, little woman knew her pretty darn well. At the house, Maria took one look at her face and shooed the children and dog toward the back door. "Nice day, *niños*. We play outside for now. Do homework later."

Kate didn't argue with that plan.

She flopped down on the sofa and kicked off her shoes. Fatigue washed over her, a riptide dragging her toward depression herself.

Her specialty was working with trauma survivors. It was rewarding work but they were a population prone to suicide attempts. She'd known the day would come eventually when a client took his or her own life.

But not Josie!

Her chest hurt. She felt nauseated. If only she hadn't put Josie's appointment off for a week. They could have talked about this breakthrough, whatever it was. She could have helped Josie deal with it, maybe slowed down the pace a bit so she wasn't overwhelmed by whatever it was.

What the hell was the big breakthrough anyway?

She'd always wondered if there was more going on with Josie. Bipolar disorder was biologically based, but it was challenging to tease out how much the mood swings were also affected by life events, past and present. Brain chemistry alone didn't quite explain the depths of some of Josie's depressions.

Then again, each time she'd gone through a depressive episode, she'd dealt a bit more with her issues regarding her cold and controlling mother and had made definite strides toward a healthier approach to life. This last shift had been the biggest stride yet. Josie had really gotten it on a deeper level that you can love someone, and know that someone loves you in their own way, but that didn't mean you had to let their negative behavior affect you.

Had that new perspective somehow opened up a can of worms, something buried in Josie's unconscious mind perhaps? Such dissociated memories did happen, despite society's resistance to accepting that reality. The human mind was remarkably adept at defending itself against anything that might overwhelm it, and if need be, it would build walls around a bad memory.

Usually such memories surfaced gradually, giving the person time to process them. But sometimes they came surging back with a vengeance, especially if the person poked at them, trying to get them out into the light of day.

Tucking her bare feet up under her on the sofa, Kate shook her head.

Josie was the type to do just that. She was not a patient woman. If something had started to surface, she wouldn't have waited until her next therapy session to explore it. She would have tried to dig it out of her unconscious mind by force.

And Kate had come full circle back to her own guilt. If she had seen Josie last week, she could have slowed her down, warned her against trying to force her psyche to open up too quickly.

Kate took a deep breath, trying to loosen the tight band around her chest.

You are not responsible for your clients' psyches or actions. You can only help them heal. You can't make them heal.

The words were an old mantra, learned two and a half decades ago from her first clinical supervisor, Sally Ford. Usually they helped Kate put things in perspective.

This time, not so much.

Josie was the one who had needed to reschedule, she reminded herself.

I should have squeezed her in somehow.

Kate sighed and leaned her head back against the sofa cushions.

You can only make the best decision possible with the information you have at the time.

Another of Sally's mantras.

At the time that Kate had left her first message for Josie, the woman had been in a very good place. And she had told her to call right away if she felt the least bit down.

At least, that's what Kate thought she had said. But it had

been almost two weeks since she'd left that message, the evening of Edie's play. Maybe she'd only thought about saying that, but hadn't actually said it.

Skip's key in the front door lock saved her from further ruminating and self-incrimination, for now at least.

She met him at the door. He wrapped his arms around her without saying anything. She rested her cheek against his chest and listened to the solid thumping of his heart.

She wished she could stay there forever, but after a few minutes she pulled back. Taking his hand, she led the way to their favorite spot on the sofa. "I know it must have been suicide, from your tone earlier."

"Looks that way, I'm afraid."

"Was there a note?"

"Don't know. The report Dolph got his hands on didn't say anything about a note. But there was a bottle of booze and two empty pill bottles."

"Josie didn't drink. She knew it was a bad idea, both because of the meds she was on and her tendency toward depression."

"Darlin'," Skip's voice was gentle, "she wouldn't care about that if she was trying to kill herself."

Kate's gut twisted. "True," she said softly. "How did they find her?"

"Neighbor got worried and she called it in."

"What made her get worried?"

Skip broke eye contact, looked across the room at nothing. "The report didn't say."

Despite her pain, warmth spread through her chest. This man loved her so much, he was almost as upset as she was. She took his hand and squeezed it. "Can you find out if there was a note?"

He turned back to her. "Yeah, I can have Dolph ask his contact." He lifted her hand to his lips and kissed her fingertips.

She gave him a small smile. "Thanks."

"I'd better go relieve Maria," Skip said, "so she can get supper started. I'll see what homework the kids have."

"Would you mind supervising their baths tonight? I think I need to go to bed early."

Worry turned Skip's hazel eyes to a muddy brown. "Early as in after supper?"

She tried to imagine getting through dinner–eating, talking with the children–then shook her head. She was exhausted. Even sitting upright for that long felt beyond her. "I'm not hungry. I think I'll get ready for bed and then read for a while."

He opened his mouth, then closed it again. "I'll take care of the kids. You take care of you."

"Thanks, sweetheart." She leaned over and gave him a peck on the cheek. "I'll be okay, in time. I... I just need to deal with this."

She pushed herself to a stand and headed for the bedroom.

CHAPTER THREE

Despite going to bed at a ridiculously early hour, Kate didn't feel particularly rested the next day. Her sleep had been fitful, punctuated by vague dreams she couldn't remember in the morning.

She muddled though her morning client sessions, then half-heartedly ate her sandwich as she returned phone calls.

At the end of the day, she checked for messages, hoping there wasn't anything pressing. She just wanted to go home and crash.

"Mrs. Huntington," a crisp, clear, female voice, "this is Nancy Hartin."

Kate's stomach clenched. Her hand flew to her mouth.

Josie's mother? Holy crap!

"My husband and I would like to meet with you. We have some unanswered questions about..." The voice faltered. "About our daughter. Please call me back as soon as possible." Couched as a request but really an order. The woman gave her phone number.

Kate fought back nausea. Were the Hartins planning to sue her? Failure to prevent a suicide was one of the three most common grounds for malpractice suits–right up there with sexual malfeasance and breach of confidentiality.

She sat rigidly in her desk chair. The last thing in the world she wanted to do was talk to the Hartins. She honestly wasn't sure she could make herself do it.

The thought of calling her friend Rob flashed into her mind. Maybe he could call Mrs. Hartin back and explain, as Kate's lawyer, that due to confidentiality she couldn't talk to her.

She shook her head. That was the coward's way out. And perhaps she could give these grieving parents some comfort.

But still she couldn't make herself dial the number. She decided to call Rob after all, for moral support and to get his take on it.

"Franklin."

"Hey there. Are you still at the office?"

"Walking to my car," Rob said. "What's up?"

"Uh, I lost a client last week... to suicide."

"Oh no! Tha..." Road noise in the background drowned out some of his words. "Are...kay?"

"Not really. I only found out about it a couple days ago. It's hit me pretty hard. I've never had this happen before. And now the parents are asking to meet with me. I'm not sure what I should do."

"Hm, any inkling why they want to meet?" The road noise made it hard to assess his tone.

Kate swallowed hard. "Not really. Although if my client's descriptions of her mother were accurate, she isn't planning on a mutual consolation session."

"You think she blames you?" he asked.

"Most likely."

The slamming of a car door. The background noise disappeared. "Maybe I should sit in on this meeting."

If only you could!

"I'm not sure how to do that legally, because of the confidentiality thing."

"Which doesn't die with the client." Silence for a beat. "You could tell them you can't talk to them for that reason."

Kate took a deep breath. "I thought of that, but it seems kind of cruel. They may just be looking for some answers. That's what her message said..." A thought struck her. The Hartins might also be able to answer some of *her* questions and help her figure out what happened.

"Well, if you meet with them, be careful what you say. They

may be fishing for evidence for a malpractice suit."

"That had crossed my mind. I'll be careful."

They said their goodbyes and disconnected.

Biting hard on her lower lip, Kate dialed the Hartins' number. Mrs. Hartin answered on the second ring. In a brisk, business-like tone, she asked to meet on Saturday.

Kate hesitated, thinking about the logistics of child care. She didn't know if Skip had any plans for the day. Did Maria have another date with her young man? Not so young really, she mentally corrected herself.

"That will probably work," she said into the phone. "We can meet at my office." She wanted this encounter on her own turf. "But I'll have to check to make sure either my husband or nanny can watch my children."

"Why wouldn't the nanny be able to watch them?"

"She's normally off duty on the weekends."

A few seconds of silence. Kate imagined Mrs. Hartin contemplating why one would be so generous with servants.

Stop it! The woman just lost her daughter.

"Very well," Mrs. Hartin said. "Call me if there is a problem. Otherwise we will be at your office, say at noon."

"Mrs. Hartin, may I ask why you want to meet with me? You do realize that there are limits on what I can share with you."

Another beat of silence. "I'd prefer to wait and discuss it in person."

Kate swallowed the lump in her throat. "Okay. I'll call if there's a problem."

~~~~~~~~~

At noon on Saturday, Kate ushered the Hartins into her office. She had placed two straight-back chairs in front of her desk. The goal here was not to make these people all that comfortable.

She went around her desk and sat down. "You do understand that there may be very little I can tell you. Confidentiality constraints may keep me from answering your questions."

Mrs. Hartin gave her a stiff nod. Mr. Hartin just stared at her, his eyes red-rimmed, his mouth set in a grim frown. Josie had described him as a reserved man, not particularly demonstrative but caring in his own way.

Kate's heart went out to him, and even to his wife. At the same time, she found them scary.

Mrs. Hartin cleared her throat. "I understand, Mrs. Huntington, that you compared me to a dog in your last session with my daughter."

Shock and confusion vied for dominance. Fortunately, Kate was adept at hiding her emotions. With a neutral expression on her face, she said, "I'm afraid I cannot discuss the specific content of my sessions with my clients."

"Not clients, Mrs. Huntington." The woman's tone was sharp. "Client. A client. *My* daughter."

"Technically, I cannot even confirm that a specific person is my client."

"Bullshit," Mr. Hartin said.

Kate stared at him for a beat, trying to figure out what made this man tick.

Mrs. Hartin ignored him.

"I'm not trying to be difficult," Kate said. "The rules of confidentiality in my profession are very strict. Due to the stigma attached to being in therapy, therapists cannot even say whether or not someone *is* their client. If possible, I will try to answer your questions, in general terms."

Mrs. Hartin leaned forward. "And what does that code of ethics say about taking measures to prevent a client from committing suicide."

Kate felt the clinical detachment kick in. She'd dealt with hostility from families more than once before. "We are required to do so," she said in a calm voice, "if we have reason to believe that a client is *actively* suicidal."

"Well, obviously my daughter was actively suicidal," Mrs. Hartin said, "since she committed suicide!"

Kate was very glad that she'd set this meeting up in her

office. The setting was helping her stay grounded in her professional persona.

"*Actively* is one of the key words in that sentence, but so are *has reason to believe*. The last three times that I was in communications with your daughter, she was not depressed, much less suicidal."

She was waltzing on thin ice even admitting to "communications" with Josie but the whole thing was becoming a bit ludicrous. The Hartins knew she was Josie's therapist.

"Again I will point out, Mrs. Huntington," the woman said, "that she *was* actively suicidal, *since* she committed suicide."

"Ma'am, I am a therapist, not a mind reader. If someone is acting totally fine around me, showing absolutely no signs of depression…" She trailed off intentionally, implying that this was the case with their daughter. "It is possible that your daughter's mood deteriorated after my last communication with her and she did not call me to report this."

Mrs. Hartin sniffed loudly. "Is that how you phrase it, Mrs. Huntington, that she should 'report' her mood shifts to you?"

"No, that is the formal language I am using with you. With my clients I *warmly* encourage them…" Did this woman even know the definition of *warmly*? "…to contact me whenever they are feeling down. But if they do not call me, there's nothing I can do. I can't read their minds from across town!"

"So what about the dreams?"

Kate's heart pounded.

Dreams! What dreams?

She hoped she'd successfully hidden her surprise. Josie had mentioned dreams in her last session, but how the hell did her mother know that?

The abrupt change of subject would have been more effective if Mrs. Hartin hadn't given her a smug look.

Awareness dawned. Kate sat back, feigning a calm she didn't feel. Elbows on the arms of her desk chair, she tented her fingers in front of her chin. "Mrs. Hartin, your remarks lead me to believe that you have found your daughter's journal. There is no guarantee that I know everything that is contained in that journal."

The woman's face remained neutral but her eyes lit up with glee.

Kate caught herself before she shook her head. *Even now, with your daughter's body barely cold, it's all about having the upper hand, being in control.*

"What has happened to Josie's dog?" She wanted to know the answer, but she was also hoping the question would inject some humanity into the interview.

"The creature was barely alive," Mrs. Hartin said. "We instructed the veterinarian to put it down."

Kate's stomach twisted. She wasn't able to keep the horror off of her face, and she wasn't sure she cared.

The glint was back in the woman's eye. "Don't worry. The vet insisted she would care for the *mutt* for free."

Of course, her daughter's dog should have been a purebred. One of the many ways Josie had defied her mother was by insisting on rescuing mutts from the pound, starting with Buster in her teens.

Mrs. Hartin sniffed. "She said she'd find it a home, should it survive."

Kate was dying to know what had brought the dog to a state of being barely alive, but she wasn't willing to show her ignorance to this woman.

"Mrs. Huntington, our lawyer has advised us that we could file a lawsuit against you," Mrs. Hartin said. "Our main reason for coming here today was to determine whether or not that was appropriate."

Kate narrowed her eyes and studied the woman across the desk. Mrs. Hartin wanted her to beg. And that might or might not fend off the lawsuit.

But even though she felt guilty about Josie's death, the logical, professional part of her brain knew that all the things she'd said to the Hartins were true. She wasn't about to grovel and give this bitch any satisfaction.

Josie, you were so right. Your mother is truly a piece of work.

"I believe I have already made my position clear. I was unaware of any depression or suicidal inclinations."

"So in other words," Mrs. Hartin said, a sneer in her voice, "you are unable to accurately detect the mood state of your clients and are therefore incompetent."

Kate's chest tightened. She gritted her teeth. She opted not to dignify the woman's words with a response.

After a moment, Mrs. Hartin continued, "I do have her journal. And obviously she was a lot sicker than you thought she was. She speaks of recurring dreams, nightmares really, of feeling haunted at night by dark shadows." The woman stared at her, waiting for her to defend her incompetence.

Kate glanced at Mr. Hartin. The whites of his eyes were now more red than white. His cheeks had sagged. He swallowed hard and looked away.

Her heart ached. She blinked once to relieve the stinging in her eyes. She wasn't about to let herself cry, or even look like she was about to, in front of Mrs. Hartin.

The woman frowned. "Well, young lady, what do you have to say for yourself?"

Sorry, the parental tone may have worked on Josie. Not so much on me.

Kate took a deep breath and leaned forward. "Mr. and Mrs. Hartin, I wish I could tell you more and perhaps give you some modicum of comfort. But I can't get specific. Let me try to explain some things in more general terms."

Mr. Hartin made a noise, somewhere between a snort and a harumph. Mrs. Hartin gave him a quelling look, which he ignored.

"I often suggest to clients that they keep a journal. It serves several purposes. It gives them an emotional outlet, and also helps them consolidate an insight by writing down their thoughts and feelings as they are happening, or shortly thereafter. Sometimes the client shows me their journals, but not always. Indeed I emphasize to them that the journal is for their benefit. I don't want them writing with my reactions in mind."

She stopped to take a deep breath, choosing her words, which were mostly aimed at Mr. Hartin. "Normally, the things a client journals about, they do bring up in therapy and we work on it. They may or may not note in the journal how the issues have been resolved, or even that they *have been* resolved. Nor are they likely to write about the good things going on in their lives."

Kate looked directly at Mr. Hartin, waited until he made eye contact. "A client's journal only shows the dark side of their life, not the good side, and in recent times your daughter was in a good place."

Mr. Hartin's eyes grew shiny. He gave her a small nod.

Mrs. Hartin sniffed again. "Father Phelps was right."

The name took Kate by surprise. "Father Samuel Phelps? At St. Bartholomew's?"

"Yes," Mr. Hartin said, his voice raspy.

Mrs. Hartin lifted her chin. "Father Phelps said that nothing good would come of Josephine being in therapy."

Kate seriously doubted the priest had said that. She knew Father Samuel. He had been the pastor of her parents' church for decades–the church she had grown up in.

He had most likely said something similar and Mrs. Hartin was twisting his words, perhaps unintentionally. People often heard what they wanted to hear.

Kate resisted the temptation to respond.

"What I don't understand," Mrs. Hartin said, "is how a girl, who is, quote, 'in a good place' can end up committing suicide."

Honestly, I don't either. Kate caught herself before she said the thought out loud.

"Do you know what Josie's diagnosis was?" she asked.

Mrs. Hartin narrowed her eyes at her. "She said that you told her she was bipolar."

Kate resisted pointing out that the diagnosis had been confirmed by two doctors, Josie's psychiatrist and her GP.

"Let me explain some things about bipolar, again in general terms. It is a biochemical imbalance that causes fluctuations in mood, from very high to very low–"

"Manic-depressive," Mr. Hartin said.

"Yes, that's the older name for it. These moods can be aggravated by what's going on in the person's life and/or their psyche, but the direct cause of the mood swing is usually more about brain chemistry than anything else."

"In other words," Mr. Hartin said, "it's not related to how the person feels about life."

"Not how they *really* feel. But once the chemistry gets a solid grip on the person's brain, they may experience feelings that are not based on the reality of their life. Or their true feelings about life events may be greatly intensified by the brain chemistry."

Mr. Hartin nodded.

Mrs. Hartin made a soft *tsk*ing noise under her breath. Her nose went up in the air. "We will be consulting with our lawyer next week." She stood. "We will decide then whether or not to pursue a lawsuit."

Mr. Hartin and Kate both stood as well.

Kate breathed in through her nose to calm herself, willing her tense jaw to relax. "I was very fond of your daughter. My condolences to both of you for your loss."

Mr. Hartin's mask cracked. For a second, Kate thought he was going to cry. "Thank you," he mumbled. Then his face pinched back into its unhappy frown.

Kate's chest ached. She wished she could do something to relieve this man's pain.

Mrs. Hartin gave her husband a sharp look. She turned on her heel and abruptly left the office. He trailed after her.

Kate waited until she heard the slam of the outer waiting room door. Then she sank into her desk chair. Burying her face in her crossed arms on the desk, she gave in to the tears she'd been fighting for the better part of two days.

CHAPTER FOUR

Kate felt better after her good cry. As stressful as the meeting with the Hartins had been, saying the things to them that she needed to hear herself had helped them sink in. She wasn't a mind reader. She couldn't be expected to know what was happening with clients if they didn't tell her.

Halfway home, she caught herself humming to the song on the radio. Her throat tightened. She flashed back a decade to the time right after her first husband's death.

She had caught herself humming to the radio then, but it was weeks after his death, not days. Back then she had seen it as a good sign, that she would survive the crushing blow of Eddie's death.

Now it made her feel guilty. How could she so quickly dismiss Josie's death and get on with her own life, as if the woman had never existed?

She wished she had more answers, for the Hartins and for herself. She wasn't likely to get those answers though, not unless Josie left a suicide note. And maybe not even then.

Driving home by rote, she prayed to God for peace.

Anger came instead. How could God let this happen? Where was He when Josie needed him?

She got no answers to those questions either.

Sunday morning she begged off from going to church, telling Skip she felt like she was coming down with something.

Coming down with something all right–full-blown depression. She'd had another fitful night, punctuated again by vague but disturbing dreams, and had woken more tired than she'd been when she went to bed.

She dragged through the day, going through the motions of being a mother and wife. Several times, she caught Skip giving her worried looks, especially when she picked at her dinner. It took a lot for her to lose her appetite.

She wanted to reassure him, but she couldn't drum up the energy to do so.

She knew intellectually she would be okay eventually, maybe soon even. The grief for Josie had to run its course.

Another Sally maxim came to mind. *No way around grief but through it.*

She knew the more one tried to fight it, to force themselves to let go and move on, the longer the grief process would take.

Monday morning saw some improvement. She was able to concentrate better than she had on Friday, and focusing on her clients' problems helped her put aside her own. She went into her last session of the morning feeling like she was beginning to get her equilibrium back.

Carol Foster suffered from major depressive disorder, similar to bipolar in the depths of the depression and its biological roots, but without the mania. Kate had been her therapist for years. Most of the time she was relatively stable, but every now and then she would plunge into depression again.

Unfortunately, this was shaping up to be one of those times. *Dear Lord, not now.*

Kate went through the suicide assessment questions with Carol. Had she had thoughts about dying lately? Yes. Did she have a plan for how she would kill herself? No. Did she have anything in the house she could hurt herself with should she feel the impulse to do so?

Carol gave her a weak smile. "Just my antidepressants."

Kate's heart rate shot up. Her stomach clenched. "Have you been hoarding them?"

Carol shook her head. "The prescription's only for two weeks at a time, and I can't get it refilled until two days before I run out. It's a pain to be constantly running to the pharmacy, but at times like this, I'm glad my doctor set it up that way."

Kate's stomach relaxed some. *Okay,* that *sentiment's a good sign that she wants to live.*

Carol could always stop taking the pills and eventually accumulate enough for a lethal dose. But that would require a level of planning this client had never exhibited before.

"You know I'm Catholic," Carol said, "and suicide's a sin."

Of course Kate knew that. She and Carol had discussed her religious beliefs before. Why did the woman feel the need to remind her now?

My God, she's trying to reassure me!

Kate hid her dismay behind a gentle smile. "I know you would never plan to kill yourself, but I have to check. And we do need to guard against a possible impulse at a particularly low moment."

Which is probably what happened with Josie.

There probably wouldn't be a note then. People who committed suicide on impulse rarely left one.

Kate yanked her mind back to Carol. That's where her focus should be, not on Josie nor her own need for answers.

"Yeah," Carol was saying, "I know I'll come out of this eventually. It's just hard while I'm in it."

"Do you feel like maybe you should go into the hospital for a few days?"

Kate's stomach tightened again. She hated that she was asking the client that question. She was supposed to be figuring that out, not Carol. But she was off her game at the moment, and this client knew herself pretty well.

Carol cocked her head to one side, then shook it. "I can hang in there, but maybe I could come in again later this week?"

"That's a good idea." Kate got up and fetched her appointment book from her desk. Her schedule was fairly packed but she'd give up her lunch break, if need be.

When she sat back down, Carol pointed to the book. "You know, there's an app for that."

Kate smiled, a genuine smile of relief. Carol couldn't be too far under the cloud of depression if her sense of humor was peeking out.

"Don't you have a smart phone?"

"I do," Kate said, "although I resent it most days. It isn't right that my phone is smarter than I am."

Carol gave her a smile, a little stronger than the last one.

Kate tapped the book. "Old habit learned from my mentor way back when. Don't trust computers with client info. They can be hacked."

Carol actually let out a soft chuckle. "Ah, thus the bank of file cabinets against the wall."

Kate's heart rate finally returned to normal. She quietly blew out air as she looked for an opening in her schedule later in the week.

At the end of the day, Kate was relieved that there were only two messages in her voicemail. The first was a routine confirmation of a schedule change. The second was from a colleague. It gave her pause.

"Hey, Kate, this is Jo Ann Reinhold. I have a client I'd like to refer to you. She's dysthymic and had a pretty rough time growing up. I think there may be more going on there in the childhood trauma department. So since that's your specialty, I'm thinking you might be a good fit for her. Give me a call." Jo Ann gave her number and signed off.

Kate cringed. Dysthymia–chronic, low-grade depression, that could potentially turn into a full blown depressive episode.

I'm just not up for this right now.

She punched her colleague's number into the phone. "Hey, Jo Ann," she said when the woman answered. "I'm sorry but I can't take your referral right now."

"You sure you can't fit this gal in?"

"I'm pretty booked up. Why do you want to refer her?"

"She's great to work with, but we've gone about as far as I can take her. There are some vague signs of possible sexual abuse, but no conscious memories. You have the skills to get to that stuff better than I can."

One part of Kate's mind was intrigued. Another part was screaming, *No, no, no!* Out loud, she said, "How depressed does she tend to get?"

"Not terribly most of the time, but here's the interesting part. She always gets fairly depressed at the same time of year."

"Seasonal affective disorder?" Otherwise known as the winter blues, caused by the reduced sunlight at that time of the year.

"No. It lasts for about two weeks around Christmas, and again for several weeks in the summer–which just happen to coincide with the times she would visit her grandparents every year as a kid."

Jo Ann was right. This case was right up Kate's alley as a trauma recovery specialist. The client sounded like she was a likeable person, and she was therapy-savvy, always a plus.

So why am I not excited?

Before she could analyze that question, she heard herself saying, "I'd like to take the case, but I'm too jammed up right now."

A pause. "Do you see your schedule lightening up any time soon?" Jo Ann's voice had lost a good bit of its earlier energy.

"Maybe, but I can't predict when."

"Anybody else you can recommend?"

Kate thought for a moment, then gave her two names.

"I've heard of them. They'll do, I guess. But they're not as good as you."

Kate faked a chuckle. "Flattery will not make more hours appear in my week."

Jo Ann laughed. "Figured it was worth a try. I may hang on to this gal for a little while, and see what bubbles up. Would you call me if your schedule opens up?"

"Sure. Good talking to you, Jo Ann."

"Same here. Take care."

Kate hung up the phone and then stared at it for a moment. Why had she done that? She'd turned down a client she could have taken, could have helped.

She sucked in air and blew it out again on a long sigh. She could always call Jo Ann back in a few days and say things had loosened up.

I just need more time to get over Josie.

But she found herself hoping that Jo Ann would have transferred the client to someone else by the time she called her back.

~~~~~~~~~

Skip decided to get the bad news over with as fast as possible. Maybe by knowing for sure that her client had committed suicide, Kate would be able to move on.

She was apparently on the same wavelength. While still kicking off her shoes, she asked, "What did Dolph find out?"

Skip took her hand and cleared his throat. "There was a note, but the family asked that the contents be kept confidential."

Her face sagged. She dropped down onto the sofa. Skip sat down beside her.

"What else did he find out?" she asked.

"They found a third bottle of pills in her medicine cabinet, also almost empty, even though it was a new prescription. With the cocktail she took, she didn't want to survive."

"No, I wouldn't imagine Josie would mess around." The sadness in her voice made his chest hurt.

"When she set her mind on something," Kate continued, "she tended to do it right. What was the other prescription for?"

"Clonazepam."

Kate's eyebrows went up. "Who was the prescribing doctor?"

"Don't know," he said. "It's a wonder she hasn't succeeded in killing herself before."

"She's never tried before."

He arched his own eyebrows. From what little he recalled from a training workshop on suicide when he'd been a state trooper, there were usually one or more unsuccessful attempts in the person's history. "Seriously?"

"She's felt suicidal a few times, but she'd never attempted it. For one thing, she was raised Catholic. The Church considers it a mortal sin to take your own life."

He squeezed her hand and dropped his gaze, then looked off across the living room, hoping she wouldn't ask any more questions.

He should have known better.

"There's something else, isn't there?" she said.

"No, it's nothing important, not really related to what she did."

"Tell me."

He shook his head, fully aware that she wasn't going to let it go.

Kate pulled her hand loose from his. "Damn it, Skip, I don't need you to protect me!"

He snorted. "Says the woman who's been depressed for the last week."

She narrowed her eyes at him. "What is it?" she said through gritted teeth.

"Her dog. It was locked in its crate…"

She flopped back against the sofa. "Holy crap." Her tone was sharp, not sad.

Not exactly the reaction he'd expected.

She drummed her fingers against her lips, her expression thoughtful. "Her mother hinted that the dog was in bad shape, but I didn't dare ask them for more details. What was in the police report?"

He winced. "You sure you want to know?"

"Yes, and I'll explain why after you tell me."

Skip suppressed a sigh. "He was found in his crate. Food and water dishes were empty." He decided against describing the feces and urine. She'd figure that out for herself. "It was the dog's howling that got the neighbor's attention."

"Anything on how long she'd been dead before she was

found?"

"Dolph couldn't get the autopsy report. But the detective's report said she had probably been dead twelve to thirty hours."

Kate looked at him, her eyes growing wide. "She did not kill herself."

Wondering if that was denial talking, he said, "How do you know?"

"She loves dogs and she was big on animal rights. She'd never leave her puppy like that."

Skip noted the mix of present and past tense. Kate's mind still hadn't digested the reality of her client's death. "Maybe it was an impulse thing."

Kate shook her head. "No. Even if she had the impulse to kill herself and decided to do it, she would have done something about the dog. She would not leave him to starve in his crate."

Skip sat back and put his arm around her shoulders. "Darlin', are you sure this isn't wishful thinking?"

She tensed.

"Sorry," he said quickly. "I'm just playing devil's advocate here. What could she have done with the dog?"

"My guess is the neighbor who reported the howling is the same one who's dog-sat for her before when she was traveling. It would have been an easy thing to go next door and say she wasn't feeling well. The woman would have taken the dog for the night."

Skip still thought she was grasping for straws, but he nodded. "You want the agency to investigate."

She pulled back a little and looked up at him, a small smile on her face. The first one in several days. "Thanks for offering, but there are some things I can check out first."

His muscles tensed but he managed to keep his voice calm. "Such as?"

"Such as calling her doctors tomorrow to see who prescribed the clonazepam. If I remember correctly, it would be a duplication of her other meds, and they might not mix all that well. And I want to check something else out."

His jaw clenched. He tightened his arm around her. "You're not going to do anything dangerous." A statement, not a question, or rather a gentle order.

She actually chuckled. His heart did a funny little flip and he breathed out a soft sigh.

"I don't think I have anything to fear from an elderly priest," she said.

"Could her death have been accidental?" Skip asked. "Maybe a bad interaction of the drugs. That would explain the dog being crated."

"But not the suicide note." Kate tapped an index finger against her lips. "Unless she'd written that at an earlier date, when she *was* feeling suicidal. I don't suppose we know where the note was found."

"Nope."

Kate sighed and relaxed against him.

Skip used his free hand to tip her chin up and lowered his mouth to hers.

An exaggerated throat clearing from the direction of the kitchen doorway.

They looked up. Maria was standing there, trying to look stern and failing miserably. "Dinner ees getting cold, you two."

Kate jumped up. "Let's eat. I'm starved." As if to prove the point, her stomach grumbled loudly.

Skip followed her into the kitchen. He was still pretty sure that her client had committed suicide. But if the belief that she hadn't was bringing Kate out of her slump, he wasn't about to argue.

~~~~~~~~

On her way to work on Tuesday, Kate called both Josie's psychiatrist and her regular doctor. She didn't get through to either of them, which was no surprise. She left messages asking if they had prescribed clonazepam for Josie.

With a few minutes to spare before her first client, she did some quick research in her reference books on drug interactions and side effects. Her suspicions were confirmed. Clonazepam was a powerful and addictive benzodiazepine, used for seizures and panic disorder. It would not have mixed well with the other meds Josie was taking. One of her doctors might have prescribe it to replace her Xanax, except for the fact that it would have interacted negatively with the mood stabilizer she was on. Kate was quite sure neither doctor would take her off of her mood medication.

She was about to close the reference book when the word *suicide* caught her eye.

Holy crap! One of the possible side effects of clonazepam was increased risk of suicidal ideation.

It was highly unlikely then that either of her doctors would have given her that prescription. Had she gone doctor shopping, expressly to get some additional meds in case she decided to kill herself? Kate found that hard to believe.

But there was a suicide note.

Had Josie gone to a new doctor who prescribed the clonazepam without asking about other drugs she was on? Also unlikely.

But if a doctor had been that careless, the clonazepam might have triggered suicidal impulses. Still, she would *not* have left the dog in his crate like that.

Arrghh!

Kate took a deep breath and mentally shoved Josie's case aside. Time to focus on her living clients.

At lunchtime, there were messages from both doctors confirming what Kate had surmised. Neither had prescribed the clonazepam.

Next step was to talk to Father Phelps. She called her childhood parish in Parkville, one community over from Towson, on the outskirts of Baltimore City.

"St. Batholomew's Catholic Church. How may I help you?" The voice was female and elderly–probably one of the legion of retiree volunteers who took turns manning the front desk in the office.

Kate asked for an appointment to see Father Samuel Phelps

and was relieved when she was able to get one for the next day at twelve-fifteen.

Then she called Rob. It went straight to voicemail, which meant he was either in a meeting or in court.

"Hey, I can't make lunch tomorrow, but I do want to touch base with you about my client's parents. I could do lunch on Friday if you're free then. Call me. And sorry about bailing on you for tomorrow but something's come up that I need to check out."

As she disconnected, a shiver ran through her. The end of that message was reminiscent of the last one she had gotten from Josie–the one she now wished she hadn't erased.

CHAPTER FIVE

Kate arrived early for her appointment with the priest and decided to look around the church for a few minutes, for old times' sake.

The cavernous sanctuary smelled of furniture polish and candle wax, with a hint of incense. Off to the left, a middle-aged woman lovingly polished the pews. She returned Kate's nod of greeting without missing a beat in the smooth motions of her cloth over the already lustrous wood.

The stained-glass windows were even more beautiful than Kate had remembered them. Of course a child, and then rebellious teen, would not have appreciated them as she could now. She made a slow circuit of the outside aisles, staring open-mouthed at each richly-colored scene from the scriptures.

She stopped at the rows of mostly unlit votive candles near the altar. Some flickered with a soft flame. A few sputtered as they burned low.

A strange mix of peace and mild anxiety grew in her chest. Her fingers fumbled a bit as she struck a match and lit a candle for Josie. Her childhood religion had both comforted and confused her. In adolescence, the confusion had briefly turned to disdain.

As a young adult, she'd described herself as a lapsed Catholic. She and Eddie Huntington had sporadically attended the Episcopal parish where they had been married. Eddie had loved the old joke: *Catholic Light, same rituals, half the guilt.*

Kate smiled to herself.

Now she and Skip belonged to that same Episcopal parish.

They'd started attending to give their kids a religious base but had become members mainly because of the current priest.

"Katie O'Donnell. How the heck are you?" rang out through the church, startling her out of her reverie.

She turned and smiled at the elderly priest hobbling toward her, leaning heavily on a brass-headed cane. "Father Sam!" The name the children had always called him popped out.

He motioned for her to come to him and held out his arms.

She willingly stepped into them and returned his hearty hug.

Then he took her by the shoulders, his forgotten cane clattering to the floor. "Lemme get a look at you, girl. Why you haven't aged a bit, still as pretty as a picture."

Kate let out a small snort. "Don't you know it's a sin to lie, Father?"

Age had not been kind to the priest's appearance. The thick silver hair she remembered from her youth had been reduced to wisps of white fuzz. His skin was leathery and craggy with deep wrinkles.

What did I expect? He was middle-aged when I was a teenager.

But above those weathered cheeks, his eyes still sparkled with the same *joie de vivre* Kate had always admired.

"You want to talk here or in my office?" He gestured with his right hand toward the pews, then looked at the empty hand, confusion on his face.

Kate bit back a laugh as she reached down and scooped up his cane.

"Oh, there it is. The confounded thing is always falling down on the job." He chuckled at his own joke.

Kate laughed out loud. She'd forgotten how delightful the man could be.

Then her mood sobered as she remembered the reason for her visit. "In your office would be better."

His expression grew serious as well. "Of course." He turned and led the way.

When they reached the doors leading from the sanctuary to the church offices, Kate had to fight the temptation to jump in front of the old man and hold the door for him. He would be offended. She tried to look nonchalant as he fumbled his cane into his other hand, then pulled on the door handle. The heavy, carved door submitted slowly to his efforts.

Finally he had it open and stepped back so she could precede him into the hallway beyond.

As they walked past a secretary's desk, the forty-something woman behind it asked, "Would you like some tea, Father?"

"Yes, please. That would be excellent."

"And for you, Mrs. Huntington?"

"Sounds wonderful."

"I'll bring it in a minute."

They settled in Father Sam's cluttered office, on either side of a large mahogany desk. The visitor's chair was a leather wing chair, in a rich shade of burgundy. The room smelled of old books.

"Huntington. Yes, it's coming back to me. You married that Protestant boy."

Kate smiled. "Yes, but he died. I'm re–"

"Of course, how could I forget. Your parents stopped by to see me when they were in town for the funeral. A terrible thing. He must have been a good man. Your parents were very fond of him."

Kate's chest ached for a moment with the old pain. "It was a horrible time, and I still miss him sometimes. But I'm remarried now, and quite happy."

"But you're using the first husband's name?"

"It's complicated." She decided she might as well explain, since she wasn't bringing up Josie Hartin until after their tea arrived. "I still use Huntington professionally, since I'd already established my reputation as a psychotherapist under that name. Elsewhere I go by Kate Canfield."

"So this is a professional visit."

Kate hid a smile. The old priest might have a spotty memory, but otherwise his mind was still quite sharp.

"Yes, and it's a little... I'm not sure what to call it... difficult, awkward? Because of the confidentiality. One of your parishioners was my client. From my end, I'd like to ask that this discussion have the seal of the confessional, so that I can tell you some things in confidence."

Something had clicked in the old man's eyes. They turned troubled. "Josephine Hartin."

"Yes, Father."

A light rap on the door. "Come in," Father Sam called out.

The secretary entered, carrying a small tray with two steaming cups and a sugar bowl. She made no effort to clear a spot on the desk, just put it down on top of the clutter. "Do you want cream, Mrs. Huntington? I can get some from the rectory."

"No, no." Kate reached for one of the cups. "This is fine."

"Thank you, Julie," the priest said as he leaned forward to doctor his tea with a heavy dose of sugar.

"Thanks," Kate echoed.

They both sat in silence until the door had closed behind the woman.

"Father Phelps, I have to get back to my office in a little while, so I'll cut to the chase."

The priest's brow furrowed. "I'd prefer you call me Father Sam. Father Phelps sounds so stuffy."

Kate chuckled softly, then leaned forward in her chair. "Look, I know there's a limit to what you can tell me, but I don't believe Josie killed herself. I think she was murdered."

A chill ran through her at the sound of her own words in her ears. It was the first time she had said *murdered* out loud in reference to Josie. It brought home the enormity of what she now suspected had happened.

Father Sam's eyes had gone wide. "Who would want to kill Josie?"

"That is the big question, but first let me address why I think it wasn't suicide. I'll tell you what I can, and then you let me know if there's anything you feel comfortable adding. And again, please keep this confidential. You can't even share it with her family."

"I understand, Katie."

She took a deep breath. "Josie was doing really well. The day before she was found, which may have been the day she died, she left a cheerful message on my voicemail. So it totally blew me away when I found out she was dead. My husband's a private detective. He has contacts with the police. He found out that it was deemed a suicide. But he also told me that her dog was locked in his crate and was near death by the time the body was found."

Father Sam winced. "That doesn't sound like Josie."

"That absolutely is not her. She would never do that to a dog, especially not her own."

"She might not have thought it through. Just assumed someone would find her right away."

"Maybe, but there's something else. One of the almost empty pill bottles they found in her apartment was for a drug that would have interacted negatively with her other meds. I checked. Neither her psychiatrist nor her regular doctor prescribed it."

The priest rubbed his chin. "Would this drug, mixed with the others, could that have killed her accidentally?"

"Not likely. She would have to intentionally take way too much of each. The interaction tends to build up over time with normal doses, and it was a new prescription, recently filled."

Father Sam blew out air and sat back, his tea forgotten.

"Had you seen Josie recently?" Kate asked.

He nodded. "She only comes to church now and again. But she did come to see me a few weeks ago. I can't remember exactly when, but I can find out."

"Would that discussion be considered a confession?"

He squirmed in his desk chair, then sat up straighter. "No, not really. But I consider all meetings with parishioners about their personal matters as pastoral counseling sessions, so the same rules apply for them as they do for you."

He stared at the ceiling above her head for a moment. "I think I can share some things with you. And I too would like you to keep what I say confidential."

Kate nodded.

"She wasn't in a good place when she came to see me. She was having some disturbing dreams and she wasn't real sure what to do about them."

Kate's stomach churned. Why would Josie tell Father Sam about the dreams and not her therapist?

"I knew she was in therapy," the priest said, "but I hadn't realized you were her therapist. I asked her if she had told her therapist and she said no, that it wasn't safe. I asked her what she meant by that, and she couldn't seem to explain it. She said she just felt terrified at the thought of telling anyone about what happens in the dreams."

"Did she tell you?"

"No. She started to, said they were dark and shadowy. Then she got really nervous and practically bolted out of here."

Kate sat back against the stiff leather of her chair. "What the hell does that mean?" She winced internally when she realized she'd let the *hell* slip out.

But Father Sam didn't react to it. "I have no idea. I've been trying to figure it out myself, ever since she died." He paused, took a deep breath and then let it out. "You realize I can't bury her in sacred ground as a suicide?"

"That was the first thing that made me wonder about her death," Kate said. "She may not have gone to church regularly, but she was still Catholic enough to believe that suicide is a mortal sin."

That and sheer stubbornness had kept Josie from going that far in the past. She'd often said that she wasn't willing to let her bipolar disorder win. But maybe the fight had gotten to be too much.

Still there was the dog issue. But Father Sam had made a good point. Maybe she'd assumed she'd be found sooner. Did she have an appointment with someone to come to her place?

"Earth to Katie."

"Sorry, I was just trying to put together the pieces."

The priest smiled at her, his eyes twinkling again. "You always did love puzzles."

Kate smiled back, realizing he was right. As a kid, she'd loved puzzles of any kind–jigsaw puzzles, crossword puzzles. Now she made her living sorting out the mysteries of what was going on in her clients' psyches. And far too often in recent years, she'd dealt with the mystery of a murder.

Did she really want to get involved in another one?

"Can't think of anything else helpful," Father Sam said.

She pulled out her wallet and extracted one of her business cards. "Will you call me if you do think of anything?"

"Surely, and you keep me posted. I'd love to be able to tell her parents she can be buried in their plot at the New Cathedral Cemetery."

Kate suppressed a chuckle. The *New* Cathedral Cemetery wasn't all that new anymore, having been founded in the 1800s. But it was the most prestigious Catholic cemetery in the area, so she wasn't surprised the Hartins had a family plot there.

The priest showed her to the door. "Where are you going to church these days, Katie?"

"St. Catherine's in Towson."

He looked puzzled for a moment, then his face cleared. "Ah, St. Catherine's *Episcopal*. Catholic Light, same rituals…"

"Half the guilt," they said in unison.

They both laughed, then Father Sam pulled her into a warm hug.

Kate's stomach growled as she drove back to her office, reminding her that she'd never eaten lunch during her lunch break. She pulled into a fast food drive-thru and ordered a quarter-pound cheeseburger and fries, promising herself she'd do an extra aikido workout this weekend to make up for the calories.

Waiting in the line of cars that was barely inching forward, she tapped her fingers on the steering wheel. She really needed to know more about that clonazepam prescription. Who had prescribed it, and was it even prescribed for Josie? But she couldn't keep bothering Skip and Dolph every time she needed more information.

Maybe she had enough to get Dolph's old partner at the Baltimore County police department to open the case as a homicide investigation. Judith Anderson was a lieutenant now, so she certainly had the clout, if Kate could convince her there was enough evidence to counter the assumption of suicide.

Maybe she could borrow Dolph one more time, to get her in to see Judith. But first she had to free up some time during a weekday. Police lieutenants worked nine to five, unless they had an important case going on, in which case Judith wouldn't have time to see her anyway.

She mentally reviewed her schedule for the next two days. Carol was coming in again tomorrow at two. She had to see her for sure, but her three and four o'clock clients had been in a good place lately. Maybe she could postpone them to next week.

Anxiety and guilt blindsided her. What if one of them went into a downward spiral while they were waiting to see her again, like Josie had?

Don't be ridiculous.

Neither of those two clients was prone to depression or suicidal ideation. And besides, wasn't she ninety percent convinced now that Josie hadn't committed suicide?

She gripped the steering wheel. She needed to find out, one way or the other, for her peace of mind.

And so Josie could rest in peace.

CHAPTER SIX

Dolph Randolph was wearing his usual uniform–a white dress shirt and dark slacks, slightly rumpled–when he met Kate in front of the police station Thursday afternoon. They greeted each other with a hug. Then he leaned forward and opened the door for her.

Kate stepped into the station's outer lobby. Despite the heat emanating from the mass of bodies, as well as from the air vents, Kate felt a chill. She rubbed her goose-bumped arms.

The last time she'd seen this lobby it had been virtually deserted, late on a Sunday evening, after the most harrowing weekend of her life. She shuddered at the memory of their race against the clock to save her former boss, Sally Ford, from a serial killer.

Today, the lobby was teeming with a cross-section of human-kind, from the well-dressed businesswoman impatiently checking her watch to the disheveled and jittery young man who looked to be in desperate need of whatever substance he was addicted to.

At the panel of bulletproof glass that separated the reception desk from the masses, Dolph spoke quietly to the female officer.

She broke into a wide smile. "Of course I remember you, Detective Randolph."

A buzzer sounded, almost drowning out the click of the door unlocking.

Dolph returned the woman's smile. "Thanks, Officer Browning." He opened the door to the inner sanctum of the precinct and bowed slightly in Kate's direction, making an after-you gesture with his arm.

"It's good to have connections," she whispered as she walked past him.

He chuckled. "A good memory for names helps too."

They made their way to the detectives' bullpen, and the lieutenant's office beyond it. The door was ajar.

Dolph rapped a knuckle against it, then stuck his head into the opening.

Kate heard an exaggerated groan.

"What do you want, Dolph?"

He signaled to Kate to follow him and stepped into the office.

Judith Anderson stood behind a desk as cluttered as Father Sam's but not nearly as elegant. Her eyes lit up. "Hey Kate, how are you?"

Kate snickered. "I'm good, and something tells me I might have gotten further with my request if I'd come alone."

Judith snorted. "Well, since you've already brought the old goat in here, you both might as well sit down." She gestured toward two metal chairs with beige vinyl seats that were theoretically cushioned.

Kate sat down, then shifted to try to find a comfortable spot. None seemed to exist.

Judith broke into a rare grin. "Keeps my people from lingering in here when they should be on the streets."

Kate returned the smile. "How have you been, Judith?"

The lieutenant dropped into her desk chair. "I'm good, but I doubt you came by just to inquire about my health."

"You know anything about the Josephine Hartin case?" Dolph asked.

Judith shrugged. "Not much. It was a suicide."

"Last I heard," Dolph said, "that was still tentative, pending the tox reports."

"Okay. So what about that case?"

Kate leaned forward. The hard vinyl under her butt squeaked. "I have reason to believe that it wasn't a suicide. I knew the young woman but…," she intentionally paused, "I can't tell you how."

She knew the lieutenant would make the appropriate assumption.

Judith nodded. "So why do you think it wasn't a suicide?"

Kate filled her in on the cheerful phone messages, and pointed out that Josie wouldn't have left her puppy locked up in a crate to starve like that. "And she was having strange dreams." This was skirting the edge of violating her promise to Father Sam. But Josie's mother had also mentioned the dreams, and Kate didn't consider her meeting with the Hartins as confidential, since they weren't clients.

"In that last phone message, Josie said something about checking something out. I've got a gut feeling that whatever that something was, it may have been related to those dreams."

Judith was quiet for a moment, then she shook her head. "Can't say that's enough for me to open the case up as a homicide."

"I'm not asking for that," Kate said, although she had hoped for it. "But there are a couple other things that are off, and I can't tell you about them unless I'm sure they mean something. I need more information from the police file."

"Could you get the file for us to look at?" Dolph said.

Judith looked from one to the other of them, then blew out air. She stood. "Be back in a minute."

After she'd left the office, Kate said in a low voice, "Doesn't she have minions now to fetch files for her?"

"Yeah," Dolph said, "but she wants to look at it first before she shows it to us."

That made sense. "I don't even necessarily need to see it, if she's uncomfortable showing it to me. I just need some questions answered."

Dolph ran a hand through his gray hair, highlighted with a few remaining streaks of its original rust color. "Well, I want to see the thing. You've got me intrigued now. I didn't know before why Skip asked me to check into the case."

Kate's stomach clenched. "Dolph, you've got to keep it to yourself that—"

He held up a hand. "I know, Kate. I'm not gonna blab about

your connection to the woman."

"Sorry. It's just that confidentiality doesn't die with the client, but…"

"But it's more important to find out if the gal was murdered, and if so, by whom."

Kate nodded. "Still, the Hartins are powerful people. I don't want to give them grounds for a malpractice suit." Especially since they were already considering one for not preventing the suicide.

"What do you need to ask about?" Dolph said.

Kate dug a small notepad and pen out of her purse. "Prescriptions and the note."

He nodded.

Judith came through the door, leafing through a file in her hands.

"That was quick," Dolph said.

"It was still on Baxter's desk. As you said, pending the tox screens."

Dolph's bushy eyebrows flew up. "And he just let you have it without an argument?"

"No, he's not in." A flash of a smile. "I borrowed it."

Dolph shook his head. Kate gathered from his expression that Baxter and Judith were not friends.

"I don't want to cause any trouble," she said.

"Don't worry. I outrank him now." There was a glint in Judith's eye as she dropped into her desk chair. "What do you need to know?"

"There were three pill bottles found," Kate said. "I need to know the drugs, the doses, and who prescribed them. And whether they were completely empty."

Judith shuffled through the papers in the file. "Here's the two that were beside her on the floor." She read off the generic names for Depakote and Xanax, then the doses.

Kate wrote it all down. The dose for Xanax was relatively low.

"Both were empty. Prescribing doc was a guy named John Montgomery."

"He's the psychiatrist I–" Kate caught herself. "And the third one?"

Judith leafed through a couple more pages. "It was in the medicine cabinet. Clonazepam, 20 milligrams."

Kate stopped writing. That struck her as a high dose. "You're sure?"

Judith looked again. "Yeah, that's what it says. Doc was a Gerald Kraft. Two pills left in it, even though it was only filled on March tenth. Wait a minute!"

Kate's head jerked up. "That was probably the day she died."

Judith was already back to the first page of the file. "Yeah, that was the coroner's best guess at the scene, that she'd been dead between twelve and thirty hours before she was found." She was rifling through papers again. "Autopsy didn't narrow down the time of death much. Between nine-thirty a.m. on Tuesday, the tenth and one a.m. on the eleventh."

Icy fingers danced down Kate's spine. "I got that message from her at noon on the tenth."

Judith grabbed her own pad and jotted a note. "Are you sure that's when she'd called?"

"No, but it had to have been between eleven and twelve. There were no messages when I checked at eleven. Wait a minute. Why was the original time span estimate so wide?"

More rifling through the file. "Heat was turned off in her apartment."

Kate flopped back in her chair. "That slows down the whole rigor mortis and such, doesn't it?"

"You've been watching CSI again, haven't you?" Judith said in a teasing tone.

Kate ignored the attempt at levity. She was re-examining the pieces that had fallen into place, making sure she wasn't trying to jam them in where they didn't really fit. "She would *not* have turned the heat off, not with her dog there. By the way, do you have the name of the veterinarian who took her dog?" She wasn't sure the vet could tell her anything useful, but she wanted to make sure the pup was okay.

Judith leafed through papers in the file and read off a name and address.

"What earthly reason would this young woman have for turning the heat off just before committing suicide?" Dolph brought them back to that question.

Judith rattled a piece of paper. "We're forgetting here that she left a note."

Kate held out her hand. "May I see it?"

Judith didn't hand it over. "It's a copy. The original would be in the evidence room. The parents wanted us to keep the contents confidential."

Dolph let out a low chuckle. "We've already got plenty of secrets going here."

Judith frowned at him. "I like my rank."

"I'm not going to tell anybody," Kate said.

That was a fib. She might very well tell Skip. And maybe Father Sam, if she didn't think the note really was meant to be a suicide note. Even if she couldn't prove that Josie didn't commit suicide, if the priest was convinced she hadn't, he'd bury her in consecrated ground. That would mean a lot to him and to Josie's parents.

Judith relented and handed the page to her.

Kate took a deep breath, bracing herself, then looked down at the paper. She thought it was Josie's handwriting, although she'd only seen it on checks.

I can't take this anymore. No one really understands what it feels like. Not even Kate. She calls it a roller coaster. She's right, up to a point. It takes you up a mountain, which is exciting at first, then dangles you over a cliff, totally out of control. Then it plunges you down, and you can't stop it. It bores right down into the ground, until you feel like you are buried alive, the earth pressing down on you, suffocating you in depression.

Kate stopped and swallowed hard. Josie had said similar words in her office, but somehow reading this, in the woman's own hand, knowing these were her last thoughts… She made herself keep reading.

Ironically, I think the out-of-control highs are sometimes worse. Kate says that may be because the out-of-control feeling reminds me of being a kid, unable to control what was happening to me. She's probably right. All I know is I hate that feeling. I'd give anything never to feel it again.

And most people are able to get off the roller coaster at times. I never do. Sometimes there's a brief lull in the middle, for a week or two, but then it starts right back up again. Kate calls it rapid cycling.

I call it the roller coaster from hell. Today, I'm ready to throw myself off that damn cliff.

By the time Kate got to the last word, her eyes were blurry with tears. She blinked them back.

Statistically, bipolar patients sometimes committed suicide while they were manic rather than depressed, but she'd never quite understood why they would do that when they were feeling up. Now she did.

She opened her mouth. A croak came out. She cleared her throat and tried again. "Can I get a copy of this? I swear I won't show it to anyone else or tell anyone its contents."

There was something about the note that bothered her, but she wasn't sure what. She didn't want to say anything to Judith until she'd had time to think about it. And make sure her own feelings weren't getting in the way.

Judith didn't respond. She gave Kate a hard, calculating look.

Kate tried not to squirm. "I assume the parents verified this is Josie's handwriting."

"Yes." Judith continued to examine her, as if she were a specimen under a microscope. Kate had a feeling that look worked really well when interrogating suspects. It was making her want to confess to something, just to get Judith to stop looking at her that way.

Finally Judith heaved a sigh. "Okay, but you had better not

let it get away from you. And Dolph, this whole conversation never happened."

Dolph shrugged innocently. "Who, me? I just stopped by to see if my former partner wanted to come over for dinner this weekend. Sue's making your favorite dish."

Judith was now narrowing her eyes at him. "Are you trying to bribe an officer of the law with meatloaf?"

Dolph chuckled. "Which night?"

Judith stood up, closing the file but leaving the note out. "Saturday." She picked up the note and moved toward her office door, then looked back over her shoulder at Kate. "You coming?"

Judith led the way to the copy machine, Dolph bringing up the rear.

Kate had just folded the copy of the note in half and put it and her notepad in her purse when a male voice called across the bullpen. "Hey Anderson, did you take the Hartin case file?"

Judith gritted her teeth, pivoted and strode across the bullpen. Kate and Dolph followed in her wake.

She grabbed a middle-aged man by the arm and dragged him to a far corner where the desks were unoccupied. "It's *lieutenant* to you, asshole," she hissed in the man's face. "And what the hell are you doing calling out the name of a sensitive case right in the middle of the bullpen?"

"Uh, nobody'll think anything of it." He stammered a little. Then he pulled loose from her grasp and shrugged his suit jacket back into place. "And what the hell do you think you're doing manhandling me?"

Judith pinched her lips together. "I'm overseeing this case until further notice. Let me know the instant the tox report is in."

She turned on her heel and almost collided with Dolph. "You two better get out of here," she said under her breath.

Dolph nodded. "Good seeing you, partner." He faked a jovial tone.

Kate kept quiet, afraid to make a bad situation worse. The other cop, Baxter no doubt, was staring at them from several feet away.

Dolph took her elbow and they left the bullpen without saying another word.

Once out in the main lobby, Kate said, "I didn't get a chance to thank her."

"I'll tell her Saturday night. Besides, she doesn't need your thanks. You may be helping her in the long run."

"How, by giving her more work?"

Dolph held the outer door open for her. "If you end up keeping a murder from being dismissed as a suicide, she'll be grateful. She's got this funny idea that crimes shouldn't go unpunished."

"So she's really coming over for dinner?"

He gave a half shrug. "She comes over every couple of weeks. We're good friends. She just pretends to hate to see me show up here, 'cause that usually means I'm about to complicate her life."

"Well, I can thank *you*." Kate stood on tiptoe on the sidewalk and pecked him on the cheek. "Thanks, Dolph."

He grinned at her. "No problem. I like to keep the boss's wife happy."

Skip greeted her at the door with a hug and a kiss. Kate dropped her briefcase and purse on the floor and wrapped her arms around his neck, deepening the kiss.

When she was almost out of air, he broke the kiss and leaned back a little to look down into her face. "Whoa, you're in a better mood tonight. I take it Dolph was able to get you in to see Judith."

"Yes, and I have some computer research to do after dinner." She leaned down and retrieved her briefcase and purse. "You've been coming home early the past few days. Things that slow at the agency or were you just worried about me?"

"Yes, and yes."

She shook her head and gave him a mock-exasperated look, then changed the subject. "Where are the kids?"

"Billy's doing his homework, and Edie is, quote, 'helping' Maria with supper, i.e., talking her ear off."

Kate tilted her head toward the kitchen and picked up the

cadence of her daughter's voice. She couldn't make out the words but the tone was strident. No doubt she was regaling Maria with the latest horrible thing that someone had done to one of her friends.

Edie was an easy-going child in many ways, but she had a keen sense of justice. She would become irate over things that happened to other people, often getting more upset than they did themselves. Kate was convinced she would become a lawyer like Rob, her honorary uncle.

The kids seemed to be okay for now so she took Skip by the hand and led him to the sofa, their favorite spot to sit and talk.

Once they were settled, Skip's arm draped around her shoulders, she turned slightly toward him. "Sweetheart, you don't need to worry about me."

He gave a slight shake of his head. "And how am I supposed to not worry about you. I love you."

"Okay, okay, it's natural to worry about the people we love, but you should know by now that I can handle my emotions. Heck, that's what I do for a living, teach people how to handle theirs."

"Yeah, but this is something new you're dealing with. And besides, you worry about me. For years, you were downright obsessed about the risk in my job."

"True," she said. "Okay, so you're right. You can't just stop worrying. So what can I do to reassure you?"

"This…," he waved his hand back and forth between them to indicate he meant the conversation, "…is helping. And the fact that you seem to be in a better place tonight."

"I am. I'm not sure that Josie was murdered, but checking into that possibility is making me feel like I'm *doing* something about her death."

A gentle smile played across his lips. He reached over with his free hand and hooked a stray curl behind her ear. "That's so you."

She let out a small chuckle. It was definitely her favorite coping mechanism, to find something to do about the problem, whatever it may be.

"So how'd the meeting with Judith go?" he asked.

Kate had promised not to reveal anything about the note so she left that out for now, but she told him about the heat being off in Josie's apartment. "Can you figure out any sane reason why she would do that?" It was still full-blown winter in early March in Maryland.

Skip was quiet for a moment. Then he shook his head. "No, but how sane is someone who's about to commit suicide?"

"Oh, she would have been quite sane. Maybe not thinking straight but not delusional."

Skip nodded slightly. "A killer might turn the heat off, to mess with the signs of what time the death occurred. And maybe to keep the smell down for as long as possible. To delay the discovery of the body."

Kate grimaced. She hadn't thought about the smell. That made sense.

"I've got the name of the doctor who prescribed the clonazepam," she said. "But I need to research how to contact him."

"He isn't going to be able to tell you much. He's got confidentiality constraints just like you do."

"He can at least admit if someone is his patient, and I'm hoping he'll tell me how long she'd been seeing him. That might give me a feel for... I don't know what. But it's an avenue to explore."

Skip nodded again. "Let's think about the dog and the crate for a minute here. Why would he be in the crate?"

"He was still a puppy. She complained about him chewing everything he got his teeth into if he was left unsupervised."

Skip gave Toby, who was lying at their feet, a pointed look. "We can relate to that. So she probably crated him whenever she went out, and maybe at night."

"Yeah. So she'd either just gotten home and he was still in his crate, or somebody got in during the night."

"Unlikely it was a break-in," Skip said. "The dog would have barked and woken her up."

"Maybe he did and she surprised an intruder."

He gave a half shrug. "Possible, but how would a stranger know about her meds, and how would they keep the dog quiet while they went to all that trouble to set it up like a suicide?"

"Maybe it wasn't a stranger. Maybe it was somebody she knew, and the dog knew."

"Could be. It's also possible someone used some ruse to get her to let them in, then pretended to be afraid of dogs, so she put the pup in the crate."

Kate leaned back against his arm and stared across the living room, imagining each of those scenarios. "I'm assuming there was nothing missing from her apartment, but I should check that out with Judith. If that's the case, then robbery wasn't the motive. Why would a robber take the time to set up a fake suicide, and then not take anything?"

"Judith reopened the case as a homicide then?"

"No, but she took the case away from the guy who had it. I got the impression they were not on friendly terms." She told him about the confrontation between Judith and Baxter.

"Okay, let's circle back around to my worrying," Skip said. "I get it that you can handle your emotions, but murderers are another story. By all means, check out this doctor. That should be safe enough, but any poking around beyond that should be done by the agency."

Kate noted his gentle tone. He was trying so hard not to be pushy or overprotective. But still she felt resistant to involving him or the agency any more than she already had, and she wasn't sure why. For now, she opted to use money as the excuse. "I don't want you paying people to check this out, not until I'm sure it wasn't a suicide." That note was hard to dismiss.

"I've been weighing each step I take, though," she added to reassure him. "Making sure it doesn't put me in danger."

"Okay, but keep in mind, things are slow right now, and we pay our people salaries, so it's not a big deal to work on this for free. I could assign Manny Ortiz to help you out."

That was tempting. Manny had been her bodyguard on several

occasions before when things had gotten dicey. He was quite bright, and they had a good rapport. "I'll keep that in mind, if and when I've got something more concrete."

Skip hooked a finger under her chin. "Okay, but you be careful."

She tried to nod, but he held onto her chin and leaned down. As their lips brushed, warmth spread through her chest, loosened her tight muscles. She opened her mouth slightly, inviting him in. The warmth moved downward, a tingling feeling in its wake.

"Mommy, Daddy," Edie yelled. "Dinner's ready."

They jolted apart, thinking she'd come into the room. But they were still alone.

"Dat's not what I mean." Maria's voice came from the kitchen. "When I say call your parents to dinner, Edie, I mean you go to where dey are and tell dem, in a normal voice."

"Sorry, Maria," Edie said, not sounding the least bit contrite.

"Go upstairs and *tell* your brother to wash up and come eat."

"Okay." Edie bounced out of the kitchen and bounded up the steps.

Kate managed to hold back until the child was out of sight, then she burst out laughing.

Grinning, Skip pushed himself to a stand and offered her a hand up.

~~~~~~~~~

Her office phone rang as Kate was about to go into her first session of the morning. She checked caller ID, and froze at the sight of *Esq.* at the end of an unfamiliar name. She grabbed the receiver before the call went to voicemail.

"Kate Huntington."

"Mrs. Huntington, my name is Kathy O'Connor. I'm an attorney, and I represent Mr. and Mrs. Phillip Hartin. I–"

"Ms. O'Connor, I'm sorry to cut you short, but I have a client waiting. My attorney is Robert Franklin. Could you call him please and explain your business to him?"

A couple beats of silence. "Certainly, Mrs. Huntington. I know

Rob Franklin. I'll give him a call. Have a good day."

"Thank you. You, too." She disconnected, then muttered, "It *was* a good day, until you called."

CHAPTER SEVEN

Kate shook her head to clear it. She had to get to Carol Foster. The day before, the woman had still been severely depressed. Kate had wanted to hospitalize her, but she'd promised not to hurt herself. They'd settled on her coming in again this morning instead. Fortunately a cancellation in Kate's schedule had made that feasible.

Ten minutes into the session, Kate was seeing no signs of improvement. Carol had called her psychiatrist, but he didn't have an opening to see her until Monday afternoon. He had called in a stronger dose of her current medication.

Problem was, when people were this depressed, such simple errands as going to the pharmacy sometimes felt beyond them. "Have you picked up the new prescription?" Kate asked.

Carol dropped her gaze to her lap. "Not yet. I'm gonna get it on my way home."

"It will take time for that to kick in." Kate kept her voice gentle, even though her heart was pounding in her chest. "I'm thinking it might be a good idea for you to go into the hospital. They can keep you safe while they get your meds adjusted."

Carol shook her head vehemently. "I hate the hospital. The staff either acts like I'm crazy or I'm a small child. Last time, one nurse kept saying, 'Now dearie.' I wanted to slug her."

Kate's mouth went dry. She wasn't convinced this woman would make it through the weekend. Her mind blanked. She couldn't think of anything to say.

"What about that thing you had me sign once?" Carol said.

"Promising I'd call you if I felt like hurting myself."

"Are you making that promise?"

Carol looked away. She twisted her hands together. "Yes."

Kate didn't believe her. Terror raged through her system, blood pounding in her ears. She still couldn't think of what to say, so she opted for the truth. "You're scaring me, Carol."

Carol's gaze flicked in her direction, then away again. "You don't have to be worried about me." Her voice was low, deflated.

That scared Kate even more. Her hand shook as she reached up to brush hair back from her face. Should she consider an involuntary admission?

Probably wouldn't work since the client would just swear to the emergency room doctors that she wasn't suicidal, and it would blow Carol's trust in her.

These times when Carol waxed suicidal had been easier to deal with back before her husband had jumped ship. Yes, it was hard living with someone who had such a severe mental disorder, but still… It wasn't like his wife wanted to be depressed or that she had any control over the mood swings.

Carol was staring at her. "Are you okay, Kate? You seem really nervous today."

Kate's throat tightened. A voice in her head said, *The client's not supposed to be worrying about* you!

Since she was doing such a crappy job of hiding her anxiety, she might as well use it. "I told you, you're scaring me."

Carol sighed, then sat up straighter in her chair. "Look, I promise I won't hurt myself this weekend. I've been this low before, and I always pull through. I know I will this time too. I just have to tough it out."

"How about we arrange for a friend to come over and stay with you?"

Carol rolled her eyes. "I don't want a babysitter. I've got several new books on my tablet. I'm gonna curl up and read all weekend, not even try to do anything else."

That sounded very depressed, but safe. "Okay, but I do want

you to sign an agreement. I know you keep your word, so that will make me feel better."

It isn't about you *feeling better,* the voice in her head said.

No, she answered the damn voice, *but guilt about letting me down might just keep this woman alive!*

When a client was suicidal, you used whatever worked.

Kate grabbed a pad from her desk and wrote out the agreement, then passed it to Carol, along with a pen.

"I don't think I'm gonna go back to work today," Carol said as she signed it. "I'm gonna go home and take a nap."

Adrenaline jolted through Kate again. There wasn't much else she could do though. Again she considered the involuntary admission, and again rejected it as not feasible. Two doctors were required to sign off on such an admission. Carol's psychiatrist would be one, but Kate didn't see them convincing a doctor who didn't know them that this woman was actively suicidal. Not if Carol was saying she was fine.

Kate understood the need for that two-doctor requirement. It helped prevent abuses of the system by family members who just wanted to get someone out of the way. But it also made it difficult to hospitalize someone who was legitimately suicidal.

Kate took the pad back with a trembling hand.

At the office door, Carol gave her a hug. "I'll be okay. You'll see."

Dear God, I hope so.

As Carol walked across the waiting room toward the outer door, Kate recalled the conversation with Skip the night before. She'd told him she could handle her own emotions, but she wasn't all that sure she'd be able to cope if she lost a second client to suicide.

She bolted after the woman. "Carol, wait."

Grabbing one of her cards from a holder on the end table, she scribbled her cell phone number on the back, all the while thinking, *What am I doing?*

She never gave out her personal numbers. She used an

answering service as a buffer. Clients called them with an emergency, the service called her, and she called the client back.

She handed the card to Carol. "Just in case," she said in a low voice so her next client, sitting in a chair a few feet away, couldn't hear her.

At noon, before she left for her lunch date with Rob, Kate called the only number she'd been able to find for Gerald Kraft, MD. The previous evening, she'd searched the Web but found no office address or number, only the one residential listing in that name.

As the phone rang in her ear, she told herself she wanted to know what the doctor had to say before she met with Rob. It might influence her response to whatever threat the Hartins were now making. She shook her head. The reality was that she was procrastinating. She dreaded finding out what that lawyer had been calling about.

"Hello." A male voice.

"Dr. Kraft?"

"Yes."

"My name is Kate Huntington. I was hoping I could talk to you about one of your patients."

"I don't have patients anymore, young lady."

What the heck did that mean? "So you didn't start seeing a Josephine Hartin recently?"

"Ms. Whatever-your-name-is, I retired two years ago."

Ah, that explained the lack of an office address. "Did you have a Josephine Hartin for a patient before you retired?"

"Name doesn't ring a bell. Who are you anyway?"

"Uh, Ms. Hartin is deceased. I'm looking into her death." Neither was a lie; they just weren't the whole truth.

"Sorry to hear that, but I can't help you." His tone was crisp.

"Could you check your records?"

A beat of silence, then air being expelled into the phone. "They're locked up in a storage unit."

"Okay, I might be able to come at this from another direction." Kate paused, deciding how much to say. "Ms. Hartin filled a prescription for clonazepam the day she died. The label on the pill bottle said you were the prescribing doctor."

"And when was this?" the man asked, his voice now cautious.

"Not quite two weeks ago."

"What?" the man barked into the phone. "I sure as hell didn't write that prescription."

~~~~~~~~~

Rob sat in his and Kate's favorite booth at Mac's Place and wondered if they'd gotten their wires crossed.

The manager came out of the kitchen door and sketched him a quick wave as he hurried off to deal with some problem. After all these years, it still seemed a little weird that Mac himself wasn't here to greet them when they came in for their weekly lunch date. But the man seemed a lot happier since turning the restaurant over to a manager and becoming an operative of Skip's private investigations agency.

Rob had ordered their usual crab cake sandwiches and sides and was contemplating calling Kate when he spotted her coming through the restaurant's door. She headed his way. Wishing he had better news for her, he rose and swallowed her up in a bear hug.

She wrapped her arms around his waist and hung on for an extra beat. "Sorry I'm late." Her words were muffled against his chest.

They settled onto the benches of the booth, across from one another. "How are you doing?" Kate asked.

"I'm okay. How are you?"

Kate shrugged. "I was doing better, until that lawyer called. What did she say?"

"You're not gonna like it. Her clients are filing suit, and she hinted broadly that what they really want is your file on their daughter."

"What? No way."

"Yeah, that's what I told Kathy."

A waitress appeared next to their booth, two glasses of iced tea in her hands. She put them on the table. "Your crab cakes should be out soon."

Kate gave her a smile that didn't reach her eyes. "Thanks."

Once the waitress had gone, Rob said, "I told her that was unethical, and I couldn't quite understand why they were asking for it."

Kate tilted her head slightly in a half nod. "I understand. They're looking for answers. But they're not going to find them in my notes. And what they would find would just cause them more pain. Not to mention that I would never do that to Jo... uh, the client. She would not want her parents seeing what she said about them."

Rob stirred sugar into his iced tea, delaying what he had to say next. "They may be able to subpoena the file."

Anger sparked in her eyes. "I'll fight them on that, but I don't know how else I can defend myself against a suit. I had no inkling that she was suicidal, and I'm not convinced now that she was." She told him about the dog issue that had first made her skeptical and the prescription supposedly written by a doctor who was retired and swore he'd never written it. "That's what made me late, talking to him. I called Judith on the way over here. She gave me the pharmacy's address from the pill bottle label. I'm going to see what I can find out from the pharmacist."

Some of the tension in Rob's chest released. "I hope you're right. If Judith reopens the case as a homicide, they'd have no grounds for a lawsuit. Otherwise, I don't know how we'll fight it."

"Yeah, either I didn't know she was suicidal or I knew and didn't do anything about it. I'm guessing the former's a little less damaging. But their attorney will have a field day making me look like an idiot."

He wished he could contradict that assessment, but she was right. "If your insurance company wants to settle out of court, I'd suggest letting them."

She nodded. "That would get around the subpoena for the

records."

Rob's chest tightened again. "Crap! Then the parents won't agree to settle, because the records are what they really want."

The waitress brought their food. Kate stared down at her crab cake sandwich and grimaced. "I've lost my appetite. Could I get a box for this?"

The young woman gave her a puzzled look. "Sure."

Rob's stomach churned. It took a lot for Kate to lose her appetite. If they were cutting lunch short, he might as well take his sandwich back to the office and deal with some of the paperwork piled high on his desk. "Make that two boxes."

While they waited, he studied Kate's face, especially her eyes. They were the quickest way to judge her stress level. Not as bright blue as they usually were, but not the washed-out gray that indicated total overload either.

She narrowed her eyes at him. "I'm okay."

"You're not doing anything dangerous, are you?"

"No. I've already had this conversation with Skip. At this point I'm just doing some legwork." She looked at her watch. "Want to come with me to that pharmacy?"

He hesitated. The paperwork called, but he sensed she hadn't told him everything. "Sure."

The waitress brought them two styrofoam containers. They boxed up their lunches and headed out of the restaurant.

Rob dropped an arm around Kate's shoulders and gave her a reassuring squeeze.

～～～～～

The pharmacy was an independent one, in an older building. Kate and Rob made their way down somewhat dingy aisles to the pharmacy counter in the back.

Kate was trying to decide how to broach the subject. There really wasn't a subtle way to do it. At the counter, she asked to speak to the pharmacist about a confidential matter.

That got the attention of a middle-aged man wearing a white coat. He removed the reading glasses from the end of his nose and motioned them down to his end of the counter. "May I help you?"

"I hope so," Kate said. "I'm looking into a prescription that was filled here on March tenth for a Josephine Hartin."

A petite woman glanced up from counting pills at a bench along the side wall. Then she lowered her gaze to her task again.

The pharmacist tilted his head. "I can't really give out any information about our customers."

Kate leaned forward to get a better look at the plastic name-tag pinned to the pocket of his white jacket. It read *Dwayne Keller, PharmD*. "I understand, Dr. Keller, but there's something irregular about this prescription. It's for a controlled substance, and the doctor whose name is on the pill bottle swears he never prescribed it."

The pharmacist's eyes went wide. His Adam's apple bobbed as he swallowed. "Uh…"

Rob leaned forward and said in a low voice, "We're asking because Ms. Hartin died of an overdose of various drugs, including the one from here."

Dr. Keller blanched. "Do you have the prescription number?"

"Yes." Kate pulled out her notepad and read it off.

The pharmacist punched keys on a computer keyboard. His skin paled even further. "Just a moment."

He went through a doorway into a tiny glass-walled office area. Resettling the reading glasses on his nose, he started rummaging through a file cabinet drawer. After a moment, his face registered relief as he pulled a slip of paper out of a file.

He came out of the office, but instead of returning to the counter he stepped over to the woman, who now had her back to them and was straightening items on a shelf along the back wall. The pharmacist showed her the slip. "Do you remember this customer, Sybil?"

The woman glanced at the paper. Shiny auburn hair bounced on her shoulders as she shook her head. "No. We get too many people through here."

Rob raised his eyebrows at Kate. They both looked around.

Herds of customers were distinctly lacking.

The pharmacist lowered his voice. All Kate could hear was an indistinct rumble. The woman shook her head again.

He returned to the counter. "We've got the prescription on file, but neither my assistant nor I remember the customer."

"Could we get a copy of the prescription?" Kate said. "To compare it to the doctor's signature?"

The man hesitated.

"Look," Rob said, "we already know all the information that's on it, so what can it hurt?"

The pharmacist shrugged. He lifted a hinged section of the counter and walked over to a copy machine. Punching in a code that apparently bypassed the need to feed it coins, he copied the prescription slip.

"I wonder how much action that machine gets," Kate whispered, "now that most printers have scan and copy functions."

Rob, the technophobe, gave her a blank look.

Kate snickered softly.

The pharmacist walked over to them.

Kate held out her hand. "Could I see the original?"

Again a moment of hesitation, then another shrug. He handed both pieces of paper to her.

She held them next to each other. There were a couple of faint lines on the original that the copier hadn't picked up, but otherwise the copy was clear.

She handed the original back to the pharmacist. "Isn't twenty milligrams a high dose for clonazepam?"

He nodded. "It's the highest dose given. Is, uh, was this woman heavy?"

"No, average build."

The pharmacist scratched his cheek and glanced at his female assistant, who once again had her back to them. "If she'd been taking it for a while, she might have built up some tolerance, so the doctor had to increase the dose."

Kate opted to let that go. She seriously doubted that Josie had been taking the drug for any length of time. "Thank you." She held out her hand.

The pharmacist shook it, his worried eyes not quite meeting hers. "We didn't do anything wrong. We followed protocol."

"No one's saying otherwise, sir," Rob said, also offering his hand. "Thanks for your help."

Once out on the sidewalk, Kate stopped, took a deep breath and let it out slowly.

Rob scrubbed a hand over his broad face. "You realize he thought we were police detectives."

"Yeah, but we never said we were. It's a trick Skip told me about. Just say your investigating or checking into something, and people tend to assume you're a cop."

"Still, I'd rather Judith not know about this little visit of ours."

Kate shook her head. What she was supposed to be keeping from whom was getting quite complicated. "I won't tell her you were along if you like, but she knew I was coming here. I called her for the name of the pharmacy, remember? And I already told her the doctor claimed he didn't write the prescription."

"Okay. I'd better get back to the office."

Kate didn't answer him. She pulled out her cell phone and notepad. She flipped to the page with Dr. Kraft's phone number.

When he picked up, she said, "Doctor, this is Kate Huntington again. Can I stop by your house around five-thirty this evening for a couple minutes? I have something to show you."

A long stretch of silence, then an audible sigh. "I suppose."

She thanked him, disconnected and pocketed her phone.

"I gotta get going," Rob said again. "Keep me posted." He gave her a quick hug. "And Kate, be careful!"

"What? I'm only talking to a doctor. That's all."

Rob gave a slight shake to his head, then turned toward his car.

~~~~~~~~~

At five-twenty-nine, Kate pulled up in front of a huge, brick house on a shaded side street one block off of Ruxton Road. She adored her old Victorian, that she and Eddie had so lovingly restored, but nonetheless she felt a shot of envy at the sight of the beautiful home, nestled amongst well-kept bushes and pine trees in the ritziest section of Towson.

Must be nice.

Then she chastised herself. She could be living like this if she wanted to. Eddie's life insurance had left her a moderately wealthy woman. But she preferred to keep her brokerage account, now well over the original million dollars, just for emergencies and for the kids' college tuition.

She wouldn't know how to act in this neighborhood anyway. She and Skip were certainly middle class, might even be considered upper middle class. She had advanced degrees and was a professional. He owned a thriving business. But they both came from working-class roots, and she knew she would find rubbing elbows with the upper crust rather intimidating.

She opened her purse and glanced in at the copy of the prescription. Taking a deep breath, she got out of her car and walked up the brick walkway.

An older woman, somewhere in her mid to late sixties, answered the door. "Yes?"

"I'm here to see Dr. Kraft. He's expecting me."

The woman broke into a smile and opened the door wide. "Come on in, my dear. He's down the hall in his study."

Kate assumed she was the doctor's wife. The woman led her across a living room the size of a small skating rink. It was crowded with expensive-looking furniture, most of which were probably antiques. Kate suspected some old money had supplemented the doctor's earnings, which were no doubt substantial in their own right.

As they neared the hallway, Mrs. Kraft said in a low voice, "Try not to tire him, my dear. He's dying, you know, of brain cancer."

Kate managed to stop her hand before it flew to her mouth, but she apparently wasn't able to mask her surprise completely.

The doctor had stood up from his desk chair, smiling

pleasantly–another elderly man shrunken by age like Fr. Sam. The smile collapsed into a sagging, sorrowful expression at the sight of her face. He made a come-in gesture with his hand.

Kate entered the room and sat down in the chair in front of the desk.

"I'll get you two some tea, dear," Mrs. Kraft said from behind her.

The doctor's face softened. "That would be wonderful, Lavada. Be careful with the hot water."

Footsteps receded. The doctor walked around the desk and gently closed the door.

"Lavada," Kate said. "What a lovely name. Was your wife named after someone?"

"No, her father just liked the name. He tended to march to a different drummer." The answer sounded rote, his voice distracted. The doctor settled into his desk chair. "She told you I have brain cancer, didn't she?"

Pain squeezed Kate's heart. Her eyes stung. This poor man, with so much wealth, was going to die, and only a few years after retiring.

He shook his head. "It's not me. She's the one with cancer."

This time, Kate's hand made it to her mouth before she could stop it. "I'm so sorry."

He blinked, his eyes now red-rimmed. "Thank you." He looked away. "I'm six years older than her. The statistics say she should be the widow, not me."

Kate nodded, not sure what to say to that.

The doctor cleared his throat. "But that's not why you're here. You found out more about that prescription?"

"Yes." Kate extracted the copy from her purse and handed it to him.

He fumbled for reading glasses on his desk and put them on. After examining the paper carefully, he peered over the top of his glasses at her. "It looks like it came from my prescription pad and that's my signature, but I didn't write this."

"Any idea who could have, sir?"

He held up an index finger, then leaned back in his chair and opened the center drawer of his desk. "Dammit!" He quickly searched the other desk drawers, then shook his head. "It's gone. Most of my prescription pads are in the storage locker with my records. But I keep one here, just in case..." His voice trailed off and he stared across the room again, blinking hard.

Just in case your wife's in too much pain later. Out loud, she said, "In case an old patient needs a prescription."

Dr. Kraft turned back to her, flashed a half smile, then rose from his chair. "I'll be right back."

Kate entertained herself by reading the titles of the books on the shelves that lined the walls. The doctor had very eclectic tastes–everything from Proust to Dan Brown–and of course multiple volumes of medical reference books.

Her cell phone chirped in her purse. She pulled it out and checked caller ID. *Carol Foster!*

Heart in her throat, she answered it. "Carol, what's up?" She tried to sound cheerful, praying the woman just needed a pep talk.

Sobbing, then a small voice, "You were right, Kate. I should've let you put me in the hospital. I can't stand this, but I don't want to die."

"It's gonna be okay," Kate said. "I'm glad you called."

The doctor came through the door. "Lavada doesn't remember, but she must have thrown it out–"

Kate held up her hand. "We'll get you some help. It will be okay. Just stay on the line with me." She grabbed a piece of paper on the doctor's desk and turned it over, then snatched up a pen and scribbled on the back, *Suicidal client. Call police. Send them to...*

Damn. Her appointment book, with contact information for her current clients in the back, was in her briefcase in the car.

She interrupted the sobbing from the other end of the line. "Carol, what's your address? I'm coming over to help you."

"I don't want to interrupt your evening."

"I hadn't even gotten home yet. Out running errands. I'm

happy to stop by."

Sniffling. "Okay." Carol gave her the address and Kate wrote it on the paper and handed it to the doctor.

He glanced at it and nodded, understanding in his eyes.

Kate mouthed *thank you* and bolted for the door. "I'm headed your way, Carol. Stay on the phone with me while I drive. Keep me company, okay?"

Another soft "Okay."

CHAPTER EIGHT

Kate heaved a sigh as she buckled her seatbelt. She started the car. The clock on her dashboard read seven-forty. Skip would be frantic.

But she hadn't dared try to call or text him before this. Any reminder that Carol was keeping her away from her family would have heaped guilt on top of depression and sunk the client even lower into the pit.

She'd arrived just in time to keep the police officers from forcibly hauling Carol off. She'd showed them her therapist's license and told them she would take it from there. She'd called Dr. Montgomery and he'd started the machinery moving to get Carol hospitalized.

She sat with Carol, making awkward small talk, until the call came through that the doctor had found her a bed at Sheppard Pratt.

"I can get myself there," Carol said.

"But then your car will be in their lot, racking up parking fees." Kate didn't want it to be too easy for her to leave the hospital prematurely. "It's on my way home. I can drop you off."

And so she had broken yet another of her rules separating her professional and personal lives and had chauffeured her client in her own car to the hospital. Fortunately Dr. Montgomery had met them in the admissions department and had taken charge of Carol.

Kate put her car in gear and pulled around to the parking attendant's booth. She handed over her money, contemplating how parking was never free in Towson, even when you were doing someone a good turn.

Once out on Charles Street and headed toward home, she instructed her Bluetooth to call Skip.

"Where the hell have you been?"

Kate tamped down a surge of irritation. "I'm sorry I couldn't call sooner. I was trying to keep another client from committing suicide."

Silence. "Did you succeed?" Still testy but not as angry.

She exhaled slowly. "For now. She's being admitted to the hospital as we speak. I'm ten minutes away."

"You scared the crap out of me." She suspected the kids were in earshot or he would have said something stronger than *crap*. "Your message from earlier said you'd be a little late because you were checking something out. I figured that it was related to the case you're investigating, and I started freaking, thinking you'd stumbled on the... person responsible."

"No. I went to see the doctor whose name is on–" She shook her head slightly and sighed. "It's complicated. I'll explain when I get home. But no, I wasn't in any danger." Her throat tightened. "And I'm sorry. It didn't occur to me that you'd think that."

A half-beat of silence. "Maria made a plate for you. It's in the fridge."

"Be there in a few minutes. Love you."

She was pretty sure she imagined the slight hesitation before he said, "Love you too."

The lingering fragrance of popcorn hit her as she walked in the door. Disappointment clogged her throat. She'd missed Friday night family time, when they all snuggled together to watch a video or played a board game on the floor of the living room.

Toby insisted on romping around her feet, almost tripping her as she made her way toward the sofa. She wasn't in the mood for his antics. She patted him once on the head, then pointed to his favorite spot by the sofa. "Go lie down."

He gave her a mournful look. She pointed more emphatically. "Go!" He slunk away.

Good. Now I can add guilt for hurting the dog's feelings to the heap.

Sighing, she dropped her briefcase and purse on the sofa and followed her nose to the kitchen. Peaches appeared beside her, her own nose high in the air, sniffing.

Skip was pulling a plate out of the microwave. He set it on the table with a flourish. "Your dinner, madame."

The cat tilted her head up at him and meowed loudly.

"Not your dinner, little miss. Yours is over there." He pointed to the cat's dishes in the corner of the kitchen.

Kate gave him a tired smile. Apparently her easy-going husband had gotten over his anger.

Kicking off her shoes, she dropped into a chair. "Thanks."

He sat across from her as she dug in. Maria's delicious chicken enchiladas were gone in record time. It had been a long stretch since lunch.

Wait, she'd never eaten lunch. The styrofoam container was still on the backseat of her car, the food now garbage since it had been off ice for too long.

"Judging by your appetite," Skip said, "your client is okay now."

"Not okay, but safe."

He grimaced. "That had to be scary, having a close call like that so soon after..." His voice trailed off as he watched her face with worried eyes.

"Very scary. But there have been some new developments in Josie's case." She told him about the visit to the pharmacy and then the doctor's home.

She suddenly realized she'd left the prescription behind when she'd raced off to Carol's place. "Crap."

"What?"

She shook her head. The police could always get another copy from the pharmacy. "Never mind. The doctor's wife has early-stage dementia. He thinks she threw a prescription pad away."

"But maybe somebody swiped it from his desk," Skip said.

"Hey, since things are slow, let me assign Manny to look into who has access to their house."

Kate's hesitation was brief. The agency had the resources to check that out far easier than she could. She nodded. "Probably someone comes in to clean at least, and they may be getting some home nursing support. You keep saying things are slow. Is the agency in trouble?"

"No," he said. "We get these lulls now and then. But that's why I'm volunteering Manny and not myself. It's my job to go out and drum up new business so I'll be pretty busy next week."

She nodded again, then remembered the other big development that day—the one she'd been trying to ignore. She took a deep breath. "Josie's parents are suing me for malpractice."

Skip's mouth fell open. He cursed under his breath.

"Yeah., that was pretty much my reaction." Kate's stomach clenched. "I've only been sued once before. That false memory case when you and I were dating."

"What's Rob's take on it?"

"Not good. They really want my records on their daughter, which I'm not about to give them." She swallowed hard. She now had a keen understanding of the saying, *between a rock and a hard place.*

She shook her head to clear it and changed the subject. "Where are the kids?"

"Maria's overseeing baths. Guess I should go check on them and do story time."

Kate gave him a small smile. "You know, Edie can read quite well herself now."

Skip frowned. "I'm not givin' up story time until she's twenty."

"You gonna drive to her college dorm room every night?" she said with a slight snicker.

His mouth quirked up on one end. "Maybe." He pushed up from his chair and headed for the stairs.

Kate rinsed her dirty plate and put it in the dishwasher. Then she trudged to the bedroom. Shedding her office clothes, she found herself reaching for her bathrobe instead of the shirt and jeans thrown over the antique chair next to the bed. She shuffled back out to the living room, struggling to find the energy to go upstairs for tuck-in.

Skip passed her on the stairs. He raised his eyebrows at the sight of her robe but made no comment.

After kissing the kids goodnight, Kate headed back downstairs. She was tempted to beg off from her evening chat with Skip and go straight to bed, but there was something she wanted to broach with him, something that had been lurking in the back of her mind all afternoon. She was finding it hard to believe she was even considering the idea.

She settled on the sofa next to Skip. He wrapped an arm around her shoulders, pulling her up against his side.

"Sweetheart," she said, "maybe this isn't the best timing if things are slow at the agency, but I'm thinking about cutting my practice back to part-time." Or perhaps closing it completely, but she could barely acknowledge that thought much less say it out loud.

He leaned slightly away and looked at her, his eyebrows in the air. "Why?"

"I could spend more time with the kids."

He studied her for a moment, his eyes slightly narrowed. "That's not the real reason."

She looked away from his gaze, which wasn't helping the jumble of emotions roiling in her stomach. "I've just been wondering why I'm stressing myself so much with a full-time practice. I could take a small draw on the brokerage account–the interest only, so the capital's still there for the kids. We wouldn't see any reduction in income." She glanced back at him.

His face had softened. "Darlin'," he said in a gentle voice, "it sounds to me like you're having a bit of a mid-life crisis."

~~~~~~~~

Kate was still stewing over Skip's comment on Saturday morning. She'd tried to hide the fact that she'd been somewhat offended by it. Therapists didn't have mid-life crises. They were supposed to be more together than that.

Sitting at the kitchen table, she took a sip from her second cup of coffee and admitted to herself that he might be right.

The house was quiet, except for the sounds of children's laughter coming from the backyard. It was a typical late March day–the sun warm but coupled with a brisk, chilly breeze. Skip had bundled the kids up and taken them and the dog out back to romp around in the fresh air.

The phone on the kitchen counter rang. She got up and grabbed it from its charger. "Hello."

"Hey, you coming over to help me paint?" her friend Rose said in her ear.

"Crap! It totally slipped my mind. I'm sorry. I'll throw some clothes on and be over in half an hour."

"Okay. I'll get things set up."

Kate quickly changed her clothes, then stuck her head out the back door.

Skip paused in his game of tag when he saw her. Billy collided with his leg.

"You're It, Daddy."

"You okay with watching the kids today?" Kate called over to him. "I forgot I was supposed to help your partner paint her living room."

"Not a problem. See ya later, darlin'."

"Bye, kids."

"Bye, Mommy," Edie yelled.

Billy tugged on Skip's pants leg. "Come on, Daddy, you're It."

"Say goodbye to your mother."

Billy waved. "Bye, Mommy."

"Now run for your life." Skip roared and made a monster face.

Shrieking, the children took off across the yard, Toby bounding after them.

Rose Hernandez was not the most likely confidant for Kate,

even though they were good friends. But she was the most handy one at the moment.

Kneeling next to the living room wall, Kate dipped her brush into the paint bucket and carefully edged along the top of the white baseboard.

Rose's short, sturdy body was perched near the top of a ladder beside the adjacent wall. She stood on her tiptoes and stretched to paint the edge of the wall just below the high ceiling. "You think we're gonna need a second coat?"

"Hm, don't know about the rolled areas but this part that I'm doing with the brush isn't covering all that well." They were putting light blue paint over a forest green color that had made the room way too small and dark. "Hey, maybe we should switch places, and I should do the top parts."

Rose scowled down at her, the intended effect diminished somewhat by the flecks of blue paint on her face and the kerchief covering her bun of black hair. She turned back to the wall and stretched again to edge another section. "Not so sure I would've gone for this home-ownership thing if I'd realized it was so much work."

"Getting the house the way you want it is a lot of work at first." Kate dipped her brush in the bucket again. "After that it's not so bad."

A loud crash and extensive gruff cursing came from the vicinity of the garage.

"What's Mac doing in there?" Kate asked.

"Putting up shelves so we can get the rest of our boxes out of storage."

Kate snickered. "Sounds like the shelves are putting up a fight." She smiled as she ran another line of blue along the wall above the baseboard. It was Mac's favorite color. He'd been her friend since childhood, and he'd met Rose through her. The younger woman had been one of the police officers assigned to protect Kate when Eddie's murderer had tried to kill her as well.

"Hey Rose, do you ever wonder if you'll be a private detective forever?"

The younger woman tilted her head to one side without turning around. "Well, I'll probably want to retire eventually, but it's hard to imagine right now."

"Do you ever question if it's the right career for you?"

Rose shot her a quick glance, one eyebrow at a forty-five degree angle. Then she went back to painting. "Nope. I preferred being a cop, in theory. But the reality involved too much bureaucratic BS and boring paperwork. Going private was definitely the right thing to do."

They worked in silence for a couple of minutes, Kate struggling again with the jumble of emotions she'd experienced the night before. "Can you imagine yourself burning out on it though," she finally said, "maybe twenty or so years down the road?"

"Maybe." Rose climbed down to move the ladder over to the last section of wall. "In twenty years I'll be about the age that Dolph is now."

Kate sat back on her heels. That was a mind-blowing thought. Then she did the math. Rose was right. In twenty years, she'd be pushing sixty. She hadn't found her niche as a private detective until her thirties, so perhaps she would dodge the whole mid-life crisis thing.

Kate, on the other hand, had been a therapist her entire working life. Maybe she really was having some kind of crisis.

"Where's all this coming from?" Rose said over her shoulder.

"Uh, I may be burning out a little."

"This related to the case Skip's got Manny working on?"

Kate turned her head and narrowed her eyes at Rose's back. "What'd he tell you?"

"Not much. Just that he needed Manny to check on some things related to one of your cases." Rose glanced over her shoulder. "So what's going on with you?"

Now that she'd gotten them onto the topic, Kate wished she hadn't. Normally Rose hated discussing feelings, but of course, today she would have to be persistent.

Kate shrugged, even though Rose had her back to her again. "I guess I'm just questioning why I'm working so hard, when I don't need the money."

"So what would you do instead? Let Maria go and keep house?" Rose's tone was just shy of incredulous.

"No, I would never let Maria go, not unless she wanted to leave," Kate quickly reassured Rose, who was Maria's cousin. "She's part of the family."

"Not sure she'd appreciate having you underfoot all day."

Kate finished edging up to the doorframe while trying to imagine the scenario of herself as a lady of leisure. She shook her head slightly and propped her brush on the side of the bucket. Struggling to her feet, she grabbed for the frame to keep from losing her balance. Her knees cracked.

"Hey, watch the doorframe." Rose pulled a rag out of her pocket and tossed it to her. "I don't want to have to paint the trim."

Kate rubbed the blue fingerprints off the white frame. "I could spend more time with the kids."

Rose was half turned on the ladder, looking at her. "But they're in school a good part of the day."

"I could do other things. Maybe teach at the university part-time."

"Yeah, you could."

Kate frowned. "You're not helping all that much."

Rose's eyebrow was in the air again. "What do you want me to say? If you're burned out, then find something else to do. But you might want to wait a bit. Make sure this isn't just a reaction to this case that's causing you problems."

Kate shook her head, then gave her friend a half smile. Rose might not be long on sympathy, but her advice was probably on target.

Rose climbed down the ladder. "Come on. Let's grab some lunch while the first coat dries."

~~~~~~~~

Kate had been unable to reach Judith Anderson over the weekend. She called her from the car on her way to work Monday.

When Judith answered, Kate filled her in on the visit to the pharmacy, and Dr. Kraft's claim that he hadn't written the prescription. "I got an emergency call while I was at his house, and I raced out of there without the copy of the prescription. Should I go back to get it?"

"No," Judith said. "I'll send a uniform to do an official interview. Be good to have the doc's statement on record, in case it does start to look like a homicide."

Kate gritted her teeth. It was already looking like a homicide, in her opinion. "What about gathering forensic evidence at Josie's apartment?"

A pause, then Judith blew out air. "I can't really spare any techs right now. And the apartment's probably already been cleaned."

"Do you mind if I go over and take a look?" Kate said.

Silence for a beat, other than the rumble of voices in the background. "In other words, can you take my name in vain in order to get in?"

"Well, yeah. That would be helpful."

"You can tell the building manager that the police have no objections to you entering the premises, but don't make it sound like he's got to let you in."

Kate considered calling her on the assumption that the building manager would be male, but thought better of it. "Okay, I think I'll stop by there after work."

"Kate, don't you think you're grasping at straws some here?"

The echo of Skip's words from a week ago irritated her, but she managed not to snap at Judith. "Maybe, but I've got to know what really happened."

"Okay. Just be careful."

Kate made a face at her dashboard. She was getting really tired of hearing those words.

At lunchtime, Kate checked her messages.

"Hey it's me." Rob's voice. "Just heard from Kathy O'Connor."

Kate's stomach twisted.

"The Hartins are getting more blatant about demanding the records. I told Kathy that wasn't an option for you ethically. Call me when you can so we can talk strategy."

Kate groaned. She dropped into her desk chair and put her hands over her face.

What a mess!

There was no strategy to deal with this. The insurance company would want to settle out of court, but the Hartins weren't going to accept a settlement that didn't include the records. When she refused to turn them over, the insurance company might then say that she was being uncooperative, which was grounds for them to refuse to pay the claim.

So she would end up going to court and fighting with these grieving parents in front of a judge, very possibly on her own dime.

She lifted her head.

Unless I can find them some answers before then.

CHAPTER NINE

Kate met the condo complex's manager at Josie's place at five-fifteen. She had called earlier and used the same ploy as she had with the pharmacist, implying she was associated with the police investigation but stopping short of impersonating an officer of the law.

"These aren't rentals." The manager, who had indeed turned out to be a man, unlocked the door. "Ms. Hartin owned the condo."

That made sense. Josie had a trust fund, set up by her grandparents. She'd worked at the gallery because she'd enjoyed it and because the owner was a friend of hers.

They stepped through the condo door. A strange medley assailed Kate's nostrils–ammonia mixed with a flowery fragrance often found in cleaning products, and underneath it, the cloying odor of decaying meat and an echo of urine and feces. She swallowed hard, struggling to control her gag reflex.

The manager waved a hand in front of his face. "Guess the place could stand to be aired out a bit more." He walked over to the sliding glass door that led to a balcony and opened it wide.

A cool breeze made the air more bearable. Breathing through her mouth, Kate slowly walked around the room. She avoided the smudges and random stains in the middle of the cream-colored carpet.

The man pointed to more dark stains in one corner that was empty of furniture.

"That's where the dog crate was. The police took it away."

Kate tilted her head and contemplated that. Why would they

take the dog crate? "What else did they take?"

He gave her a funny look.

She realized too late that she'd blown her cover as an associate of the police. But she opted not to try to explain. "Was there anything else missing?" she asked instead.

The man shook his head. "Nope, her purse was on the desk, next to some book. They took both of those away. And there was some expensive jewelry in the bedroom. Mrs. Hartin's assistant came and got it last week."

"So they've had a cleaning crew in. Have they said anything about putting it on the market yet?"

He shook his head again. "Ain't been no cleaning crew. This is the way it was when we found her."

Kate stopped in her tracks. She scanned the neat room. No, more than neat. With the exception of the stains on the carpet, the place was spotless.

That was out of character. Josie was not a good housekeeper. It was one of the many things she and her mother argued about. Her mother kept trying to send their cleaning staff over to straighten the place up. Josie always refused. Kate suspected she was messy out of defiance.

So what did it mean that Josie had cleaned the place before killing herself? Some kind of putting-life-in-order ritual?

But that didn't fit with leaving the dog in the crate. If she'd killed herself on impulse, that was one thing. But if she'd taken the time to clean, she would have taken the time to think through the consequences to the dog as well.

"Sir," she was blanking on the guy's name, "I think we need to dust for prints, to be on the safe side here. I'll have a man come by tomorrow morning. His name is Manuel Ortiz."

The manager shrugged. "I'll be in the office by nine."

"Thank you. Sorry for disrupting your evening."

Kate followed the manager out of the building. He sketched her a small salute and headed down the sidewalk. As Kate walked toward her car, she felt a chill on her neck. But the early evening air wasn't all that cold.

When she reached the driver's side door, the creepy chill came again. Was someone watching her? She turned and scanned the parking lot. No one was in sight. A slight breeze rustled through the small trees surrounding the lot, casting wavering shadows.

She shook her head.

Get a grip, Kate!

~~~~~~~~~

Skip's hair had fallen over his forehead as he ate. He left it there, using it as a veil to watch his wife.

Kate had made it home just in time for dinner. She picked at her food, a vacant look on her face.

"Mommy," Billy yelled, "you're not listening!"

"Oh, uh, that's nice."

Skip narrowed his eyes at her. In a low voice, he said, "He was telling you about being picked on by the older kids."

Her face turned pink.

Skip's annoyance melted at her chagrined expression. "Son, you need to settle down. Mommy's a little preoccupied with work stuff right now."

Billy pursed his lips and glared at him. The boy had a temper to match his mother's.

"It's hard being an adult sometimes," Skip said. "We can't always be everything we want to be for everybody." The message was aimed at Kate as much as Billy.

She flashed him a grateful half-smile.

Billy crossed his arms and pouted.

As they finished eating, Maria tilted an eyebrow at Skip. He hid a grin. The Hernandez cousins had very expressive eyebrows.

"*Niños*, you help me with dishes."

Clearing the table and loading the dishwasher were usually tasks that Skip and Kate did together, but the kids knew better than to protest when Maria used that tone.

It bought Skip and Kate a few minutes on the sofa before they had to start the bedtime routine. He settled down beside his wife and threw an arm around her shoulders. She was staring off into space.

"What's the matter, darlin'?"

"Nothing. I'm okay."

Skip stifled a sigh. She was *not* okay. "Want to talk about your client's case?"

She shrugged. "I tried again to get Judith to reopen the investigation. No dice." She turned slightly toward him. "Can I borrow Manny tomorrow morning?"

"Sure. He's available to help whenever you need him."

She gave him a small smile. "Thanks."

He'd figured she would be more receptive to Manny's help than anyone else's. She and Manny had developed some kind of bond from previous times he'd been her bodyguard. Skip didn't completely understand it, but his gut said it wasn't anything he needed to worry about.

"What do you need him for?"

"To check for fingerprints in Josie's condo. I stopped by there on my way home. The place was spotless, but the manager said no cleaning crew had been in."

She fell silent for a few moments.

"So?" Skip asked.

"Josie was a slob."

"So maybe somebody cleaned up to get rid of forensic evidence."

"Yeah," she said.

The kids bounced into the living room. Skip gave up on the pulling-teeth process of getting Kate to talk. He pushed up from the sofa and herded the children up to their rooms.

After homework had been checked, baths supervised and stories read, he descended the stairs. Kate wasn't in their usual spot on the sofa.

He found her in the bedroom, already getting ready for bed. Silently, he followed suit. Once in bed, he wrapped his arms around her and gathered her against his side, but he hesitated to go further.

She sighed.

He slid a hand down her side to her hip. She didn't move or make a sound. He slid it back up and cupped her breast.

No moan or curling closer to encourage him.

A lump formed in his throat. He swallowed, but it refused to go away. She had been doing better. Now she seemed obsessed with proving her client hadn't committed suicide.

He moved his hand again to her side and pulled her closer still. Inspiration struck. "You've convinced me. The woman didn't kill herself." He truly believed that. There were too many inconsistencies.

She pulled back a little in his arms and looked up at him. "Really?"

"Really. Let us help you prove it."

She gave him a small smile. "Thanks for lending me Manny. But a lot of this stuff, it might not make sense to anyone who didn't know her. Like about the clean condo, for instance."

She snuggled back down, spooning against him.

He rubbed her back and felt her body relaxing, moving toward sleep. His groin ached but he would be happy with her sleeping well. "I love you," he whispered.

She abruptly flipped over and clung to him, her face turned up toward his. "I love you." Her voice was low and fierce.

She stroked his chest. His skin quivered beneath her fingertips.

He stared into her eyes, shiny with unshed tears. Did she want him to make love to her after all? He kissed her lips gently.

She deepened the kiss.

He sought her breast and closed his mouth over it. Her back arched and she moaned out his name. His mouth curled into a smile against her skin.

He sucked a bit harder for a moment, while his hand explored elsewhere. She was starting to writhe and moan. He rolled over on top of her, bracing himself on his elbows so as not to crush her with his weight.

Her eyes were the indigo blue of arousal. "Thank you for putting up with me," she whispered.

He grinned down at her. "My pleasure."

Kate found herself smiling as she drove to work the next day. The sun shone through her windshield and her favorite CD was playing.

Life was good.

Her throat closed. How could she be happy when Josie was dead?

She shook her head. This was no different than any other sad dilemma a client presented in her office. She worked to put up the barriers of detachment that normally insulated her own life from her clients' woes. Whoever had killed Josie, for whatever reason, that wasn't part of her own life. It was Josie's life, not hers.

Reality slammed past her defenses for a moment. *Not Josie's life. Her death!*

Kate pressed her lips together and gripped the steering wheel. Nothing was to be gained from feeling guilty about Josie's death.

She forced herself to sing along with the song coming from the speakers in her car.

At lunchtime, Kate listened to Manny's message. "Hey Kate, that place was wiped down clean as a whistle. Which smells funny in my book. Nobody gets every fingerprint when they're just dusting."

She picked up the receiver of her desk phone and punched in Judith's office number, which she now had memorized.

"Anderson."

"Hi, Lieutenant. I've got some things to report." Kate told her about the out-of-character, spotless apartment and Manny's inability to find any fingerprints at all.

"I agree with your guy," Judith said. "It's smelly. But still not anything concrete we can use to justify a homicide investigation. By the way, that doc swore he'd never heard of you or Josephine

Hartin or any recent prescription for clonazepam."

"What?" Kate screeched.

"Yeah, so I sent a detective by that pharmacy, and the prescription has mysteriously disappeared from their files. They have no clue what we're talking about."

"But I saw it! He—"

"Calm down, Kate. I believe you. They're all covering their butts."

Kate banged her fist on her desk. "Damn it! They're so afraid they'll get implicated in some lawsuit, they'd destroy evidence."

"I think the old man is mostly covering for his wife. And protecting his own reputation. Not so sure about the pharmacist. I may go down there and talk to him myself."

Kate held her breath, afraid to say something that would discourage Judith from doing so.

"Still can't make it an official investigation," Judith said into the silence. "But I'm inclined to shake this guy's tree and see what falls out."

"Would you let me know what you find out?"

A pause. "Probably." Judith disconnected.

Kate glanced at the clock on her office wall, then dialed another number. She made an appointment with Josie's veterinarian for seven that evening. Toby didn't know it yet but he was getting his yearly check-up a few months early.

Her stomach grumbled, wanting to know where lunch was.

But she had one more call to make. She got Liz Franklin's voicemail. "Hey Liz, since your husband's in court tomorrow, I suddenly have a gaping hole in my schedule. Would you be interested in meeting for lunch? Give me a call."

She winced a little, wondering if that sounded like Liz was just the pinch hitter, when Rob wasn't available for their usual Wednesday lunch. Then she shrugged. Liz would probably understand.

In truth, she was glad Rob wasn't available so she could get together with Liz instead. In many ways she and Rob were closer, the friendship having grown initially out of working together on the cases of mutual clients. But after all the harrowing things the three of them had been through together–before and since her remarriage to Skip–she and Liz were pretty tight as well.

And there were some things that women understood better than men. Like guilt.

CHAPTER TEN

Kate held back her tired sigh. Her last client of the day walked to the outer door of the waiting room and turned to give her a little wave as she left.

A small cough.

Kate jumped and jerked around toward the sound.

A woman rose from a chair in the corner of the waiting area. She smoothed down the skirt of her navy wool suit and cleared her throat.

Belatedly, Kate realized it was Nancy Hartin. Grief had aged her a decade in the last couple of weeks. Her face sagged and the frown lines at the corners of her mouth were etched more deeply. Her blonde hair–pulled back in a neat chignon–was dull, with gray roots showing around her face. Her clothes hung on her too-thin frame.

The woman cleared her throat again. "May I have a few minutes of your time, Mrs. Huntington?"

Kate resisted the urge to look at her watch. If she didn't get home soon, she'd miss out on time with the kids before her appointment with Josie's vet.

"Sure. Come in to my office." She gestured toward the door.

Nancy Hartin settled into the chair across from her desk.

Kate sat down in her desk chair and waited.

Mrs. Hartin uncrossed and re-crossed her legs. "My lawyer will be furious if she finds out I'm here, but I had to come and ask you again to please let me… us, see Josephine's file."

"My lawyer won't be too happy about this meeting either."

Kate paused, choosing her words carefully. "Mrs. Hartin, I can only begin to imagine your pain. But you need to believe me when I say that seeing Josie's file will not help. There is nothing in there that gives any hint of why she died." She avoided saying the word *suicide*, since she was no longer convinced that her client's death was self-inflicted.

Mrs. Hartin gave her a stern look, but the grief shadowing her eyes diminished the effect.

Kate's chest ached. She tried to put herself in this woman's shoes, imagining if Edie had... Her mind rebelled against the thought. She leaned forward. "There is something that might help both of us to find some answers."

The woman's eyebrows went up but she remained silent.

"You have her journal. There may be something in there that would shed some light on what happened."

Nancy Hartin straightened her spine. "I've read the journal, cover to cover, twice. There are no answers there. But there are indicators of your incompetence. Apparently my daughter was afraid to tell you certain things."

Kate's heart raced. *What things?*

She made herself pause to think through her words. "It's quite possible, Mrs. Hartin, that something in the journal will click with something Josie said in therapy. I may be able to interpret it differently than you have."

The woman stiffened. "Are you implying that you knew my daughter better than I did?"

In some ways, yes.

Kate managed to keep her face neutral. "No. But the things she journaled about were most likely related to the things she talked about in therapy. Something that seems insignificant to you, well, I might recognize it as a clue."

For a moment, she thought the woman would burst into tears. With an effort, Mrs. Hartin gathered herself, both figuratively and literally. She rose from her chair.

"Sorry to have troubled you, Mrs. Huntington. I can find my

way out." At the door, she turned. "I will get those records, one way or another."

I'll burn them first.

Out loud, Kate said, "I'm only fulfilling my responsibility to a client. Confidentiality…" She caught herself before saying *does not die with the client.* "It's imperative that clients know what they say in therapy is completely confidential. I have to honor that for Josie's sake."

Mrs. Hartin's head tilted back, her chin in the air. "Josephine would not want me to suffer needlessly."

"No, she would not," Kate said in a gentle tone. *Which is the other reason why I cannot show you her file.*

Nancy Hartin stared at her for a moment, her face pale. Then she pivoted on her heel and left.

~~~~~~~~~

I'm a miserable excuse for a mother.

Kate's guilt had taken the bit in its mouth and was running full tilt as she drove to the veterinarian's office.

Once again, she had been preoccupied at dinner, and had said the wrong thing in response to Billy's tale of his day at school. And he had exploded.

Skip had scolded the boy for his temper tantrum, but his eyes kept flicking toward her the whole time he was chastising their son. They said loud and clear, *What's gotten into you?*

Edie had that solemn look on her face that Kate hated. Too many things had already happened in the child's life that had rattled her sense of security.

When Kate had told Skip after dinner that she was taking Toby to her client's vet, as an excuse to get in to talk to her, he had just nodded. Then he'd gone off to check the kids' homework.

Kate's mind turned to Billy. He'd been so volatile lately. She remembered him mentioning being picked on by some older kids. Was that a random event, or was her son being bullied? She added 'call Billy's teacher' to her mental to-do list for the next day.

Her GPS informed her that her destination was coming up on

the left. She swung into the parking lot of a small strip shopping center. The vet's office was on the far end.

Toby let out an excited woof from the backseat when she opened her door.

"You may not be so thrilled about this outing when you find out what's coming," Kate told the pup as she reached in to release his harness from the safety tether. She had barely grabbed his leash when he bounded out of the car. He dragged her across the lot to the building.

"Has Toby had his puppy shots?" The dark-haired vet looked to be in her early forties. She was a bit taller than Kate, with broad shoulders for a woman, and an equally broad smile. Her tone was disgustingly cheerful for this late in the day.

"Yes, last year," Kate said. "I meant to grab the records before I left the house but I forgot. I think he's due for some boosters."

Dr. Blake nodded and stroked the dog's ears. He calmed down some and licked her hand.

The poor pup had been shaking ever since the vet's assistant had hefted him onto the examining table. He had apparently made the connection between the cold metal under his rump and the pain of injections.

Dr. Blake examined Toby. He licked her face when she leaned down to listen to his heart with her stethoscope.

"Sorry," Kate said.

"Don't be. I never mind doggie kisses." The vet straightened and put the stethoscope in the pocket of her white jacket. She rubbed the pup's ears again. Toby looked like he might swoon.

"He seems quite healthy. I can't give him any booster shots, however, without knowing what he's already had. Can you fax us the record? And then you can bring him in next week for the shots he needs."

"Sure. I'm still debating though if I want to change vets. The one we have been going to is nice enough..." She trailed off, letting the woman fill in the blanks with whatever her mind conjured up as a reason to be discontent with one's vet. "You were recommended by Josie Hartin."

Dr. Blake's smile faded.

"Such a tragedy," Kate continued. "I understand you have her dog. Someone said the poor thing almost died."

The vet's cheerful demeanor returned. "Oh no, he wasn't that bad off. Just dehydrated some. But he did look a mess when he came in. You want to see him?"

"Could I? I mean, I don't want to keep you from other patients."

"No problem. You're my last appointment of the day." She wrapped her arms around Toby and lifted him off the table and onto the floor. "Not sure I'll still be able to do that, big boy, once you finish filling out."

"You mean he's going to get bigger?"

"Probably not too much taller, but he'll get heavier over the next year, as his muscles and organs finish maturing."

"Ugh. He already eats more than my daughter's pony does."

Dr. Blake laughed. "Come on. You can bring Toby along. Sphinx likes company."

She led the way out of the examining room and through another room lined with shelves of medications and supplies. "Sphinx is our only overnight guest right now," she said over her shoulder as she pushed open a door.

As soon as Kate spotted the dog in his crate, she understood his name better. He lay on his stomach, his back legs along his sides, front legs partway out in front–exactly like the Sphinx in Egypt.

Toby rushed past her, almost yanking the leash out of her hand. He yipped and dropped playfully down in front of the crate.

Sphinx had risen to his feet. He made a sound halfway between a woof and a sharper bark. It sounded almost like he was talking to Toby, inviting him to play.

"Is it okay if we let them out back for a few minutes?" the vet asked. "Sphinx has been kind of depressed. Maybe a playmate will cheer him up."

"Sure," Kate said, thinking she couldn't have asked for a better opportunity.

Dr. Blake opened another door and flipped a light switch next to it. A floodlight illuminated a fenced-in area in back of the building. "Come on, Toby."

Kate unhooked the leash from her dog's harness. Toby took off for the steps down to the yard.

Dr. Blake crossed to Sphinx's crate and opened its door. The dog stepped out. He tilted his head to look up at the vet, and then turned and bounded for the still open door. A moment later they heard happy yips and barks coming from the yard. The vet closed the door but stayed next to it, nudging aside the flimsy curtains across its window to keep an eye on the dogs.

"This isn't the best set-up for boarding. The fenced area isn't really adequate. I'm hoping to move soon to a better location. Part of what Josie did for us was take the boarded dogs for longer walks."

It was news to Kate that Josie had done anything for the vet. "Had you seen Josie recently?"

"Yes, a few days before..." Dr. Blake stopped and cleared her throat. "She'd recently started volunteering here, mainly on the weekends, coming in to care for the boarded animals."

"Did she seem depressed to you lately?"

"No, just the opposite. She seemed really happy to be around the dogs and cats. She'd bring Sphinx and he'd play with the dogs outside. The ones that were boarded that is. The ones who were recuperating from illness or an operation, she would walk them more sedately by themselves."

"She definitely loved animals." Kate was letting the vet assume she and Josie had been friends. She hoped she wouldn't ask for any details of their relationship. "Do you think she was okay otherwise? I was kinda surprised when I heard she'd killed herself."

"Me too. I was downright shocked." Dr. Blake didn't elaborate.

She watched the dogs cavorting in the yard from the window in the door.

"What's going to happen to Sphinx?" Kate asked, mostly to get the conversation started again.

"I've got the word out. Someone will adopt him eventually. I'll keep him here until they do."

"Isn't there a shelter around here?" Kate knew there was. It was where they had gotten Toby.

"Yeah." The vet seemed to hesitate. "But I feel like I owe Josie this. I want to make sure the person adopting Sphinx will love him like she did."

Kate's throat tightened. "You'd grown fond of her."

Dr. Blake turned from the door. Her eyes were shiny. "Yes, even though she'd only been volunteering for a few weeks. She was a special young woman."

Kate nodded. "I thought so too," she said in a low voice.

After she'd said goodbye to the vet and pried Toby away from his new friend, she headed across the parking lot toward her car. The dog had not yet learned how to act on a leash. He darted off in whatever direction struck his fancy, sniffing and exploring.

She was about to yank him away from yet another patch of tall grass when he lifted his leg. "Okay, boy, that's a legitimate excuse to dawdle."

As she patiently waited for the pup to empty his bladder, she once again felt that creepy feeling on her neck. She glanced nervously around the parking lot. It was starting to mist. The lights around the lot created circles of white edged with haloes of rainbow colors. The pavement glistened. There were few other cars on this end of the lot, although there was still activity at the other end near the grocery store.

She tugged on the leash. "Come on, Toby. We've gotta go." She hustled him to the car and opened the back door. Normally she would have used the rag she kept on the floor to dry his paws, before letting him jump up on the upholstery. But not tonight. She gestured for him to climb in, then slammed the back door and hurried around to the driver's side. When she was inside with her own door closed and locked, she let out her breath.

She shook her head. Tiny droplets fell from her hair onto the shoulders of her raincoat. "Get a grip, Kate," she said out loud.

The dog whined in the backseat.

He's picking up on my nerves.

"It's okay, boy." She leaned over between the front seats and struggled to get his safety tether hooked to his harness.

Starting the car, she mentally shrugged off the fear. She'd been imagining things.

Driving home, she wasn't sure if she was more relieved or disappointed by her chat with the veterinarian–relieved that her own assessment of Josie's mood just before she died was accurate, but disappointed that she hadn't learned anything more that was helpful to solve the case.

It occurred to her that she should talk to Josie's boss at the art gallery. And maybe some of her artist friends.

And how the hell am I going to fit that in between seeing clients and taking care of my kids and paying some attention to my husband!

Suddenly she felt overwhelmed. Her life was too busy. Maybe it would be a good idea to cut back on her office hours.

She gave herself a mental kick in the head. *You wouldn't be so stressed out if you weren't trying to play detective.*

She arrived at home just in time to give out goodnight kisses and tuck the children into bed.

Billy seemed to be already asleep but she suspected he was faking. She sat down on the side of his bed and waited. After a minute or two, he opened one eye, then clamped it shut again.

"I'm sorry I've been preoccupied lately, kiddo."

He half opened his eye again, watching her. She leaned down and kissed his cheek. "Love you."

When he didn't move or say anything, she started to push off the bed.

He lurched forward and hugged her around the waist. "Love

you too, Mommy." His voice was slightly muffled since his face was half buried against her stomach.

This was a bit out of character, but she opted not to say anything. Best not to ask questions and get the child stirred up at bedtime. She gave him a tight squeeze. "Go to sleep, little boy."

He settled back down on his pillow. She pulled the covers up to his chin.

"'Night, Mommy," he mumbled, now legitimately sleepy.

Her shoulders sagged as she closed the door to his room. She had to get a grip and start acting like a mother again.

She sighed and headed for her daughter's door.

Skip was in their favorite spot on the sofa. Legs stretched out in front of him, head back, eyes closed, he was half asleep by the time he felt Kate's weight settle beside him.

He slitted one eye open and looked over at her. She had a leg curled under her and a strange expression on her face.

"Tired?" she asked.

He opened his eyes all the way. "Some. I've been chasin' new clients all week. The guy I took out to lunch today insisted I have a couple beers with him. I've been groggy ever since." Except for an occasional beer or glass of wine in the evening, he wasn't much of a drinker.

He maneuvered his arm around her shoulders and pulled her closer. "How are you doing?"

She sighed. "I wish I knew. I felt kinda relieved driving home. The interview with the vet didn't give me anything new, but Dr. Blake agreed that Josie didn't seem depressed recently."

"So what's next?"

"I'm not sure. I'm running out of leads. It occurred to me that I should talk to the woman who runs the art gallery where she worked, and maybe her friends."

Skip stifled a groan. Supposed friends could all too easily be secret enemies. "Why don't you let my crew check out her friends?" He tried to keep his tone light, but wasn't sure he'd succeeded.

"How will you know who they are?"

He wiggled his eyebrows at her. "We have our ways."

She gave him a small smile. "I think I should talk to her boss though."

He dropped his head back against the sofa. His eyes drifted closed again. How dangerous would that be? The boss was a female, and Kate knew aikido. But still...

"Take Manny in with you," he said. "He's getting bored, just following you around."

He felt her jerk away. His eyes flew open.

"You have Manny following me?"

Aw, crap! If he hadn't been so tired, he wouldn't have let that slip out.

She shifted further away from him. "Damn it, Skip. I don't need a bodyguard."

That's a matter of opinion. Pulling his feet in, he pushed himself up straighter on the sofa. "Uh, I didn't have anything else for him to do. Figured he could be handy, you know, if you needed him for anything."

She narrowed her eyes at him.

Yeah, he wouldn't have bought that feeble line either. He took her hands in his. "Look, darlin', I know you can take care of yourself under normal circumstances. But if you're right and your client was murdered, well, there's somebody out there who could become quite desperate if you get too close to the truth."

She pulled her hands free, then crossed her arms across her chest. "No wonder I've been getting the creepy feeling that someone's watching me. I don't want him following me around."

His gut twisted but he knew better than to push too hard. "Okay, not all the time. But will you call him to go with you when you're investigating?"

She opened her mouth, then closed it again. "Maybe. I mean it depends on what, or who, I'm checking out." Most of the anger had gone out of her tone.

He considered protesting that Manny should go with her whenever she was talking to someone involved in the case. Any of them could turn out to be the killer.

"Honestly," she said, "I don't think the gallery is going to lead to anything. But I've got to check out all possibilities, right?"

"Yeah, but you really should take Manny with you. Somebody murdered Josie. That's the premise we're working with here, are we not?"

She blew out air. "Okay, I'll take Manny with me to the gallery. But where do I go after that?" She looked up at him, pain and something else he couldn't name in her eyes.

His chest tightened. The temptation to say what he was thinking–drop it and get on with your own life–was strong. He resisted it. "Basic rule of thumb in investigating–when you're stuck, go back to the beginning."

She shook her head slightly. "I can't even remember off the top of my head where I started. Wait, it was with Father Sam. Maybe I could learn something more from him."

Skip relaxed some. The old priest was probably harmless.

Kate settled back against his shoulder. After a moment, she said, "Hey, do you know what's going on with Billy? Do you think he's being bullied?"

Skip would have welcomed the change of subject, if it had been any new topic other than that one. He stared off into space for a moment. He hated that he couldn't protect his son from what he himself had been through as a kid.

He swallowed hard. "Yeah, it's looking that way."

She took his hand and squeezed it. "I'll send the teacher a note tomorrow, ask her to call us."

He looked back at her. "Give her my cell number. I don't have any appointments, so she can call me whenever she has a break."

She held his gaze for a moment, then heaved another sigh. "Sometimes I wish Billy didn't take after me so much. All that intensity makes him an easy mark for the bullies."

He smiled. "I wouldn't have him, or you, any other way."

She smiled back at him, a mischievous glint in her eyes. "You too tired to have some fun?"

Suddenly wary, he said, "What did you have in mind?"

She pulled her hand loose from his. "A little race."

He cocked one eyebrow at her.

"To the bedroom." She dug her fingers into the ticklish spot on his side.

He squirmed away. "Hey, I'm bigger than you."

She jumped up and bolted for the bedroom. "Yeah, but I'm faster," she threw back over her shoulder.

He shoved off of the sofa and ran after her. But he let her get to the edge of the bed before he tackled her. They fell onto the bed. Her laughter was the best thing he'd heard in weeks.

CHAPTER ELEVEN

On her way to Liz's favorite Italian restaurant the next day at noon, Kate realized that she felt lighter than she had in days, maybe weeks. She might be running low on leads in her investigation, but maybe, just maybe, she was coming out the other end of the grief process.

She beat Liz to the restaurant. The hostess showed her to a table close to the door, so she could keep an eye out for her friend.

The waitress brought a basket of bread sticks and Kate ordered two glasses of iced tea.

The tea and Liz arrived at the same time. She flopped down in the chair opposite Kate. "Ugh, feels good to get out of that office for a while." To the waitress, she said, "I'm having the meatless lasagna with whole grain pasta, and a salad. Do you know what you want, Kate?"

Kate smiled across the table at her health-conscious friend.

She'd love to order the lasagna, but she was experiencing some slowing of her metabolism with age. Since she'd skipped several of her aikido workouts recently, she'd better keep things lo-cal. "I'll have the soup and salad special." The waitress nodded and left.

"So how are you?" Liz said in her booming voice, which always seemed so incongruous coming from her petite body.

Kate looked around, but no one seemed to be paying attention to them. It was one of the things she liked about this restaurant. The tables were spaced a decent distance apart, with plants or half-partitions separating them, providing diners a fair amount of privacy. "I'm okay. How about yourself?"

Liz tilted her head and raised her eyebrows. "I'm fine. But I've gotten the distinct impression lately from my husband that you're not. Of course, I've learned not to ask, since it almost always has to do with a mutual client so he can't tell me much."

Kate leaned forward. "This time I'm his client," she said in a low voice. "I'm being sued because one of my clients supposedly committed suicide."

Liz's eyebrows shot even higher. She put her hand on top of Kate's on the table and gave it a squeeze. "Oh, sweetheart, that's gotta be rough."

Kate blew out a soft sigh. "It has been, but I'm starting to feel a little better. The woman was prone to depression." She was choosing her words carefully, keeping her comments about Josie vague. "But she wasn't in a bad place at the time she died. Or at least she didn't seem to be."

"So you've been feeling guilty and wracking your brain, trying to figure out how you missed the cues."

Kate let out a small laugh. "You know me too well, Liz."

The waitress brought their food and they ate in silence for a few minutes. Deciding her soup was too hot, Kate pushed it aside and started on her salad.

"You've dealt with guilt before," Liz said between bites of lasagna.

She certainly had. Eddie had died because of one of her cases, and another client's miscalculation had put her family and friends at risk and led to the death of one of those friends.

"That was different," Kate said. "The evil, for lack of a better word, was being perpetrated by someone else, and I just happened to draw that evil to innocent people. I could eventually step back from it and realize I wasn't responsible for the actions of others. But I'm supposed to try to keep my clients stable enough that they can function in the world, and not become suicidal."

Liz gave a slight shake of her head. "Key word is *try*. You're still not responsible for their lives or actions."

"Yeah, I know that intellectually." Kate stabbed at her salad with her fork. "There's more. I'm not convinced the client really did kill herself. I've been checking out some things that don't add up. She mentioned in a phone message something about a 'breakthrough.'" She made quote marks in the air while she chewed a bite of salad. "We'd had some problems with scheduling. So since she seemed to be in a good place, I put her off for a week. I can't help wondering if something about that breakthrough led to her death–"

"And maybe if you'd seen her that week, you could have headed her off," Liz said.

"Yeah, but now that I'm saying it out loud... Again, she's responsible for her actions."

"Exactly. But you're the one who's always saying that emotions aren't logical."

Kate nodded. "I have been feeling better about it lately. Sometimes it just takes some time for emotions to work themselves out."

"That will be a hundred dollars, please," Liz said with a grin.

Kate laughed. "I keep telling you that you should have been a shrink instead of an actuary."

"Nah, I like playing with numbers. They're very concrete. No emotions involved."

Kate tried her soup again. Now it was a little on the cool side so she ate it quickly.

Liz had finished her lasagna and was working on her salad. "Hey, maybe I can help you investigate. Do you need a background check on your client or any of your suspects?"

Kate contemplated that as she finished off her own salad. There was the whole confidentiality-doesn't-die-with-the-client thing, but that paled by comparison to the idea that a murderer would get away with cutting Josie's life short.

"It wouldn't hurt," she finally said.

Liz pushed aside her salad plate. "Let's go then. My tablet's in my car."

~~~~~~~~

Skip's cell phone vibrated on his desk. He picked it up. "Canfield."

"Mr. Canfield, this is Mrs. Langdon." Her voice was crisp. She sounded like she was in her fifties, maybe older. "Sorry I couldn't call you back sooner. The children are at lunch now, so I have a few minutes."

"Thanks for getting back to me, Mrs. Langdon. My wife and I have some concerns. Billy has been telling us that some boys are picking on him out on the playground."

"I haven't observed anything."

"Well, he's mentioned it a few times, and he's been very volatile lately."

"We have strict rules against fighting, Mr. Canfield."

What does that mean? The comment seemed a bit of a *non sequitur*. Then he got it. "I don't think anyone has done anything physically to him, at least not yet. They're taunting him, calling him names."

Another pause, the thwap, thwap of papers being spewed from a copier or printer in the background. "Well, kids need to learn to handle social interactions, even negative ones."

Skip's jaw clenched. Just their luck that they'd get the teacher with the antiquated attitudes about bullying. He tamped down his anger. "He's a second grader, Mrs. Langdon, and I get the impression these boys are at least two years older."

"Still, it's often best to let kids sort these things out for themselves, as long as they're not resorting to violence."

Skip's hand fisted around the phone. He struggled to keep his voice even. "I disagree. I was bullied as a kid myself."

"And it probably made you stronger."

"No, it just made me miserable. I'm not willing to see my son go through that."

A longer stretch of thwapping noises and a phone ringing in the distance. "Well, the kids have free play in a few minutes. I'll keep an eye on Billy and see if anything inappropriate is going on."

That almost sounded like she didn't believe Billy's reports. Skip started counting to ten. He only made it to six.

"I have to go, Mr. Canfield. The kids will be dismissed from the lunchroom in a minute."

"Thank you for your time," he managed to squeeze between gritted teeth.

He disconnected and sat back in his chair. Then he jumped up and pocketed the phone. He was at his office door before he remembered his gun. He couldn't take it on school grounds.

Pulling the .38 out of its waistband holster, he turned back to his desk and deposited the pistol in a drawer. He locked the desk and jammed his keys in his pocket.

Then he headed to his partner's office to tell her he was going out for a while.

After he'd succinctly explained his errand, Rose cocked one of her expressive eyebrows at him. "Want company?"

He knew why she was offering. She was afraid he'd blow. He wasn't real sure that he wouldn't. His usually easygoing personality seemed to fly out the window whenever there was a threat against his family. "Sure. Come on."

In the parking lot, Rose opened the passenger door of his SUV and climbed in. "You know there is something to what the teacher said."

"What do you mean?" Skip started the engine and headed for the lot exit.

"You can't fight all of Billy's battles for him."

"No, but I can fight this one. I know what it's like to be picked on by bigger kids. You feel so helpless, and scared senseless. 'Cause you don't know just where they'll stop. A couple times I thought they were gonna kill me."

"How is Billy going to feel about you coming to his rescue, in front of the other kids?"

He opened his mouth, then closed it again. It was a good question. Although he had longed for his father to intervene directly with the bullies, he also would have been mortified by such an intervention. But he'd been a good bit older than Billy, in middle school.

"He's too little to be dealing with this," he said.

"Oh, I think we should be checking it out, but you might want to hold back some. Assess the situation before barging in."

An image flashed into his mind of them lurking around the edges of the school playground. "We're likely to get arrested as pedophiles."

Rose shook her head. "No, we check in with the school office first, but then we watch from a distance."

Skip had to insist on talking to the principal before they were allowed to go to the playground to observe Billy's class. By the time they got there, with visitor badges now pinned to their shirts, the kids were being called inside. Skip spotted Billy at the far end surrounded by three bigger boys.

His fist clenched at his sides.

"Take it easy, partner," Rose said.

The words were no sooner out of her mouth than Billy shoved one of the boys away from him. The three of them fell back, laughing.

Movement out of the corner of his eye. An older woman— Mrs. Langdon, he presumed; he'd missed back-to-school night last fall–walked briskly across the asphalt, headed for the confrontation.

Skip took off at a lope to catch up.

She had Billy by the arm by the time he got there. Tears were streaming down the little boy's face.

The older boys were standing a few feet away, laughing. "Sissy," one of them called out.

"That's quite enough," Mrs. Langdon said. "Billy, I'm going to have to take you to the principal's office."

"It's not my fault," Billy yelled. "They started it. They called me a faggot."

Skip suspected his son didn't even know what the word meant, but he knew it was intended to be derogatory.

"I think all the boys need to go to the office," Rose said from beside him.

Skip nodded. "That sounds like a good idea."

Mrs. Langdon rounded on them. "The rules are very clear. Physical aggression is not allowed. Billy shoved the other boy."

Skip ignored her. "Billy, how many times have these boys picked on you?"

"I don't know. Lots." The child wiped his wet face with the jacket sleeve of the arm his teacher wasn't holding.

"When did it start?" Skip asked.

Billy's lower lip trembled, but he took a deep breath. "After Christmas break."

Skip narrowed his eyes at the teacher. *And where were you the last three months?*

"We were just havin' some fun with him," the boy who'd been shoved said.

The boy next to him jabbed him with an elbow.

"Come on, Billy," Mrs. Langdon said.

Skip crooked his finger at the other boys. "You're all coming too."

"We don't have to," the elbow-jabber said.

"Oh, I think you do," Skip said in a low, firm voice.

Rose had stepped around behind the boys.

"You better not touch us or my dad'll sue you," the jabber said.

Skip pegged him as the ringleader. He leaned over and stared the boy in the face. "You better hope that I don't *have* to touch you."

The boy paled.

"Move!" Rose barked from behind him.

All the boys jumped.

"We will all go," Mrs. Langdon said, as if it had been her idea all along.

~~~~~~~~~

Kate was feeling like her normal self as she drove back to her office. Liz hadn't found much on Josie. Only that she had been moved from the elementary school at St. Batholomew's to Bryn Mawr when she was in second grade. All Kate had known was that her client had attended private school. She had assumed those schools had been Catholic, considering her parents' staunch beliefs. But Bryn Mawr made sense too. It was a top-notch girls school, one of the best in the country.

Liz had also checked out Father Samuel Phelps. Kate hadn't been surprised when his record with the church was squeaky clean. The Hartins also seemed to have no skeletons in their closets, although Kate knew from her professional experience that things could happen behind closed doors that never made it into any official record.

Gerald Kraft, the doctor who'd claimed that he hadn't written the clonazepam prescription, had never had any disciplinary action against him by the AMA. Nor had he ever been sued for malpractice.

Kate got back to her office with only five minutes to spare before her first afternoon client was due to arrive. Racing into her office, she threw her raincoat in the general direction of the coat rack in the corner and reached for her desk phone to check her voicemail.

The outer door opened and closed. Her client was here.

Fortunately, there were no phone messages. Kate pulled her makeup case out of her purse to freshen up a bit.

A rap on her half open office door. Her head jerked up. She dropped her lipstick tube on the desk.

A woman who looked to be in her mid thirties stood in the doorway. Her gray suit was impeccable. Not a strand of her strawberry blonde hair was out of place. "Mrs. Huntington?"

"Yes." Kate picked up the lipstick and capped it. "Can I help you?"

"I'm Pernette Wells, Mrs. Hartin's assistant." The woman's tone was carefully neutral. "She asked me to deliver this to you." She held out a shoe box-sized package, wrapped in plain white paper.

Kate took the package. "Thank you."

The woman gave a stiff nod and left.

Kate waited until she heard the snick of the outer door closing. Her hands trembled as she tore away the wrappings and opened the box.

Inside was a bound book, about six by nine inches. Its cloth cover was black with bright flowers on it.

Josie's journal.

CHAPTER TWELVE

On the way home, Kate promised herself she would put aside the journal, literally and figuratively, until after the kids were in bed. She'd been neglecting her family obligations too much lately.

Several messages had required return phone calls at the end of her day, and she'd only had time to peek at the last entry in the journal, hoping it would miraculously reveal the "breakthrough" Josie had referred to in that phone message, or at least give some hint as to what she was "checking out." The entry indicated she had figured something out and was both excited and scared to pursue it, but otherwise it was frustratingly vague.

"Enough," Kate said out loud as she pulled up in front of the house. She mentally closed the door on all thoughts of Josie.

This time, Skip was the one who seemed preoccupied over dinner.

Billy squirmed in his chair as Edie chattered on about her day. Finally he interrupted. "Daddy and Aunt Rose were awesome, Mommy. They made the bad boys go to the principal's office with us. And I didn't get in trouble for shoving Jimmy Henshaw after all."

Kate raised her eyebrows in Skip's direction.

He gave a slight shake of his head. "I'll explain later." He turned to Billy. "Remember what I said, son. It's always better to walk away from a fight when you can."

"But they were all around me, Daddy."

"I know, son, but for future reference."

Billy subsided into a mild pout.

Edie jumped into the silence with more about her riding lesson after school. "Miss Linda says I'm doing a whole lot better, and Fiddlesticks didn't try to buck once today."

"That's great," Kate said. "Hey, did you get all your homework done yet?"

"Almost. I have some math left to finish."

"Get to it right after dinner, and I'll check it before bedtime."

"Okay, Mommy."

Kate turned to Maria, who had been rather quiet throughout the meal. "How are things going with your gentleman caller?"

Maria looked confused for a moment, then flashed a smile. "Good. He take me to dinner this Friday, wid his children."

"How old are they?"

"Ten, twelve and fifteen."

"Have you met them before?" Kate asked.

"No. Dis is first time." Maria ducked her head. "I am a little nervous. What if dey no like me?"

Kate wanted to reassure her, but she knew realistically that the kids might resent someone they perceived as a replacement for their mother. "How long has he been widowed?"

"Four years," Maria said.

"If they don't like you," Edie piped up, "then they're just crazy."

The adults laughed. "I agree," Kate said, her chest swelling with pride for her daughter. She suspected Edie knew the implications of the situation. If this man's kids liked Maria and the romance progressed, they might very well lose her as a member of their household.

But her little Edie was the poster child for fairness–she wasn't going to put her own selfish interests above Maria's happiness.

"Come, *niños*," Maria said. "You help me clear de table, so your mama and papa can talk."

Apparently Maria had caught the undercurrents earlier. Kate's anxiety about this romance eased some. Her housekeeper was no fool where people were concerned.

~~~~~

Skip started to lead the way to the sofa, then thought better of it. He didn't want the kids to hear them. He turned toward the study instead.

Kate sank into the desk chair behind the computer desk. "So how'd you end up going over to the school?" she asked in a low voice.

He nudged the door closed and perched on a corner of the desk. "When I caught up with his teacher, she gave me this song and dance about letting kids work it out for themselves." An echo of his earlier anger churned in his gut. "That's the same BS the school gave my folks when I was a kid. 'Boys will be boys,' the principal said when my father complained about the bullying." He noticed his hands were balled into fists and willed them to relax.

"So you and Rose went over there."

"Yeah, and we witnessed the boys picking on Billy. He shoved one of them, and Mrs. Langdon was going to have *him* punished for fighting." His jaw clenched, then released again at the memory of what had come next. "We made sure that the older boys were marched off to the principal's office too."

"What happened?"

"The principal read them the riot act for picking on a kid younger than them. She basically called them wimps." He grinned a little at the mental image of the chagrined expressions on those boys' faces.

"You know Mrs. Langdon's attitude isn't the norm anymore," Kate said. "But teachers are so overworked these days, it's hard for them to have to monitor the kids' behavior constantly too."

"I know that, but the teachers were all huddled together in a group, talking to each other. They weren't even paying much attention to what the kids were doing. That is until Billy shoved the other kid."

Kate didn't say anything.

"The principal wants me to speak at the PTA meeting next

Tuesday," he said. "She wants to start an anti-bullying campaign." Butterflies fluttered in his chest, taking him by surprise. He wasn't usually self-conscious about talking to groups of people. But this topic was a different story.

Kate smiled up at him. "Wow. That's wonderful, sweetheart."

"Can you come to the meeting?"

"Of course." She took the hand that had been resting on his knee and gave it a squeeze.

He squeezed back. "Guess we'd better check their homework and then get baths going."

"Okay, but I may not be going to bed on time tonight."

"Oh?"

"Josie's mother sent her journal to my office this afternoon. I want to check it out."

He grinned down at her. "I'm impressed by your restraint that you didn't tear into it the minute you got home."

"Trust me, I wanted to. But I'm trying to be a little more balanced about this whole thing."

~~~~

Skip had volunteered to supervise baths so Kate could get started on the journal.

She carried the box over to the sofa and pulled the book out. Skimming through it, she found the entry for a month before Josie's death and started reading there.

Almost every day, Josie wrote about the roller coaster of emotions that was bipolar disorder. Some of the entries were rather disjointed. But she hadn't been writing a memoir. The journal was intended for her own eyes only.

Kate stopped to study the entry a few days before her last session with Josie. It was the first mention of the dreams in that month's sample of entries. They had probably been mentioned earlier. She would go back later and look for more details about them in the earlier entries.

February 27

Last night, I had the dream again. I really need to remember to tell Kate about them. But every time I even think that, I get so anxious. My hand is shaking as I'm writing this.

I hope this doesn't mean another round of depression. I'm just now coming out of one, and that would be so unfair. Usually I get to have some fun in the in-between times, before the mania gets too out of control to be comfortable.

That implied that the dreams triggered her depressive episodes, or maybe they only announced them. With bipolar it was hard to tell when the person's moods were related to life events and when they were just brain chemistry taking over.

Kate turned the page.

February 28

Today I volunteered at the vet's office. I was downright giddy getting ready this morning. I hate to admit it but my crush on Laurie Blake is getting worse. I got that feeling again today. We were chatting at lunchtime, all relaxed and friendly, then suddenly she closed down. I have no clue what is triggering that reaction. What am I doing that makes her withdraw like that? Has she picked up on my crush maybe?

And I also have no clue about who the hell I am. Or rather what am I? Straight or gay?

When I dated guys I was plenty turned on by them sexually, but I never loved them. Not in this deep longing way that I love women sometimes. Note to self: bring this up with Kate next time. Maybe she can help me figure it out.

"Yes I could have," Kate said under her breath. But Josie had brought up her mother instead, in that last session. Was that a dodge, or had the mother stuff really been more pressing? There was no denying that Josie experienced a major shift that day regarding her mother.

Kate's chest ached that she'd never been able to help Josie understand her attraction to women. The young woman had brought it up before and had been quite conflicted about it. But she hadn't called it a "deep longing."

Most likely Josie was indeed bisexual, but the words *deep*

longing were telling. Kate suspected they indicated transference. Something about the women Josie was attracted to reminded her of her mother on an unconscious level–in Laurie Blake's case, it was probably the shutting down and distancing. Then the childhood longing for love and attention is triggered, confusing and complicating any real romantic attraction.

Correction, *was* triggered. Past tense.

Kate's eyes stung. Josie'd never had a chance to sort that out. And now she'd never have a chance at a healthy romantic relationship with someone, male or female.

Kate blinked back the tears and made herself keep reading. The next day's entry described the telephone conversation with her mother that Josie had brought up that Monday in therapy. Mrs. Hartin had once again insisted she was sending her maid over to clean Josie's condo. Josie had just as adamantly told her she wouldn't let the maid through her front door.

Kate felt a momentary pang of sympathy for that poor maid. How often had the servants been caught up in the tug of war between mother and daughter?

Damn it, Mother! Why do you do this to me? I can feel the dark tendrils of the depression curling around me. Damn it to hell! I hate this!

So it had been her mother issues more than the dream that was triggering the depression this time. Or at least that had been Josie's take on it.

The following day's entry was written after her therapy session. She described the analogy Kate had made with Buster, her childhood dog. She seemed excited about the breakthrough.

The depression is gone. Poof! I feel lighter than I have in eons. I really think I can handle Mother now and not let her get to me. Bless you, Kate!

This time a tear broke loose, making a dark, wet spot on the white page. Kate leaned back and swiped at her eyes. She didn't want to leave tear stains in the journal that she would eventually have to return to Mrs. Hartin.

Josie really had turned a corner that day. Kate's brain was off and running, crafting a treatment plan for advanced recovery–strategies for managing the bipolar mood swings better, now that the worst of the client's psychological issues were getting resolved. There were adjustments she could make to her lifestyle, and ways she could better identify when her mood was headed up or down.

Reality slammed on the brakes. The client was dead. There would be no advanced recovery.

Kate's throat closed.

Reading the journal was harder than she'd thought it would be. She leaned her head back against the sofa and gave in to the tears. They streamed down her face.

A soft clearing of a throat. Her head jerked up.

Skip was watching her with worry in his eyes. "You okay, darlin'?"

"No, but thanks for asking. The kids ready for goodnight kisses?"

"Yeah."

She swiped at her wet cheeks with her fingertips, then pushed herself up off the sofa. She was almost past Skip when he touched her shoulder. She turned toward him.

He wrapped his arms around her and tucked her head under his chin. "That's not your life," he whispered. "This is your life."

She held on tight.

~~~~~~~~~

Kate's stomach churned as she drove to work the next day. She was starting to relate to the roller coaster of emotions that had been Josie's life. She'd been feeling so much better yesterday, until she'd read those entries in the journal.

She tried to rationalize the guilt away, with little success. Not only had she not followed up with Josie on the dreams, but apparently her client didn't trust her enough to tell her she was having doubts again about her sexual orientation, and that she was interested in a possible new relationship.

Was Dr. Laurie Blake a lesbian? Kate had no idea.

She reminded herself that the latest confrontation between Josie and her mother had pushed these things aside in Josie's mind during that last therapy session.

"You are not a mind reader," Kate said out loud.

No, but you're supposed to pick up on nonverbal cues.

No doubt Josie assumed there would be plenty of future sessions to explore those other issues. Just as Kate had assumed there would be time to come back to the dreams that Josie had mentioned and then veered away from discussing.

For her own self-preservation, she wanted to stop reading Josie's journal, but she couldn't. Not when there might be answers on those pages. Answers that would ultimately give her and Josie's parents some peace, and might get them to stop trying to get their hands on Josie's file.

Answers that might keep someone from getting away with murder.

She had tucked the journal into her briefcase this morning. She couldn't read it at lunchtime and risk being upset when she had to deal with her afternoon clients. But if she didn't have too many phone calls to return at the end of the day, she would read some before leaving for home.

Perhaps then her evening ritual of figuratively closing the door on her clients' issues would work with Josie as well, and she could go home to a peaceful evening with her family.

The plan didn't work. At the end of the day, she did indeed have some time to read in the journal. But what she found out was too disturbing, and also too exciting, to let it go when she walked out of her office door.

She was mentally rehashing the entry as she headed toward the parking lot where her car was parked. The hair stood up on the back of her neck. That creepy sense of being watched was back.

She stopped and looked around. The sidewalk was relatively crowded with workers from the surrounding office buildings, who were now rushing to their cars to get home in time for dinner. Which was what she should be doing.

Only a few people were moving more slowly. A young couple sauntered hand in hand toward a nearby restaurant and a woman in a black jacket and red knit scarf–the latter a little excessive since the evening was not all that chilly–was staring into the window of a shop down the block. A rather disheveled man of indeterminate age lingered at the corner behind her. He too was overdressed for the weather, in an old Army coat. Was he homeless? The red-scarf lady turned away from the store window and stepped over to a car parked at the curb. She opened the passenger door and climbed in. She'd probably been killing time, waiting for her ride to show up.

Kate did another slow turn, scanning the hustling crowd of pedestrians. Then she pulled out her cell phone as she started moving again toward the corner where she would cross the street. "Hey, Manny," she said when he answered. "Where are you?"

"Heading home. Do you need me to do something?"

"Never mind. It can wait until tomorrow."

"What?"

"Nothing." She didn't want to tell him she'd thought he was still following her, against her express orders to Skip about that.

"I need to think this next move through a bit more," she said, ad-libbing. She had no next move–yet. "I'll call you tomorrow if I need your help."

"Okay. 'Night, Kate."

"Have a good evening."

She pocketed her phone and glanced up. The crosswalk signal flipped over to the little stick man walking. She stepped off the curb.

"Look out!" a woman screamed from behind her.

Kate jumped and whirled around, braced for an attack of some kind. A whoosh of air plastered her skirt to the back of her legs.

She twisted around again as horns blared and tires screeched. A car had run the red light. Fortunately the other drivers had managed to stop or swerve out of the way.

A woman appeared at Kate's elbow. "That was too close for comfort. I can't believe the way some people drive these days."

Kate placed her hand over her pounding heart. "Were you the one who yelled?"

"Yeah." The woman patted her own chest. "I was right behind you, about to step into the crosswalk, when I saw that jackass wasn't gonna stop."

"Thanks for yelling. I wasn't even looking his way. I would've walked right into his path."

Vehicles and pedestrians had only paused a few seconds to bear witness to the potential tragedies the speeding driver came close to causing. Both cars and people were again rushing past. Kate and the other woman had to wait through another cycle of the traffic light before crossing over.

CHAPTER THIRTEEN

March 5

I'm getting some inklings of what the dreams may be about! I've started having bits and pieces of… something during the day. Not sure if it's a memory or what. It's completely dark, like in the dreams. I'm cold and scared, and really little. There's a flash in the darkness. It blinds me, and then it's gone. The second time I… I guess "remembered" is as good a word as any. The second time I remembered it, I heard voices in the distance.

Kate read the words again while waiting for Skip to finish the kids' stories. She turned to the next day's entry.

March 6

I went to see Father Sam today. I just had a gut feeling that he might know something helpful. But he didn't. I asked him why my parents took me out of the school at St. Bart's. He didn't remember, said he wasn't sure they gave a reason. He'd always assumed it was because Bryn Mawr would improve my chances of getting into a good college.

Then I tried to tell him about the dreams. But the anxiety got so overwhelming that I had to get out of there. I should call him and apologize for bolting on him like that, but the mere thought of having to explain why has me reaching for my Xanax bottle.

Skip came down the stairs and joined her on the sofa.

Kate closed the journal and slipped it into her briefcase at her feet.

He circled her shoulders with one arm and pulled her close to him. She snuggled against his side and sighed.

But her mind wouldn't let it go.

Why hadn't Fr. Sam mentioned that Josie asked about the school switch? Had the next topic of conversation–the dreams–and Josie's abrupt bolting from his office, had that overshadowed the school discussion sufficiently that it hadn't even registered in the priest's elderly brain?

Skip had said to go back to the beginning. She now had two reasons to go see Father Sam again.

"Glad to know I'm such scintillating company," Skip said from beside her.

"Oh, sorry, sweetheart." She turned her face up to him.

He was smiling, a teasing light in his eyes. He leaned down and brushed her lips with his.

She shoved aside all thoughts of Josie and focused her attention on the deepening kiss.

~~~~~~~~~

Kate showed her client to the door of her office. Her waiting room was full of people. She looked around, trying to remember who she was supposed to see next.

Who were all these people? She didn't even know half of them. And some of the others were clients who had finished therapy years ago.

She couldn't remember any of their names. What kind of therapist was she?

"Next," she called out.

A woman rose from a chair against the wall and moved forward, her gait dragging. Her skin was pale, translucent, the area around her eyes bruised with fatigue.

As she came closer, Kate recognized her.

"Why did you put me in the hospital?" Carol's words were angry but her tone was sad. "You know I hate it there."

Kate reached out. Her hands went through the woman's body.

A scream caught in her throat. Tears streamed down her face but she couldn't move, couldn't talk. She started shaking, more and more violently.

"Kate! Wake up!"

The shaking eased as her eyelids fluttered open.

"You're havin' a bad dream, darlin'."

A dream. Carol isn't dead. Kate shuddered.

Skip gathered her against his chest and held her tight. "You wanna tell me about it?" he said softly, his breath stirring her curls.

Did she? Not really. Because then she would have to admit to her doubts about herself. She shook her head against his chest.

He eased his hold on her and held her slightly away from him to look into her face. His expression said loud and clear, *Are you sure?*

He knew her too well. Normally she used language to sort out her feelings. It was what she did professionally, what she was used to. Who she was.

That last thought hit her in the solar plexus. She gasped, then immediately pushed the thought aside. She was not her job. She was Kate Huntington-Canfield, wife and mother. Psychotherapy was only her profession.

Oh really? a little voice smirked in the back of her mind.

She told it to shut up. She couldn't think about all this now, or she'd never get back to sleep.

Skip was still watching her face.

"It's okay. I was dreaming about the client that I had to hospitalize this week." It was the truth, just not the whole truth.

He looked down at her for another second, then rolled onto his back, taking her with him, snug against his side. "You wanna mess around to get your mind off of her?" His tone was teasing.

She lifted her head and smiled up at him. "I always wanna mess around, but it's late. We both have to work tomorrow."

"How about a back rub to help you get back to sleep?"

"Mmm," she purred. "You are way too good to me."

He grinned. "Yes, I am, but I get plenty in return."

Do you? The thought startled her, sent a small chill through her core. She couldn't bring herself to say it out loud.

Skip had maneuvered her onto her side and was caressing her

back in warm soothing circles.

She tried to empty her mind, but sleep evaded her. Finally, she intentionally slowed her breathing, pretending she was asleep.

He eased over onto his back. Soon, soft snoring told her that at least one of them would get some decent rest tonight.

Father Sam couldn't see her at lunchtime the next day, but he was willing to stick around for a while at the end of the day. "It's not like I have a long commute," he'd said with a chuckle. "The rectory's right across the courtyard."

When Kate arrived at the church at five-twenty, the office door was locked. She peered through the glass window at an empty desk and a darkened hallway beyond. She rang the bell.

After a minute, the priest shuffled into sight.

He pushed the door open and tried to hold it that way so she could pass by him into the building, his manners no doubt demanding that ladies go first. But his elderly muscles were no match for the automatic closer mechanism.

Kate grabbed the inside handle. "Lead on, Father."

Once he had gingerly settled himself into his desk chair, he said, "So, to what do I owe this pleasure, Katie? Two visits in as many weeks after decades of neglect." It could have been a rebuke but his eyes were twinkling.

She smiled at him. "I know you want to get to your supper, so I won't keep you long. I have Josie's journal and it's given me some new information."

"Oh? Something that supports your theory that she didn't die by her own hand?"

She thought about that for a moment. Not really, since the memory that had been bubbling up in Josie's psyche could have sent her into another depression.

"I hope so." Leaning forward, she rested her elbows on the edge of the priest's desk. "Josie was starting to remember something. Something that happened when she was little. And she had a gut feeling that it had to do with St. Bartholomew's."

Kate was intentionally paraphrasing her client's words to indicate more of a connection to St. Bart's than Josie had implied.

Father Sam tilted his head. "She thought something happened here?"

"Not necessarily." Kate let those words hang in the air, waiting to see what Father Sam might reveal.

"What did she remember?"

"Nothing all that specific. She'd asked you about why her parents took her out of school here. Do you remember any more about that?"

He shook his head, then dropped his gaze from her face to his cluttered desk. "I don't even remember discussing that with her."

Her gut said he was lying. A lump grew in her throat.

Gut feelings aren't always right, she told herself.

"Who was in charge of the school back then?" she asked.

He raised his eyes from the desk to look straight up at the ceiling. After a moment, he said, "I don't recall."

Another lie. When trying to remember something, people usually looked up and to their left or their right, as they searched the hemispheres of their brains for the information.

She decided to let it go. Liz would be able to track down the names.

Father Sam was now looking directly at her. "Katie, you may be messing with something dangerous here. You've convinced me that she didn't commit suicide. I'll tell her parents that Josie can be transferred to their plot at New Cathedral Cemetery."

"Thanks, Father Sam. That will be a big comfort to them." She managed a smile that she hoped looked genuine. Her chest ached at the thought that the old priest was lying to her.

What did that mean? And who else might have some memory of Josie's short tenure at St. Bart's school?

"Who was the youth director then?" she asked.

Father Sam stared across the room. He shook his head. "It's a pain getting old, Katie. I can see the woman's face in my mind's eye, but I can't recall her name."

"Never mind. I can find it."

Something flashed in his eyes and then was gone, so fast she couldn't interpret it.

She rose and extended her hand. "Thanks for your time, Father."

He also rose and took her hand, but instead of shaking it he held it between his two. "Be careful, Katie. I don't want anything happening to you. Indeed, I wish you'd let this go and let the police take care of it. It's not safe to be trying to track down a killer."

This time her smile was more genuine. "I'll be careful, Father. You get to your supper. I can see myself out."

Once in her car, she stopped to analyze that final exchange. Father Sam seemed genuinely concerned for her. And he was right. Chasing murderers was dangerous. But coupled with the sense that he had lied to her, she couldn't help wondering if he was trying to warn her off.

Then again, he came from a generation that saw women as the weaker sex. So maybe he really was just worried about her.

Grr! Dear Lord, save me from men who want to protect me.

She mentally did the math. Josie had recently turned thirty-one—yet another bone of contention between her and her mother, that she was not married with children by her thirties. Josie would have been in second grade roughly twenty-four years ago. That would have been the early nineties.

She instructed her Bluetooth to call Liz's cell phone.

"Hey, Kate." Liz's booming voice filled her car.

"Hey there. You said to call if I thought of anything else you could do. Do you mind looking something up for me?"

"No problem."

"Could you find out who was in charge of St. Bartholomew's Catholic grade school twenty-four years ago?"

"Pish, give me something hard to do! Hang on."

Kate imagined her friend stretching out her arms, pretending to crack her knuckles before tackling her laptop's keyboard. Any kind of computer research was mental ambrosia for Liz, even if–maybe especially if–it involved some mild to moderate hacking. But this time, Kate only needed her superior research skills.

"Sister Michelina Larsen."

"That was quick. Can you find out where she is now?" Kate prayed that the woman was still alive.

"Okay, give me a sec." The soft clacking of keyboard keys, then Liz rattled off an address. "That's a retirement home for nuns."

"I'm driving. Can you email that address to me?"

"Email? How quaint. I'll text it to you."

"Wait! Which is harder to hack into?"

"They're both pretty easy if you know what you're doing. Why so paranoid?" Liz's tone morphed to worried. "What are you getting into, Kate?"

"Never mind. Text is fine. I've just had this weird feeling lately that someone is watching me."

A pregnant pause. "Aren't you the one who's always saying to trust those gut feelings?"

Kate let out a short, humorless laugh. "You're not helping with my paranoia."

"How's Skip feel about you investigating a potential murder?"

"He's assigned Manny to help if things get dicey, but so far I'm only interviewing priests and nuns."

Another beat of silence. "Be careful, okay?"

"I will be. I am. Thanks for checking on that for me. Bye."

"Take care of yourself." Liz disconnected.

When Kate pulled up in front of her house, she turned off the car but she didn't get out. Instead she grabbed her cell phone from the passenger seat, checked the text Liz had sent and called the number for the nuns' retirement home where Sister Michelina Larsen now lived.

The call went to voicemail. An elderly, female voice asked her to leave her name, number and who she was calling for.

Deciding to try again in the morning, Kate disconnected

without leaving a message.

~~~~~~~

She only had slightly better luck the next day. The same qua-very voice from the voicemail recording answered in person. Kate asked for Sister Michelina Larsen.

"She's not here right now, I'm afraid. She's visiting her sister in Chicago."

"When is she due back?"

"Monday evening. Shall I have her call you on Tuesday?"

"Yes, please. Tell her I'm a former parishioner of St. Bartholomew's and I have a couple questions for her." Kate gave the elderly nun her cell phone number.

Hanging up, she wracked her brain trying to think of what else she could do at this point. Nothing came to mind except to keep reading Josie's journal.

She glanced at her watch. That would have to wait until later. It was time for her first session.

At the end of the day, Kate stole a few minutes before going home to read the last few journal entries before Josie's death. Over the weekend, she hoped to find time to go back to the beginning of the journal and read the whole thing. It was so hard reliving her dead client's life through the journal, but it was the best chance she had of finding more leads.

She flipped a page over.

March 8

I think I've got it. And my gut says it ties in with that face I used to get flashes of. Kate's always saying to trust my gut. Now I just have to find him.

"Come on, Josie. Who is *him*?" Kate muttered under her breath.

And what's this about flashes of a face? Yet another item that Josie had never mentioned to her.

She turned the page and there was the last entry, made the day before Josie left her final message on Kate's voicemail.

March 9

I had the dream again last night, and I'm pretty sure I'm on the right track. It's related to those flashes. I get scared silly inside at the thought of pursuing this. I know what Kate would say to that–it's the little kid part of me that's scared. The adult can handle this!

The adult actually feels excited about all this, and it's so nice! It feels different from the mania. It's REAL excitement!

The next page was blank, as were the rest of the pages in the little booklet.

Which flashes was that last entry referring to? The flashes of the man's face in the past, or the more recent glimpses of memory, in which there were flashes of light?

Kate sat back in her desk chair. Tears stung her eyes.

Josie had made substantial psychological progress those last two weeks of her life. She had been using the things Kate had said to guide her, but she was essentially doing it on her own. This was exactly what a therapist wanted to see. The main goal of her job was to work herself out of a job.

No doubt, that would have happened with Josie, probably within the next few months.

If she had lived.

~~~~~~~

Saturday dawned sunny and warm. Mother Nature had finally gotten the memo that it was spring.

The kids wanted to play outside. Kate sent them to their rooms for sweaters, and then they all went into the backyard.

She took Josie's journal with her and headed for the Adirondack chair at the far end of the yard. It was the one she had sat in each evening during the weeks after her first husband's death.

As soon as she sat down, sadness washed over her. Maybe this chair wasn't the best idea. It had too many associations.

Then again, sad probably was the most appropriate mood for reading the journal. She opened it at the beginning. The first entry was nine months ago.

She skimmed the pages, looking for references to flashes of a man's face, stopping to read more carefully whenever the dreams were mentioned. The sounds of her children whooping and hollering faded into the background.

There were entries for almost every day, sometimes several a day. Occasionally there would be gaps.

At the halfway point there had still been no mention of a man's face. Kate stuck her finger between the pages to hold her place and flipped to the back to re-read the next to the last entry again.

… that face I used to get flashes of.

Those words *used to* triggered a memory of the first session with Josie three years ago. She'd encouraged her new client to keep a journal, to help her sort out her feelings. Josie had said that she used to do that when she was in therapy before, and it had been helpful.

A shadow fell across the page. Kate looked up. Her daughter was standing in front of her.

"Can I go ride Fiddlesticks today, Mommy?"

"Not today, sweetie," Kate answered without really thinking about it.

"But it's such a pretty day," Edie whined. "And I already got most of my homework done for Monday. I'll finish tonight, I promise."

Kate's chest tightened. Homework had been the furthest thing from her mind. She'd said no as a knee-jerk reaction because she was too absorbed in the journal to be bothered with taking Edie to the horse farm where her pony was boarded.

Rustling in the leaves and a longer shadow fell across her lap, announcing Skip's arrival.

She tilted her head up at him, shading her eyes with her free hand. "Can you keep an eye on Billy? I'm going to take Edie out to the farm."

"Woot!" Edie turned and raced toward the house to change into her riding clothes.

"No problem," Skip said.

She struggled to get out of the tilted seat of the chair. Skip offered a hand up. She fumbled the journal, almost dropping it. Her finger slipped out from between the pages.

Crap! Now I'll have to re-read part of it to find my place again.

She slid it into the pocket of her jacket. She could read while Edie was riding.

Oct. 22

I ran into Father Bill today. He seemed kind of embarrassed or shy or something. Maybe he doesn't like to be reminded of his priest days. He might be ashamed of having left the priesthood to get married, although why he would feel that way, I can't fathom.

Kate glanced up from where she was perched on the paddock fence. Edie, in jodhpurs, riding helmet and boots, was happily trotting Fiddlesticks around the ring.

I hope he doesn't regret that. The girls and I at school used to call him Father What-A-Waste. He's gained some weight and lost some of his hair, but he's still a good-looking man. I always liked him; he somehow seemed heroic to me–

"Look, Mommy. Watch this!"

Kate raised her head. Edie was heading the pony toward a jump along the side of the worn path of the ring. The jump's top rail wasn't very high, but her riding teacher had only recently begun to work with her on jumping.

The little girl kicked the pony's sides. Fiddlesticks broke into a reluctant canter.

"Edie! No!"

Too late.

The pony's front legs left the ground.

Kate held her breath. She let it out when it looked like pony and child would clear the jump.

Then Fiddle's back hoof struck the top bar. It fell off its pegs, as it was supposed to do, but the contact had thrown the pony off balance. He staggered sideways, and Edie tumbled off.

The sound of helmet hitting wood stopped Kate's heart.

CHAPTER FOURTEEN

The emergency room pediatrician at Sinai Hospital was examining Edie. He looked in her ears with his scope, then asked her to follow his finger as he shone a light into her eyes.

Kate stood in the doorway of the small room, where Edie could see her. But she was also watching the glass doors separating the pediatric emergency center from the rest of the hospital.

The doctor glanced at Kate. "Any nausea?"

"What's that?" Edie said.

"She threw up in the car coming here," Kate said.

Edie's cheeks turned pink.

"It's not your fault, sweetie," Kate said, feeling like crap inside. "Bumps on the head can make us sick sometimes."

Her ears registered the faint whoosh of the doors opening. She looked up as Skip entered the emergency center. He saw her and strode in her direction. The storm clouds on his face did not bode well.

"She just seems to have a mild concussion." The doctor slipped his scope into his pocket. "Keep her quiet for the rest of the weekend. If there's no more nausea, she can go to school on Monday, but no phys ed or running around during recess, at least for this week."

"What's a concushion?" Edie asked.

The doctor smiled at her. "Concussion. It means you rattled your brain cells around inside your skull, and it will take a little time for your brain to heal, so you don't want to jostle it again for a while."

Kate felt a smile tugging at her lips despite the ominous presence of her angry husband behind her. It was a great explanation of a concussion for a nine year old.

Edie glanced up and her face brightened. "Hi, Daddy."

"Hey, Pumkin," Skip said from behind Kate. "I hear your pony jumped without you."

"Aw, Daddy. I made it over the jump, but Fiddle hit his foot and stumbled."

"And where was your mother while all this was happening?" Skip muttered next to Kate's ear.

Anger flared in her chest, at the same time that guilt twisted her gut. Even if she'd been watching Edie's every move, she probably couldn't have stopped her from the impulsive attempt to take the jump.

She tamped down her temper and turned to Edie. "No more jumping except during lessons until Miss Linda says you're ready."

"No more jumping, period," Skip said.

"Daddy!" Edie whined.

Kate gritted her teeth and resisted the urge to turn around. As scary as the last hour had been, while she'd raced Edie to the hospital and tried to wait patiently for a doctor to see them, she didn't see the need to curtail the child's riding lessons.

"We'll discuss that another time," she managed to get out in a relatively calm voice.

"Well, she's good to go." The doctor stood up from the stool next to the examining table. "You all check out with the nurse up front, please."

"You take care of the bill." Skip's voice was terse. "I'll take her home."

Although she wasn't crazy about his tone, the idea was sound. The passenger floor of her car was not a pretty sight right now. Nor did it smell all that good.

~~~~~~~~

Skip managed to wait until the kids were bedded down, but it wasn't easy. First she's oblivious to the fact that Billy's being bullied, and now Edie's hurt on her watch. Enough was enough!

She was in their usual evening spot, sitting on the sofa. But her expression said she wanted to be anywhere but there.

She held her palms out in front of her as he approached. "Look, I know I should have been paying better attention–"

"You said you were looking down. You were reading, weren't you?" He'd seen her slip that journal into her pocket, but he didn't want to falsely accuse her.

She dropped her hands and nodded.

"What were you reading?" He knew the answer but he was going to make her say it.

She looked down at her lap. Then she brought her gaze back up to his face, where he stood looming over her. "Josie's journal," she said in a flat voice.

His jaw clenched. "Enough, Kate! You have got to let this go."

She stared up at him. "Would you please sit down. I'm getting a crick in my neck."

He scowled at her and took the armchair across from the sofa.

She showed no surprise that he hadn't sat down next to her, as he usually would.

"I understand that you're pissed," she said in a low voice. "Your child got hurt."

"*Our* child got hurt."

"Our child got hurt. But I'm not sure I could have stopped her even if I'd been looking her way at that moment."

"But the point is, you were supposed to be watching her, not absorbed in that damn journal."

"You watch her every second when you take her?" Her tone was angry.

That made him even madder. He was the one who had a right to be pissed. *She* was supposed to be contrite.

He breathed in slowly through his nose. This wasn't getting them anywhere. In an emphatic tone he said, "You need to let me assign Manny to investigate this, so you can get back to focusing on your own life."

She sighed and looked away. "If only it were that simple. This isn't just about justice for Josie." She caught her lower lip between her teeth for a moment, an old nervous habit. "It's affecting my work. I…" Her voice dropped to almost a whisper. "I don't trust myself anymore."

Even in profile, he could see the pain in her face. Some of his anger drained away. "Let us find the killer, Kate. It's what we do."

She shook her head slightly. "A lot of this stuff, it won't mean anything to anybody else. I'm catching things because I knew Josie, her issues. When I have something more concrete, then somebody else could probably take it from there. But not yet."

He ground his teeth. He wasn't willing to let this drag on. "I want our lives back to normal. I want the mother of my children to be focused on them again. I insist that you let us handle this."

Her eyes flashed. "You insist? Or what?"

He blew out air. "Poor choice of words." He ran fingers through his hair, then grabbed a hunk and tugged.

Her face softened. She leaned forward. "Look, I promise I will try harder to segregate all this from my personal life. I'll work on it during my lunch hours, and a little bit after work, but I'll focus on home when I'm here."

He didn't say anything, wasn't sure what to say really.

"Skip, I wish… I've tried to forget about it, but I can't." Her voice was low. "This is the best I can do right now."

Her deflated tone tugged at his heart. He wanted this done, but he was no stranger to grief. After his father's death, he'd gone a little nuts. Blown his career with the Maryland state police by erupting at his captain. Granted the man was an ass, but still…

"You'll let me know as soon as there's anything the agency can do? The sooner this gets resolved, the better."

"Amen to that." She smiled for the first time all evening. "Is it time for make-up sex yet? Or do you need to yell some more?"

The last of his anger melted. His mouth quirked up at the corners. "Hmm, sex versus yelling?" He held out both hands, palms up, and moved them up and down, weighing those alternatives.

"I could probably yell some more, but I think I'll take the sex. You better make it extra good, though."

Her smile turned to a full-fledged grin. "I think I can manage that," she said in a low, sultry voice.

~~~~~~

Ironically Skip ended up having to work on Sunday. The CEO of one of his biggest clients, a major insurance company, was in town just for the weekend and wanted to meet with him over lunch. It bordered on a command performance, and Kate told him she totally understood that he needed to go.

She hadn't taken the kids to Sunday school, since Edie was supposed to be taking it easy. But the child seemed to be doing fine. Kate watched from across the kitchen as Edie sat at the table drawing in the sketch pad they had given her for her birthday. Without having to look, Kate could guess that it was another picture of a horse.

Billy's laughter could occasionally be heard over the sound track of the video he was watching in the living room.

Kate leaned her butt against the counter and took a swig of coffee from her mug. Yes, she'd promised to focus on family when she was home, but Skip being gone for part of the day had shot the heck out of family time. With nothing else to focus on, her mind kept wandering back to Josie's case.

It dawned on her that she'd never talked to the owner of the gallery where Josie worked. Nor had she heard back about Manny's efforts to track down her friends.

She grabbed the phone from its base on the counter and called Manny.

"Yo, Kate. What's up?"

"Hey, Manny. Sorry to bother you on a Sunday morning, but I was wondering if you'd had any luck tracking down Josie Hartin's friends."

"Yes and no. I checked out the artist crowd she hung with. I'd say they were more acquaintances than close friends. Some of them hinted that they found her a bit too intense, which I thought was really sayin' something, coming from that crowd."

Kate wasn't totally surprised. In addition to her bipolar disorder, Josie had some symptoms of borderline personality disorder. She tended to be needy and yet volatile in her relationships. She was definitely intense, although those borderline tendencies had been getting better in recent months.

Manny cleared his throat. "Most of them said she was pretty tight with that gallery owner she worked for. But I didn't talk to her. Skip said you wanted to interview her yourself."

"Yeah, I do." She knew that Josie's boss had been one of her few close friends. From what Manny was saying, maybe she was her only close friend. "But I haven't gotten around to it yet. I was thinking about going down there today."

"I can go with you."

"No, I don't want to make you work on a Sunday."

"Humph. I've been bored silly lately. Except for the few things I've checked out for you, I've mostly been sitting around the office waiting for things to pick up."

She pursed her lips, debating with herself. She'd promised Skip she would take Manny with her, but would he have to pay the man overtime on a Sunday? And it seemed so unfair to ask Manny to work on his day of rest.

"Kate, it isn't good for me to have so much time on my hands," Manny said in a low, intense voice.

That made the decision for her. She was one of the few people outside of AA who knew that Manny was a recovering alcoholic. She could understand how being at loose ends might lead to temptation.

"Okay. Do you have the address?"

"Yeah. Lemme find it." Rustling noises for a moment, then he was back. He gave her the address, and she jotted it down on the pad lying next to the phone's base.

Kate glanced again at Edie, trying to assess if an outing to an art gallery would qualify as too much excitement. Probably not.

"I'll meet you there in an hour. The kids will be with me. Is that okay?"

"*No problema.*"

Kate disconnected. "Sweetie, how's your head feeling?"

Edie looked up from her drawing. "It's okay."

"How would you like to go see an art gallery today?"

Her face lit up. "Really?"

"Really. But you've got to promise to not get too excited or be too active, okay?"

"Sure, Mommy."

Art gallery struck Kate as a bit of an overstatement when they arrived at the address. The gallery was in the first floor of an old rowhouse on a side street in Fells Point, a rather bohemian area in downtown Baltimore known mainly for its bars.

Manny was leaning against a streetlight pole near the entrance, which sported a red sign reading *Hiliau's Gallery, Paintings and Other Works of Fine Art.*

He stepped over and pulled the door open for them.

"Kids," Kate said. "You remember Mr. Manny, don't you?"

Edie said a shy hello, but Billy had already raced ahead into the building.

Kate stepped in after him and quickly cased the big front room. Reasonably child-friendly—no nudes and nothing breakable within Billy's reach. Nonetheless... "Billy, do not touch anything, you hear me?"

"Okay, Mommy," the boy shouted.

"Inside voice please." Kate looked around for her daughter.

Edie was already completely enthralled. She was moving slowly down one wall that was covered in landscapes, her head bent back, mouth hanging open.

Billy's outside voice had brought them to the attention of a staff member. A big-boned, middle-aged woman, with graying hair and dressed in a brightly colored tee-shirt and jeans, crossed the room toward Kate.

The woman's smile was warm and welcoming. "Can I help

you?"

Not sure how long Billy would be content with looking at pots and pictures, Kate opted to get right to the point. She extended her hand. "I'm Kate Huntington. Are you Marilyn Hiliau by any chance?"

The woman's smile faltered for less than a second. "Yes, I am." She took the offered hand and shook it.

"I'm a friend of Josie Hartin's. Could I talk to you for a few minutes?"

The smile faded. The woman glanced at Manny.

"He's with me. He'll keep an eye on the kids, keep them from breaking anything." Kate looked at Manny, hoping he was okay with this plan.

He nodded once. "Come here, little man," he said to Billy. "You wanna see the pots on the high shelves?"

Kate glanced at the Native-American pottery, each on its own small shelf extending from one wall. "Don't let him get within reach."

Manny chuckled and swept Billy up into his arms.

Marilyn Hiliau's expression had turned wary, but she gestured toward a door leading into the rest of the building. "Let's go back to my office."

They walked down a hallway and through a room full of empty frames, packing crates and several large rolls of bubble wrap.

Office also turned out to be an overstatement. Kate suspected it had once been a large closet. It contained a small metal desk, overflowing with piles of papers, and an old wooden desk chair that squeaked when Ms. Hiliau sat down in it.

The woman gestured toward a straight-back chair, half in the oversized doorway and half hanging out into the larger room. "Have a seat."

The ornate woodwork of the doorframe caught Kate's eye.

Marilyn Hiliau followed her line of vision and chuckled. "This house used to be a brothel. The big front room was for entertaining guests, well, until it was time to entertain them another way more privately. This room…" She gestured with one hand to encompass the larger room. "It was the madam's bedroom."

Billy's voice echoing in the front room reminded Kate that she might not have much time. She leaned forward and took a deep breath. "Ms. Hiliau, I'm not sure where to start so I'll just dive in. I'm looking into Josie's death, because I don't think she committed suicide."

The woman nodded as tears pooled in her eyes. "Call me Marilyn. And neither do I."

Kate gave her a small smile. "And I'm Kate. I knew Josie fairly well, but I didn't know her artist friends."

Marilyn shrugged. A tear broke loose. She swiped it off her cheek with her fingertips. "I don't know that she had many friends, besides me. We were pretty close."

"Why don't you think she killed herself?"

"Because she was getting better. Yeah, she had a down spell recently, but it wasn't as bad as some of her previous depressions. And that last week or so, she was excited about something, but she wouldn't tell me what."

"A new art project maybe?" Kate asked to keep the conversation going.

"No. She would have told me about that. She became quite secretive about it all, but she said she might soon be free of the past."

"That's all she said?"

Marilyn nodded.

Damn! Why did you have to be so cagey, Josie? "Back to her friends, there wasn't anyone else she might have confided in? Was she dating anyone?"

Marilyn narrowed her eyes at her. "I thought you said you were her friend."

"I am. I was–"

"Wait! *Kate.* You're her therapist, aren't you?"

Kate smiled. "I can neither confirm nor deny that information."

It was the line her graduate school ethics professor had suggested for such situations. It covered one's butt legally without actually lying.

Marilyn smiled back. "So you knew her well, but not all aspects of her life."

"Exactly. What about dating?"

"Not anyone recently. The last guy she was involved with, that ended badly."

Kate nodded. She knew about that romance.

Marilyn tilted her head to one side. "Uh, I'm assuming you know that she was bisexual."

Kate wasn't quick enough to mask her surprise.

"I guess not."

"No, I knew that she was," Kate said. "But I'm surprised that she called herself that."

"She didn't. That's my word. She tended to fight the homosexual tendencies." Marilyn stopped, swallowed hard. "She'd become interested in a woman lately. Oh, she didn't say anything to that effect, but she talked about the gal all the time. Her dog's veterinarian."

Kate nodded again. "Do you know how far things had gone?"

"Not very would be my guess. I think she was still trying to find out if, one, the woman was gay, and two, was she interested. But she also said that Dr. Blake acted strange at times."

That fit with Josie's comment in her journal about the vet "closing down."

Had Josie asked Dr. Blake if she was a lesbian, and the vet had been offended by the question? That would hardly lead to a rage sufficient to commit murder, and setting up a suicide was not an impulsive action. And if the vet was the killer, she was also an extremely good actress. Her reactions the other night had seemed genuine.

"Could the vet have a partner," Kate asked, "male or female, who got wind of Josie's interest and was jealous?"

Marilyn scrunched up her face. "That's a stretch."

Kate thought so too. But she made a mental note to talk to the vet again. She was searching her mind for more questions to ask the gallery owner, when Edie came through the doorway into the packing room.

"Mommy, there's a picture out here I really like. Can we buy it?"

Kate suppressed a groan. She seriously doubted an original painting was within their budget. She looked at Edie's pleading face. Maybe, if it wasn't too outrageously expensive, she'd take the money out of the brokerage account.

Manny came through the door behind Edie. He had Billy by the hand. "Sorry. She got past me when I was trying to keep this guy entertained."

Kate rose from her chair. "That's okay. I should be apologizing to you, for saddling you with babysitting duty."

Manny shrugged. "*No problema.*"

"Come on, Edie. Show me this picture."

They trailed out to the front room, and Edie led Kate to a small painting in a corner, halfway up the wall. It was of two dogs, a black mutt of indiscriminate parentage and a copper-colored Labrador. Except for the color, the Lab looked just like Toby. The dogs were romping together in the grass, sunshine highlighting the red in the Lab's coat. Despite the Impressionistic style–the use of tiny dots of color to build the images–the scene was very realistic. Kate had to resist the urge to reach out and pat the dogs' heads.

A choking sound behind her had her turning around.

Tears streamed down Marilyn Hiliau's face. "That's one of Josie's." She stepped forward and lifted the framed painting off its hook.

Kate tried to get a look at the price tag. "How much is it?"

"For your little girl, it's free." Marilyn handed it to Edie, who took it reverently, her eyes wide, her mouth a small o.

"I can't let you do that," Kate said.

"Yes you can." The woman's voice was fierce. "Just find out what really happened to Josie."

CHAPTER FIFTEEN

Maria surprised them by returning home from her weekend off at dinnertime on Sunday.

Kate was heating up leftovers while Skip was upstairs overseeing the preparation of backpacks for school the next day, making sure all homework was accounted for.

"Aren't you having dinner with Eduardo tonight?" Kate asked. She always felt a little weird saying the man's name, since she had sometimes teasingly called her first husband Eduardo.

"No," Maria said. "I tell him I need time to tink."

"Think about what?"

Maria stood still in the middle of the kitchen, staring into space for a moment. Then she shook herself and said, "He propose to me today."

Kate's mouth fell open. "He asked you to marry him?"

That's a little quick, Señor Eduardo. She kept that thought to herself.

"*Sí.*" Maria clasped her hands together in front of her. "I not sure what to do."

"Do you love him?" It wasn't a question Kate had dared to ask before, but Maria seemed to be inviting input.

The little woman tilted her head to one side. "I tink I do."

Kate's stomach knotted. "You only *think* so?"

Maria nodded once, firmly. "*Sí.* I do. But it so complicated with de children and all." She stared meaningfully across the room.

Kate turned. Her son was standing in the doorway. "Billy, go tell your sister to wash up for dinner, and you do the same." It wouldn't buy them much time, but…

"Okay, Mommy." Billy bolted for the stairs.

Skip stepped into the doorway. "All set for tomorrow…" His voice trailed off as he stared at Maria.

Kate turned back to her. Maria had covered her face with her hands and was crying.

"Oh my God!" Kate grabbed her by the shoulders and guided her to the table, ignoring the ding of the microwave behind her.

Skip pulled out a chair for Maria. They all sat down.

"What is it?" Kate asked gently.

Maria swiped at her cheeks with the back of her hand. Skip fished his handkerchief out of his pocket and handed it to her.

"*Gracias.*" She blew her nose, then looked at them with sad eyes. "I no want to leave you."

For a selfish moment, Kate was tempted to encourage her to turn down the marriage proposal. She couldn't imagine their household without Maria.

She pushed her own feelings aside. "You will still be a part of our family, always."

Maria teared up again. "I no can imagine not seeing Billy and Edie every day. Dey like my own children."

Kate leaned over and hugged her. "We'll work something out so you see them regularly. Don't let that stop you from grabbing at this… chance for love."

At having your own life, she thought but didn't say out loud.

Skip grinned. "We'll be happy to dump the rug rats on you as often as you like."

Maria smiled, even as a fresh tear broke loose and trickled down her cheek. "You tink I should do it then?"

"I think you should do whatever you want to do," Kate said. "Whatever will make you happy."

Skip nodded.

Maria's head bobbed up and down. Then she rose from her chair. She held up Skip's handkerchief. "I do laundry tomorrow.

Kate, you set table. I heat up food."

Skip chuckled. Kate shot him a mock glare. She was such a lousy cook that the two of them conspired to keep her away from food preparation as much as possible. But even she could heat up leftovers, for Pete's sake.

As Edie said the blessing at the dinner table, Kate looked across the table at her housekeeper. A poignant sadness washed over her.

Cherish this, a little voice inside her said. *It won't be the same soon enough.*

Monday morning, Kate woke up with a minor epiphany. After a moment, she realized it was really the completion of the thought she'd had Saturday. It had been driven out of her mind by Edie's accident.

Josie "used to" keep a journal and she "used to" have flashbacks of a man's face. Kate needed to find those old journals.

She hustled through her morning routine so that she was ready for work by the time the kids were headed out the door for school. She left right behind them.

She opted to wait until she got to her office to make the call. It might be too distracting while driving.

That turned out to be a good decision because she never got past Pernette Wells. The PA refused to even tell Mrs. Hartin that Kate was on the phone.

"As I understand it, Mrs. Huntington," the woman said in that snooty voice of hers, "you and the Hartins are engaged in a legal dispute and all communications should go through attorneys."

Kate opened and closed her mouth, trying to think of what to say next. *What the hell does a woman who doesn't work need with a personal assistant, anyway?*

As if the woman had read her thoughts, she said, "Now if you'll excuse me, I have to attend to some details for a charity function Mrs. Hartin is hosting this coming weekend."

"So soon after her daughter's death?" Kate blurted out.

"It has been in the works for months. She could hardly cancel. Now good day, Mrs. Huntington."

Kate disconnected and stared at the phone for a moment.

I'm sure people would understand her cancelling when she's grieving her daughter.

Or would they? She'd just gotten a glimpse of the pressures a woman of Mrs. Hartin's position experienced. All too much of her life was dictated by the conventions of her class.

She recalled her envy of Dr. Kraft's luxurious home in Ruxton. *You all can have it!*

She dialed Rob's office. Fortunately, he was in. She gave him a quick summary of her earlier meeting with Josie's mother and the arrival of the journal.

He was silent on the other end of the line.

"Now I need the other journals. There's something in this one that hints at some earlier flashbacks, of a man's face. I need to find out more. This man may be the key. He may even be the killer."

"Kate, the Hartins are suing you for malpractice because they want your records. Do you realize how much leverage you will lose if you ask them for these journals?"

"Yes, except that Mrs. Hartin really wants answers. If the answers are in those journals, she'll give them to me, but I can't get past her assistant to even talk to her."

A sigh from the other end of the line. "I'll call their lawyer, but don't hold your breath."

They said their goodbyes and disconnected.

Kate checked her watch. Time to get her head oriented toward dealing with clients.

At lunchtime, she checked her messages. Nothing from Rob. Ignoring the couple of requests to reschedule appointments–she could call them back tonight–she read through the last entries in the journal again.

This man's face, it was the only real lead she had right now, at least until she could catch up with Sister Michelina. She had to get her hands on those earlier journals.

Maybe they were still in Josie's condo.

Kate jumped up and grabbed her purse. If she hurried she could get there and back before her first afternoon client arrived at one.

On the way, she remembered that she wanted to talk to the veterinarian again. She called and was informed by Dr. Blake's receptionist that they only had one evening time slot left this week. "I'll take it," Kate said, making a mental note to write it in her appointment book when she got back to the office.

The condo manager was on the phone when she entered the management office. She crossed her arms and resisted the urge to tap her foot.

He fell quiet, as if waiting for something.

"Are you on hold?" Kate whispered. "I need to get into Josephine Hartin's condo again. Could I get the key? I'm pressed for time."

The man waved a hand at her. "Yeah, I'm here, Frank. No that wasn't what I ordered. I need a truckload of topsoil, not fill dirt."

Kate despaired of getting his attention before she had to get back to her office.

He opened a drawer and rummaged in it while he continued to argue with the supplier on the phone. Finally he pulled out a key and tossed it to her. "Bring it back," he mouthed.

"Of course." She hurried out the door and across the wind-swept complex, not bothering with her car for such a short ride.

Once inside Josie's condo, she paused and looked around. Where to start? Her bedroom? No, older journals would probably be stored somewhere. In a box in a closet, or on a bookshelf maybe. She didn't have time to search closets, but she could look over the bookshelves in the study.

A quick rummage through the books on the middle shelves turned up no journals. She crouched down and searched the lower shelves. Finally on the top shelf, she noticed a couple of books tilted on an angle across an empty space. She pulled them out.

They were novels.

She stood on tiptoe and felt around the bare spot on the shelf. Her fingers came away dusty. Whoever had cleaned the rest of the apartment hadn't bothered with the bookshelves.

So had they removed whatever had been in that spot, or had Josie?

Kate pulled over the desk chair and climbed up on it so she could see the shelf. There were lines in the dust that indicated several books had sat there at one time. Probably recently.

She stood on tiptoe to see better. The chair wobbled under her and she grabbed the shelves for support.

A soft thud came from behind the bookcase.

She gingerly climbed down off the chair and tugged the books off the next lower shelf. A fleeting glimpse of something sliding down behind the books and another thud.

She pulled the books off the next shelf more carefully, one at a time. Wedged behind them was a small book. She reached in and got her fingers on the spine.

Pulling it out, she prayed that it was what she thought it was. She blew the dust off of it and opened the front.

October 10th, continued – The fight with mother was one of the worst we've had...

She flipped through the pages, searching for a year. At the beginning of January, she found it–2008. Yes, this was one of Josie's earlier journals.

But what had happened to the rest of them? Did the Hartins have them?

She glanced at her watch. She was out of time.

Back in the manager's office, Kate handed over the key. "Have the Hartins packed up any of their daughter's things yet?"

He shook his head. "Not that I know of."

"Has anyone else been around, asking to look at her condo?"

His eyes flicked up and to his right. After a beat, he shook his head again. "Nope."

Odd. A negative answer shouldn't have required even that

much thought. "But someone was around?" she asked.

He nodded. "I saw somebody in her corridor a few days after she died. They turned away quickly. I don't even know if they were there to get into her place, or had anything to do with her."

"Male or female?"

The manager closed his eyes for few seconds, as if calling up the details of the memory in his mind's eye. "Can't really say for sure. Could've been a woman or a short man. They were all bundled up in a coat and a scarf around the head. Didn't get much sense of their build and never saw the face."

Kate thanked him and headed back for her office.

She prayed no traffic cops were hanging out along her route.

At the end of the day, she hastily jotted down the phone messages from her voicemail. She'd return the calls later. She spent the next forty-five minutes skimming through the first part of the old journal.

She was about to stop when she turned one more page, and there it was.

November 23rd

I thought I saw him today, the old man I see in my head sometimes. I was walking across the grocery store parking lot. I could only see his profile, but I was sure it was him. Then he turned and it wasn't him at all. Yeah, he had the scraggly beard, but his face was fuller, and the eyes weren't right. They were blue, not brown, and softer.

I haven't had those flashes in a while. I hope they don't start up again. They're creepy, and scary. He's yelling in my face. I can't remember the exact words, but I've apparently done something wrong.

Mother and I had another fight today...

That was it. Nothing more about the man's face.

Kate sighed, then glanced at her watch. Time to put all this aside and go home to her own life.

She returned phone calls via her Bluetooth on her way home.

How had she ever survived without this gizmo?

One call was in response to an inquiry from a potential new client, referred to her by a colleague. She was relieved when she got his voicemail. Being circumspect in case others in his household had access to his voicemail, she said, "Hi. This is Kate Huntington returning your call. I'm very sorry but I'm not taking on anyone new right now. My schedule is booked solid. Let me know if you need a referral to someone else."

The booked schedule was a lie. She had two empty time slots this week, one of them the next afternoon. But she had plans for that one, if Sister Michelina called her back by then.

And she wasn't willing to take on new clients right now.

She'd adjusted somewhat to her new normal and was able to focus okay in sessions. The feeling that she was on the verge of making a mistake had eased some. But she still felt like she was walking on a tightrope with clients.

No, not exactly a tightrope—more like she was walking along the top of a wall. There was room to plant her foot firmly, one in front of the other, but she had to concentrate and be very careful. One misstep and she would plunge off one side or the other.

Her old smooth confidence was gone, and with it most of her enthusiasm for her work.

As she pulled up in front of her house, she mentally slammed the door on thoughts of clients and work. She was going to have a good evening with her family!

~~~~~~~~~

Kate's phone rang as she was driving to her office the next day. The display on the dashboard said *Rob's cell*.

She answered the call. "Good morning."

"Good morning to you," Rob said. "You sound more chipper than you have in a while."

"Skip keeps reminding me that I have a life. I'm trying to heed that advice."

"Good, because you're not going to like what I have to say."

Dread twisted in her gut. "What?"

"Kathy O'Connor says she'll be happy to ask the Hartins for the journals, as soon as you hand over their daughter's records."

"Crap. She won't even *ask* them?"

"That's what she said, but technically she's supposed to inform them of anything relevant to the case."

"So she may or may not mention it to them."

"Yeah." Rob cleared his throat. "You know, you could probably get away with turning the records over to make this lawsuit go away. Technically, breach of confidentiality is illegal, but it's a civil matter, not a crime." His voice was gentle. "The client can't exactly sue you, and I can write up something for the Hartins to sign promising they won't either."

Kate shook her head, even though he couldn't see her. "Rob, that goes against everything I stand for." She stopped to swallow the lump forming in her throat. How could she explain? "For lawyers or doctors, confidentiality is a practical, legal matter and/or a privacy issue. For therapists, it's different, almost sacred. Clients have to be able to trust that what they're telling us will never, ever be revealed to anyone, and especially not to the very people they are complaining about in therapy. Besides, the Hartins aren't going to find any answers in my records. They'll just find more grief."

"Why do you care if the contents hurt their feelings?"

Kate's temper flared. She tamped it down. "I'm not doing this to spare the Hartins. It's my *duty* to protect Josie's confidentiality. She would be horrified if her parents, especially her mother, knew what she had said in therapy."

A beat of silence, then Rob said, "I understand."

"Hey, maybe we could tell them I'm considering settling out of court but I want to meet with them in person first? Then I could ask Mrs. Hartin about the other journals."

The sound of air being expelled in a sigh. "Maybe."

Hmm, not exactly enthusiastic, is he? That ticked her off even more. He was willing to bend the rules and turn over confidential records but objected to some mild trickery to get a chance to even *ask* the Hartins for the journals?

But she didn't want to fight with Rob. She opted for a more conciliatory approach. "I did find one of the older journals at her condo. Maybe I should look through that first."

"Yeah. See you tomorrow for lunch?"

"That's the plan." She faked a cheerful tone. "See you then."

"Take care, Kate."

She hadn't taken the time to pack a lunch that morning so she ran out to a nearby deli to get a sandwich to go. Halfway back to her office she thought to turn on her cell phone, which she left off during sessions.

It immediately beeped, indicating a message. She stopped abruptly in the middle of the sidewalk. Someone ran into the back of her.

"Sorry." The person ducked their head and hurried past her. She barely glanced up–just got a quick impression of red against black–as she accessed her messages.

An elderly female voice, this one firm and no-nonsense, informed her that she was Sister Michelina Larsen and she had returned from her family visit. Please call her back.

Kate hit redial while crossing the street to her building, but she kept an eye out for speeding cars this time. As the phone rang a second time, she had that creepy, being-watched feeling. She looked around. The sidewalk was teeming with people. No one seemed to be paying any attention to her.

Someone picked up the phone on the other end. After greetings were exchanged, Kate asked for Sister Michelina.

Kate was just inside the door of her building when the same voice from the message said, "Hello."

"Hello, Sister. My name is Kate...O'Donnell." She wasn't real sure why she gave her maiden name. "I attended St. Bartholomew's as a child. I have some questions about the school, and I was wondering if I could meet with you."

"It's been a long time since I was at St. Bartholomew's."

"I know, and perhaps you won't be able to help me, but I'd appreciate a few minutes of your time. Could I come there to see you this afternoon at four-thirty?"

She took the stairs rather than the elevator to her second floor office. She didn't want to lose the connection.

She was starting to fear that the call had been dropped despite that precaution. Then Sister Michelina said, "I suppose that would be fine. Do you like tea?"

"Yes, Sister, I do."

"Fine. I'll see you then."

Kate pocketed her phone and searched in her purse for her office keys. She glanced down. A piece of white paper stuck part-way out from under her outer door.

She crouched down and grabbed its corner. Pulling it out, she stood.

It was half the size of a regular sheet of paper, with writing on it in block letters, all caps.

SOME PEOPLE MIGHT SAY THAT POKING YOUR NOSE WHERE IT DOESN'T BELONG IS A FORM OF SUICIDAL INTENTIONS.

CHAPTER SIXTEEN

Kate's knees wobbled. She grabbed for the wall. Her heart raced as her mind flashed to eight years ago, when someone had been sending anonymous notes threatening her baby daughter.

Those notes had also been in block letters, all caps. But the person who'd sent them couldn't be behind this one, not unless they could send notes from the grave.

Kate fumbled to get her key in the lock. She opened the outer door carefully and was greeted by an empty waiting room. She knew no one was there. The note was meant to scare her off. Its sender probably wouldn't do anything else yet. Not unless she ignored the note's message.

Still she searched her office, checking the closets and behind furniture. Nobody lurking behind the loveseat, and nothing seemed to have been disturbed.

Rustling in the waiting room. Her heart jumped into her throat. *Sheez! It's your client.*

She peeked out. "Be with you in a minute," she said to the woman who was settling into a chair and reaching for a magazine.

Kate closed the door and quickly hit the speed dial number on her phone for Manny.

"Yo, Kate. What's up?"

"Can you follow me this afternoon? I need to drive over to Essex to interview somebody."

"Who? They dangerous?"

"No. It's a nun. But I want to make sure no one is following me."

And I want you close by, just in case.

"Sure. What time?"

"Come to my office at three-forty. And thanks, Manny."

"*No problema.*"

~~~~~~~~~

Kate and Sister Michelina made small talk in the parlor while they waited for the tea to be served. A somewhat younger nun arrived with a tray. The ceramic teapot and teacups were simple, plain white, but the cookies on a matching white plate looked homemade and were elaborately decorated with swirls of icing.

Sister Michelina thanked the nun, then gestured toward the plate. "Sister Mary Francis loves to bake. Try one. They're delicious." She leaned forward to pour the tea.

Kate ate one of the cookies. It was indeed excellent. Her stomach grumbled for more. She reined it in. She wasn't here to eat cookies.

"Sister, I did go to St. Bartholomew's as a child, but it was before you were there at the school. The person I'm interested in was Josephine Hartin. She would have been in the first grade a couple years after you started there. Do you remember her?"

"I certainly do." The nun's tone was firm but her eyes were wary. "You said *was*. Is Josephine okay?"

"I'm afraid not, Sister. She's passed away." Kate hated the euphemism but she couldn't just blurt out that Josie was murdered. She didn't want to give the old nun a heart attack.

Sister Michelina closed her eyes and crossed herself.

Of its own volition, Kate's hand followed suit.

"She would only be in her thirties," the nun said.

"Yes. She was thirty-one." Kate took a deep breath and let it out slowly. "She supposedly committed suicide, but I have reason to believe that she was killed."

Sister Michelina's expression sagged. "Oh my." She narrowed her eyes slightly. "Who are you exactly?"

"A friend of hers." Kate hated lying to a nun, but she couldn't say she was Josie's therapist. "I'm looking into her death."

"Aren't the police investigating?"

"No. But they will if I can find enough evidence that it was indeed murder."

Despite the slow build up to the M word, the nun's eyebrows flew up. She sat back in her chair and ran one hand over her lap, smoothing the skirt of her light blue modified habit. Then she reached for her teacup on the small table next to her chair. It rattled a little in its saucer as she struggled to pick it up.

Age or nerves? Kate wasn't sure which. Maybe some of both.

"How can I help you?" Sister Michelina asked.

"Josie left St. Bart's school in second grade. Do you remember why her parents moved her?"

The sister looked away. "We assumed it was to go to a better school. She transferred to Bryn Mawr, I believe."

"But it was during the school year, an odd time to make such a change. Did anything happen that precipitated her parents moving her?"

Sister Michelina shook her head. Too quickly. "Not that I recall."

That's funny. Your memory was excellent a minute ago. Kate let out a small fake laugh. "I'm surprised you remember Josie at all."

The sister gave her a faint smile. "Oh, well, she was a very sweet girl."

No doubt the nun had encountered many sweet girls in her career as a schoolteacher and principal. "What made Josie stand out?"

"Oh, she was so bright and friendly... and..." Sister Michelina's eyes flicked in Kate's direction.

The confident, no-nonsense personality had morphed into something else. Kate wasn't sure what, but she was sure that the nun was lying. "So sweet?" she prompted.

"Yes, sweet." Sister Michelina rustled in her chair. "That's really all I remember about her."

Why were priests and nuns suddenly lying to her? The obvious answer popped up. Josie was at St. Bart's in the early nineties. It was quite conceivable that the Catholic Church was still hiding sexual abuse cases involving clergy then.

Father Sam?

Kate's chest hurt at the thought.

Sister Michelina cleared her throat. She was now watching Kate intently.

Kate leaned slightly forward. "Who else was at St. Bartholomew's back then, who might remember Josie?"

The sister looked away again. She was silent for so long that Kate thought she wasn't going to answer. Finally she said, "Father Bill. I can't remember his last name at the moment. He was assistant pastor and worked with the youth. But not usually with the younger children."

Kate had a hunch. "Do you remember any older man there, a parishioner maybe or staff member, who had a rather scraggly beard?"

Sister Michelina shot her a sharp glance. "No," she said, again too quickly.

Kate rose. "Well, thank you for your time. If you remember anything else about Josie, give me a call." She held out a slip of paper with her name and cell phone number on it.

The nun looked at the slip for a beat, then took it and stood. She tucked the paper into a pocket in her skirt.

"Thanks for the tea, and tell Sister Mary Francis I thoroughly enjoyed her cookies."

"Take some for the road," Sister Michelina said.

"I think I will." Kate picked up two cookies, one with pink icing and one chocolate. She wrapped them in a napkin from the tray.

The nun led the way to the front door of the building. "Let me know what you find out. I'd, uh, like to... I don't want to believe Josie committed suicide."

Kate thought about the note that had greeted her at her office earlier. "Sister, I am quite sure she did not."

Out on the sidewalk and headed for her car, she had that prickly feeling on her neck. But this time she knew who was watching her. She pulled out her phone and hit Manny's speed dial number.

"Yo."

"Are you behind me?" she asked.

"Half a block back," Manny said in a low voice.

She didn't have to ask if he'd seen anyone else following her. He would have said so right away. "Do you like chocolate?"

"Uh, yeah. Why?"

"I'm leaving you a present on that bench up ahead. A little thank you for having my back today."

She disconnected, pocketed her phone and then extracted the pink iced cookie from the napkin in her other hand. Tucking the napkin around the chocolate one, she dropped it on the bench without slowing her pace.

As she was climbing into her car, her cell phone rang. She answered.

"Wow. Where'd you get that cookie?"

"Retired nun baked it."

"Seriously?"

"Yup."

"Wonder if she'd break her vows and marry me."

Kate chuckled and disconnected. She started her car and headed for the Baltimore Beltway.

She hadn't felt this positive in a long time. It wasn't like she had some hot lead, but at least she was making progress. And the note, as scary as it was, offered proof that someone had killed Josie. Someone who didn't like it that Kate was investigating.

A shiver ran down her back.

She would take the note to Judith tomorrow. Maybe now the homicide lieutenant would be willing to re-open the case, and Kate could "stop poking her nose" into things.

Another chill ran through her. She should ask Manny to follow her around tomorrow and make sure no one else was tailing her.

She rounded a curve and the remnants of her good mood evaporated. The rush hour traffic had been heavy but moving steadily along. Now brake lights were blinking on a few hundred feet ahead. All four lanes of cars slowed to a crawl.

After creeping along for fifteen minutes, the source of the problem came into view. Blue lights flashed ahead, next to a tractor trailer that was stopped at an odd angle in the far left lane.

Loud rumbling. Movement flashed in her peripheral vision. Kate jumped in her seat. A tow truck rattled past her on the shoulder. She blew out a breath and willed her heart to settle down.

The traffic stopped moving completely. Up ahead, the tow truck jockeyed around the tractor trailer. Certainly they weren't going to try to tow that semi with that little truck!

She tapped her fingers on the steering wheel and mentally went back over the interview with Sister Michelina. The woman's demeanor had changed completely when discussing Josie's time at St. Bart's.

Kate needed to track down this Father Bill the nun had mentioned. She suddenly sat up straighter in her seat.

Wait! Father Sam had implied that the youth director back then was a woman. He'd said he could see her face but couldn't remember her name. Had he been thinking of Sister Michelina and was confused about who was in which role? That was certainly possible considering his other memory gaps.

But he'd remembered that young Katie O'Donnell had loved puzzles. Memory certainly did get fickle with age.

Kate glanced at the dashboard clock. Another ten minutes had ticked by.

Crap! She was going to be late for dinner. Well, Skip couldn't blame her for a traffic jam.

She squinted into the sun setting on the horizon. It looked like some vehicle was being winched onto the tow truck's flat bed. When she registered its squished condition, she felt guilty for cursing her own fate.

Better to be stuck in traffic than to be the driver of that car.

She said a silent prayer that its occupants were okay, but she doubted they were.

She considered calling home, but decided to wait. If the traffic cleared out quickly enough she might still make it by six. Once she was rolling again, she'd call and explain about the accident and give Skip her ETA.

A voice in the back of her head said, *You don't have to say you were working on the investigation. You could just say you were running an errand.*

The lie was tempting but she told the voice to shut up.

Her stomach growled. She fed it the remaining cookie. It rumbled again, letting her know that was wholly inadequate. She told it to shut up too.

The cars ahead of her started easing forward. Slowly she crept toward the accident scene. As she got closer, she saw that it wasn't as bad as it had seemed. No one looked to be bleeding, but there was debris across three of the four lanes. Cars crawled past in the far right lane, the drivers' rubbernecking slowing the process further.

She glanced at the clock again. Five after six. She was now officially late for dinner. But even with the Bluetooth she didn't want the distraction of making a call until she was past this mess.

Her cell buzzed. Her dashboard screen read *Manny.*

She answered it. "Hope you didn't have a hot date tonight."

A low chuckle. "Skip just called me. Wanted to know if I was with you. I told him you'd gone to interview some nun over in Essex and we were now stuck in traffic."

So much for the option of lying about where she was coming from when she encountered the backup. Not that she would have anyway. She'd never outright lied to Skip before, and now wasn't a good time to start.

But why hadn't he called her if he was worried?

"There is hope," she said into the phone. "I can see the accident scene now. Maybe another ten minutes tops and we should be past it."

"Good."

"Hey, Manny, can you stick with me tomorrow?"

"Sure. Where we going?"

"Just to my office. Meet me there in the morning, say at eight-forty-five. I'll explain then." She didn't want to get into the note right now, as her turn to edge past the accident was rapidly approaching.

"Sure. You want me to follow you home now?"

She hesitated, hating to tie him up any longer. "No. Head on home."

"Okay. See ya tomorrow."

Once she was past the accident and sailing down the highway again, she instructed the Bluetooth to call home.

"*Hola.*" Even after nine years in the U.S., Maria still answered the phone with the Spanish greeting.

"Hey, Maria. I got stuck in a traffic tie-up, but I'm on my way now. You all go ahead and eat without me. Just stick a plate in the oven for me."

"Skip eat already. He leave for PTA meeting a few minutes ago."

Holy shit! His presentation's tonight! How could she have forgotten that?

"Okay, stick that plate in the fridge instead." Her stomach protested loudly. "I'll go straight to the meeting. You okay with the kids?"

"Sure. We doing homework now."

"Thanks a million." Kate disconnected and wondered again how they would get along without Maria if she decided to marry Eduardo.

Damn, I can't believe I forgot the PTA meeting. Guilt twisted her already unhappy stomach.

And she noted that she'd been cussing a lot lately, if only in her own head. Half an hour ago, she'd been feeling good about her investigation, but now...

She should let this go. Especially in light of that note!

She shook her head. She knew she couldn't. If her suspicion about a child abuse cover-up at St. Bart's was true, there was more at stake here than justice for Josie.

But the potential price tag for finding Josie's killer was starting to scare her.

CHAPTER SEVENTEEN

The principal was introducing Skip when Kate slipped into the school auditorium. She moved down a side aisle and found an empty seat.

Skip stepped up to the podium on the small stage.

She gave him a little wave. He looked her way and his jaw clenched.

Her stomach churned. *He's pissed.* She could hardly blame him.

He squared his broad shoulders and leaned forward toward the microphone. "Y'all might not believe this but I used to be the shortest kid in my class."

A ripple of chuckles rolled through the room. Despite her anxiety, the corners of Kate's mouth quirked up.

"I was picked on a lot. One kid, the leader of the bullies, particularly hated my guts. It wasn't until recently that I realized it was because he envied me, and felt threatened by me."

His delivery was smooth, like he was chatting with the audience.

Kate was impressed. He'd obviously practiced the presentation carefully.

Where had she been while he was doing that? *Not paying attention obviously.*

"I went back home for a high school reunion last summer," Skip said. "It was very enlightening. The bullies were still pushing people around, making trouble. They had made my life miserable from the age of eleven until I graduated from high school, but for the first time I realized they were miserable too. My psychologist wife…" He paused, looked her way.

She couldn't quite read his expression.

"She could tell you better than I can the dynamics of bullying. All I know is it's born out of insecurity, and it breeds insecurity. Both the victim and the bully suffer." He cleared his throat.

"My daddy tried to advise me on how to handle the bullies. But this was back in the days when adults figured kids should 'work it out for themselves.'" He made air quotes.

"Well, we didn't work it out, because bullies have no desire to work it out. Eventually I had a growth spurt and I was bigger than them. They left me alone after that. But my entire adolescence was marred by the experience. I came east to college and never moved back home. That hurt my folks, that I was so far away, but I couldn't bring myself to go back there and deal with the bullies again.

"Last summer, I realized they were still overgrown adolescents, now in their forties. One was successful. Two of them weren't. But they were all unhappy. The insecurities that had caused them to become bullies had never been addressed." He looked around the room that had fallen silent. All eyes were on him.

"Again, I'm not the best person to tell you how to stop the bullying, but it needs to stop. Both the victims and the bullies need some kind of intervention. It's not a little thing, or something kids can work out for themselves. It's a big thing. It damages the victims, and leaves the already damaged bullies without the help they need."

He ducked his head. His hair fell down onto his forehead. He skimmed it back with a long slender hand. "Thank you for your attention." He walked down the steps from the stage and headed Kate's way.

Her chest felt like it might burst with pride.

The people next to her scooted over, leaving an empty seat. Skip stepped past her and lowered himself into it.

She took his hand. He tensed.

It felt like he'd slapped her. She pushed words past the lump in her throat anyway. "That was great."

He glanced sideways and relaxed a little. He squeezed her hand, then let it go.

It was almost eight-thirty by the time they got home. The PTA meeting had run long as a lively discussion ensued on how to address the bullying issue.

Kate had wished she could contribute more, but Skip had already said most of what she would have pointed out, that bullies were insecure and they needed help as much as the victims did. She made a mental note to search out some research on best practices for bullying intervention programs and send it to the principal.

Skip's SUV pulled over to the curb in front of their house. She parked behind him, and they both climbed out. They walked up the porch steps in silence.

The house was quiet, the kids already in bed. Peaches appeared out of nowhere and rubbed against their legs, meowing pathetically as if she were starving. Kate knew better. Maria would have fed her before retiring to her third-floor apartment.

No appearance from Toby, which meant that Maria had put him in the laundry room where he normally slept, or Billy had snuck him into his bedroom again.

Kate stopped in the living room and turned to Skip. "Sweetheart, I would have been home in time, if there hadn't been an accident on the Beltway."

He looked down at her for a long moment, his eyes the murky brown they became when he was worried or pissed. She had no idea which he was right now.

"You could've called." His voice was neutral, too neutral.

Butterflies fluttered in her stomach. "I was going to. I did, once I was past the accident. It was a little tense, with people rubbernecking and such."

And besides, you had already called Manny. But she didn't particularly want to bring that up. She was hoping she didn't have to admit that she'd completely forgotten about the PTA meeting.

"Look," she took both of his hands in hers, "tonight was important to you, and I haven't been supportive enough about all this. I'm sorry. But I was so proud of you up there. Your speech was perfect."

He looked down at her for another moment, his face unreadable. Then he blew out air and pulled her to him. Wrapping his arms around her, he rested his chin on the top of her head. "Thanks for coming straight to the meeting."

She slowly let out the breath she'd been holding. She was off the hook. Ignoring the nagging guilt that lurked under her relief, she relaxed against his solid body.

Her stomach growled. She pulled out of his arms and took his hand to lead him to the kitchen. "I never had dinner. You want anything?"

"I think I'll have a beer."

That surprised her a little. Skip almost never drank, except at parties, and then not much. Tonight had taken even more out of him than she'd realized.

She opened the fridge and got him a beer. "Did I tell you how excellent your speech was?" she said as she handed it to him.

He finally grinned at her, his first smile of the evening.

Smiling back, she fished her dinner plate out of the fridge and put it in the microwave. When it dinged, she brought the plate and a fork to the table and dug in.

Five minutes later, the plate held only a few smears of sauce and Skip was grinning at her again.

"You definitely know how to enjoy food." He chugged the last of his beer. "I think I'm gonna take a shower."

He usually showered in the morning. An evening shower indicated it had been a particularly stressful day. He said the hot water helped him relax. Tonight she figured it might also help wash away those high school memories.

While she waited, she might as well do some research. She sat down at the computer and called up the website Liz had found for her–the historical archives of St. Bartholomew's Catholic Church. She skimmed for any references to a Father Bill.

In the section from the early 1990's, she spotted a picture over the name, Father William Coleman. No wonder Josie had called him Father What-A-Waste. He was a handsome young man. He'd be in his fifties now.

Wait a minute! Josie wouldn't have been calling the priest that in first or second grade. When had she crossed paths with him as a teenager?

Kate glanced back at the computer and froze as another face jumped out at her from the screen.

A man with hard, brown eyes and a scraggly beard.

CHAPTER EIGHTEEN

Guilt rode shotgun as Kate drove to work the next day. She'd intended to tell Skip about the threatening note after his shower, but she'd lost her nerve. He'd had a stressful evening, she'd told herself. He didn't need to be worrying about her right before bedtime.

They'd snuggled together, spoon-style. He'd kissed her on the temple. "Do you mind if we don't make love tonight? I'm beat."

"That's fine." She was secretly relieved. Making love would have made her feel worse.

Now she couldn't tell Manny about the note, or show it to him, for fear he would mention it to her husband. And the longer she went without telling Skip, the worse it would be when he finally found out.

Oh the tangled web we weave...

Kate instructed her Bluetooth to call Judith Anderson. She got past the precinct's receptionist by saying that she had information related to one of the lieutenant's cases. It was true, even if the case wasn't active right now.

But Judith wasn't in. Kate left a message saying she would come by at lunchtime with some evidence. Hopefully the detective would be there so she could pick her brain some more, but regardless she wanted to get the note to her as soon as possible. Kate was hoping it would give Judith sufficient cause to re-open the case.

Manny was waiting in the hallway outside her office.

She unlocked the door and they entered the waiting room. "I

hate to ask this of you, Manny, but could you hang out here today, as my bodyguard?"

"No problem. You got reason to believe you're at risk?"

"Nothing concrete," she said, hating the lie. "But I think I'm getting close to something on this case, and I've had the niggling feeling for days that someone was following me." That at least was true, although she suspected it was her imagination.

"Anything I can investigate?" Manny asked.

"Not yet. I've got Liz Franklin doing some computer research for us." She'd shot off a quick email to Liz the previous evening, asking her to check out Father William Coleman and the man with the scraggly beard. The archives had identified him as Gary Jones, the janitorial supervisor in the late 1980s to early 1990s. And while Liz was at it, could she find out where Josie went to high school? It might not have been Bryn Mawr.

"After work," Kate told Manny, "we may have something to go on."

At lunchtime, Kate returned a phone call that couldn't wait and then told Manny she needed to make a quick trip to the police station.

"Why don't you ride with me?" he said. "Then we don't have to worry about getting separated in Towson traffic."

She agreed.

Manny didn't ask what was in the large manila folder she clutched as she sat in his passenger seat. He got her to the precinct in record time.

Kate fished a twenty-dollar bill out of her purse. "You want to get us some fast food for lunch while I'm in there?"

He tilted his head to one side, studying her. "Sure," he finally said.

The young officer on the front desk—a male this time—informed her that Lieutenant Anderson was in and could see her.

"Thank you, Lord," Kate whispered under her breath.

She succinctly told the lieutenant when and where she had

found the note, and what it said, then handed over the envelope.

Judith opened it and fished the note out by pinching the top edge between the fingernails of her thumb and index finger. She studied it for a moment, then slid it back in the envelope. She got out a large evidence envelope and wrote on it. Then she slid Kate's envelope into the larger one. "You need to leave this alone. It's gotten too dangerous."

"Does that mean you'll reopen the case?"

Judith gave her a pained look. "We're pretty busy right now."

Kate gritted her teeth. "Come on! You can't tell me to let it be and then say you aren't going to investigate either."

"Let me see what our lab finds when they examine the note. We'll take it from there."

Kate wasn't sure what that last sentence meant, but she let it slide. Checking her watch, she decided not to bring up the other stuff she'd found out from the journals. No point in making herself late getting back to the office if Judith wasn't interested.

A small voice in her head said she was being petty, but she was too pissed to listen to it.

Then she spotted a cardboard box in the corner. The label said *J. Hartin.*

"Is that the stuff from Josie's condo?"

"Yeah. I haven't gotten around to taking it back to the evidence room."

Kate resisted the temptation to ask why she'd gotten it from the evidence room in the first place. The lieutenant wasn't as disinterested in the case as she pretended to be.

What the hell's going on here?

"Anything interesting in there?"

Judith started to roll her eyes, aborted halfway, then sighed. "Not much. Just her phone and such."

Kate sat up straighter in her chair. "Her cell phone? Can I see it?"

"It's password protected."

"So your lab can't break the password?"

"We don't normally need to. We get the phone records from the carrier."

"So who did she call that last day or two?"

Judith sighed again. "We never requested the records, since it was ruled a suicide."

Kate made herself count to five–she didn't have time to go to ten. "May I see the phone?" She held out her hand toward the box.

Judith hesitated a moment. Then she stood and walked to the table where the box rested, opened it and extracted the phone. She turned it on and, carrying it by its edges, brought it to Kate.

Kate took it and tried several possible passwords, beginning with Buster, then Sphinx. When she ran out of ideas, she stared at the phone for a moment, wishing she could break it open like an egg and spill out its secrets.

She noticed an odd sheen on the surface. Placing the phone flat on her palm, she tilted it this way and that. The sheen had a pattern to it, left by the oil from Josie's finger.

B is for Buster. She carefully touched the top left corner of the pattern and traced the letter B. The phone unlocked.

Judith had been watching her silently. "Why didn't I think of that?" she said, letting it slip that she'd been trying to unofficially unlock the phone's secrets.

"Dumb luck, and I have the same kind of phone. I remembered that it has the option of using a pattern on the screen to unlock it, rather than a password."

Kate went to recent calls. Her own office number was the last one. Before that were three calls in a row to and from the same number. But there was no name next to it. She dug in her purse for a pad and pen and wrote the number down. They were the only calls Josie had made or received that morning.

Kate glanced at her watch. She was out of time.

Judith held out her hand for the phone. "I'll look it over and let you know if I find anything useful."

"But you won't reopen the case?"

Judith stared at her. Her cop mask slipped for a second, and

Kate saw worry and frustration in her eyes. "I can't. And I can't tell you why."

Kate reluctantly turned over the phone.

As she started to rise, Judith reached out and put a hand on her arm. "Be careful."

"I will be. I have one of Skip's men with me, as a bodyguard."

Judith nodded, her mouth set in a grim line.

In Manny's car, Kate held the chicken sandwich he'd bought for her in one hand and fished her own phone out of her pocket with the other. She'd silenced it before entering the police station, and it had vibrated several times while she'd been in Judith's office.

She checked missed calls. Four of them, all from Rob.

Crap! She'd completely forgotten that it was Wednesday and she had a lunch date with him. She checked voicemail. Four messages, increasingly frantic.

Her stomach churned. She dropped the sandwich onto its wrapper on her lap and called Rob back.

"I am so, so sorry," she said as soon as he answered. "Something happened and..." Her throat closed. She'd never before forgotten their lunch date, not in the decade plus that they had been meeting for lunch on Wednesdays.

"Are you okay? What happened?" Rob's voice was anxious, not angry.

But she wasn't sure the anger wouldn't come when he found out she'd just plain forgotten.

"Yes, I'm fine. I, uh, received a threatening note, but keep that under your hat because I haven't had a chance to tell Skip yet."

Manny shot her a sideways glance.

"Threatening as in?" Rob asked, his tone even more worried.

She repeated the words of the note to him.

"When did this happen?"

Her stomach clenched, but she couldn't lie to her best friend. And Manny was sitting right beside her. He'd know she was lying. She could only hope that Rob was in an understanding mood. "Yesterday. I took it to Lieutenant Anderson during my lunch break."

"Why haven't you told Skip?" Now his voice sounded ominous.

With good intentions, she and Skip had kept things from each other in the past, trying not to worry the other one. As Rob knew, that hadn't worked out so well, had even put them in danger.

"I'm going to tell him tonight. He had a presentation at the PTA meeting last night, about bullying. I didn't want to upset or distract him before that. And he was kinda stressed afterwards." This was probably more than she should be saying in front of Skip's employee. Manny could be trusted to be discreet, but still...

Guilt and anxiety surged through her. She felt lightheaded and nauseous.

What the hell am I doing?

Tears stung her eyes and it took all she had to fight them back. She was falling apart. Where was the confident, forthright woman she'd once been?

"You okay?" Worried voice again.

"Yeah, I'm fine," she managed to get out without her voice shaking. She took a deep breath to steady herself. "I'm kinda burned out, I guess. Trying to do too much."

"So Judith is going to take over the investigation now. You can let it go and get back to your own life."

"Uh, not exactly." She glanced over at Manny.

His eyes were on the road ahead as he drove. "I see nothink, I hear nothink," he said in a credible imitation of Sergeant Shultz from the old show, *Hogan's Heroes*.

A chuckle bubbled in her chest but she suppressed it. She knew she was dangerously close to losing it, and that chuckle might just turn into hysteria. She gave Manny a small smile instead.

"I think she's unofficially looking into it," she said to Rob, "but she said she couldn't reopen the case. And she couldn't tell me why."

"Hmm," Rob said, then fell silent for a beat. "Somebody from above is pulling strings."

Something clicked in her brain. "That fits. I don't have any real evidence of this, but priests and nuns are lying to me right and left, so—"

"So the logical conclusion is that the Church is hiding something. They definitely have the power in this state to pull strings."

"The question is who are they protecting?" Kate's chest hurt again at the thought that Father Sam might be a child abuser. The guy with the scraggly beard, Jones, might very well be part of it, but the Catholic Church wouldn't go to such lengths to protect a janitor. The clergy had to be involved.

"So you're going to keep investigating?" Rob asked.

She wanted to let it go. She'd proven that it wasn't suicide, which should be easing her guilt and helping Josie's parents feel better. "Wait! What if the influence to squelch the case is coming from the Hartins? Maybe Mr. Hartin did something they're trying to hide."

A sigh from the other end of the line. "I guess that answers my question. Maybe they want the records to make sure Josie didn't say anything that would incriminate them."

"Yeah, but don't they realize that forcing me to give the file to them means it might be read in court?"

"I don't think they're going to take it all the way to court," Rob said. "They're trying to pressure you into turning over the records, to make the case go away."

If she was being honest with herself, she really didn't think the Hartins were trying to cover anything up. If they were worried about something in her records, they wouldn't be drawing attention to them by trying to get them from her. No, they wanted answers.

She was on the right track. Josie's death had something to do with St. Bart's. "Yes, I need to keep investigating, but I've got Manny's help and protection now. That will make it easier."

Manny smiled beside her, his eyes still on the Towson traffic.

"There's more at stake here," she continued. "If the Church is covering for a sexual abuser, then he's still out there abusing children."

"Good point," Rob said. "Be careful, sweetheart."

"I will. And thanks for not being mad about me missing lunch."

A slight pause. "Just don't do that to me again." His tone was a bit sharp. "Last time you didn't show for lunch, you'd been attacked by a killer."

"Oh my God! You didn't think–"

"I didn't know what to think. I was just scared out of my wits."

Kate's eyes stung with tears. She swallowed the sob threatening to escape her throat. "I'm so, so sorry."

"Shh, it's okay. You're safe, so no harm done."

"I promise I'll never stand you up again."

They signed off, and Kate put her phone away. She stared at the chicken sandwich on her lap, then wrapped it back up. Maybe her stomach would settle down enough before her next client that she could eat at least a few bites to get her through the afternoon.

She should feel relieved that Rob hadn't yelled at her, but guilt was the dominant feeling. Just because she'd dodged the bullet of his wrath didn't mean she hadn't screwed up.

She was beginning to feel like she had bipolar disorder herself. She needed to get a grip, and soon.

CHAPTER NINETEEN

A text was waiting on Kate's cell phone at the end of the day. Liz had located a current address for the janitor and the priest, and a phone number for the latter. If the janitor had a phone, it was a cell.

She hadn't had any luck with the mysterious phone number from Josie's phone that Kate had sent to her earlier.

Not a landline. Checked major cell phone providers, the text read. *No luck. I can check other providers, but might be a throw-away cell. If so, untraceable. Sorry.*

Kate blew out air.

Damn! A dead end!

She texted back thanking Liz and telling her not to bother continuing the search. If the phone was traceable, the police lab would find its owner.

Kate sagged in her desk chair. She had a bad feeling that Liz was right. And she'd had such high hopes that the phone number would lead them to whoever Josie was "checking something out" with that day.

Sighing, she picked up the older journal. She'd read in it for a few minutes before going home.

She was about to call it a day when she turned the page.

December 12th

I had a dream last night, a different one. This one was that dude with the scraggly beard. He was yelling in my face stuff like "Now look what you've done" and "You've ruined every-thing." When I strain to remember what this might be about, I get a vague sense of opening a door–I'm real small–and some-one yells, "No! No lights!"

And I'm just as anxious when I think about this dream as the other one. I think I'm going to call my doctor and see if he can give me something for the anxiety, and maybe something to knock me out at night.

Kate skimmed through the next twenty or so pages, but there was nothing more about Scraggly Beard, or the dreams.

At home, she opted to get it over with quickly. Once she had greeted Maria and the kids, she led Skip out of the kitchen. "I've gotta tell you something," she said in a low voice so the kids wouldn't hear her. She gestured toward the study.

After they had settled in the room with the door closed, she took a deep breath. "It happened yesterday afternoon, but I didn't want to upset you before your presentation, or after for that mat-ter when you seemed to need to decompress."

Skip was silent, his eyes slightly narrowed.

"And before I tell you, I want you to know that I've already done some things to deal with it, so that I'm safe." She cleared her throat. "I got a threatening note yesterday afternoon. That's why I called Manny to guard me."

His jaw tightened. Not a good sign.

"I took the note to Judith," Kate quickly added, "during my lunch break today."

He clenched his fists. "What did the note say?"

She repeated the threatening words.

He sucked air through gritted teeth. "Manny's sticking with you like glue until Judith finds the murderer."

"I agree with the Manny and glue idea, but Judith isn't inves-tigating. Not officially at least."

His mouth fell open. "What?"

"Yeah, that was my reaction. She wouldn't say why but appar-ently she's being pressured to keep the case closed."

He stood up and paced a few steps in the small room. "You're leaving this alone. The agency will take over from here."

Kate measured her words carefully. "I would appreciate any help you all can give, but I need to be involved. As I've said before, I'm the one who knew Josie, who will realize what some things mean. Things that others may dismiss as irrelevant."

He paced back toward her. "Okay, but you're strictly consultant status. We do the footwork."

She pulled in air and blew it out softly. She was glad that Skip hadn't yelled at her for not telling him about the note sooner, but she wasn't going to be shut out of the investigation, or be put on the shelf as a "consultant."

"I can't agree with that. I need to see people's faces and body language as they're interviewed."

Skip's fists clenched again. She could hear his teeth grinding.

She pushed the desk chair back a bit so she could look up at him more readily. Her throat tight, she prayed that he would understand how important this was to her. "There's more to this than just Josie's death, or even my safety." She told him about her suspicions that abuse had occurred at St. Bartholomew's back in the nineties, and had been covered up. "If I'm right, then the abuser or abusers are still out there, hurting more children. I can't ignore that."

He stared down at her. "You keep Manny with you at all times when you aren't home here with me."

"Not a problem. I have no desire to get hurt. Actually, could I have the use of a second bodyguard? So I can sometimes send Manny out to investigate some things."

"I thought you just said you had to be there."

"Most of the time I will, but there might be some stuff he can track down for me."

Skip huffed out air, then threw his hands in the air. "I should know better than to try to buck you when you've got the bit in your mouth like this."

Kate smiled at him. "I believe you are mixing your horse metaphors there, sweetheart."

He shook his head, then extended his hand to her. "After the kids are in bed, let's go over what you have so far, so I can see how the pieces fit together."

"Or don't," she said as she let him pull her to a stand. "So far, only a few of the pieces are fitting together."

While Skip did story time with the kids, Kate started sorting out what she already knew. Thinking of her favorite fictional detective, she pulled a pad out of a kitchen drawer and sat down at the table.

She didn't have any index cards, like Kinsey Milhone used, but she could list what she knew or suspected. She bypassed the reasons why she believed Josie hadn't committed suicide and went straight to clues as to who might have murdered her.

1. J had recurring dreams. Something happened in the dark. She was terrified of even talking about the dreams.

2. She left a message about some kind of breakthrough the day she was murdered.

3. Her gut feeling was that the dreams were related to earlier flashbacks of an angry man's face, with a scraggly beard. An earlier journal entry gave more specifics: man said she had done something wrong, had ruined something.

4. Scraggly Beard may very well be the janitor at St. Bart's back in 1980s to 90s.

5. J asked Fr. Sam why her mother pulled her from St. Bart's school. I asked same question. Felt like Fr. Sam might be lying.

Kate looked at the *might be* and then scratched it out. She was kidding herself, not wanting to admit that Father Sam might be involved somehow. She inserted *was* above the word *lying.*

Okay, what else?

She thought for a moment, then put pen to paper.

6. One of prescriptions for drugs found in her system was for clonazepam. Doctor on label says he didn't write it. Both doctor and pharmacy now claim no knowledge that the prescription ever existed.

She tapped the pen against her lips.

7. Last journal entry indicates she was checking out something related to another hunch.

8. She made or received three phone calls morning of her death from a certain number. Liz can't trace number. Probably a throwaway cell phone. (Judith checking this.)

9. Father William

Kate couldn't remember his last name off the top of her head.

9. Father William Something (see St. Bart's Archives) was also at St. Bart's at the time Josie was in the school there.

10. Liz checked on Fr. Bill and the janitor. (Have address for both, phone # for Fr. Bill; janitor has no land line.)

11. Did Josie know Fr. Bill as a teenager? If so, where?

12. Sister Michelina also seemed to be lying when I asked her about Josie. She mentioned Fr. Bill was youth pastor, but he didn't work with the younger children. Was that last comment of hers relevant?

Had her tired brain forgotten anything? She chewed on the end of her pen.

A hand descended on her shoulder. She jumped.

Skip squeezed the shoulder, then sat down at the table next to her. "Who's Sister Michelina?"

Kate told him, then explained anything else in her notes that didn't make sense to him.

"You've made good progress," he said when she'd finished.

The knots in her stomach relaxed some. She was perversely pleased with the compliment.

"Is that everything?" he asked.

"I'm not sure. Give me a minute." She read over the list again, then added next to #3: *She dreamed once about this man. That dream also made her nervous.*

Skip took the list from her and read it over again. "We should add the threatening note."

Kate handed him the pen.

He scribbled a #12 about the note on the page. Then he stood up. "I'm going to scan this on the computer and email it to Liz, Manny and Rose. That way we'll all be on the same page."

"Sounds good."

"Then," he paused, the gold flecks dancing in his hazel eyes, "it's time for bed."

She grinned at him, her knotted stomach and muscles relaxing some more. "*That* sounds good too."

~~~~~~~~~

Her mother was yelling about the broken vase on the dining room floor. Kate knew her brother Jack had knocked it off the sideboard, but she was trying not to be a tattletale. Her mother's anger scared her, made her feel guilty even though she hadn't done anything wrong.

Bridget O'Donnell planted her hands on her hips. "Don't you be protectin' your siblings now, Katie. Who broke it?"

Skip was suddenly there, telling his mother-in-law that Kate shouldn't be involved in the investigation. It was too dangerous.

"Harumph," her mother said. Then she turned on her heel and marched away, bellowing Jack's name.

Kate's insides tightened. She felt like she might throw up. She hadn't said his name. She hadn't told.

Kate jerked up in bed. The dream had been so real it took a moment for her to orient herself.

The guilt remained, free-floating.

I didn't tell on Jack.

In real life, she had. The incident had really happened and fear of her mother had trumped filial loyalty. She had squeaked out Jack's name, and then her mother had turned and marched off in search of him.

Her body shivered, but the room wasn't cold. Somehow she knew her unconscious mind was trying to tell her something.

That's it! Josie's anxiety.

She'd been threatened into silence, maybe even told to forget whatever had happened.

It was a common tactic of abusers, to tell the child victims they wouldn't be believed, that people would blame them, or that their parents would somehow be harmed by the truth. And suggesting to a traumatized child that the whole thing should be forgotten played right into the mind's defensive tendency to block out anything too emotionally overwhelming.

Some of the pieces fell into place. They clicked together nicely. Josie had been abused, at St. Bart's. Probably by the janitor, but there had to be someone else involved. The Church wouldn't work so hard to protect a lowly janitor.

Please don't let it be Father Sam, she prayed silently.

She laid back down carefully, amazed that Skip had slept through her jerking around. Staring at the ceiling, she planned her course of action.

Tomorrow she would have Manny go talk to the janitor. Manny wasn't particularly tall, but he was muscular and could be quite scary when he wanted to be.

She would look into Father Bill some more. But first she really needed to talk to Mrs. Hartin, for several reasons.

Once she'd figured out how to accomplish that, she was finally able to drift off to sleep again.

~~~~~~~~

"Franklin," came from the speaker on her dashboard.

"I need you to call that O'Connor woman, the Hartins' lawyer."

"Well, good morning to you too, Miss Obsessed."

"I'm sorry." Kate shook her head as she negotiated her car through the morning rush-hour traffic. She'd been saying those two words a lot lately.

She started over. "Good morning."

"Now what am I supposed to tell Kathy O'Connor?"

"Tell her that I have some answers for Mrs. Hartin, but I have to see her in person. Today at lunchtime, if possible. My office or I'll meet her somewhere."

"And what are these answers?" Rob asked.

"That threatening note for one. It proves that Josie was murdered."

"Maybe. Or it may just mean that someone's worried you'll uncover something else while you're poking around."

"Like what?"

"It bothers me that all records of that prescription disappeared from that pharmacy. What if someone there is peddling stolen drugs?"

"I don't see how that could have led to Josie being killed."

"That's my point. They may just be worried because you're asking questions about that prescription, so they sent that note."

Kate shook her head, even though Rob couldn't see her. She didn't want to hear that the note might not be solid proof that Josie was murdered. She pulled into the parking lot across from her office building. "Maybe. But I still have some questions for Mrs. Hartin."

"Okay. I'll see what I can set up. You mind if I sit in?"

Kate wanted him to so badly. It hit her that she'd felt pretty alone with all this. But she'd been the one who'd been shutting the others out for the most part, convincing herself that she was the only one who could investigate, the only one who knew Josie and would understand the clues. Was that some kind of unconscious penance for letting Josie down?

"Kate, you there?"

"Sorry. I'd love to have you sit in since Mrs. Hartin's kinda scary, but she's not likely to open up if you're there. I'll call you as soon as it's over."

"Okay. I should be around all afternoon. This is a catch up on paperwork day."

Kate disconnected and climbed out of her car. As she walked to her office, she felt lighter than she had in days. She hoped the feeling lasted this time.

She was really, really tired of guilt.

CHAPTER TWENTY

Kate groaned quietly when she saw who Skip had sent as her second bodyguard, while Manny was off interviewing the janitor. Correction, Skip probably hadn't sent him. Mac Reilly, who was leaning against her outer office door, had no doubt volunteered for the job.

He was his usual scruffy self, with a two-day-old beard and wearing a faded Army T-shirt and blue jeans. He was going to scare the bejesus out of her clients.

She loved Mac dearly. They'd grown up together. But in that lay the other part of the problem. He tended to play the overprotective big brother at times.

"Hey, sweet pea," Mac greeted her with his childhood nickname for her.

"Good morning." She pasted on a smile even as her mind was scrambling for a way to get him to leave. But she knew he wouldn't.

And he shouldn't. She was in danger, and she was way too vulnerable in the office. Also, if someone came after her here, a client could end up getting hurt as well.

That thought made her heart race.

The only thing she could think of was to call her clients and tell them not to be alarmed by the scary-looking guy in her waiting room. She had no clue what excuse she could give for why he was there.

She unlocked the door and led the way into her waiting room.

Skip sat at his desk staring at the list of pieces of information his wife had gathered. He admitted to himself that Kate was a good detective. Which shouldn't be surprising since she spent her days piecing together the psychological puzzles of why people did and felt what they did. That had to be tough to do, since you couldn't see or touch the psyche.

He wasn't about to tell her she was a good detective though. No need to encourage her. She seemed to stumble over more than enough dead bodies as it was.

She had thought the nun, Sister Michelina, had been lying to her, or at least withholding information. And everything pointed toward something that had happened at that church back when Josie was a kid. It'd be worthwhile to re-interview the nun.

He checked his watch. Kate would be in session right now. He called her cell phone and left a message. Then he made another call, to schedule an appointment with Sister Michelina.

When the elderly nun came on the line, he identified himself as an investigator looking into Josie Hartin's death.

She didn't sound particularly surprised by that, but she was a bit resistant. "I haven't seen Josephine in decades, young man." Her tone was crisp. "I'm sure it would be a waste of your time to talk to me."

Skip pushed, and finally the nun agreed to see him on Saturday, mid-afternoon.

~~~~~~~~~

Kate was almost her old confident self with her clients. She only second guessed herself a couple of times during her morning sessions.

Even the session with Carol Foster had gone well. "I just feel blah now," the woman had said. "That usually means the depression is lifting and I'll feel better soon."

Kate gave the client an encouraging nod. *You and me both, sister.*

She'd been checking messages between each client and had heard nothing back from Rob. So she was a bit surprised when she ushered Carol out of her office and saw Nancy Hartin sitting in her waiting room, surreptitiously eyeing Mac.

Kate showed the woman into her office and gestured toward the loveseat in the corner sitting area, where she normally talked to clients.

Mrs. Hartin glanced at her desk, back at her and then headed toward the loveseat. She settled onto it, crossing her legs and smoothing down her skirt. "My lawyer informs me that you have some answers." Her tone was an odd mixture of haughty and anxious.

Kate realized that she no longer found the woman intimidating. She had a pretty good idea where the Hartins' skeletons were buried. She leaned forward. In her best therapist voice, she said, "I need to ask you a couple things first."

Mrs. Hartin hesitated, then gave a small nod.

"Why did you take Josie out of St. Bartholomew's school in second grade?"

Mrs. Hartin turned her head away. She bit down on her lower lip.

The gesture was so out of character Kate had trouble hiding her shock.

"I have a good reason for asking," she said softly. "It may very well be related..." She stopped, not sure she wanted to say more just yet.

"We let everyone think it was because Bryn Mawr would give Josephine certain advantages, but that wasn't the real reason." Nancy Hartin paused and sucked in a deep breath. It came out on a shudder. "I was taking her to school one day and she said to me, 'Do I have to go with the man who makes me take my clothes off today?'"

Kate had been suspecting something like this, but still her throat tightened.

A tear meandered down Mrs. Hartin's carefully made-up cheek. She dropped her gaze to her lap. "Her voice was so innocent, as if she were asking if she had to eat her vegetables. I tried to get her to say more, but she got this scared look on her face. She said she'd made it all up."

Mrs. Hartin raised her head. "But how does a seven-year-old make something like that up?"

"She didn't," Kate said gently.

"I know. I took her back home and called the school, told them she was sick." The words were now tumbling out. "But my husband poo-pooed it, said it was just a child's lively imagination. I took her to our family doctor, without Phillip's knowledge."

She stared straight at Kate now, her eyes begging for understanding. "The doctor said she hadn't been abused. I thought I'd gotten her out of there in time, before anything really bad had happened." She looked away again, gnawed on her lip. "But when she was a teenager and started struggling with depression, I wondered."

If only you'd told Josie about it, then she and I would have both known what we were dealing with.

Kate didn't voice the thought. She knew what Mrs. Hartin's reasoning had been. It was the common belief of the time, and still believed by all too many people today. If one just didn't think about the trauma, they would be fine.

She changed the subject. "Mrs. Hartin, I need to see the rest of Josie's journals."

The woman's head jerked up. "There was only the one."

Kate shook her head. "Josie had been journaling for months, and she'd also kept journals a few years ago, when she was working with that other therapist."

"The most recent one was the only one the police found. I asked specifically about that."

Kate told her about the dusty vacant spot on the bookshelf and finding one of the older journals down behind other books.

"Do you think Josephine got rid of them?" Mrs. Hartin asked.

"No, I think someone stole them." Kate shook her head again in frustration. "And probably destroyed them."

"Why do you think that?"

"Because there are references in that old one and the current one that imply something happened to Josie back then." Kate decided against describing the man with the scraggly beard. Mrs. Hartin might remember the janitor, and who knows what a distraught mother would do to try to find out what he knew. Time enough later, after she got Manny's report, to point a finger at Mr. Jones.

"I think whatever happened was the cause of her recurring dreams, and that she'd been told not to tell anyone, maybe even told to forget what happened. So whenever she got close to remembering, it made her very anxious."

Mrs. Hartin's lips formed an angry line even as more tears leaked out of her narrowed eyes. "Not *told*. You mean she was threatened."

Kate knew there was no way to make this easier for the woman. She was facing the reality that her little girl had gone through some horrible experience, and she, her mother, had failed to protect her.

"Brainwashed would probably best describe it," Kate said. "A combination of threats of dire consequences if she told, followed by reassurances that everything would be okay if she kept quiet."

She leaned forward and took a chance. Reaching out a hand, she rested it lightly on Nancy Hartin's arm. "You did get her away from whatever was going on. And you took her to the doctor. A lot of people wouldn't have done that. They would have preferred to hang on to their denial."

"Yes but I didn't get her away completely." Her voice was harsh with self-recrimination. "I wanted to change parishes but Phil wouldn't do it. There were too many influential people who went to St. Bartholomew's, he said. He needed those contacts."

So Mr. H can stand up to his wife when he really wants to. Too bad he's only assertive when it comes to his business, not his daughter.

Kate kept those thoughts to herself as well.

Mrs. Hartin shook her head. "But I never let her out of my

sight when we were at church. I kept her with me in the sanctuary, wouldn't let her go to Sunday school." The woman's voice broke on a sob. She buried her face in her hands. "She was always so nervous when we were going to church. She'd cling to me. I knew in my heart of hearts that something…had already happened."

Kate moved over to sit next to the woman on the loveseat. She laid a hand on her shoulder. Mrs. Hartin turned toward her and let Kate wrap her arms around her. She sobbed for several minutes.

When the crying seemed to be ebbing, Kate let go and sat back. "What happened at St. Bart's wasn't the only cause of Josie's depression. It probably wasn't even the main cause. It just aggravated her bipolar disorder. And bipolar is biologically based. There's pretty good evidence that it's genetic."

Mrs. Hartin gave a slight nod as she dried her eyes with tissues from the box Kate kept on the table next to the loveseat. "See, that's what I don't understand," she said when she'd sufficiently regained her composure. "Nobody on either side of the family has ever had any mental disorders."

Kate seriously doubted that, but bipolar was often missed in earlier generations, especially if the person tended more toward mania than depression.

She slipped back over to her own chair, facing the loveseat. "Tell me, who made the original Hartin fortune?"

"My husband's grandfather. He was an old man by the time I met him, but he'd been quite the dynamo in his day. Very charismatic and…" She trailed off, her mouth forming an o.

"No doubt he was also depressed at times," Kate said. "But he would have hid that, forced himself to push through it."

"So why couldn't Josephine do that?"

Kate stifled a sigh. When would that belief die, that people with mental disorders should just buck up and deal with it?

"Because she wasn't a man born in the late 1800s. She was a woman born in the 1980s. In Josie, the mania took the form of creativity, came out in her artwork." Kate was waltzing close to the line of confidentiality, but she didn't think her dead client would mind if the knowledge helped her mother to finally understand her.

Mrs. Hartin dabbed again at her eyes with a tissue. "I kept pushing her, thinking I could make her stronger."

"She was strong, in her own way, and courageous."

Unfortunately, the latter trait probably got her killed. Another thought that Kate kept to herself.

She changed the subject. "Josie didn't go to high school at Bryn Mawr, did she? Why did you move her again?"

"Because she rebelled, in eighth grade. Said she hated Bryn Mawr, all the pressure and emphasis on academics." Mrs. Hartin's voice rose, became sharper. "I pointed out..." She trailed off, then sighed. "We fought about it repeatedly. She wanted more time to spend on her artwork, said the local public high school had a really good art department. We ended up compromising, when she refused to go to school completely. I agreed to her transferring to the Catholic high school, and getting her private art lessons."

Her eyes went wide. "She *was* strong, wasn't she? Otherwise she wouldn't have bucked me so much. She would've caved into my demands years ago."

Kate gave her a wry smile. "Exactly."

Mrs. Hartin chuckled softly, then her face sobered again. "I really was proud of her," she said in a low voice. "But I was afraid if I told her that, then she'd think it was okay, the way she was living. But living that way made her happy."

The tears started up again. "There were so many things I should have said to her."

Kate leaned over and patted her hand. "That's one of the hardest parts of the grief process, the shoulda, woulda, coulda's. Tell me, do you believe in heaven?"

Mrs. Hartin's eyes went wide. "Of course I do."

"Then you know that Josie is there now, and that she's forgiven you."

Another startled look. "How could she be in heaven? She killed herself."

Crap! Forgot to tell her about the note.

Hadn't Father Sam contacted them about burying Josie in hallowed ground? Maybe it had slipped his elderly mind.

Or maybe he's the one who sent the note.

Kate suppressed a shudder. "I seriously doubt she did kill herself," she said out loud. "I received a note a couple days ago, threatening me if I didn't stop investigating her death."

Mrs. Hartin stared at her. "You've been investigating?"

Double crap!

Kate hadn't thought through how to handle this. She didn't want to say too much and maybe get Judith in trouble, or have the Hartins start confronting people prematurely.

"At first, I was just trying to figure out why Josie would kill herself when she seemed to be doing so well. But I've found some indicators that it wasn't suicide. Only circumstantial stuff so far. My husband's a private investigator. He's helping me look into it. When we have something more concrete, we'll take it to the police."

Mrs. Hartin nodded. "And the note confirms that she didn't kill herself."

"I think so." At least it confirmed that someone had secrets they didn't want revealed. "I'd prefer that you not tell anyone that we're investigating." She was tempted to add, *not even your husband.* But she hated to ask a woman to keep something from her husband, even though she suspected it wouldn't be the only secret in their relationship.

Mrs. Hartin nodded again. "So you really think Josie's forgiven me?"

It was the first time Kate had heard her use her daughter's preferred nickname.

"Yes, I do." She gave the woman a warm smile. "Especially if she's been listening in on this conversation."

Mrs. Hartin gave her a small smile back. She gathered her purse and jacket, then rose from the loveseat and offered her hand.

Kate stood and shook it, giving an extra squeeze before letting it go.

Josie's mother's face sagged. "Now all I have to do is forgive myself."

~~~~~~~~~

There were no messages on her office voicemail for a change, but her cell phone had two. The first was from Manny. "Hey Kate, the janitor claims he doesn't remember back that far. I think he's lying through his teeth, but I doubt we'll get him to admit to anything. I'm headed back to your office now."

The second message was from Skip. "Hey darlin', I was looking over your list again. I'm gonna follow up with that nun."

A warm feeling washed over her. Skip had offered to help from the beginning. Why had she stubbornly resisted? She'd let her guilt and grief isolate her.

Well no more of that!

She remembered she was supposed to call Rob.

He was in an emergency meeting with a client, his admin assistant informed her. She asked Fran to tell him she'd call him that evening. She stuck her head out into the waiting room.

Mac jumped up from a chair. She walked over to him. "Sorry for the boring duty, Mac. Manny's on his way back here to relieve you."

"Don't mind being bored." Mac grabbed her hand before she could turn away. "You okay?"

She studied his weathered face. His eyes were full of worry.

I sure have been putting those who love me through the wringer lately.

She gave him a peck on his leathery cheek. "I'm okay. Thanks for caring."

He took a step back. "Now ya don't have to go all mushy on me." The glint in his baby blues said he was teasing.

She smacked his shoulder, then realized she'd been neglecting him and Rose lately. "Hey, why don't you guys come over for dinner tonight?"

He flashed her a grin. "Sounds good."

"See you then." Kate went back into her office and glanced

at the wall clock. She only had ten minutes left before her next client was due. Grabbing her lunch bag out of her bottom desk drawer, she plopped down in her chair.

While munching on her sandwich, she called up her personal email account. Skip had copied her when he'd sent the list to the others. She clicked on the attachment and read the list through again.

There were little lines on the scanned image, indicating the edges of the sheet of paper she'd written the list on–from a pad smaller than the standard eight and a half by eleven inches.

Something nudged at her memory. She'd seen lines like that before. Where?

She looked at her watch. She was out of time. Closing her email, she stood and went out to fetch her first afternoon client.

Halfway through her three o'clock session, her brain coughed up the connection. It was all she could do to concentrate on her clients for the rest of the afternoon.

Once her last client had left, Kate pulled Josie's latest journal from her briefcase. It took a few minutes of leafing through it to find what she was looking for.

A very thin edge of a page that had been cut out. She realized there were actually several pages missing, cut cleanly from the book, probably with a razor blade. The page before ended in a complete sentence. The page after started with a new entry– three days later.

She pulled out the file from her briefcase that contained the information related to her investigation. Extracting her copy of the suicide note, she found what she had expected. There were faint lines around the edges.

Judith had said the sheet in the case file was a copy of the note. Kate would bet her brokerage account that the original was on a smaller piece of paper, say about the size of a journal.

She re-read the entries before and after where the pages had been removed. The entry before talked about coming out of a depression. In the one after, three days later, Josie was bemoaning the beginnings of a new manic episode.

Then she skimmed through the note. Viewing it not as a suicide note but as part of a journal entry, it fit neatly between the other two entries. Josie had often waxed introspective about her disease in those short periods of normalcy as she swung from depressed to manic.

The killer hoped no one would make the connection to the journal.

It had almost worked.

So why had this journal been left behind when the others, the older ones, had been taken? Was the killer afraid that others knew Josie kept a journal?

That had to be it. If there was no journal in the apartment, that might have raised questions about the suicide.

The hair stood up on the back of Kate's neck. The killer had calmly sat in that apartment and read through the journal, searching for a believable 'suicide note'—while Josie's body was shutting down from the overdose cocktail she'd been given. Then the killer had thoroughly cleaned the place to remove any forensic evidence of his presence.

She wasn't just looking for a murderer, she was looking for a cold-blooded one.

Feeling ill, Kate stuffed the journal into her briefcase and gathered the rest of her things to go home.

CHAPTER TWENTY-ONE

It was a beautiful spring evening, warm and dry, the sky glowing to the west, and Rose was in the bosom of her adopted extended family. But she was having trouble relaxing.

She wasn't nearly as confident as Skip was that Kate would take this well. She exchanged a look with her husband, standing next to Skip at the grill.

Mac shook his head slightly and took a swig from the beer can in his hand.

Rose huffed out a sigh.

He's right. Not our business.

Her cousin headed toward the back door of the house. Rose followed her into the laundry room and through the living room. In the kitchen, Maria handed her a big bowl of potato salad.

Rose had carried it out to the table and was coming back through the squeaky screen door, shooing the dog out of her way, when she heard Kate greeting Maria in the kitchen. By the time she got around the corner, the master bedroom door was closing.

"She changing clothes," Maria said as she gave Rose two more bowls to carry outside.

Rose hurried to get them on the picnic table, then hovered just inside the back door in the laundry room. The least she could do was warn Kate so that she wasn't totally blindsided.

Kate came through from the living room in jeans and a loose cotton shirt. "Hey, Rose," she said as she breezed past her.

"Brace yourself," Rose said, then turned and almost collided with Kate's back. The warning had come too late. Kate stood frozen in the back doorway, staring at her children sitting at the picnic table.

"Hey, don't let that mutt out here!" Skip yelled from the backyard.

Toby was indeed trying to nose his way past them. Rose blocked him with one knee, then shooed him back into the house.

Kate's movements were stiff as she walked toward the picnic table. She glanced back over her shoulder, her eyebrows arched in a questioning look.

Rose gave her a slight head shake. She wasn't about to be the one to explain.

"Why don't you want the dog out here?" Kate asked, her voice strained, her eyes flitting back to Billy's scratched and bruised face.

"Toby stole one of the hamburgers," Edie answered from her spot next to her brother.

Kate gestured toward Billy. "What hap–"

Skip raised a hand in the air. "Hold that thought. The burgers are ready."

"Hey, sweet pea," Mac called over. "You want a beer?" The corners of his mouth quirked upward.

Rose gave him a quelling look.

"No," Kate said, "but I think I'm gonna have a glass of wine." She turned and marched back into the house.

Rose joined her husband and Skip by the grill. "I'll take a beer," she said to Mac.

He leaned down and pulled one from the cooler at his feet.

Rose took the dripping can. She narrowed her eyes at Skip. "You two might think this is cause for celebration, but I doubt she's gonna see it that way."

Skip shrugged. "It's a guy thing."

Rose snorted and went to the table to sit down next to Edie. She popped the beer open and took a healthy sip.

Kate returned, a bouquet of wineglasses held by their stems in one hand, a bottle of red wine in the other. Maria followed, her hands full of several bottles of salad dressings.

They all settled around the picnic table. Kate poured wine for herself and Maria. She looked at her husband.

Skip held up his beer can. "I'm good."

Kate very deliberately put the extra empty wineglass off to one side.

"I wanna say grace," Billy yelled.

Kate opened her mouth. "Inside voi–"

"We're not inside, remember?" Skip gave her a lopsided grin.

Kate glared at him, but she kept quiet as Billy said the blessing loud enough that God and all the angels were sure to hear him.

Everyone started passing bowls and loading condiments onto their burgers. From the way she was devouring her food, Kate's normal voracious appetite had apparently returned, despite the current tensions.

Rose nodded slightly. A good sign that she was coming out of the funk she'd been in for the last few weeks.

Skip glanced at his wife's plate periodically. When most of the food had disappeared from it, he said, "Billy, tell your mom what happened today at school?"

Rose started to take a sip from her can. Billy bounced up and down on the other end of the bench. She barely avoided inhaling beer.

"Those guys were pickin' on me again, Mommy, but I did what Daddy told me. I told them they'd better stop or I was tellin' the teacher. Then Freddie Perkins, he slugged me." Billy stopped to shovel a forkful of beans into his mouth.

Kate gave Skip a hard look.

He kept his gaze on Billy. "What'd you do, son?"

"It really hurt. A lot more than I thought it would." Billy touched his bruised chin. "But it also made me mad. So I slugged him back. We was whalin' on each other when I remembered what else Daddy had told me, so I started hollerin' real loud."

"*Were* whaling. What'd you yell?" Kate said, but her gaze was not on her son. She was watching her husband, her eyes narrowed.

Rose glanced at Skip. The glint in his eye said he was enjoying the retelling of the story, which they'd already heard before Kate got home. But he was maintaining a neutral expression otherwise.

"Somethin' like, 'Leave me alone, you big bully.' Freddie landed a couple more punches but I got him good a few times too. Then the teacher came runnin' up and she said we were all in trouble." Billy stopped, looked at his mother, his face puckered with anxiety.

Kate gave the boy a small smile.

"She dragged us to the principal's office, just like Daddy said she probably would. And I told Mrs. Grant what Daddy said to say."

"Which was?" Kate said, again narrowing her eyes at her husband.

"That I told them to stop pickin' on me and that I was gonna tell the teacher, but when Freddie hit me, my Daddy said I had the right to offend myself."

Rose fought to keep a straight face. "Defend, Billy."

"Right, so I defended myself."

"What did the principal say?" Kate asked.

"Nothin'. She just sent me to the nurse. But I heard later that Freddie's parents had to come to school to get him and that maybe he'd been suspended."

Kate's eyes widened. "Do they suspend kids in elementary school?"

"Apparently they can," Mac said, "for fightin'."

"I called the principal when I got home," Skip said, "to make sure Billy wasn't in any trouble. Everything's cool."

"Daddy says they prob'ly won't pick on me anymore, but if they do, I should do exactly the same thing."

"And what are you *not* going to do?" Skip said, his voice firm.

"Throw the first punch," Billy answered.

Maria, sitting beside Kate, had been silent throughout this whole exchange. Now she smiled at Billy. "Chocolate cupcakes for dessert. I bake dem special."

Kate turned to her and frowned.

"Yippee!" the kids shouted in unison.

Rose exchanged a look with Mac across the table. His baby-blues sparked with amusement. He grinned at her.

No, Mac! Don't do it!

Mac raised his beer can in the air. "To Billy."

Kate swiveled around and scowled at him.

Rose shook her head.

~~~~~~~~~

After Rose and Mac had left, it took longer than usual to get the kids settled down. Sugar and chocolate were not the best combination close to bedtime.

But the delay gave Kate time to get over her irritation at Skip and Mac.

When the children were finally tucked in for the night, their parents went out back to finish cleaning up from the cookout. As they carried the last of the dirty paper plates and empty serving bowls inside, Kate said, "I'm not comfortable with rewarding Billy for fighting, even in self-defense. It's like we're advocating fisticuffs to deal with conflicts."

"Not conflicts, darlin', bullies," Skip said. "With them, it's often necessary."

She frowned but didn't say anything. She wasn't sure how she felt about the whole situation. She headed back outside to check that they'd gotten all the trash.

Skip trailed behind her. "Kate, we can hardly advocate total non-violence when their father carries a gun. I've told the kids repeatedly that I only use it, or my fists, when I absolutely have to, in defense of myself or others."

She shook her head. Butterflies of worry fluttered in her chest. "It's hard to know how to deal with bullies. These kids may beat up on Billy worse the next time they get him alone."

"Maybe." Skip took her hand and led her to the picnic table. They sat across from each other. He kept her hand. "Bullies only understand one thing, power. They want it, which is why they lord it over others. But when somebody fights back, it tends to have one of two effects. Either it scares the bully off, or it wins their respect."

Tends to... Kate's throat tightened. "Most of the time," she said out loud, "but not always."

"Yeah, but it's a good bet."

She struggled to tamp down her maternal angst. "I guess I'll bow to your judgement on this. You've had more experience with bullies than I have."

"Yeah, but you've got all them fancy degrees," Skip said in a teasing tone.

She snorted softly. "They haven't been doing me much good lately."

"What do you mean?" She couldn't see his face well in the moonlight, but his tone was now serious.

She blew out air, debating if she wanted to admit to her insecurities out loud, even to Skip. She took a deep breath. "I've been second guessing myself a lot at work, ever since Josie's death."

"Even after you knew it was murder, not suicide."

"Yeah, well, reading her journal, I've realized there was a lot of stuff I missed."

"You missed, or she didn't tell you?"

"Mostly she didn't tell me."

"So how can you know something somebody doesn't tell you?"

"But why couldn't she tell me? I'm supposed to gain the client's trust so they can open up to me."

Skip reached across the table and captured her other hand. He gave both hands a gentle squeeze. "Kate, the client has an hour a week. They're gonna pick and choose what they talk about, depending on what's most important to them right then. Am I right?"

Kate sighed again. "Yeah, you're right. But clients tend to be resistant to digging down to the deeper stuff. I'm supposed to catch that and gently push them to go there."

"But you can't read minds, if they choose to keep something from you."

"That's just the thing though, they shouldn't feel the need to keep something from me."

He shook his head. "Look, I've never seen you in action in your office, but you've been my psychological consultant on enough of my cases. *I* know that *you* know your stuff."

Warmth filled her chest. She smiled up at him. "It's been better this week. Thanks for the pep talk."

Her throat tightened as it struck her how little she'd been truly present with Skip lately, except in occasional fits and spurts. Too many of their evening talks, that were the mainstay of their emotional intimacy, had been dominated by her preoccupation with this case.

She wished Josie Hartin had never come to see her. Then she wouldn't be dealing with this all-consuming quest to find–

"You need to learn to separate work from home better." Skip had read her thoughts, as he had an irritating habit of doing.

"I used to be really good at that. I have this mental routine. When I switch on my car in the evening to drive home, I switch off all thoughts of clients."

Skip rose from his side of the table. "So why'd that stop working?"

She pondered that as she stood and they walked toward the house. "Probably because I haven't been doing it very consistently lately. When I finish with clients for the day, I switch to detective mode instead of home mode."

He dropped an arm around her shoulders. "Which is fine, until you actually get home."

"Yeah, I guess I need a new mental routine for this situation."

He stopped just inside the living room and grinned down at her. "I've got an idea. When you get home, I'll kiss you like this." He gave her a tender but chaste kiss on the lips. "That's the signal to stop thinking about anything but home."

She leaned against him. "Hmm, that sounds good."

He gestured toward their spot on the sofa. She noted the permanent indentation in the sofa cushions and smiled to herself. They moved in that direction.

"Then after the kids are in bed," he said, "we can talk about the case, compare notes."

They settled on the sofa. She snuggled close to his solid body.

He smiled down at her. "And when it's time to put all that aside again, I'll kiss you like this." He wrapped his arms around her and claimed her mouth again. Nudging her lips apart, his tongue went exploring.

Heat stirred in her core and spread rapidly through her body.

But we haven't compared notes yet, a little voice said in her head. She told it to shut up. Warm, tingling sensations enveloped her.

They finally broke apart, gasping a little. Kate expected Skip to rise and take her off to the bedroom. Maybe even sweep her into his arms, although he did that less and less these days. At forty-eight, his back was starting to complain about such activities.

She realized she had loved this man for the better part of a decade. It actually felt much longer. She couldn't imagine life without him—without this sense of closeness, as if they truly were two halves of a whole. Independent beings, but not quite complete without each other. She had loved Eddie Huntington dearly, but her life with him now felt as distant as her childhood did.

It registered finally that Skip had made no move toward the bedroom after all. He had relaxed back against the sofa. His arm tightened around her shoulders, pulling her up against his side.

She rested her hand on his broad chest, over his heart. Its solid thud, thud under her palm reassured her, grounded her even further in her own world. She silently vowed not to let Josie's case overwhelm her again. She'd keep trying to find out who murdered her, but she would not *obsess* about it.

"Guess I was a little premature with that second signal there tonight," Skip said with a chuckle in his voice.

So we're going to compare notes after all. She raised her head and grinned up at him. "That's okay. You can give it to me again in a little while."

The gold flecks danced in eyes.

How did she get so lucky? The warmth in her core expanded again. She tamped it down for now.

"I've got a follow-up interview scheduled with your nun on Saturday afternoon," Skip said.

"That's good. I figured something out today." She told him about the missing pages from the journal.

"Hmm," he said, "pretty clever way to get a suicide note in the victim's own handwriting."

"Yeah, and it almost worked. Both the police and Josie's parents bought it as a suicide note." Her eyelids were starting to droop. She looked up at him. "I'm thinking it's time for that signal again."

"Let's move this to the bedroom first." He gently disentangled himself and stood up, then reached down a hand and pulled her to a stand.

She leaned against him. "Suddenly, I'm so sleepy." Then she added in a teasing tone, "I'm not sure I can stay awake to do anything."

"We'll see about that." He brushed a thumb across one of her breasts.

Even through cotton shirt and bra, the gesture puckered her nipple. The warmth in her core expanded yet again. This time she gave it free rein.

He brushed the thumb back the other way. A current of electricity jolted through her, leaving a lingering tingle in its wake. Her knees turned to jelly.

She sucked in air. "Yeah, but now I'm not so sure I can walk to the bedroom."

"Is that a hint?" He reached down and circled her wobbly knees with one arm. Sweeping her up, he started across the living room. Then he groaned and began to stumble along in an exaggerated stagger.

She laughed and smacked his shoulder. "Stop that. You're breaking the mood."

He grinned down at her and wiggled his eyebrows. "Don't worry, darlin'. I *know* how to recapture it."

CHAPTER TWENTY-TWO

When Kate awoke the next morning, she was alone in the king-sized bed. Glancing at the clock, she realized she had overslept.

She hurried through her morning routine of shower and makeup. As she ran a comb through her unruly curls, she smiled at herself in the mirror.

Life is good.

She braced herself for the guilt, but it didn't come this time.

Also good. I'm getting damned tired of feeling guilty!

She donned her office attire and headed for the kitchen to grab a quick breakfast.

Halfway to the office, her cell phone rang. She didn't recognize the number on her dashboard screen, but she answered the call anyway.

"This is Dr. Blake's office," a young female voice said. "I'm calling to remind you of your appointment this evening at six."

"Huh?"

"For Toby, for his shots."

"Oh yeah."

Dang! She'd forgotten to put the vet appointment in her book, and it had completely slipped her mind. Indeed, she wasn't even sure she'd put Dr. Blake on that clues list she'd made for Skip.

"So we'll see you at six?" the voice said.

Kate hesitated. Keeping the appointment meant missing dinner with Skip and the kids. And on Friday night to boot. It was one of her favorite times of the week. They could relax, not worry about homework or having to deal with work again the next day. They usually let the kids stay up an extra hour.

"Ma'am, are you there?"

"Yes, uh…" She'd miss dinner but she'd be home early enough for family time. "I'll be there."

"Good. See you then." The young woman disconnected.

Kate instructed her Bluetooth to call Skip. It went straight to voicemail. He must be on the phone. "Uh, sweetheart, I need to go out for a little while this evening. It's kinda complicated so I'll explain when I get home. But I just wanted to give you a heads-up. I should be home by seven or seven-fifteen at the latest. In plenty of time to snuggle up with you and the kids and watch a video."

She disconnected, praying that her husband wouldn't be mad at her.

And the knot of guilt in her stomach was back. She sighed.

Is it possible to get used to feeling guilty?

At lunchtime, she barely had a chance to eat, much less look at Josie's journal again. Two clients had left rather frantic messages, and another had requested to have her Monday appointment rescheduled to later next week. With the weekend looming, Kate couldn't ignore any of the calls.

By the time she'd returned them, snatching bites of her sandwich in between, she only had time for one more phone call. She really wanted to track down this Father Bill and set something up to meet with him. He had been at St. Bart's during the relevant time and might know what happened to Josie there.

Could he have been the abuser?

Possibly. But her impression from Josie's journals was that she had trusted the priest. Maybe she had confided in him, either as a child or when she crossed paths with him later when she was in high school.

Kate punched in the work number Liz had dug up for him.

As she waited for the call to go through it occurred to her that the abuse didn't necessarily happen at St. Bart's. It could have happened anywhere, and little Josie was just thinking about it on the way to school that day when she asked about going with the man who made her take her clothes off.

Or was she indulging in wishful thinking because she didn't want Father Sam to be the abuser? Mrs. Hartin had said that Josie was nervous at church after the day she'd blurted that out. But the little girl could have been picking up on her mother's anxiety.

A receptionist answered her call and directed her to William Coleman's office.

Kate glanced at the clock. It was almost one. Her first afternoon client was probably already out in the waiting room.

Another young woman picked up the phone. Kate quickly gave her name and asked to speak to Mr. Coleman.

"Uh, may I ask what you're calling about?"

"It's personal. Tell him it's about St. Bartholomew's Church."

"Okay. I'll see if he's back from lunch yet."

Kate drummed her fingers on the desk.

What did priests do when someone reported abuse during a confession, either as the abuser or the victim? By Maryland law, they would be mandated to report the abuse. But would a priest really do so? The confidentiality of the confessional was considered a sacred vow. Maybe Bill Coleman wouldn't tell her even now, assuming he knew anything useful.

"I'm sorry," the young woman said in her ear. "He isn't back yet. Can I take a message?"

Kate hesitated. She really wouldn't be reachable for the rest of the day. And she didn't want him calling her back this evening, during family time.

"Just tell him I called and that it's important that I reach him. I'll try him again later."

"Okay, I'll tell him," the woman said cheerfully, then disconnected.

Kate hung up her desk phone and raced out to her waiting room to apologize to her client for running late.

The woman looked distinctly nervous. She was watching

Manny, who sat at the opposite end of the waiting room, his head back against the wall, eyes closed.

He seemed to be asleep, but Kate knew he wasn't.

"It's okay," she said to her client. "He's a friend of mine." She didn't offer any more of an explanation. There was no way to explain the presence of a beefy man in her waiting room, other than the truth. And she wasn't about to scare the woman even more by telling her that she'd received a threatening note.

We have got to get this resolved soon.

Not only was it costing Skip's agency money to pay Manny but having him around was not good for her clients, especially the paranoid or anxious ones. Which was over half of her client load.

At the end of the day, she had only one message.

The male voice was sharp. "Mrs. Huntington. This is Phillip Hartin. What part of 'we are suing you so you should communicate only through our attorneys' don't you understand. Leave me and my wife alone."

Kate gritted her teeth, wishing now that she had asked Mrs. Hartin to keep their meeting confidential. How much had she told her husband? Maybe very little. But she might have come home upset enough that he'd noticed. Did Mr. Hartin really care all that much about his wife's feelings, or was he just pissed because Kate wasn't following the rules?

Or did he have something to hide? Kate shuddered at the thought that he might be able to perpetrate such a premeditated crime against his only child. As bad as things could get in highly dysfunctional families, rarely did parents intentionally kill their children.

She shook her head and quickly gathered her things. She needed to get going.

On the way to the parking lot, she asked Manny to check out Mr. Hartin the next day. "Liz did a background check and he came up clean, but see if you can dig up anything else on him."

"Will do." Manny sketched her a small salute and headed for

his car to follow her home.

When Kate pulled up in front of the house, Skip's truck wasn't parked out front. Once she was on the porch, she waved to Manny. He waved back and drove away.

Too late, she realized she should have asked him to wait and follow her to her appointment with the veterinarian. She could call him and ask him to come back. Or was she being a wuss?

It was still daylight, she would be around other people the whole time, and she would have a large dog with her. Was anybody really likely to mess with her?

A quick glance at her watch. Five-thirty-five, and it took a good twenty minutes to get to the vet's office. She raced inside to get Toby.

Edie was stretched out on the living room floor, drawing in her sketch pad.

"Where's Maria?" Kate said.

"Out back with Billy," Edie said without looking up.

"I've got to take Toby to the vet's to get his shots. Tell Maria not to wait dinner for me, and tell your dad that I'll be home by about seven-ish."

"Okay, Mommy."

"Don't forget now," Kate said back over her shoulder as she went into the study to get the record of Toby's vaccines.

She checked her watch again. With Friday afternoon rush-hour traffic, she'd be very lucky if she made it to her appointment on time.

Why hadn't the dog greeted her at the door like he normally did? "Toby, where are you, boy?"

As she went into the laundry room to get his leash and travel harness, she found her answer. He was outside with Maria and Billy, chasing the frisbee the little boy was tossing in the air.

Kate stuck her head out the door. "Sorry to break up your fun, Billy, but I need Toby." She whistled and the puppy loped over to her. Snapping the leash on his collar, she debated whether to explain to Maria where she was going.

There really wasn't time. She just waved and led the dog toward the front of the house. Edie would deliver her messages.

The clock on her dashboard read two minutes after six when Kate pulled into the parking lot of the small shopping center where the vet's office was located. The lot was crowded with people stopping off to run errands or get groceries on their way home from work. Rather than take the time to hunt for something closer, Kate headed for the far side of the lot where spaces were plentiful.

She parked, grabbed her cell phone off of the central console and her purse from the passenger seat, then jumped out of the car. Stuffing her phone into the pocket of her slacks, she opened the back door. She leaned in and unhooked Toby's harness from the safety tether connected to the seatbelt. "Come on, boy."

He licked her face, then jumped out of the car.

"Ick," she muttered as she led him at a jog toward the vet's office. She liked dogs and Toby was a sweetie, but she'd never be able to think of being licked in the face as a kiss.

Her anxiety over being late was all for nothing. It was almost six-thirty before her name was called. Or to be more precise, Toby's name was called.

She and the pup followed the vet's assistant into one of the examining rooms.

The assistant lifted Toby onto the table. "Dr. Blake will be right with you."

The vet came in a minute later, a piece of paper in her hand. Kate recognized it as the list of vaccines she had turned over to the receptionist when she'd arrived.

"Sorry, to keep you waiting, Mrs. Huntington. We're running behind schedule. A couple of emergencies earlier."

Kate caught herself before she blurted out, *I know how that goes*. She didn't want to have to explain that she was a mental health professional who also sometimes had emergencies that threw her off schedule.

Dr. Blake was looking down at the paper. "It's really too soon to give Toby his booster shots."

"Well, uh, I didn't want to wait too long, and maybe forget."

Okay, that sounded pretty lame.

"Yeah, but over-immunizing animals can actually compromise their natural immune systems."

"Oh, I didn't know that."

"Most people don't. In this case, more is not better."

"Okay, well..." Kate fumbled for something to say. She'd counted on a little time, while the vet gave Toby his shots, to lead up to her questions.

Dr. Blake was lifting a shivering Toby down to the floor. Once he was there, he gratefully licked her hand. "We'll just reschedule you for June." The vet turned to leave the room.

"Wait, Dr. Blake."

The woman turned back.

"Can I take up a little of your time anyway? I wanted to ask you a couple things, about Josie Hartin."

The vet's eyebrows went up. "Oh?"

Kate opted for honesty. "I have a confession to make. I was using Toby's shots as an excuse to see you again. Some evidence has been uncovered that suggests Josie didn't commit suicide."

"The overdose was accidental?"

"No, she was murdered."

The vet's eyebrows flew up again. "Oh!"

"Yes, and I've been looking into it. Well my husband and I. He's a private detective." Kate hoped that would make her seem more legit, not just a nosy friend of the deceased.

Dr. Blake leaned a hip against the examining table. It was a casual pose but her eyes had gone wary. "How can I help?"

"I'm not really sure. Had she said anything to you about something she was investigating?"

The vet stiffened, then cocked her head to one side. "No."

"Was anything upsetting her that you knew of?"

The vet's body was now rigid, her face a neutral mask. She shook her head.

Is this what Josie meant about the woman shutting down?

Dr. Blake frowned. "As I said before, she seemed to be in a good mood right before..." Her voice trailed off.

"I know, but maybe a little further back than that. Had she indicated she was thinking about confronting someone about something?"

"No." The word came out a little too vehemently. "She hadn't been coming here that long. We were really just getting to know each other."

"I know Josie was very fond of you."

The vet didn't respond.

"She seemed to have a crush on you."

"A crush? What do you mean?"

Kate was in a quandary. She was skirting on the edge of confidentiality already. Without thinking it through, she blurted out, "Dr. Blake, are you gay?"

Now the vet's eyebrows were almost touching her hairline. "What's that got to do with anything?" Her tone was angry, but her body had actually relaxed a little.

Butterflies fluttered in Kate's chest. How safe was this, confronting the woman when they were alone in the room? She strained to hear signs of human activity outside the room. Had the staff gone home?

Would Toby protect her? That seemed unlikely since he was currently rubbing against the vet's leg, begging to be petted.

Dr. Blake suddenly stood up straight.

Toby jumped back and whined softly.

Heart beating faster, Kate wrapped the slack in the leash around her hand to keep the dog near her. "Well, are you?"

Dr. Blake planted her hands on her hips. "Yes, as if that's any of your business."

"That's what I meant, about Josie having a crush on you."

The vet's face was unreadable as she digested that. "So Josie was gay."

"More likely bisexual."

"I have a partner." The tone was terse. "We've been together for six years."

Even though Dr. Blake was visibly angry, Kate couldn't help feeling that she was less uptight than she had been a few minutes ago. Was there something else this woman was worried about?

"Did Josie know that?"

"Not that I know of. I don't hide my sexual orientation but I don't flaunt it either."

"Thank you for your candor, Doctor." Kate was hoping to mollify the woman, but her words seemed to have the opposite effect.

Dr. Blake narrowed her eyes. "You're her therapist, aren't you?"

"She told you she was in therapy?"

"Yes." Suddenly the anger drained out of the woman's body. Her shoulders slumped. "She said you were great." Her voice was soft now. "That you really cared."

"I'm sorry for the interrogation. I started out trying to figure out why she killed herself, but now... There's a murderer out there." She didn't know what else to say.

"And you want justice for Josie. So do I, Mrs. Huntington. Honestly, if I knew anything that might help, I'd tell you."

Kate's own shoulders slumped. "Okay. Well, if you think of anything, can I give you my cell number? Would you call me?"

"Of course."

Kate rooted in her purse for a business card. Dr. Blake handed her a pen. She wrote her cell phone number on the back and gave it to her. "Thank you for your time."

The vet moved aside as Kate and Toby headed for the door.

"Mrs. Huntington." The anger was back in Dr. Blake's voice.

Kate pivoted, bracing herself physically.

"Get the bastard!"

Kate relaxed, feeling a bit sheepish. "I'm gonna try to."

As she and Toby left the building, dusk was moving toward full dark. The parking lot was far less crowded, with only a few cars scattered near the grocery store at the other end of the shopping center.

Kate moved quickly across the lot to her car, tugging on Toby's leash each time he tried to stop and sniff.

It dawned on her that the vet had asked if the overdose was accidental. How had she known that Josie died of a drug overdose? That hadn't been in the obituary. How readily available would that information be to the general public? Had the police talked to Dr. Blake before the case was ruled a suicide? They must have, since she ended up with Josie's dog. But police officers didn't usually volunteer much information.

She flashed back to her first conversation with the Hartins. They had discussed the dog's fate with the vet. So somewhere in there, Laurie Blake could have learned the cause of death.

She yanked Toby away from what was apparently a particularly enticing odor. "Sorry, boy." They needed to take him for more walks and work on his manners on a leash.

At the car, she opened the back door. The dog jumped up on the seat and she leaned in to hook his travel harness to the safety tether that was attached to the seatbelt. This rig gave him some leeway to move around on the seat, but theoretically would help keep him safe in an accident. She hoped that never got tested.

She'd no sooner gotten the tether hooked and was pulling her head back out of the car when Toby erupted, utilizing his ability to jump around and barking loudly.

Kate clapped her hands over her ears. "Sheez, pup, will you settle down."

In the next instant, she was face down on the asphalt, a heavy weight in the middle of her back. Toby's barking became frenzied.

Adrenaline shot through her system.

"Shut up, mutt," a deep voice growled. Then hot, rank breath on her cheek.

Dear God, no!

Her body shuddered under the weight. Her throat closed. She tried to push away the panic as her mind madly scrambled for an aikido move that would unseat someone whose knee was planted in your back.

Her assailant grabbed her hair and turned her head sideways. A glint of metal in her peripheral vision.

I'm dead! Holy Mary, Mother of God, watch over my children!

Sharp pain shot from her nose up to the top of her skull. She thought she might pass out. Part of her wished she would, before this creep did whatever he was going to do to her. She was help-less–her hands pinned under her, her assailant's weight firmly holding her down.

Something warm ran along her upper lip and into her mouth. Coppery. Her own blood.

Her stomach heaved.

Hot breath against her ear this time. "Thought you were told to butt out." The voice was gravelly. "Do I gotta cut off yer nose to get ya to leave things alone."

Then the weight was gone from her back. Toby was still bark-ing like a crazed dog, twisting and turning in his harness.

She pushed herself up. On hands and knees, she stared at the dark liquid dripping onto the pavement. Her head swam. She had to move, get away, or at least get in a position where she could fight back. Her assailant was probably nearby.

She'd no sooner had the thought than something hard con-nected with the back of her head. Horrible pain exploded in her skull. Her vision blurred. She fell forward.

Toby's barks faded away.

CHAPTER TWENTY-THREE

Skip looked at his watch again. "When did Mommy say she'd be home?"

Edie scrunched up her face. "Seven-ish."

"And she said she was going to the vet?"

"Yes, Daddy, to get Toby his shots." Her tone was impatient. *Better not ask her again.*

Eventually the child's impatience would turn to anxiety when she realized the implications of her mother's absence.

Because it was now seven-twenty-five.

He'd called Kate's cell phone at seven-fifteen. It rang several times and went to voicemail. He'd texted her. No response. Which made no sense. If she was sitting in the vet's waiting room she could text him back. If she was on her way home, she'd have answered with her Bluetooth.

Then he'd called their veterinarian's office. The receptionist there had informed him that Toby did not have an appointment that evening, and he wasn't due for any shots until June.

He'd also called Manny who reported that he'd followed Kate home and she'd waved to him from the porch so he'd left. "She seemed to be in a big hurry to get home, but she didn't say anything about going out again."

Worry and fury were doing battle in Skip's chest. Why had she ditched Manny and lied about where she was going? How could she be so reckless?

He got up off the sofa and walked into the kitchen to get away from the noise of the video playing on the TV. He took out his cell phone and replayed Kate's message from that morning.

"Uh, sweetheart, I need to go out for a little while this evening. It's kinda complicated so I'll explain when I get home. But I just wanted to give you a heads-up. I should be home by seven or seven-fifteen at the latest. In plenty of time to snuggle up with you and the kids and watch a video."

Edie appeared in the kitchen doorway. "Aren't you gonna watch the movie with us, Daddy?" There was a bit of a whine in her voice.

No wonder. Now she has two preoccupied parents.

"In a minute, Pumkin."

She went back into the living room.

Skip sat down at the kitchen table and tried to sort this out. The phone message didn't quite jive with what Kate had told Edie. It did imply that she was going to come home and then go out again, but why didn't she just say she had to take the dog to the vet? How could that be "kinda complicated?"

Did this have something to do with Josie Hartin's case? Worry overrode his anger.

He punched Manny's speed dial number on his phone, then quickly disconnected. What the hell could Manny do? There was nothing *to do.*

He had no idea where his wife was. He grabbed a hunk of hair and yanked.

All he knew was the dog was with her. He hoped that was enough of a deterrent if anyone truly meant her harm.

He glanced at his watch again. Seven-thirty.

Based on her message, she was only fifteen minutes late. No need to panic yet.

Yeah, right!

He tried her cell phone again.

~~~~~~~~

Something rough and wet ran up her cheek. Hot breath in her ear. She jerked away.

A whining noise. The rough wetness on her neck. It tickled.

She opened one eye. Dark, blurry shadows.

Where the hell am I?

Pain came roaring back, memory right behind it.

She rolled over on her side, tried to focus her eyes.

Another whine, then a bark.

Sharp pain shot through her head. "Shush, Toby."

Her vision cleared enough to make out that the poor dog was dangling half out of the backseat. His front paws were on the asphalt, his harness holding his back end inside the car.

He stretched his nose toward her and licked her face, whined again.

"It's okay, boy," she said, even though it wasn't.

She managed to sit up. The blurry image of a dark parking lot tilted to one side. Her stomach churned. She leaned over, gagging, but there was little in her stomach. Every dry heave shot ice picks through her brain.

She closed her eyes and swallowed, willing the gagging to subside.

Toby whined.

She opened her eyes. When the world stopped spinning, she scanned the area around her. This end of the parking lot was deserted. Her eyes searched the pavement near her. Her purse was gone. But her keys were just under the edge of the car.

She picked them up. Pushing herself up on her knees, and trying to ignore the pain ripping off the top of her head, she managed to shove the dog back up on the backseat. "Stay, boy."

Grabbing the armrest on the inside of the back door, she pulled herself partway upright, then got her feet under her and stood up. The parking lot did another slow spin.

Please, Lord, don't let me pass out.

She closed the back door and grabbed for the handle of the driver's door. The panic she'd been holding at bay now overwhelmed her. She ripped the door open, jumped in and hit the lock button.

The thunk of the doors locking was somewhat reassuring. But

she had to get out of here.

She looked down at the keys still clutched in her hand. Her eyes went out of focus. There was no way she could drive.

"Call 911." No response from her Bluetooth.

Panic threatened to swamp her again. Her cell phone was gone.

Wait, no. It's in my pocket.

She patted her pocket to make sure. Yes, the phone was still there. Had it been damaged in the fight?

What fight? He knocked you out, a voice in her head said.

Oh yeah, the car needed to be on for the Bluetooth to work. She fumbled the key into the ignition switch and turned it. The engine roaring to life in the quiet night made her jump.

She looked at the dashboard clock. Eight-fifty.

My God, Skip will be frantic.

But first things first. "Call 911," she said again.

Nothing happened.

She fumbled the phone out of her pocket to make sure it was on. It was. Her fuzzy brain remembered that the phone needed to be within a certain distance from the Bluetooth. She laid it on the console.

"Call 911."

A disembodied voice said, "911. What is the nature of your emergency?"

"I've been mugged."

"Are you safe now, ma'am?" The voice was calm and urgent at the same time.

"Yes, I think so."

"Where are you?"

"At the vet's."

"Can you give me the address?"

Kate had no idea what the address was. "I don't remember. It's in a shopping center. I used my GPS to get here."

"Are you hurt, ma'am?"

"Yeah. He hit me in the head, and cut my nose."

"Stay on the line, ma'am. I'm sending the police and an ambulance. The police can track you through your cell phone signal."

Kate's eyelids were drooping. She shook her head, then wished she hadn't when pain shot through her skull.

"I can't stay on the line. I've gotta call my husband." A thought meandered into Kate's mind. "Please contact Judith Anderson. This is related to a case of hers."

A half beat of silence. "Okay, but you need to stay on the line, ma'am."

"I'll call back. Disconnect. Call Skip."

Kate's head lolled to one side.

Toby whined in the backseat.

~~~~~~~~~

Seven minutes of nine. The credits were rolling on the Disney movie.

Bile rose in Skip's throat. His insides were tied in knots. He looked at his kids, stretched out on their stomachs on the living room floor.

My God! Their mother may be dead. Pain surged through his body, threatened to explode his chest wide open.

Edie rolled over on her back. "Where's Mommy?" she said in a sleepy voice.

He opened his mouth, not at all sure what he would say. His cell phone buzzed. He snatched it off the coffee table.

Kate's cell, the screen read.

"Kate, where the hell are you?" he yelled into the phone.

"I don't know." Her voice was plaintive, her words slurred. "I'm so scared." Toby barked in the background.

Oh my God!

"Where are you?" He tried to calm his voice without completely succeeding.

"At the vet's."

"No, you're not. I called the vet."

Silence, then, "Not our vet. Josie's vet." Her voice sounded a little steadier.

He glanced up. Edie was standing in front of him, biting her lip. Billy clung to his sister's arm.

He took a deep breath. "Darlin', where is Josie's vet?"

"I don't remember the address." The words were slurred again.

"Are you hurt? What happened?"

Edie was crying now.

"It's okay, Pumkin. It's gonna be okay." Into the phone, "Kate?"

"I called the police. They're on the way."

"Good, good." He tried to smile at his kids. He had no idea how successful that effort was.

"Kate, did you use GPS to get there?"

"Yeah."

"Call up recent addresses on the GPS."

A long silence. His heart pounded.

"Okay."

"What's it say?"

"One, one two... Can't read it. There's two more numbers. My vision keeps going in and out on me."

"What's the street name?"

"Delaney something."

Probably Delaney Valley Road.

"Okay, you're doing fine, darlin'. The vet's office? Is it in a house, an office building, a mall?"

"No. It's a little shopping center."

"Okay, I'll find you. Hang on!"

He jumped up and headed for the door. Halfway there it dawned on him that Maria wasn't home. Would it be better to leave Edie in charge, or take the kids with him?

There was a killer out there, who'd attacked Kate. He didn't dare leave them alone.

"Come on, kids." he gestured for them to hurry. "We need to go get your mother."

Once in his truck, he called Rose.

"What's up, partner?"

"I need your help." He tried to keep his voice calm, for the sake of the kids. "I'm on my way to pick Kate up. I may need you to–"

"What? Manny checked in earlier and said she was home. Who's with her?"

He didn't want to go into details with little ears listening from the backseat. "Nobody. It's a long story."

"Is Kate okay?" Rose's tone was sharp. "What's going on?"

"Not sure. I'm on the way to get her. The kids are with me."

"What do you need?"

Skip almost lost it.

I need my wife! Struggling to keep his voice even, he said, "I need you to come get the K-I-D-S."

"Daddy, I can spell!" Edie said from the backseat.

"I know, Pumkin."

"I can spell too, Daddy," Billy yelled.

An hysterical bubble of laughter rose in his throat. Skip desperately shoved it down. "I know, son."

He gave Rose the partial address.

"We'll find it!" she said.

CHAPTER TWENTY-FOUR

Toby went ballistic, almost covering the sound of knuckles rapping on glass.

Kate jumped. Her eyes flew open.

A young man's face stared at her through the window of her car. "Ma'am, you called 911?"

A siren in the distance.

Still some instinct told Kate to be wary. "Who are you?" she mumbled.

Toby kept barking.

"S'okay, boy," Kate told him.

The man held a badge up to the glass. "Police, ma'am."

"Good." Kate drifted off to sleep.

Sharp rapping. Toby barking.

"Ma'am, unlock the door!"

"Who are you?"

"Police, ma'am." A badge mashed against the window.

"'kay." She fumbled for the unlock button.

~~~~~~~~

"Stay here!" Skip ordered. He jumped out of his truck and hit the button on his key fob to lock it.

"I'm her husband," he kept shouting as he pushed past police officers. Ten feet from her car, his way was blocked by a very large and determined sergeant.

Skip tried to see past the man's bulk. The dog was barking nonstop, the silhouette of his head bouncing around in the back-seat, but no other silhouettes.

"I'm her husband. I gotta see her." He choked on the lump in his throat. "Is she okay?" He managed to get past it.

The cop pointed toward an ambulance twenty feet away. "She doesn't seem to be seriously hurt."

Suddenly Edie was at his elbow. He grabbed her arm. "I thought I told you to stay in the truck?" He heard the harshness in his voice.

Edie started crying.

A knot coiled in his stomach. He swept her up, held her tight and kissed her damp cheek. "It's okay, Pumkin. Mommy's fine." He ran back toward his truck.

Mac's Hummer came to a screeching halt next to it. Rose jumped out of the passenger side and ran to meet Skip.

"Is Billy in my truck?" he yelled.

Mac was out of the Hummer, peering into the SUV's window. "Yeah," he called out.

Rose reached Skip. He set Edie on her feet and handed his keys to Rose. She took the child's hand.

"Toby," Edie said through her sniffles.

"Come on, honey, we'll get the dog." Rose led her toward Kate's car.

Skip turned and tore off toward the ambulance.

Mac had beat him there and was hovering near where Kate sat on the side of a gurney. One paramedic dabbed at the blood on her face with a wad of gauze, while another was trying to convince her to go to the hospital.

The small crowd around his wife was keeping Skip from getting a good look at her.

But Mac's face was a mask of fury. Except for his eyes, which were shiny with unshed tears. "Who did this, sweet pea?"

"I don't know." Kate's voice, a bit slurred.

Skip shoved past one of the paramedics and froze. Kate's face was a mess.

"Most of the blood's from her nose, sir," the young woman doing the dabbing said to him.

"Kate, are you okay?"

She looked up and made a choking sound. Throwing her arms out toward him–and almost backhanding the nearest paramedic in the process–she fell forward.

He grabbed her, dead weight against him. Had she fainted? Then he heard her sobs, coming from where her face was buried in his shoulder.

Oh my God! This time it was a prayer of thanksgiving.

Mac stepped over next to them. "Is she okay?" His normal growl had gone up an octave.

"She doesn't seem to be seriously hurt," one of the paramedics said. "But she really needs to go to the hospital to have her head looked at."

Again, hysterical laughter threatened to erupt from Skip's throat. His wife definitely needed her head examined!

Mac was patting Kate's shaking shoulder. "It's okay, sweet pea. We've got ya now. You're safe." The man sounded like he was ready to cry himself.

Skip swallowed hard. "Mac, can you follow the ambulance in my truck?"

Mac nodded. "Sure thing."

Kate's head was shaking vigorously against Skip's chest. He ignored the message. "Thanks, man," he said to Mac.

A willowy figure emerged from the darkness. It took Skip a second to recognize the tall woman, dressed in black and white.

He left the paramedics to the task of trying to convince his wife to go to the hospital, although he doubted they'd succeed. He'd probably have to insist.

"Lieutenant, what brings you here?" He willed himself to relax his clenched fists.

"Your wife's 911 call. She told the dispatcher it was related to one of my cases."

"Josie Hartin," he said.

Judith Anderson blew out air. "Someone made good on the threat in that note."

"To a certain extent." He didn't even try to keep the bitterness out of his tone. "She's got a notch in her nose now."

Judith looked around. Silence hung in the air.

Skip was struggling to keep his anger tamped down.

But Judith was the one who exploded. "This is bullshit!" She stopped, took a deep breath. "Officially I've been told hands off, but that's on the Hartin case. This is a whole new ball of wax. New case–the assault of Kate Huntington."

The paramedics had won the battle about going to the hospital, but once in the emergency room, Kate kept asking to go home.

"We will," Skip said, "just as soon as the docs say you're okay."

The ER doctor who was examining her flashed him a look. "I'd rather keep her overnight for observation."

"No!" Kate said.

Skip shrugged at the doctor, then shook his head.

His hand had gone numb about fifteen minutes ago, but he wasn't about to pull it loose from Kate's grip. She'd clung to it during the ambulance ride, letting go only long enough for the paramedics to unload her once they'd arrived at the hospital.

"You have a concussion, young lady." This despite the fact that the doctor was probably a decade younger than Kate.

Duh! Skip thought. He'd have been shocked if she wasn't concussed.

"I'm going to order a CAT scan, to make sure there's no other damage. And you'll need a couple stitches in that nose. I'll send an intern in to take care of that." The doctor left without another word.

He'd never said whether or not Kate could go home after she'd been stitched and scanned, but Skip knew that unless his wife passed out long enough for them to tie her to a bed, she would be going home tonight.

It was after one in the morning by the time Skip pulled up in front of their house. Kate had said very little on the way home, her head turned away from him and leaning gingerly against the headrest of her seat.

He helped her out of his SUV and up to the house. Unlocking the door, he held it open for her.

The house was quiet. Rose had called him earlier to report that Maria was home from her date and the kids were bedded down. He'd given her an update on Kate's condition. The CAT scan had found no serious head injury. "Apparently her head is as hard as mine."

Rose had chuckled. "In some ways harder."

Skip had faked a little laugh. He wasn't finding his wife's stubbornness all that amusing at the moment.

Rose had said she'd swing by the hospital and pick Mac up. She'd also offered to collect Kate's car in the morning. Skip thanked her profusely.

Rose had harumphed as if she were offended. "No thanks necessary. You're family."

Now Skip guided Kate toward the bedroom. They were halfway there when she said, "I'm hungry." He changed directions and sat her down in a chair at the kitchen table. Then he went to the fridge to dig out some leftovers to reheat.

"Where's Toby?" Kate asked.

"In the laundry room, I'd assume." That's where he slept at night.

"Let him out for a few minutes, will you?"

"He's gonna jump up on you."

"I know, but I need to see him."

"Okay." Skip had his doubts about this plan but he went to the back of the house and opened the door to the laundry room.

Toby came tearing out and made a beeline for the kitchen.

By the time Skip got back there, the dog had his front paws firmly planted on Kate's lap and was vigorously licking her face. Kate had turned her head so he couldn't get to the injured side of her nose, but otherwise she made no effort to stop him.

Instead she was smiling and murmuring, "Good boy. You're such a good boy."

"Since when do you like being licked in the face?"

Toby settled down some. He lowered his head to her lap and whined softly. Kate scratched his ears. "Since this guy woke me up with a doggie kiss, after scaring that creep off before he had time to do more harm."

"You think the dog made a difference?"

"I suspect so. There were still people coming and going from the grocery store at the other end of the parking lot. The guy might have taken off anyway, but Toby's barking probably made him go sooner instead of later." The dog lifted his head and licked her cheek again. She chuckled. "Here, you better take him back to his bed before he drowns me in saliva."

Skip took the dog to the laundry room, pausing to crouch down and give him a good belly rub. "Thanks, boy," he whispered.

Back in the kitchen, the microwave dinged. Skip brought the bowl of stew to the table and set it in front of Kate.

Edie appeared in the kitchen doorway, rubbing her eyes with her fists. Her gaze fell on Kate and she ran across the room, scrambled onto her mother's lap, and threw her arms around her. "Mommy, I was so scared."

Kate held her tight, rocking a little in the chair. "So was I, sweetie, but I'm okay now. And Lieutenant Anderson is going to find the man who hurt me."

Edie pushed back to look her mother in the eye. "You cannot go outside until the lieutendent finds the bad man." Her tone was an exact match of Kate's when she was laying down the law to the kids.

Skip swallowed a chuckle, even as his eyes stung.

"*Lieutenant*, sweetheart," Kate corrected her with a smile. "And I'm not going anywhere but the bedroom for at least a day or two."

"Amen," Skip muttered under his breath. He ruffled his daughter's hair, then lifted her off her mother's lap. "Come on, Pumkin.

It's back to bed for you."

"'Night, Mommy."

"Goodnight, sweetie."

The nine-year-old allowed herself to be carried up the stairs to her room. When Skip laid her down on her bed, she hung onto him for a beat.

He pulled the covers up to her neck.

"Is Mommy telling the truth? Is she really okay?"

"Yes, Pumkin."

"Is that man gonna try to hurt her again?"

"No, Pumkin." *Not if I can help it!*

He brushed the hair off her forehead and dropped a kiss there. "You go to sleep now."

Downstairs, Kate was slowly spooning stew into her mouth. "I am so hungry, but it hurts to chew."

He pulled out a chair and dropped into it. "You're gonna be one big bruise by morning."

She nodded slightly and lifted her spoon to her mouth again.

"Judith is going to use the attack on you as an avenue to quietly investigate Josie's case. So no more poking around for you."

Kate winced, then looked up at him. Something flashed in her eyes, then her battered face sagged. "My head hurts too much to think about that right now."

Skip gritted his teeth but didn't say anything.

"I'm sorry, sweetheart." Tears leaked from her eyes. She put down her spoon.

"For ditching Manny?" His tone was harsher than he'd intended.

"That wasn't intentional. I was so rushed today that I never got around to telling him that I needed to go somewhere tonight. It didn't even occur to me until he was driving away. Then I figured I'd be okay in a lighted, busy shopping center."

"That was a major miscalculation." Anger seeped through despite his best efforts.

"Yes it was." She dropped her gaze to her half-empty bowl.

"I haven't been thinking straight for weeks. I'm so sorry I've let you down."

Her forlorn tone made his chest ache. A medley of emotions roiled in his stomach. Anger won out. "More like scared the crap out of me." He didn't try to keep the sharpness out of his voice this time.

She shuddered without looking up. Then her shoulders shook with a silent sob.

His anger melted. Eyes stinging, he reached across the table and picked up her hand. "It's okay, darlin'. We can talk about this tomorrow."

"No, let me get this out before I lose my nerve." She lifted her head. Her cheeks were wet. "I totally forgot about your presentation about bullying that night. It wasn't until I called home and Maria said something that I remembered. And I blew off a lunch date with Rob. Again, I totally forgot about it. And you both let me off the hook, which made me feel worse, not better. I don't know what's wrong with me, but I'm so, so sorry."

He went around the table and pulled her to a stand, then kicked the chair sideways and sat on it himself, pulling her down onto his lap. "Darlin', darlin', it's okay."

She burst into tears. "No, it's not. Stop forgiving me. I've been a terrible wife and mother."

He wrapped his arms around her. "Sh, sh, it's–" He caught himself before he said *okay* again. "It's gonna be fine. You're gonna be fine. Josie's death has rattled you, that's all."

She cried for another minute, then swiped her cheeks with her fingertips.

He was sitting on his handkerchief and didn't particularly want to get up, so he handed her the paper napkin from next to her bowl.

She dried her eyes and wiped her nose, then grimaced.

"Another miscalculation," he teased.

She gave him a wan smile. "The doctor said I'm probably going to have a scar."

He secretly hoped that she did, at least a little one. Maybe if she saw it in her mirror each morning it would remind her not to go chasing after killers on her own.

She leaned into him and gingerly positioned her head against his chest. "I thought I was going to die."

He tightened his arms around her, his throat too clogged to say anything.

"I couldn't fight back. My hands were pinned under me." She sniffled. "I've had this false sense that I could handle whatever happened. Just because I have a brown belt in aikido."

All the comforting words that came to mind would also encourage her to be foolish again. So he kept his mouth shut and rocked her gently back and forth while she wept.

~~~~~~~~~

Kate woke in her own bed. She had a rip-roaring headache, her nose stung, and she'd gotten very little sleep because Skip had woken her up every hour or so to make sure she was okay.

But she smiled as she looked around the room. She was alive. She would heal. And she had confessed her sins to her husband.

She wasn't sure whether or not he had absolved her of those sins, but she felt lighter for having fessed up. For about the third time in her marriage, she solemnly vowed to herself not to keep anything from Skip. Except, of course, her clients' confidences.

And that was so often the rub. She'd get involved in something, like Josie's murder, where she had to honor that confidentiality. Maybe she *should* get out of this line of work.

She shook her head, which turned out to be a very bad idea. When the pain subsided some, she decided to think about that some other time. Her brain was too fuzzy from the abuse it had suffered the night before.

The bedroom door opened and Skip stuck his head in. "You're awake?"

"Yes."

"Good, because the munchkins have breakfast for you." He pushed the door the rest of the way open and stood aside.

Edie came in, walking slowly, a lap tray in her hands.

"Scrambled eggs and Maria's biscuits," Skip said. "Not too hard to chew."

She struggled up into a sitting position, leaning back against her pillow and the headboard. "Smells wonderful," she said, even though she couldn't smell much through her damaged nose.

Billy followed his sister across the room, carefully balancing a cup on a saucer in his hands. "Coffee, Mommy," he yelled.

Kate winced.

"Billy, you really need to work on keeping your voice down," Skip said. "Mommy's head is gonna hurt for a while."

The kids made it to the bed with minor spillage. Skip took the tray from Edie and settled it in front of Kate. Then he deposited the coffee cup on it.

She picked it up and gratefully lifted it to her mouth, taking a sip. The inside of her lower lip stung when the hot liquid hit it.

That reminded her that she must look like hell.

"Can you bring me a mirror?" she whispered to Skip who had sat down on his side of the bed.

He shook his head. "Not a good idea, darlin'. Eat your breakfast."

After breakfast she was ordered to stay in bed. She had no objection to that idea. Within minutes, she was sound asleep again.

She awoke with the nagging feeling that she was missing something.

Geez Louise, Kate, you never learn! Her inner voice sounded suspiciously like Skip's.

The bedroom door eased open and Skip moved quietly across the room toward their bathroom.

"Sweetheart," she said, "when you get a chance, could you bring me my briefcase. I think I left it in the living room yesterday."

He turned and raised his eyebrows at her, his lips pressed together.

"I brought some paperwork home. Might as well get it done

while I'm bedridden."

It was the truth, sort of. Josie's journals were made of paper.

He frowned at her, but he went and got her briefcase.

For the rest of the morning, she alternated between reading and napping.

Liz called mid morning to see how she was doing.

Kate reassured her that she would be fine in due course. "Can you check out a Dr. Laurie Blake for me? She's a veterinarian."

"Sure, but Skip said Lieutenant Anderson was investigating now, unofficially at least."

"She is, but... I don't have anything concrete to tell her about this woman. I just had the gut feeling last night that she was hiding something. And you're the best computer researcher I know."

Liz chuckled. "And one that can be bought with a little flattery. I'll see what I can find out."

Kate went back to reading Josie's journals.

When Skip brought her lunch, she started to hide the books under the covers, then remembered her new vow of transparency.

He put the lap tray off to one side and sat on the edge of the bed beside her. "Darlin'—"

She held up her hand. "There are still aspects of this investigation that only I will pick up on because I knew Josie. And the sooner her killer is caught, the sooner we can relax and get on with life. You can't pay Manny to babysit me forever."

"I was seriously considering it," Skip said.

She wasn't at all sure he was joking.

"Look, I'll make you some promises, okay? One, I won't investigate anything that doesn't require my special knowledge of Josie and her life. Two, I won't *actively* do anything but read," she held up the journal, "unless I'm absolutely sure it's safe, and even then I will definitely take Manny with me. I have no desire to have another close encounter with that thug who jumped me."

"I got the impression last night that you were going to let go of this obsession."

"I am. I will. There's really only a couple things that would need my knowledge of Josie anyway, and once I've checked out those loose ends, I will gladly let Judith handle the rest."

He gave her a skeptical look. "And these couple of things are?"

She sighed. "I honestly can't remember. That's part of why I'm re-reading her journals. But something's nagging at my brain."

He turned his head, stared off across the room. "I've tried to be patient..." His voice trailed off.

Her throat closed. She grabbed his hand. "You've been more than patient. More than I deserve."

He looked back at her, his eyes muddy brown. "I want this crap out of our lives!"

She swallowed hard. "So do I."

He looked away again. Then he took a deep breath and blew it out. "You're right. That's not gonna happen until this case is solved and the killer's locked up."

He pushed himself to a stand.

She hung onto his hand for an extra beat. "You're too good to me."

He looked down at her and a slow smile spread across his face. "Yes, I am, but I can't help myself." He leaned down and gently kissed the top of her head. "I love you."

She returned the smile. "I love you too."

He shook his head slightly. "Just don't ever put me through another evening like last night."

She shuddered. "Don't worry. I won't."

.

By dinnertime, she had finished re-reading both journals. The older one had revealed no new insights. She'd stared at the suicide note for a few minutes, before skimming through the most recent journal again.

The niggling feeling that she was missing something was stronger. It was related somehow to the suicide note, she decided as she stared at it again. But she had no idea what exactly she wasn't seeing.

The newer journal had reminded her that she never had caught up with Bill Coleman. She needed to tell Judith that he might know something useful.

~~~~~~~~~

Skip didn't even think about his appointment with Sister Michelina until two hours after it was supposed to have happened. He was a little surprised that the nun hadn't called him when he didn't show up. He'd given her his cell number, and she didn't seem the type who stood for people not doing what they said they would do.

He checked his phone. No messages. That reinforced his earlier sense that she was not eager to see him.

Sure enough when he called her, she hemmed and hawed about rescheduling, claiming a busy schedule.

How busy can a retired nun be?

Finally, she agreed to see him on Wednesday afternoon.

He felt a little guilty when he got off the phone. He'd admonished Kate to turn everything over to Judith, but he was still pursuing this angle himself.

It was hardly the same thing, however. He was an experienced investigator and he carried a gun. He could certainly handle interviewing a nun!

And *he* hadn't been the one who'd been attacked at knife point.

CHAPTER TWENTY-FIVE

Kate was once again served breakfast in bed on Sunday, but by mid-morning she was tired of being prone. Moving slowly to keep her skull from coming apart, she headed for the bathroom. She showered, carefully avoiding getting the back of her head wet. The doctor had said the dressing on her wound could be removed after a couple of days, and then she could wash her hair.

She could hardly wait. In addition to the pounding headache, her scalp itched like crazy.

Her reflection in the mirror wasn't quite as scary as the day before. But she still had very little color in her face, unless you counted the vivid bruise on her forehead where she'd connected with the pavement after being knocked out.

She slowly pulled on jeans and a loose shirt, and then made her way to the kitchen.

She stopped short in the doorway. Maria sat at the table, sipping a cup of tea. "You didn't go to church this morning?" Kate asked.

Maria looked up. "I not want to leave you alone, and Skip, he really want to go."

Hm, wonder what that means.

They attended church fairly regularly, but they weren't fanatics about it. Maria, on the other hand, was a devout Catholic. She never missed Sunday Mass if she could help it.

Maria blessed her with a smile. "I tink he have *mucho* thanksgiving prayers to say."

Kate pursed her lips. Her housekeeper had been hanging

around Skip too long. She was taking on his mind-reading abilities.

"You want some tea?" Maria stood up. "Water already hot. I get for you."

Kate's protest that she could get it herself died on her lips. Her legs were feeling wobbly. "Yes, thanks." She pulled out a chair and sat at the table.

Maria returned with a steaming mug and the jar of honey.

Kate added a dollop of honey to her tea and stirred. "So how are things going with Eduardo?"

Maria gave a slight shake of her head. "I not sure."

"You still haven't given him an answer?"

"No. I say I need some time apart to tink, but he keep calling me."

"I thought you had a date Friday night?" Kate suppressed a shudder. If only Maria hadn't been out, then her children wouldn't have been subjected to the trauma of being dragged to that parking lot.

Maria sighed. "He keep pushing. So I finally go to his place for a while Friday. We had dinner with de kids."

"How do you get along with them?"

"Fine. Dey good kids."

"So what's the issue?"

"Issue?" Maria gave her a quizzical look that said she didn't understand the word in that context.

"The problem. What's making you hesitate?"

Maria shook her head again. "I not know. Everything fine 'til he ask me to marry him."

"Are you sure you love him?" Kate said then quickly added, "Feel free to tell me to butt out if I'm getting too nosy."

Maria gave her another small smile. "*Sí*, I do love him. He very nice man."

Kate waited a beat. "But?"

Maria took a sip of her tea. "Before, sometimes we go out, sometimes we with kids, but he pay *mucho* attention to me. He not neglect his kids, but he, how you say, had his eyes on me?"

"He was focused on you."

"*Sí*. Now he focused on kids. It like we married already."

Kate stomach twisted. It was what she'd feared from the beginning, but she took no pleasure in being right. "He's taking you for granted?"

"Not all de time…" Maria trailed off.

"Do you think he loves you?"

Maria had her mug halfway to her mouth. She lowered it to the table without taking a sip. "I tink dat is de problem." Her accent was thickening, a sign that her emotions were stirred up. Sometimes it was the only sign, since Maria was good at hiding her feelings.

She lapsed into silence without elaborating.

"What do you mean?" Kate prompted.

"I tink he like me but maybe not love me. I tink maybe he mostly look for a *madre* for his children."

Sadly, I think so too.

Maria went quiet again. This time, Kate let the silence settle around them.

"We get along good. Kids are great. I could have good life with them. But I wonder what we have when kids are grown and leave de house."

Kate was glad that Maria was really thinking this through. She wasn't nearly as naive about love and marriage as Kate had thought.

"When I tink about dat, then I wonder if I would be… how you say, when get more and more angry over time?"

"Resentful."

"*Sí*, I be resentful, because I would have missed out on Billy and Edie's growing-up time."

"May I make a suggestion?"

"*Sí*."

"If you love him, then talk to him about all this. Tell him you wonder if he is looking more for a mother for his children than for a mate for himself. Tell him your fears about the future."

Maria turned her head away, stared across the room at the refrigerator. "Dat not easy. In my country, men and women no talk about such things. You either love and say, '*Sí*, I marry you' or you decide not love and not marry."

"But wouldn't you talk about problems after you're married?"

"Not too much. Mostly you just put up wid each other. You have married, for better or worse."

Kate picked up Maria's hand and held it between both of hers. "But talking about it can make it better, and not talking about things can make it worse."

Maria nodded. "Okay, I try talking to him." She pulled her hand loose and rose from the table. "You want more tea?"

"No, but could you bring me my cell phone? It's in the bedroom." Walking that distance, short as it was, felt beyond her right now.

When Maria returned with her phone, Kate scrolled through her contacts. Judith Anderson had given Skip her cell phone number Friday night, and he had programmed it into Kate's contacts yesterday. "So it's really easy to pass along information," he'd said, giving her a hard look. The message had been clear–let Judith handle the investigating.

"Way ahead of you," Judith replied, when Kate suggested that William Coleman, aka Father Bill, might know something about Josie's childhood that related to the case. "I've already talked to everybody related to St. Bartholomew's, past and present."

"Did he have anything useful to say?"

"Nada. Said he barely remembered Josie, that she was a cute kid, but that's all he could recall about her."

"He should have crossed paths with her again later," Kate said. "He was at the high school she attended. I think he was in the administration."

"Hmm, he didn't say anything about that. What's you're take on that janitor?"

Kate moved in her chair. Pain shot down her back. "Ouch."

"You okay?"

"Yeah, in addition to a head five times its normal size, my back is sore where that bastard kneeled on me. The janitor's description matches a face in one of Josie's dreams and in some flashbacks she used to have."

"Yeah, Skip told me all that."

Kate took a sip of her now tepid tea. "He might very well have abused Josie in some way. He may have been the man who, quote 'made her take her clothes off.'"

"Could he be the guy who attacked you?" Judith asked.

"Quite possibly. I didn't see the guy's face, but his voice was gravelly and his breath stank."

"Gravel voice matches," Judith said. "I didn't get close enough to him to smell his breath, but he's a bit unkempt in general. And of course, he disavowed all knowledge of you or Josephine Hartin."

"Wait. There's another possibility. The guy who attacked me could've been hired by Phillip Hartin." Kate told Judith about her meeting with Nancy Hartin and the less-than-friendly call later from her husband.

Judith cleared her throat. "You do realize that this is one of the most influential men in the area we're talking about?"

"Hey, I'm just telling you what happened. Why would he object to my contacting his wife? Mrs. Hartin is certainly capable of taking care of herself." Something else was making Kate's brain itch besides her dirty scalp. "Hey, that threatening note I got, do you have it handy?"

"Hang on. It's in my briefcase." Paper rustling. "I think I know what you're going to say. This note's well written, by a person with a better education than our janitor. He dropped out of high school."

"Yeah, and even if the guy who attacked me wasn't the janitor, his speech and personal hygiene..." She shuddered slightly at the memory of rank breath against her cheek. "They didn't imply that he was a well-educated man. So we've got at least two people involved, and someone–Phillip Hartin and/or the Catholic

Church–is putting on the pressure to keep us from investigating."

A long silence. Kate was waiting to be chastised for the *us*.

Instead, Judith said, "I never said I was being pressured not to investigate."

Kate chuckled. "Yeah, well I'm pretty good at hearing what people aren't saying, Lieutenant."

A shorter pause this time. "Yes, you are." Judith's tone was lighter. "Call me if you think of anything else."

"Will do." Kate disconnected.

Hearing what people aren't saying.

Yes, she was good at that, and she had also been raised Catholic, understood the Church and its idiosyncrasies. She might be able to get more out of Father Bill than Judith had. With the police, he'd be likely to give the party line, either because he'd been told by his superiors back then to keep his mouth shut or he considered anything that Josie had told him as confidential.

Or he might claim he didn't know anything if he was involved in the abuse himself. Kate would certainly prefer that he was the abuser rather than Father Sam. But when she'd re-read the entry yesterday about Father What-A-Waste, it had definitely sounded like Josie liked and trusted him.

Kate put her hand on the table and pushed herself to a stand. Both her head and her back–which had stiffened up from sitting–protested the movement. She took her phone with her as she shuffled back to the bedroom. She needed to call clients to reschedule them. There was no way she would be working tomorrow, and maybe not on Tuesday.

It was a delight to be able to eat dinner with her family. After a long afternoon nap, she was starting to feel more like herself again, although still sore and with a splitting headache. Only once did she catch herself wishing the kids were in bed already so she could talk to Skip about Josie's case. She quickly banished that impatience and refocused on her children's chatter.

She was still deemed enough of a convalescent by Skip and

Maria to be relieved of bedtime duties. She hugged and kissed each of the children before they went upstairs for their baths.

Edie clung to her for a moment. "It's okay, sweetie," Kate whispered into her hair. "I'm safe, you're safe. We're all safe."

She felt the child's head move in a nod against her shoulder. Her heart ached. She wanted to erase Edie's memory of Friday night, even more than she wished she herself could forget it. She held the child away from her by her shoulders and looked her in the eye. "Everybody's safe and we're going to stay that way."

She knew it was a lie even as the words left her lips. Her husband worked in a dangerous profession and there were no guarantees in life. She'd always tried not to lie to her children, but the desire to restore her daughter's innocence had overridden that for a moment.

She didn't take the words back though, nor try to explain. She suspected Edie knew they were only a reassurance, not a guarantee. Despite her young age, she'd already been exposed to several examples of the fickleness of fate, and sadly of humankind's fascination with violence, starting with the senseless death of her biological father before she was born. Kate hugged Edie again and sent her upstairs to Maria, who was running her bath.

Kate made her way to the sofa and was thumbing through the last journal again when Skip came downstairs after story time. He settled down beside her and laid an arm gently across her shoulders.

"Here we devised those nice signals the other night," Kate said, "and then didn't even have a chance to use them."

"Well, we can remedy that." He turned her face toward him and kissed her tenderly.

When they came up for air, she said, "I talked to Judith today." She recounted the conversation to him. "We're pretty sure that janitor was my attacker, but there's no way to prove it."

Skip's jaw was now tight. "We'll prove it, somehow."

She read his thoughts. "Don't you go after him, not after all the scoldings you've given me about doing dangerous things."

He gave her a grim smile. "How 'bout if I take Manny and Mac? I'm sure they wouldn't mind helping me."

She shook her head. Her insides were trembling at the thought of Skip up against that knife. He could hold his own and then some in a fist fight, but knives were a different matter entirely. "Let's see if the law can come up with something first."

Time to steer the subject away from the attack on her. "I'm wondering if I can get more out of the former priest than Judith did. I could take Manny with me and have him stay in the next room. I doubt this Coleman guy would talk in front of him."

Skip frowned. "I'll go talk to him."

"Well, I was thinking that I have the advantage of a Catholic background. I know what buttons to push."

"Maybe, but I'm pretty good at getting men to talk, one guy to another."

"So you think your advantage is greater than mine?"

He wiggled his hand back and forth in a maybe, maybe-not gesture. "Probably about the same, but different. Tell you what. You take the follow-up session with the nun and I'll tackle Coleman. Then if we both come up with *nada* we'll switch off and try yet again. They really are our best bet at finding out what happened at that church and who would be willing to kill to cover it up. But don't even think about going anywhere near Coleman without Manny."

"Okay, it's a deal. I'll call Sister Michelina tomorrow and tell her I'm coming instead of you."

"Might be better if you just show up," Skip said. "She was pretty resistant to rescheduling the appointment."

"Hm, that says she does know something."

"Well, something she doesn't want to talk about. It may or may not be related to Josie's death."

Kate thought of something that Skip would need to know if he was going to interview Bill Coleman. "I rechecked the reference to Father What-A-Waste in the journal. It doesn't indicate whether or not Josie actually interacted with Coleman much at the high school. She may have just admired him from afar."

Skip was tilting his head to one side. "I didn't know there was any connection in high school. And what the hell is a Father What-A-Waste?"

Kate chuckled. "See, that's what I mean. Catholicism is its own little subculture. Catholic girls often call the young, handsome priests that behind their backs."

Skip grinned. "Okay, I get it, because of the whole celibacy thing."

"Right. Anyway there was a reference to Josie and her friends calling Father Bill that. He'd been transferred to the girls' Catholic high school by then and was in the administration. She refers to him as seeming 'heroic' but she doesn't explain that."

"If she saw him as a hero then it's unlikely he was one of her abusers."

Kate nodded, her chest aching at the thought that Father Sam was most likely the janitor's accomplice. He was the only other man at St. Bart's at the time who the Church would work so hard to protect.

Images flashed into her mind, snippets of memories from her childhood—wiggling in a pew, her starched dress scratchy against her skin; a younger Father Sam beaming down at her, as she showed him a picture she had drawn in Sunday School; staring in awe at the statue of the Virgin Mary above the votive candles; her excitement the day of her First Holy Communion. Then other memories flooded back—a nun's ruler smacking her knuckles, when she couldn't remember how to spell one of the words on that week's vocabulary list; the sense of free-floating guilt as she tried to think of something to tell the priest in confession.

She had been taught to love the Church as a child. But in her teens, she had found it lacking. Parting ways with it had been more a sin of omission than a conscious decision. Once away at college, she had slept in on Sundays like many of her classmates.

Skip cleared his throat. "Are we done comparing notes so we can move on to the other signal?"

She mustered a smile for him. "Afraid not. Going through the most recent journal again, I realized there's a page missing after the last entry."

Skip rubbed his chin. "So it wasn't the last entry after all. Is that the journal?" He pointed to the book that she had placed on the coffee table. "Judith said it was okay to keep it?"

"Yeah. She said it had already been handled enough that there was no use sending it to the lab."

His brow puckered. "Even so, that's not proper procedure."

Suddenly she knew why Judith had let her keep the journals. She turned a little more toward Skip. "I'll bet she's afraid if they're at the police lab or in the evidence room, they'll disappear, and they really are our only evidence as to what Josie was up to before she died."

He frowned. "Yeah, they might disappear if somebody in the police department is helping with the cover-up, which is quite possible since she was pressured to leave the case alone."

"But who in the police department would do that?"

He shrugged. "Someone who was involved in the original cover-up maybe? Like a beat cop who got wind of what was going on at the church but was bribed to keep quiet. And now that cop may be amongst the brass."

Kate sat up straighter. "Bribery might not have been necessary if the cop was a good Catholic."

"What do you mean?"

"Say the cop sees something, or is told something by one of the children at St. Bart's. It's unlikely that Josie was the only victim there. And a priest or a bishop tells him not to report it, that the church will deal with it quietly. It will be better for the children if they don't have to go through a trial, yada, yada."

"Yeah, that probably wouldn't fly today." Skip picked up the journal. "But it might have in the early nineties. The whole scandal about abuse in the church was just beginning to come to light then."

He leafed through the pages. "Hang on. I'll be right back."

He returned with a pencil in his hand and sat next to her again. "Oldest detective trick in the book, no pun intended." He started rubbing the side of the pencil point gently over a page in the journal.

She sucked in her breath in horror. Then she saw the faint white letters appearing and realized what he was doing. "Doesn't that screw it up as evidence in court?"

"No more than the fact that you've handled it repeatedly and carried it around in your briefcase."

She leaned over to get a better look at what his efforts were producing. Her back screamed at her. She sat back and tried to wait patiently for him to finish.

He finally put the pencil down, looked the page over quickly, then held the journal up for her to see.

She squinted at it. There were a few clear words, but not many.

.... *kid* ..... *over again*....... *terrified* ...... *.confronti ..g.*..................... *no danger.*........... *not listening.*

I .... *wrong. That's* .... *write his name,*................. *journal.* .... *find out.*................................... *paranoid* .... *days for informa.*...................... *hands.*............... *to slander.*..................*m wrong.*

The next paragraph started with something that looked like a smiley face.

W......... *in case th.*................ *I'm wrong,.. told Sphinx where* ... *going... lol.*

"Who's Sphinx?" Skip asked.

"Her dog."

"Great. So she told her dog where she was going, and then makes a joke about it. Was she an idiot?"

Kate bristled and pulled away from him some. "No, but when she was feeling even somewhat manic... Well, people with bipolar, when they're manic, can sometimes feel invincible. I don't think she was quite there, but she obviously underestimated the danger of this confrontation she was going to have."

"Obviously." Skip wrapped his arm around her shoulders

again. "Sorry, I didn't mean to insult your client."

Her flash of anger melted. "I'm the one who should apologize. I'm being hypersensitive."

He was silent for a minute, staring into space. "You know, I think that's one of the things I love about you. It was certainly something that impressed me when we were dating, that you're so fiercely protective of your clients. Once you take on a case, you're really dedicated to helping them any way you can."

"Yeah, well it makes the job more stressful sometimes. I should probably work on not being quite so 'fierce' about it." She made quote marks in the air.

He tilted his head to one side. "Nah, then you wouldn't be you."

Her chest swelled with warmth. It spread downward. She smiled up at him. "I think it's time for that other signal now."

He looked down at her, his eyebrows slightly raised. "You sure?"

"Yeah, but you need to be very gentle. I've still got a jackhammer doing its thing in my head."

He grinned. "I can do gentle. And maybe I can make you forget the jackhammer for a bit."

~~~~~~~~

Kate jolted upright in bed. Searing pain ricocheted inside her skull. She put a hand on each side of her head, praying it wouldn't explode.

Her memory had coughed up the answer to at least part of her niggling feeling.

When the pain in her skull had subsided some, she carefully slid out of bed and padded across the room to her dresser. Her briefcase was on the floor next to it.

She fumbled around in the dark until she found its handle, then carried it into the bathroom, closed the door and turned on the light. Sitting down on the closed toilet lid, she searched in the case for the piece of paper.

She stared at the suicide note and nodded her head, then

wished she hadn't.

She knew now where else she had seen those vague lines from photocopying–on the original clonazepam prescription at the pharmacy. There had been a couple of horizontal lines on it.

Had someone cobbled together a bogus prescription?

Kate dug a pad and pen out of the briefcase and wrote herself a note to call Judith about it in the morning. She was pretty sure she wouldn't forget, but a concussed brain couldn't be trusted.

In the dark bedroom, she put the briefcase back next to her dresser and carried the pad over to her nightstand.

Skip suddenly turned over in his sleep, startling her. She dropped the pad on the floor.

She barely kept from screaming in pain when she tried to lean over to get it. Feeling around with her bare foot instead, she had no luck finding it.

She'd have to trust her concussed brain after all, and even if she did forget, she'd see the notepad on the floor when she got out of bed in the morning.

CHAPTER TWENTY-SIX

Wednesday morning, Kate studied her face in the mirror. She didn't look quite as gruesome as she had. The bruise on her forehead was now a lovely shade of light purple fringed with yellow. Her nose was still a bit red and puffy, but the cut didn't look that bad. The intern had done a good job of stitching it up.

Kate made a mental note to avoid turning her back to her clients if she could. The scabs in the middle of the shaved lump on the back of her head were an unsettling sight.

She hoped her energy held out. Even though she didn't have a full day of clients, there was the appointment this afternoon with the nun to get through as well.

It had taken some major re-juggling to clear Monday and Tuesday, and to re-schedule her last two clients for today. She hoped she was fully recovered by next week. It was going to be a rough one, with shortened lunch breaks and extra sessions tacked on to the end of most days.

At least she wouldn't have the stress of driving and dealing with traffic. She was being chauffeured by Manny for the foreseeable future.

Liz called Kate while she and Manny were en route to her office. "Sorry this took so long, but I did a lot of looking for stuff that wasn't there."

"Hunh?" Kate said.

"You'll understand in a minute. Are you sitting down?"

Butterflies fluttered in her chest. She wasn't sure if they were from anxiety or excitement. Maybe some of both. "Yes."

"Okay, first Laurie Blake did not start life as a Laurie. She was Lawrence Blake until twelve years ago."

"Holy crap!" The butterflies bounced around her rib cage. "No wonder she seemed to be hiding something."

"Yeah, but would someone kill to hide the fact that they were transgender in this day and age?"

The butterflies subsided. "Probably not, especially since she was relatively open about being gay."

"Okay, well here's another secret, and this one she might kill to keep. The thing I was looking for that I couldn't find. Neither Laurie nor Lawrence Blake went to any veterinarian school in the U.S. And she's not licensed by the State of Maryland to practice as a veterinarian."

Kate realized her mouth was hanging open. She closed it.

"I finally found a record of her graduation," Liz continued, "as Laurie, eight years ago. The vet school is in Jamaica, and apparently it's not accredited in the United States."

"Maybe she couldn't get into a school in the states, or the one in Jamaica was a lot cheaper?"

"Could be," Liz said. "But that's pretty risky to set up a practice without a license. You'd think someone would have found her out by now."

Kate shoved an unruly curl out of her face. "Not necessarily. Nobody's ever asked to see my credentials, not even my landlord when I first rented the office space. She could go about her business for a very long time, maybe even an entire career, as long as nobody tried to file a complaint against her with the veterinarian licensing board."

"Still, I say that takes a lot of nerve."

"I agree, but she'd already reinvented herself by going from a he to a she. Why not reinvent herself professionally as well."

"Yeah, makes sense," Liz said. "So are you going to tell Lieutenant Anderson about this?"

"I think I have to. I might have been barking up the wrong

tree all along here."

Liz chuckled. "No pun intended. You thinking Josie's death isn't related to St. Bartholomew's after all?"

"Maybe not." Kate still believed that Josie had been abused at the church, but that might not have been what got her killed.

After signing off with Liz, Kate called Judith's cell phone. The call went to voicemail. She left a detailed message about Laurie Blake.

Kate hated to do it. If the vet had nothing to do with Josie's death, she'd just destroyed her livelihood. And maybe worse than that, if there were criminal penalties for practicing as a veterinarian without a license.

~~~~~~~~

Kate was gobbling down her sandwich at lunchtime, in between returning phone calls, when she remembered the insight about the prescription slip.

Crap! Her concussed brain *had* forgotten it. No doubt she'd find that pad kicked under the edge of the bed.

She reached for her phone, then glanced at the clock on her desk. She was out of time. Her twelve-thirty client would be out in the waiting room.

That prescription slip nagged at her all during her next two clients' sessions. Which was not good. She'd already been having trouble concentrating, thanks to her still fuzzy brain.

As she and Manny left her office at two-forty, she was considering calling Judith from the car. She shook her head and realized this was still not a good idea. When the ping pong ball of pain had stopped ricocheting inside her skull–at least it wasn't a jackhammer anymore–she said to Manny, "I need to make a stop before we head for Essex."

"Where?" he asked.

"A pharmacy." She let him assume she was picking up a medication for herself.

Okay, so investigating the clonazepam prescription didn't necessarily require her expertise, but she was hoping a personal appeal to the pharmacist's conscience would get him to open up.

At the pharmacy counter, the man recognized her before she opened her mouth. His eyes went wide. "What happened to you?"

"Close encounter with a bad guy," Kate said.

The pharmacist's sympathetic expression faded. "Look, I don't have time to talk to you right now. My assistant quit on me without notice, and I'm swamped."

Kate glanced around. Again the place was hardly bursting at the seams with customers. She suspected the assistant's defection was being used as an excuse.

"I won't keep you long, Dr...." She glanced at the nametag pinned to the pocket of his white coat to remind herself of his name. "Dr. Keller. Indeed, I'll get right to the point. I can understand why you wanted to cover up about that clonazepam prescription that wasn't handled properly, but we have no desire to get you in trouble."

The pharmacist blanched. Manny was looking at her funny but he stayed silent.

"We *do* need your cooperation," she said. "That medication was used to kill a young woman, and then her death was made to look like a suicide."

Red splotches now adorned the pharmacist's pale cheeks. "That's not my fault."

She ignored the interruption and pointed to her face. "A killer's out there, and he did this to me. We need to stop him before he hurts or kills someone else."

Dr. Keller stared at her, his eyes wide again, his mouth working soundlessly. Then his shoulders dropped. "What do you need to know?"

"What did you do with the original of that prescription?"

"I have it. I genuinely thought it was missing when that other detective was here."

Manny's eyebrows had gone up at the words *other detective*.

"That's why I denied knowing anything about it," Keller said. "But then I found it later. It had been misfiled."

And you didn't call the police because your lie had dug the hole you were in even deeper.

Kate opted not to say that out loud. It would only put the guy on the defensive. "May I see it, please?"

He nodded and went into his office. After a minute, he came back with a piece of paper and handed it to her.

She'd handled it before so she saw no reason not to again. As she'd remembered, the vague lines were there on this supposed original prescription slip–one just under the doctor's printed name and office address and another just above his signature.

She leaned across the counter a bit and pointed to the lines. "I believe this prescription was cut and pasted from another one by that doctor."

Dr. Keller went pale again. "I don't know who filled it."

"Aren't you supposed to keep good records of that, especially for a controlled substance?" She knew he was.

He nodded once, then shook his head and swallowed hard, his Adam's apple bobbing in his throat. "Please don't report me. I could lose my license. I do keep good records, but there's nothing in there about this prescription. I have no idea what happened. We have a couple part-time pharmacists that work weekends and evenings. They both denied having filled it."

"Okay, I'm going to keep this prescription slip for now." She hefted her briefcase onto the counter and slid the prescription inside the folder for Josie's case. "I'll try to keep you from getting in trouble. But when my lieutenant comes here to talk to you later, you need to answer all her questions honestly."

As they walked toward the front door of the pharmacy, Manny whispered out of the side of his mouth, "*My* lieutenant?"

"Shh."

Manny held the door for her, then followed her out onto the sidewalk. "You shouldn't have taken that prescription slip. The lieutenant's gonna be pissed."

"There's a lot of things I shouldn't be doing regarding this case, and the lieutenant would be more pissed if the slip mysteriously disappeared again."

Once Kate was settled into the passenger's seat of Manny's car, she pulled out her phone. She got Judith's voicemail again. As best she could, she explained in a message about the prescription and the encounter with the pharmacist. She disconnected.

Manny was threading his way through Towson's heavy traffic, headed for the Beltway. "Are you sure Lieutenant Anderson is okay with us continuing to investigate this?"

"I'm not sure and I'm not going to ask. She'll tell us to butt out if she doesn't want our help." Kate didn't want to tell Manny that the lieutenant was actually investigating Josie's death on the q.t., disguised as an investigation into the attack on her, and would probably welcome anything they could come up with. The fewer people who knew about the pressures from above at the police department, the better off Judith would be.

Skip was getting annoyed. He'd tried several times on Monday and Tuesday to catch up with William Coleman, at his office and at home. No luck either place. He hadn't wanted to leave a message and give the guy time to think about what he wanted to tell him, or *not* tell him. The plan had been to find out where he was, then show up unannounced. But finally Skip had been forced to leave a vague message on the man's home voicemail.

That was yesterday afternoon, and the ex-priest still hadn't called him back. Maybe he thought Skip was a telemarketer.

He might need to be a little less vague. He called the brokerage firm where the man worked. Once again, the receptionist said that Mr. Coleman wasn't available.

"When will he be available?"

"I'm not sure, sir. Would you like me to transfer you to his voicemail?"

This time, Skip said yes.

"Mr. Coleman, my name is Skip Canfield. I'm a private investigator. I'm looking into a matter that you might be able to help me with. It doesn't directly involve you, but you may have some useful information. Please give me a call as soon as possible. It's very important."

He disconnected and blew out air. He was getting the distinct impression that this dude was ducking him intentionally.

Sister Michelina herself opened the heavy door of the convent. Her jaw dropped when she saw Kate's face. "What happened to you?"

"It's a bit of a long story. May I come in?"

The nun looked up and down the street. "Yes, but I have an appointment. He should be here any moment."

"The man you have an appointment with is my husband."

"He said he was a private investigator."

"He's that too. I've come in his place."

Sister Michelina took a deep breath and let it out slowly. "You'd best come in."

"This is my bodyguard," Kate said as she and Manny stepped over the threshold. "He can sit out here in the foyer."

The nun nodded silently and gestured toward a wingback chair against one wall. Then she led the way to the small parlor where she and Kate had talked before.

There was no offer of tea and cookies this time.

As Kate took a seat, rage boiled up inside of her. At this woman, at the pharmacist, and Dr. Kraft for that matter. All these people were lying to cover their butts, or someone else's. Meanwhile a killer was getting away with murder and with beating her up.

A small, more lucid part of her brain told her that the anger was a delayed reaction to the mugging. Nonetheless, she decided Sister Michelina was a justifiable target for that anger. The nun was avoiding eye contact with her.

"Take a good look at my face, Sister," she said in a sharp tone.

The nun glanced her way, winced, then looked away again.

"I know for sure now that Josie Hartin was murdered. I received a threatening note telling me to stop investigating, and when I didn't," Kate waved her hand toward her face, "this happened." She turned her head around so the nun could see the back. "And this."

A sharp intake of air. "Who did that to you?"

Kate turned her head back around. The nun was now looking directly at her.

"I didn't see his face, but I've got a pretty good idea who it was. He's small potatoes though. Someone else was involved in whatever happened at St. Bart's when Josie was a kid. Someone the Catholic Church was willing to protect. A mere janitor they would've thrown under the bus."

Another sharp intake of air. The nun covered her face with her hands. Kate heard mumbled words, but couldn't make them out.

Not until the nun dropped her hands again. "In your Son's holy name. Amen," she whispered and crossed herself.

She leaned forward and met Kate's eye. "I was asking for forgiveness because I'm about to break one of my vows." The no-nonsense persona was back.

Sister Michelina suddenly leaned to one side and reached for a dark object on the lower shelf of a small table beside her chair.

Kate's heart went into overdrive. She opened her mouth to yell for Manny.

CHAPTER TWENTY-SEVEN

Skip called the ex-priest's office again. This time he was told that Mr. Coleman had left early. "Was he going home?"

"I'm not sure, sir. Would you like his voicemail?"

"No, thanks. I'll catch up with him later."

He disconnected and sat back in his desk chair. Rough estimate, he'd spent at least an hour now, in five-minute increments, trying to catch up with this guy. Might as well waste some more time going to his house to see if he was there. If he was, Skip could totally take him by surprise.

Which might be a very good thing, since Skip now suspected this guy knew exactly what he was calling about. Maybe the same big wheel who had stifled Judith's investigation had contacted Coleman and pressured him to keep quiet.

Skip pushed himself to a stand and headed out of his office.

Or maybe Coleman was involved in whatever happened at St. Bart's. Kate had said that Josie seemed to like and trust him. What was it she'd called him in her journal–her hero? You'd think if the guy had abused her, she'd have hated him, or at least been afraid of him. Even if she didn't remember the actual abuse, wouldn't the emotional associations still be there?

He made a mental note to ask Kate about that. But just in case this guy turned out to be something other than an innocuous, middle-aged ex-priest... Skip took out his cell phone as he walked across the parking lot to his truck. He punched his partner's speed dial number.

It rang four times and went to voicemail, which meant Rose

was interviewing someone related to the insurance fraud case she was working on. That was the only time either of them put their phones on vibrate and didn't answer them.

He left a message telling her where he was going, then disconnected. Putting his own phone on vibrate, he dropped it into his shirt pocket and climbed into his truck.

Skip drove slowly past Coleman's house. There were no cars in the driveway, but they could be in the over-sized garage attached to the large colonial. Had to be at least five bedrooms. Coleman had done well for himself in the secular world.

He circled the block and pulled his truck to the curb just beyond the entrance to their driveway.

A petite woman, almost painfully thin, with long, shiny auburn hair, answered the door. Skip guessed her to be in her mid-thirties.

"Mrs. Coleman, I'm sorry to bother you, but I need to talk to your husband about something."

The woman blinked. "My husband? What about?"

"Is he home?"

"No, not yet. He took our sons to baseball practice. What did you want to talk to him about?"

"I'm a private investigator, ma'am. I'm working a case related to where he used to work. He might have some information that would be useful."

"Where he used to work? He's only ever worked at Brown and Hall Investments."

"From when he was a priest," Skip said.

Her brown eyes went wide and her mouth made a small o. Then her expression quickly shifted. She smiled and stepped back. "You're welcome to wait for him. He should be home soon." The woman held out a delicate hand in a come-in gesture.

This woman's a little too trusting for her own good, Skip thought as he entered the house.

"Would you like something to drink?" Mrs. Coleman asked. "Coffee, tea, a soda?"

"Coffee'd be good, ma'am."

"Please, call me Sybil. *Ma'am* makes me feel old." She ushered him into a spacious living room, then headed toward the back of the house. "I'll just be a minute," she said over her shoulder.

Skip studied the family photos covering most of one wall of the living room. It looked like the Colemans had five kids. In one picture, the eldest and her mother stood next to each other. If one didn't know better, they could be mistaken for sisters. There was an older boy, a teenager, and two younger ones. Skip couldn't tell which was older. They looked to be about the same age. The youngest child was another girl.

Mr. Coleman hadn't aged as well as his wife. In the later pictures, he was balding, with considerable gray in his remaining hair, and an expanding waistline.

Several minutes ticked by. Finally, Mrs. Coleman returned bearing a tray. "Sorry that took so long. I decided to make a fresh pot."

Kate was very glad she'd caught herself before screaming Manny's name. It would have been quite embarrassing to admit she'd thought a nun was going to shoot her... with a Bible.

Sister Michelina had held the book against her chest, over her heart. Then she'd put it in her lap and folded her hands on top of it.

"Which vow is that, Sister?" Kate said softly.

"Obedience." The nun cleared her throat, then tapped the Bible. "But this is a higher authority." She fell silent again, staring across the room, her eyes out of focus.

Kate knew the look well. She'd seen it on her clients' faces often enough as they stepped mentally back into the past.

"Mrs. Huntington, are you familiar with Saint Michelina?"

"No, Sister."

"I chose her as the saint whose name I would take along with my vows because she is the patron saint of mentally ill people, and of children who die before they have a chance to grow up. I had a younger sister. She was born with Down's syndrome, although we didn't call it that back then. It was just called retarded. She wandered off when my mother was distracted by something, and fell in a pond on our neighbor's property. She didn't know how to swim."

Kate's throat tightened. "I'm so sorry."

The nun turned her head toward Kate, her eyes shiny. "I vowed that day to devote my life to innocent children, for you see, I was the distraction. I was fourteen, a miserable age, and I was constantly picking fights with my mother."

"You were still a child yourself."

Sister Michelina held up a hand. "I've long since come to terms with my guilt from back then. I was a teenager, doing what teenagers do. I certainly never intended to do anything that would harm my sister. I loved her. She was so sweet." Her voice broke. A tear wandered down her cheek. She swatted at it with her hand as if it were a pesky fly.

"So I took the name of Michelina, and I vowed to teach children, help them in any way I could, and of course protect them from harm. And I failed miserably." She took a deep breath. "Yes, there was abuse at St. Bartholomew's, and yes there was a priest involved."

Kate's heart sank. *Oh, Father Sam.*

"And when they were caught, yes, there was a cover-up. I was told in no uncertain terms by two priests, a monsignor and my mother superior that I would be breaking my vow of obedience if I told a soul, ever. I was also promised that the children involved would get free counseling and the culprits would be dealt with."

None of this surprised Kate. She should have been excited to have her theory confirmed, but all she felt was sad. "And neither of those things happened," she said quietly.

The sister shook her head. "No." She paused, blinking hard. "My child, will you pray with me?"

Kate was anxious to hear more details of what had happened at St. Bart's, but one could hardly say no when a nun asked you to pray with her. "Of course."

The elderly nun gingerly lowered herself from the chair onto her knees.

Kate started to slide off her chair. Pain shot up her spine and bounced around in her head. She gritted her teeth. "I'm afraid I can't kneel, Sister. I'm still pretty sore."

"That's fine, child." Sister Michelina smiled over at her. "I'm sure God will understand." She pulled a string of beads from her pocket. "Hail Mary, full of grace. The Lord is with thee..."

Kate suppressed a sigh. It wasn't going to be a short and simple prayer. The nun was going to say the whole dang rosary.

Kate had no choice but to join in.

Mrs. Coleman placed the tray on the coffee table and gestured toward the large sofa, covered in a flowered fabric. Skip sat down, and she settled onto the edge of a matching upholstered armchair.

She poured coffee into two china cups on the tray. "Sugar or cream?"

"Black's fine. I was admiring your family." Skip gestured toward the wall of photos. "Good-looking kids."

"Thanks. Catherine, our oldest, is sixteen, a junior in high school. Samuel's a sophomore. The twins are in middle school, and Bernadette, our youngest, will start there next year."

Skip tasted his coffee. It was excellent. He took a hearty swig. "You don't look old enough to have a sixteen-year-old daughter." The woman was so slender and delicate looking, he had trouble imagining her chasing five kids around the house.

Mrs. Coleman's cheeks turned a pale pink. "Thank you. You're very kind." She picked up her own cup, blew gently on the hot liquid and touched the cup to her lips.

"Not at all, just the truth," Skip said.

Mrs. Coleman's blush deepened as she lowered her cup. "Please, have a cookie." She pointed toward the plate next to the coffee carafe on the tray. "I was a young bride. I'd just turned twenty when Bill and I married. He's a little older than me. He was thirty-eight."

Eighteen years struck Skip as a lot more than *a little older*.

The man probably hadn't been out of the priesthood all that long when the couple tied the knot.

And as good Catholics, apparently no birth control had been in use, so Mrs. Coleman was most likely pregnant within the first year of marriage. That would put her at thirty-seven or eight.

Skip drank more coffee, then set the cup in its saucer. To be polite, he took a cookie. It was a plain sugar cookie and looked to be store-bought. He took a bite. It was stale.

"Did you know Mr.... uh, your husband, when he was still at the high school?" He would have been Father then, not Mister. But his wife might not like to be reminded of that.

Mrs. Coleman's face relaxed. She smiled–the second or third smile since he'd been there, but this one looked more genuine. "Yes, I was a student there, and then I worked in the office after graduation."

Skip tried to return her smile but his own felt kind of lopsided. He wasn't Catholic, but the concept of a young woman knowing her future husband in the capacity of a celibate priest felt kind of creepy to him. Of course it wasn't all that unusual for priests and nuns to fall in love and leave the church to get married. But somehow that seemed more innocent, more chaste, than a woman just barely out of her teens becoming enamored of a priest, and he with her. *Especially* he with her.

"Would you like some more coffee?" Mrs. Coleman asked.

"Sure. It's excellent."

"Thank you." She ducked her head as she poured. "I don't skimp when it comes to coffee beans. Bill loves this dark roast the best."

Skip eyed the half cookie resting in his hand, wishing he could get away with dunking it in the coffee. It would improve it significantly. How could someone make great coffee but serve store-bought cookies that were probably well past their best-used-by date?

Then again, considering how skinny this woman was, coffee was probably a more common staple in her diet than cookies.

Skip popped the cookie in his mouth and then took a swig of coffee to wash it down.

Mrs. Coleman picked up her own coffee and sat back in her chair. She rested the cup on her jeans-clad thigh. "Things were quite calm the first year that I worked there. I was only a file clerk then. But shortly after I was made Bill's secretary, I started hearing veiled rumors that one of the male teachers might have been doing some things that were not really appropriate."

Hmm, had they miscalculated? Had Josie been abused in high school, not at St. Bart's? But wait, she was just a kid when she told her mother about someone making her take her clothes off.

Sadness weighed on his chest at the thought that the young woman might have been abused at *both* places.

Belatedly it dawned on him that Mrs. Coleman was giving him information that most people wouldn't volunteer so readily. He kept his expression bland but he was now watching the woman more closely. He took another sip of coffee. "Did anyone investigate?"

"No not really. You have to realize it was the nineties. Society wasn't as tuned in to such things back then."

Yeah, even in the nineties it would have been investigated. Internally, at least. But maybe a lowly secretary wouldn't have heard about the investigation. "Who was the priest?"

"I didn't say it was a priest." Her tone was a little sharp.

Skip didn't have to be Catholic to know that a male teacher in an all girls school was most likely a priest. "I assumed that it was."

"Well, it could have been," Mrs. Coleman said, her conversational tone sounding a bit forced. "I never heard who it was exactly, except that it was definitely one of the teachers."

That struck Skip as odd. How would she know definitively it was a teacher when she didn't know the person's actual identity? He tilted his head to one side.

The room tilted in the other direction. He blinked. The room righted itself.

What the hell? Had he just imagined that the room shifted?

He tried to recall what he'd been thinking about. Oh yeah, why was this woman telling him about some teacher accused of abusing the girls at the Catholic high school?

But Sybil Coleman had changed the subject and was now regaling him with stories about her kids. "The children are involved in so many activities. Catherine's in the drama club. That's where she is right now, rehearsing. And all my boys are quite athletic. Sam plays football. The twins are at Little League practice, and Bernadette has a piano lesson this afternoon. I need to pick her up in a little while. So I hope this won't take too long."

You don't have to keep me entertained while I wait for your husband.

The words formed in Skip's brain but it seemed like too much effort to say them. His eyelids drooped. He hoped Coleman got home soon. This woman was putting him to sleep.

"Would you like more coffee?"

"No, I'm fine." His words sounded a bit slurred to his ears. He leaned forward and placed his almost empty cup in its saucer. The dishes rattled.

Mrs. Coleman frowned at him.

As he leaned back again, the room did a slow spin.

A part of his brain was telling him that something was wrong, but a strange euphoria had settled over him.

"Another cookie, Mr. Canfield?"

"No... thank you." The words left his mouth a couple beats after he'd thought them.

The woman launched into another story about one of her kids.

CHAPTER TWENTY-EIGHT

Kate tried to be patient as Sister Michelina worked her way through the decades of the rosary. Finally the nun said the final prayer and crossed herself.

Kate rose from her chair to help the elderly woman up off her knees.

When they were both seated again, Kate said quietly, "Thank you for telling me about Father Sam."

The nun looked at her, her face puckered in confusion. "Father Sam? Well, he was one of the ones who told me to keep quiet." The confusion cleared. "Oh, you're thinking he was the abuser. No, no. It wasn't him. The other one, he took the kids into the church basement and turned out all the lights. Then the janitor would take over and make them take their clothes off..."

The other one? Panic shot through her. *There was only one other priest at St. Bart's.*

The nun was still talking but Kate wasn't listening. Father Bill was the abuser, and Skip was planning to go talk to him today.

She jumped up and bolted for the foyer. "Manny!"

~~~~~~~~

Something jiggled in Skip's shirt pocket and made a funny, purring noise. It tickled. He tried to laugh but nothing came out.

His mouth was parched. He reached for his coffee cup. His hand jerked forward, several seconds after his brain had told it to move. It hit the edge of the saucer, rattling the cup.

Mrs. Coleman snatched the cup and saucer away. "Don't you dare break that. This set was my mother's." She narrowed her eyes at him. "I think we're about ready to get started here."

Adrenaline jolted through his system, but it did him no good. His muscles were no longer reliably obeying his brain's orders.

Mrs. Coleman had a cell phone in her hand–an old-style flip phone. Her smart phone sat on the coffee table. "Bill, I need you to come home. Now! Something's happened and I need your help. Have another of the parents bring the boys home after practice." She went quiet.

Skip's pocket jiggled and purred again. It registered that his own phone was vibrating with an incoming call. He somehow managed to fumble it out of his pocket. It fell on the floor.

"It's complicated. Just get here fast, before Catherine and Sam get home." Mrs. Coleman disconnected and stepped over to where Skip was fumbling around on the floor. She kicked his phone out of his reach.

He looked up at her and his head swam. "Wha'd ya do that for?" He wasn't sure if he actually got the words out or not.

Next thing he knew he was down on the floor on all fours, his butt having slid off the sofa. That struck him as funny. He rolled over onto his back, knocking against the coffee table and rattling the china. His stomach shook with laughter that wasn't coming out of his mouth.

His brain was trying to think. He knew he was in danger, but he felt surprisingly blasé about it. His gun. He should try to get it out. His arm just flopped around when he told it to go for the pistol.

Sybil Coleman leaned over him. She knocked his arm out of the way and slid her hand under his lower back. It came out with his gun in it.

She smiled down at him. "Don't worry, Mr. Canfield. It won't hurt a bit."

~~~~~~~~~

"Skip's not answering." Kate tried and failed to keep the panic out of her voice.

"Call Rose," Manny said from the driver's seat as he sped

along Eastern Boulevard toward the Baltimore Beltway.

She did so and quickly filled Rose in on what she'd found out and what she was afraid might be happening. She choked up a couple times but managed to get it all out.

"Skip left a message that he was going to this guy's house." Rose's voice was tense. "Do you have the address?"

"Yes," Kate said.

"Okay. Mac is with me. We're on our way there now. You guys get there as fast as you can. But Kate, *you* stay in the car."

Kate didn't bother to argue. She disconnected and stared out the windshield, willing the car to move faster. But Manny was already risking life and limb as he wove in and out of the traffic.

She prayed a cop didn't try to stop them for speeding. How would they ever explain all this and get him to let them go?

That reminded her of Judith Anderson. She called the lieutenant, and once again got voicemail. Where the hell was she that she'd have her phone off all this time?

To distract herself from the panic threatening to explode in her chest, Kate pulled the more recent journal out of the file and leafed through it. She came to the last page, light gray with pencil markings, and re-read the scattered words.

She grabbed her phone again and called Dr. Blake's number. When the receptionist answered, Kate didn't give her time to say anything.

"I've got to talk to Dr. Blake right away. It's extremely important, a matter of life and death."

Half a beat, then, "Hold on, please."

Kate counted off thirty seconds. "Come on," she muttered. Her mind veered to what might be happening to Skip right now. Bile rose in the back of her throat.

What she thought she was about to find out, would it make any real difference? Only to confirm what they already suspected.

A voice in her ear said, "Hello. Who's this?"

"Kate Huntington. I need to know something. Did you get Sphinx's crate from Josie's apartment?"

"Yeah." Dr. Blake's voice was hesitant. "Are you okay?"

No!

But Kate didn't take the time to answer her out loud. "Was there anything odd about the crate, maybe something scratched on it?"

"No... Wait. Damn! I'm sorry. I'd forgotten all about that."

"What?" Kate yelled, then stopped to suck in air, trying to calm herself.

"A piece of paper, taped on the underside of Sphinx's collar. But it didn't make any sense. It said Frobill on it."

Kate flipped back a page in the journal to verify what she already knew. Josie's periods were tiny o's.

"Could it have been F-R, period, B-I-L-L?"

"Yeah, I guess so. I threw it away."

"Thanks, Dr. Blake."

"What's going on?"

"I'll get back to you." Kate disconnected and looked down again at the journal in her lap. "So you really did tell Sphinx."

"What?" Manny said.

"Josie taped a paper with *Fr. Bill* on it under her dog's collar, then hinted in her journal that she'd told Sphinx where she was going, that day she was murdered."

Manny accelerated. He laid on the horn and veered around some cars, then whipped back in front of them. His tires squealed as he took the entrance ramp onto the Beltway.

CHAPTER TWENTY-NINE

Rose sat in her car, observing the Colemans' house. She'd tried her partner's cell phone. It rang several times, then went to voicemail.

That could mean he was in the middle of a tricky interview with someone. She hesitated to go to the door and perhaps interrupt the flow of things just as Skip was about to cajole the man into confessing, to child abuse if not murder.

Then again, he also wouldn't answer his phone if he was in trouble in there.

Mac slipped into the passenger seat, quietly closing the car door. "Didn't see any activity in the back. The front windows are too far off the ground to see in."

Rose narrowed her eyes as she peered at the large colonial. "Looks like the curtains are drawn anyway."

Her phone buzzed. She snatched it up off the console between the seats. "Hernandez."

"Rose, no time to explain." Kate's voice, frantic. "I got another piece of evidence. Coleman is definitely Josie's killer."

"How far away are you?"

"We're on the Beltway. Ten minutes, unless we get stopped for speeding."

"Tell Manny we're going in. You stay in the car!"

~~~~~~~~~

"What the hell are you doing, Sybil?" A male voice, startled and angry.

The face of the father in the pictures on the wall swam into

Skip's line of vision. The man looked horrified.

Help me!

"I had to incapacitate him, Bill. He's here about St. Bartholomew's."

"Dear God," the man bellowed. "What have you done?"

They stood over Skip, arguing.

Coleman grabbed his wife by the arms and shook her. "You little fool. I told you not to do this again."

Again?

"I can't let you go to jail." The woman's voice rose into a wail. "The children need you. I need you."

"Don't you get it? Now both of us will go to jail. Where does that leave the kids?"

"We just need to get rid of him. Then everything will be okay."

"No, Sybil. I'm not committing murder. I'm a Christian. I used to be a priest, for Christ's sake."

Ironic that you take Christ's name in vain in the same breath with "I'm a Christian."

The room was getting darker. Skip could barely keep his eyes open. He found it fascinating that he was having so little emotional reaction to what was happening.

"We have to call 911," the man said. "Get him to a hospital."

"I only gave him roofies. I wasn't going to hurt him."

Roofies! Had to have been in the coffee.

The image of the woman touching her cup to her lips, then lowering it again, swam into his mind's eye.

She didn't drink any of hers.

"Where the hell did you get roofies?" the man yelled.

"From work. I got them just in case something like this happened. I knew his wife was nosing around. I was afraid they'd find out about you eventually. Look, all we've got to do is put him in his car and drive him somewhere. When he wakes up, he won't even remember that he came to see us."

Skip was pretty sure that the memory blanks caused by the date-rape drug weren't that thorough. People usually did remember where they were and what they were doing *before* they were given the drug. But he wasn't about to tell Mrs. Coleman that her plan was flawed, even if he could have managed to make his mouth muscles cooperate.

"Everything will be fine." The woman's voice was steadier, more commanding. "Go move our cars out of the way so we can pull his into the garage. That way nobody will see us putting him in there."

Silence, a male grunt, then heavy footsteps receding.

A small hand slid into Skip's pants pocket and felt around.

Hey, stop that! I'm a married man.

The hand pulled something out of his pocket. Mrs. Coleman's face swam into view. Her eyes were hard. His own truck keys dangled from her fingers. "I tried to warn that nosy wife of yours." Her voice was low, harsh. "But you two couldn't leave it alone."

His keys clattered onto the coffee table, and she moved out of his view. He managed to turn his head a little. A very little.

How much of that damn stuff did she give me?

Despite the drug in his system, his heart rate kicked up a notch when he saw what was now in the woman's hands.

She plunged the needle into the small vial and drew clear liquid into the syringe. "This will take care of you. Then I have to figure out how to get rid of your wife."

CHAPTER THIRTY

Mac had made his way along the property line and was now hunkered beside a bush at the right, front corner of the house.

Rose hunched over and raced across the grass toward the weeping cherry tree in the middle of the lawn. As she neared the tree, the garage door rumbled and slowly slid up. Startled, Rose darted behind the trunk of the tree.

A paunchy, middle-aged man came out of the garage and walked to a car parked in the driveway.

That's our killer?

He got in and started the car.

Rose debated–should she try to get back to her car and follow this guy? Mac could check out the house.

But the man didn't go very far. He pulled past Skip's truck and parked the car at the curb. Then he got up and jogged back up the driveway.

A few seconds later, a minivan backed out of the garage.

Rose braced herself to bolt for her car as soon as he was a little bit up the street. Skip was probably in that van.

But again the man pulled out onto the street, parked the van there, and got out.

She held her breath as he walked within five feet of her hiding place. He was huffing a little.

He climbed the front porch steps and entered the house.

Movement in the corner of her eye. Rose turned her head. Manny's car had pulled up behind hers further down the block.

She held her hand up to Mac in a hang-on gesture. Then she

hunched over and darted back to the street.

Manny clicked his doors unlocked. Rose climbed into his backseat for a quick conference. She opened her mouth.

Kate pointed out the windshield. "Look!"

Rose followed her line of vision. A teenaged girl, with long red hair, was crossing the front yard.

Correction, a petite woman who looks like a teenager from a distance.

"Wait," Kate said. "I know that woman!"

"Who is she?" Rose said.

"The assistant who quit without notice."

"Huh?"

Kate shook her head. "Too complicated, but if she's Coleman's wife, it all makes sense."

The woman had reached the street. She raised her hand and pointed it toward Skip's truck.

Rose sucked in air.

"She's got his keys," Manny said.

The woman climbed into the truck.

Heart pounding, Rose grabbed Kate's shoulder from behind. "Stay. In. The. Car."

The woman was pulling Skip's truck into the garage. The door slid closed behind it.

"Call 911!" Rose barked at Manny. "And keep her here." She pointed at Kate.

Rose bolted from the car. She crouched down and raced across the lawn.

Mac was moving along the front of the house, hugging the brick facade. Rose got to the garage just ahead of him. "I've got the front," he growled softly.

Rose nodded and slipped around the corner and along the side of the garage. There was a regular door on the side, with a window in it. She eased up to it and peeked in along the edge of the window. Flimsy, semi-sheer curtains gave the scene inside a dream-like quality.

The middle-aged man, Coleman, was slowly and awkwardly dragging Skip's inert body across the garage floor. His petite wife held open the back passenger-side door of Skip's SUV.

¡Dios mio! Let him be alive!

It took them awhile to wrestle the big man into the backseat. It looked like little Mrs. Coleman was doing as much lifting and shoving as her husband was. The couple finally stepped back. Coleman slammed the back door of the truck, and they both climbed into the front.

Rose already had her snub-nosed .32 in her hand. Now she turned it around, ready to break the window in the side door with the butt. She waited for the whir of the main garage door opening.

A couple quick, hard raps had enough glass out for her to reach in and unlock the door. In the next second, she was inside the garage, her gun pointed at the truck's windshield.

"Stop!"

Two gunshots exploded in the confined space, deafening Rose. She dove behind some boxes.

She could barely hear, over the ringing in her ears, Mac's voice shouting, "I shot out the rear tires."

Rose raced to the driver's side window. She pointed her gun at the head of the man. "Put it in park," she yelled, "then hands on the wheel!"

The man closed his eyes for a second. Then he shifted the truck into park. His chin sank to his chest.

Mrs. Coleman bolted out of the truck and ran for the door into the house.

Mac blocked her way and grabbed her arm. "Where the hell do you think you're going?"

The back passenger door was ripped open. Kate clambered into the truck. "Skip! Skip!"

Rose sighed. She'd known the woman wouldn't stay put.

Skip's eyelids fluttered and his mouth moved.

Rose's knees wobbled. *¡Gracias, Dios mio!*

Coleman hadn't so much as twitched. She said a second prayer of thanksgiving for that.

Unbeknownst to him, the truck's window glass was bulletproof.

~~~~

Heart pounding, Kate clung to Rose's hand, watching as the paramedics worked on her husband. He was stretched out on the Colemans' garage floor, unconscious but breathing.

"Anybody got any idea what he was given?" one of the paramedics called out.

"Roofies," Coleman said.

Kate narrowed her eyes at Mrs. Coleman. "And maybe clonazepam."

Horror on his face, Coleman tried to turn toward his wife, but the cop hanging onto the elbow of one of his handcuffed arms hampered the movement.

Mrs. Coleman–also cuffed and in the custody of another officer–gave a small nod.

The paramedic swiveled around on his heel without standing. "Is it in his stomach?"

"No. Injected," the woman said.

The paramedic spoke into the radio clipped to his shoulder, then turned to his partner, who was already drawing something into a syringe.

Kate's tense muscles relaxed some. Skip was healthy and strong, and help had arrived in time.

Rose squeezed her hand and let it go. "You ride with Manny to the hospital. I'll fill Judith in."

"Tell her Mrs. Coleman worked at that pharmacy. She'll know what that means. And I think she was following me. See if she owns a red knit scarf."

Rose nodded and jogged away.

Kate followed her path with her eyes. Judith was getting out of an unmarked car at the curb.

Movement across the street caught Kate's attention. A teenaged girl with auburn hair and a dark-haired boy a year or two younger climbed out of a car and crossed the street. At the end of the driveway, the girl broke into a run. "Mom! Dad!"

Kate's throat closed.

Two uniformed officers intercepted the kids, turning them toward the front door of the house. The girl looked back over the cop's shoulder, tears streaming down her face.

Kate's own cheeks were wet.

Father What-A-Waste in more ways than one.

CHAPTER THIRTY-ONE

Kate sat next to the hospital bed, holding her husband's inert hand and anxiously watching his still face. His eyelids had fluttered a few times, but he hadn't yet regained consciousness.

The doctors had reassured her that he was out of the woods. She'd called Rose, who'd promised to let everyone else know.

Kate's stomach was queasy and her chest hurt. Guilt, an all too frequent companion lately, lay heavy on her shoulders.

Skip had insisted on trading the nun for the ex-priest to protect her, but neither of them had honestly thought the man would be dangerous. Why had they assumed that?

She shook her head slightly. Because Josie had called him heroic, had seemed to like, even admire him.

The nun had said something about the lights going out and then the janitor made the kids take their clothes off. In the dark, seven-year-old Josie might never have realized that Father Bill was one of her abusers.

Or the traumatic amnesia had been sufficient to also block out the negative feelings about the priest. Kate had seen that often enough in incest cases. The abused child's psyche would split the abusing parent into two beings–during the day, the loving parent on whom the child depended; by night, the monster who came to her room.

Kate sighed. They would never know all the answers, since Josie was dead.

Her eyes stung. She let the tears trickle out. It was time to finish grieving for Josie and let her go.

The hand she was holding twitched. Kate's head jerked up.

Skip's eyelids were at half-mast. "Where am I?" he mumbled.

She hastily swiped the tears off her cheeks. "In the hospital. Coleman drugged you, but the doctors say you'll be fine."

He nodded slightly, then winced.

"Headache?"

"A killer of one."

Bad choice of words, sweetheart.

She let go of his hand and reached for the call button. "Let me ring for the nurse. See if she can give you anything."

"What'd they drug me with?"

"Rophynol and clonazepam."

"Clonaze... wasn't that the other drug in Josie's system?"

"Yes." Much of the tension released in Kate's body. She took his hand again and gave it a squeeze. "Sounds like your brain cells are starting to fire."

A young nurse came in with a small paper cup. She poured water one-handed from the pitcher on the bedside table into its matching plastic cup. Then she held the little cup of pills up to Skip's mouth.

He went cross-eyed looking down at it.

"It's acetaminophen," the nurse said.

With the hand Kate wasn't holding, Skip took the small cup from the nurse and tossed the pills into his mouth. She handed him the water.

His hand was less steady with that but he managed not to spill any as he lifted the cup to his lips and drank. He paused for breath, then downed the rest of the water.

He handed the cup back to the nurse. "Thanks."

"The doctor will be in to check on you soon, now that you're awake." She smiled down at him and then left the room.

Before the door could close completely, it was nudged open by a black-clad foot. Judith Anderson stood in the doorway.

"Lieutenant," Kate greeted her.

Judith stepped into the room. "How's the patient?"

"Groggy but alive." Kate blew out air, finally allowing herself to feel the full impact of her relief.

"With a killer headache," Skip added. "Did you catch Mrs. Coleman?"

Judith gave him an odd look. "Yeah, she and her husband are in custody. She lawyered up right away, but he confessed to everything. The abuse at St. Bartholomew's years ago, Josie's murder and trying to kill you."

Skip shook his head, then grimaced. "He wasn't home when I started feeling funny. The wife gave me coffee and we were talking…" His voice trailed off. "That's all I remember."

"Wait," Kate said. "That jives with something that happened before you got there, Judith. The wife was the one who confirmed that Skip had been given clonazepam, and the husband seemed horrified by that news."

"So he's protecting her," Skip said.

"Hm, seems like I'll be having another little chat with the Colemans." Judith took a deep breath and let it out. "We found camera equipment and pictures stashed in a locked room in their basement. Some of the pics are older ones, of kids."

Kate winced. "Naked?"

"Yup, and the rest were of Mrs. Coleman, with bows in her hair, posing as if she's a child."

Kate's stomach clenched. Bile rose in her throat.

Skip grimaced and squeezed her hand.

"Yeah," Judith said. "Coleman seems to think he never hurt those kids at the church, because he didn't touch them, just took off their clothes and took pictures of them."

Ah, the flashes in Josie's dream–they were flashbulbs going off.

"And the janitor helped," Kate said.

Judith nodded. "Coleman claims it was Jones's idea and it might have been. I sent Baxter," she smirked for a second, "and a couple of uniforms to pick him up. He would take the pictures, then give the kids their clothes back. Then they'd turn the lights back on and Father Bill would console them, tell them they were okay, they didn't need to tell anybody, yada, yada."

"Crap!" Kate said. "That's why Josie thought of him as, quote 'heroic.' She thought he'd saved her from the bad guy who'd made her take her clothes off."

"Jones sold copies of the photos to his pervert buddies," Judith continued. "Coleman claims that was a good thing, that it kept those men from actually abusing children even though they were committing a sin by masturbating."

"Gag me," Kate said.

Judith snorted. "Yeah, that was my reaction."

Kate recalled some of the journal entries. "In one of Josie's dreams, the janitor was yelling in her face that she ruined something. And she had the feeling that she'd opened a door and someone yelled 'No lights.' She stumbled onto their darkroom."

"That makes sense," Judith said. "I will need those journals now, and you may have to testify, Kate, about where you got them. That is, if we can't get Coleman to admit his wife did it. I doubt she'll confess."

Kate nodded, although the thought of testifying at such a trial made her stomach churn all over again.

"By the way," Judith said, "that phone number that showed up on Josie's phone from that morning, it was for a throwaway cell. The same number called your office later that morning."

"The hang up after Josie's message," Kate said.

"Yeah. That didn't tell us much, until we found the phone on the Colemans' coffee table today. It's another piece of evidence against Mrs. Coleman. And yes, she owns a red knit scarf."

"So it wasn't my imagination that I was being watched," Kate said. "One of the times I had that feeling, there was a woman in a red scarf, turned away from me, staring into a shop window."

Judith nodded. "Coleman claimed he lured Josie over to his house with a promise of information, then used his wife's clonazepam to drug her enough that she was out of it, but not unconscious. He took her back to her place, made her take the other pills and wash them down with the vodka. Then he found the page in the journal that would work as a suicide note and cleaned the condo to make sure he hadn't left any fingerprints anywhere."

"That's all probably close to the truth," Skip said, "but it was Mrs. Coleman, not him, who did all that."

"Yeah," Judith said. "I was having trouble visualizing Coleman being so cold and methodical. But Mrs. C? Yeah, I can see her doing it. And now that bogus prescription makes more sense. She worked at that pharmacy, had access to Dr. Kraft's old prescriptions that were on file. So she steals some clonazepam from there and cobbles together a bogus prescription slip to make it look like Josie had it filled."

Judith paused, staring hard at Kate. "We got a call at the precinct earlier today from the condo manager at Josie's building. He asked for Detective Huntington."

Heat rose in Kate's cheeks. She opened her mouth but couldn't think of a thing to say. She gave Judith a sheepish look. "I never said I was with the police, just that I had authorization to see her condo."

Judith shook her head slightly, then chuckled under her breath. She pulled a piece of paper from the slim briefcase at her side. "The Hartins asked him to make arrangements to get rid of Josie's furniture. When the movers picked up the desk, they found a piece of paper under it." She handed the paper to Kate. "This is a copy."

As Kate started reading, she recognized it as the last entry from the journal.

The little kid inside has taken over again. She's terrified about confronting him. The adult knows there's no danger now, but the kid's not listening.

I still kind of hope that I'm wrong. That's why I hesitate to write his name, even in this private journal. But I'll find out today. Maybe I'm being paranoid but it's too easy these days for information to fall into the wrong hands. And I don't want to slander the guy if I'm wrong.

Kate's eyes stung. The next sentence was indeed bracketed

by smiley faces.

Well just in case the kid's right and I'm wrong, I've told Sphinx where I'm going... lol.

Kate sniffled, then handed the page to Skip. "Josie did tell Sphinx." She told him and the lieutenant about the slip of paper attached to the dog's collar. "The vet didn't realize what it meant at the time she found it."

Judith looked at Skip. "You should hire her. She's a good detective."

Kate took a deep breath. "No, I get too sucked in. For some reason I can listen to people's trauma from the past and stay relatively detached, but when they're in dire trouble in the present, I become obsessed." She'd done it a couple of times before, but this time had been far worse. She had almost lost herself in the process of finding Josie's killer. "I think I'll stick to being a therapist. I've had more than enough murder and mayhem for a long time to come."

"Amen to that," Skip said with fervor. "What I don't get is how the Catholic Church could transfer this guy to a girls' high school after he was caught."

Kate shook her head. "He no doubt swore that he'd never do anything like that again."

"And they believed him?" Judith asked, her tone incredulous.

"No, but they would pretend they did. The Church authorities were all about covering things up back then. And they may have assumed that he was only interested in younger children."

"Well, they could've been right about that," Judith said. "All the pics except those of his wife were little kids."

Skip looked up at Kate. "Do you think it's the celibacy that sometimes makes priests turn to kids like that?"

Kate stifled a sigh. She'd fielded that question more than once since the Church sex abuse scandal had broken wide open. "No, but I think that celibacy is attractive to men who realize on some level that their sexual proclivities are warped. They're trying to suppress that warped sexuality and think that celibacy as a priest will help them do that."

Judith nodded. "But it doesn't work."

"No," Kate said, "the urges are too strong. It's a compulsion they can't resist, and now they're in a position of authority with ready access to children."

Out of the corner of her eye, she saw Judith shudder.

"Well, I'd better get back to the precinct and start tying up loose ends." Judith turned toward the door, then stopped. She pivoted around again. Her face softened as the cop mask dropped away. "I'm sorry you couldn't reach me earlier. I was in meetings with the brass."

Kate opened her mouth, then closed it again as it registered what those meetings were about. Judith had reported whoever had pressured her to not investigate Josie's murder. Kate prayed that there would be no repercussions for blowing the whistle. She smiled at the lieutenant.

Judith tilted her head up and down in a subtle nod and returned her smile. "Skip, I'll need to get a formal statement from you, when you're feeling up to it."

When he didn't answer, Kate glanced over at him. His eyelids were drooping.

She looked back at the lieutenant and shrugged.

Judith nodded a farewell and moved toward the door.

It crashed open and Billy ran in. "Daddy!" He dove at the side of the bed, but it was too high for him to clamber onto it.

Skip's head jerked up. He leaned over and grabbed for the boy, and almost fell out of bed. Kate braced herself against one of his shoulders.

Judith stepped to the side of the bed and grabbed the other. Together, they shoved Skip up onto the mattress.

He fell back against the pillows and closed his eyes.

Billy's face fell. "I'm sorry. I didn't mean to hurt you, Daddy."

"You didn't," Skip said, his eyes still closed. "I'm just a little dizzy."

"I hate to tell you," Kate said in a low voice, "but you're not going to feel right, off and on, for a while. Rophynol has some nasty long-term side effects."

Skip opened his eyes and grimaced. Then he rearranged his face into a smile for the kids' sake.

Edie was hanging back, holding Maria's hand.

"Come here, Pumkin," Skip said. "Give me a hug."

She let go of Maria and ran over. Kate helped the kids climb up on either side of the bed. "Sit still now. Daddy's got a bad headache."

Kate noticed that Judith had left. She'd forgotten to ask her about the message she'd left regarding Dr. Blake. She now regretted it, since the vet hadn't been involved in Josie's murder. But the woman had known what she was risking when she'd opened her practice without a license.

Kate shook her head slightly. She refused to waste any more of her life feeling guilty about other people's actions.

Maria gestured from the doorway. Kate stepped over next to her.

"Ees okay I bring de kids in?" Maria whispered. "De nurse say he awake and could see them."

"Yes, it's fine," Kate said, although she was worried about Edie. This whole experience had reinforced a somber streak in her personality that wasn't part of her inherent cheerful nature.

Kate's stomach knotted. Maybe Skip should consider a different line of work too.

She looked across the room at her husband listening intently to the children's chatter. She doubted he would go along with a career change. At least the aftereffects of the Rophynol would keep him on desk duty for a little while.

She made a mental note to watch for signs of PTSD. Skip had experienced close calls before and had suffered no ill effects afterward. But being awake but drugged enough to not be able to do anything–those helpless feelings would still be festering in his psyche even though he couldn't remember them consciously. She'd seen it before in rape survivors who'd been drugged with roofies.

Maria slipped her hand into Kate's and squeezed. "He gonna be okay." A statement, not a question.

The tension in Kate's stomach relaxed as she watched her family—Edie beaming as she told her father about her day at school, Skip nodding and then turning his head to hide a wince, Billy interrupting his sister in a too-loud voice.

Yes, he would be okay. They would all be okay in time. She said a silent prayer that there would be no more dead bodies. She would be more than happy to confine her mystery-solving talents to jigsaw puzzles.

She smiled down at Maria. Her fingertips grazed something hard. She lifted Maria's hand and stared at it. "You're engaged?"

"Oh no." Maria pulled her hand free, then rubbed the silver band with two tiny red stones embedded in it. "Eduardo call it a commitment ring. We have dat talk like you suggest. He say we start over and he court me again, as a lover, not as a man looking for a *madre* for his children."

"And how do you feel about that?" Kate asked.

Maria flashed her a bright smile. "I tink ees very good idea."

AUTHOR'S NOTES

If you enjoyed this book, please take a moment to leave a short review on Amazon and/or other book retailers' websites. Reviews help to sell books and sales help to keep the series going! You can readily find the links to these retailers at http://misterio-press.com (click on *misterio press* bookstore).

We at ***misterio press*** pride ourselves on producing top quality mysteries. Each book is proofread by several sets of eyes. But proofreaders are human. If you found errors in this book, please e-mail the author at lambkassandra3@gmail.com.

First let me say a big thank you to you, my readers! You are Kate's lifeblood. Without you, she and her friends and family would die a slow death in my hard drive. But every time you read one of her adventures, she and the gang come to life again.

Also I owe so much gratitude to my beta readers–Gina, Ralph, Angi and Sally–and to my critique partners at misterio press– Shannon Esposito and Kathy Owen. You all made this story better.

And my writing would not be at the level of quality that it is without my wonderful editor, Marcy Kennedy. I am so grateful that I found you, Marcy!

I'd better not leave out my long-suffering husband who is my final proofreader. Any errors you may have found are probably because I couldn't resist tinkering with the story a bit more after he'd proofread it.

And now for an apology–to the Catholic Archdiocese of Baltimore. To the best of my knowledge there wasn't a major abuse scandal or a cover-up in that particular diocese, although I know of a few isolated cases of abuse by priests there. I am fairly familiar with one of those cases. When the abuse came to light years after it had happened, the church authorities reacted appropriately. The priest was required to attend an inpatient sex addiction recovery program and was removed from any position where he would be likely to be around children or teens.

The people who knew this priest personally, myself included, were dumbfounded by the accusations. Those close to such priests often are. This is because these priests usually are quite sincere in their calling to the priesthood and are caring toward their parishioners.

But a part of their motivation for pursuing a vocation in the church, often operating out of conscious awareness, is a desire to suppress their warped sexuality via celibacy. This rarely works. The compulsion to act out is too strong.

This compulsion comes from the abusers' own childhood abuse. Part of the dynamic is the need to reclaim the power that was taken from them by their abusers. Now as the abuser, they are in control again. This need for power is associated with sexual arousal and the urge is often quite strong.

Abuse is also twisted up with love for many abusers. This further stymies and confuses those who know these abusive priests. "But he loves kids. He was always so involved with the youth group." Yes, he does love kids; unfortunately, in his case, that love is associated with sexual urges.

Okay, enough of that grim subject. *shudder*

I have an announcement to make. I'm starting a new mystery series!!

Now, before you get worried, I'm not abandoning Kate. But I figured she could use a little bit of a break from stumbling over dead bodies. I do have another Vacation novella planned, this one set in Hawaii (see blurb below). Hopefully I will have that out in late winter/early spring, 2016. And there will be more full-length Kate novels as well.

I'm really excited about this new series. The protagonist is…

Wait! I'll let her introduce herself. Here's an excerpt from the beginning of the first book in the series:

I'm a normal person. Granted I have a somewhat unusual vocation. I train service animals for PTSD sufferers—mostly combat vets.

But other than that, I'm just a small-town, thirty-something divorcee. About as average as one can get.

My name is Marcia Banks—pronounced Mar-see-a, not Marsha. Okay, so I don't have a totally normal name.

I live in what has recently become the third largest state, population-wise, in the country. I reside in one of its least populated areas, however, in a little town called Mayfair, Florida, population 758 (and a half—Agnes Baker is pregnant. Again).

Mayfair is in central Florida, on the outskirts of the Ocala National Forest, a forty-five-minute drive inland from I-75, which runs along the western side of the state.

The town sprang up in the late 1960's when old Mr. Mayfair started an alligator farm there. (Rumor has it that he poached the alligators from the Forest.) He plastered billboards all over the newly minted I-75 corridor, and a few on I-95 on the other side of the state, and soon vacationing families were stopping here to witness the wonders of alligator wrestling and to buy cheap alligator belts and handbags as gifts for their relatives the following Christmas.

The Mayfair Motel was built. A gas station, a small diner, some tacky souvenir shops and a ma-and-pa grocery store rounded out the town.

Sadly, the alligator farm's success was short lived. It went under in the mid-seventies, no longer able to lure tourists once

Walt Disney had plopped his mega-amusement park down next to another sleepy little Florida town–Orlando.

Mayfair had come close to ghost town status, but it's now experiencing a resurgence. People like myself, who work in jobs that don't require one's physical presence in an office somewhere, are moving here for the peace and quiet and the climate.

It's mildly chilly here in January and February, quite pleasant in March and April and again in November and December, and stinking hot the rest of the year. But to northerners like myself, the ability to throw away our snow shovels and heavy parkas makes it heaven on earth.

I moved here four years ago, right after the demise of my short and disastrous marriage to a concert pianist in the Baltimore Symphony. It's a great place to train service animals because everybody knows everybody. So it didn't take long for the residents to learn the rules. Never, ever pet the dogs I train unless I say it's okay. That's the main rule.

The one exception is my Black Lab-Rottie mix, Buddy, if he's the only dog I'm walking at the time. He's now my mentor dog and my best friend. He was my first trainee, and how he came back into my possession was the beginning of my not so normal avocation–unwilling amateur sleuth.

And here's a synopsis of the next Kate on Vacation adventure, *Missing on Maui*:

Days before Kate Huntington is scheduled to leave for her niece's wedding on Maui, she receives a desperate call from said niece. Kate's rather intense sister-in-law, Amy's mother, is at it again–alienating the groom's family, members of the wedding party and even the disgusted wedding planner. Can Aunt Kate come early and run interference?

It's an awkward situation at best, but things get a whole lot more so as young women start disappearing. Hawaii is supposed to be a relaxing paradise, but Aunt Kate is kept busy smoothing ruffled feathers and chasing down errant wedding party members.

When her maid of honor doesn't show for a rehearsal, Amy is frantic. Her friend Molly was seen in the company of a notorious local player. Is he the one responsible for the girls going missing?

As it turns out, the maid of honor has a very good reason for her absence, and Kate may just get herself and young Molly killed.

ABOUT THE AUTHOR

Kassandra Lamb has never been able to decide which she loves more, psychology or writing. In college, she realized that writers need a day job in order to eat, so she studied psychology. After a career as a psychotherapist and college professor, she is now retired and can pursue her passion for writing. She spends most of her time in an alternate universe with her characters. The portal to this universe, aka her computer, is located in Florida, where her husband and dog catch occasional glimpses of her. She and her husband spend part of each summer in her native Maryland, where the Kate Huntington series is based.

Kass has completed eight books in the series, plus three Kate on Vacation novellas (somewhat lighter reads along the lines of cozy mysteries). She is currently working on Book 1 in a new series, the Marcia Banks and Buddy mysteries, as well as the next Kate on Vacation novella, *Missing on Maui*.

To read and see more about Kassandra and Kate Huntington you can go to http://kassandralamb.com. Be sure to sign up for the newsletter there to get a heads up about new releases, plus special offers and bonuses for subscribers. (New subscribers get a free e-copy of the first Kate on vacation novella.)

Kass's e-mail is lambkassandra3@gmail.com and she loves hearing from readers! She's also on Facebook (http://www.facebook.com/kassandralambauthor) and hangs out some on Twitter @KassandraLamb. She blogs about psychological topics and other random things at http://misteriopress.com.

Please check out these other great *misterio press* series:

Karma's A Bitch
(Pet Psychic Mysteries)
by Shannon Esposito

Maui Widow Waltz
(Islands of Aloha Mysteries)
by JoAnn Bassett

The Metaphysical Detective
(Riga Hayworth Mysteries)
by Kirsten Weiss

Dangerous and Unseemly
(Concordia Wells Mysteries)
by K.B. Owen

Murder, Honey
(Carol Sabala Mysteries)
by Vinnie Hansen

Steam and Sensibility
(Sensibility Grey Steampunk Mysteries)
by Kirsten Weiss

Plus even more great mysteries/thrillers at
http://misteriopress.com/misterio-press-bookstore/